D1712991

A
LANGUAGE
of DRAGONS

A LANGUAGE of DRAGONS

S. F. WILLIAMSON

HARPER
An Imprint of HarperCollinsPublishers

Library of Congress Control Number: 2024945852

ISBN 978-0-06-335384-8

Typography by Jenna Stempel-Lobell

24 25 26 27 28 LBC 6 5 4 3 2

First Edition

For my husband, who believed in me more than I ever did;
for my parents, who gave me the precious gift of a second language;
and for all those brave enough to forgive themselves.

Here be dragons.

ONE

I'm dreaming in Draconic again.

The long, intricate sentences come to me more easily in sleep than when I'm awake, and just before I open my eyes, my mind settles on one word.

Mengkhenyass.

What does it mean?

I roll over, the haze of sleep lifting quickly as sunlight streams in through the sash windows. On the floor, tangled in a pile of blankets, my cousin Marquis snores. His father spent the night talking with Mama and Dad again, whispering about strikes and protests and dragonfire. Marquis's presence on my bedroom floor is becoming a regular occurrence.

The clatter of pots and pans rings from the kitchen below and I swing my legs off the bed as realization settles in my stomach. The Chancellor of the Academy for Draconic Linguistics is coming for dinner. Here in my parents' house.

Tonight.

I've been waiting for this day for weeks—no, months. Dr. Rita Hollingsworth is coming to see Mama to discuss her theory on dragon dialects, but it will be my chance to impress and—I almost don't dare hope—secure a summer apprenticeship in the Academy's translation department.

"Marquis!" I throw a cushion at my cousin's head. "Wake up."

Marquis grunts into his pillow. "For God's sake, Viv. I thought we were sleeping in."

"Too much to do," I reply. "I have to be at the bookbinder shop by ten."

I pull on my dressing gown and cross the room to the desk, where my professor's letter of recommendation lies crisp and smooth. The door opens with a bang and Ursa bursts in, fully dressed. Marquis groans as she tramples over him and presses her rosebud lips to his ear.

"Cousin?" she whispers loudly. "Are you awake?"

"He is now, little bear." I laugh and open my arms to her. She's soft and warm and smells of milk and honey. "Where are you going?"

"I can't tell you," Ursa replies, her eyes growing wide. "It's a secret place."

"A secret place?" Marquis sits up, a devilish grin on his face. "That's my favorite kind."

Ursa giggles and lets me untangle her hair, which is caught in the fraying ribbon that holds her class pass.

URSA FEATHERSWALLOW
AGE 5
SECOND CLASS

I turn the ribbon over in my hand and swear.

"Ursa!" I say. "You should have asked Mama to replace this by now. You *know* not to risk losing your pass."

I reach for my own pass, strung on a black velvet ribbon, and slip it round my neck. The thought of Ursa being stopped without her class pass fills me with dread. Those two words—*Second Class*—are the difference between having something and having nothing.

My sister just frowns and points a finger at the wall behind my desk. It's decorated with paper clippings: sketches by Marquis of the different dragon species, my acceptance letter to the University of London, and a watercolor painting. I brace myself for the question Ursa asks most days.

"Where is Sophie?"

I turn reluctantly toward the painting, trying to ignore the sudden longing that floods through me. My own grinning face stares back at me and, beside it, the face of my dearest, oldest friend.

"I've already told you," I say, cupping Ursa's face in my hands. "She's gone away."

I haven't seen Sophie since the summer, since she failed the Examination and was demoted to Third Class. In the space of a few weeks, she was forced to give up on our dream of attending university together and move away from her family's home in Marylebone to a halfway house in a Third Class quarter. I shudder at the memory of results day. Sophie's weak cry, the way she sank to the ground like a deflating balloon, the grim face of her father as he stooped to read the paper in her hand.

The guilt rises like a tidal wave, knocking the breath from my chest.

"Sophie's Third Class now, Ursa," Marquis says, glancing at me nervously.

I rip the painting from the wall.

"Ursa!" Mama's voice calls up the stairs. "I'm waiting for you, sweetheart."

Ursa darts from the room without a backward glance, and a few seconds later the front door slams. I drop the painting into the waste-paper bin and pull a lace blouse and trousers from my wardrobe.

"Will you let me dress?" I say to Marquis before he can mention Sophie's name.

He nods, gathering his belongings, and leaves the room. I let the tears come, hot and inevitable, as I pin up the front of my hair. Then I blink them away angrily. What I did to Sophie is unforgivable, but it's too late to change things. I made my choice—an ugly, necessary one—and now I have to live with the consequences. My sorrow is nothing compared to what Sophie must feel.

A few moments later, there's a knock. I open the door and Marquis offers me his arm.

"To the bookbinder?" he says with a cheerful grin.

He's wearing a camel trench coat and his dark hair is styled to perfection. I loop my arm through his and my anxiety subsides. The day stretches ahead, bringing us closer to the moment I'll impress Rita Hollingsworth with my portfolio. I feel a rush of anticipation. If tonight goes as planned, I'll be one step closer to becoming Vivien Featherswallow, Draconic Translator.

Fitzrovia hums with activity and I grip Marquis tightly as he sashays between the street-sellers peddling sweet treats and boxes full of trinkets. Many of them turn to greet him. Marquis, whose effortless charm and wit has brought us all sorts of privileges since we were children, is loved by everyone. A group of bearded men are inspecting a collection of antique books, holding up eyeglasses to admire the gilded edges. The familiar Bulgarian language sounds sweetly in my ears and a row of painted religious icons stare out at me from one of the stalls.

"Rebel Dragons Detained in Durham!" shouts a newspaper vendor. "Is the Peace Agreement in Peril?"

Marquis turns to read the headlines and I snort.

"In peril? It's been in place for over fifty years. As if a few rebels are going to bring it down."

The Peace Agreement between Prime Minister Wyvernmire and the British Dragon Queen allows humans and dragons to coexist harmoniously. Without that and the Class System, we'd still have overcrowding, homelessness, *and* the hunting of humans and dragons. I don't understand the sudden backlash against it.

"I heard a delicious rumor yesterday," Marquis says as we cross the street into Marylebone.

I step over a deep fissure in the pavement, the impact of a dragon's tail left over from the war.

"Hugo Montecue's current girlfriend said her brother-in-law saw a dragon *and* a plane in the sky at the same time, flying *side by side*."

"That's a lie. Dragons and planes have their own designated routes to avoid collision," I recite, opening the door to the bookbinder's. A bell rings shrilly inside.

"Well," Marquis begins, "maybe the rebels are finally getting their way. Maybe they're closer to overturning the Peace Agreement than we think."

I scoff. "If your friends believe the government is letting the rebels take to the skies, then they're bigger skrits than I thought."

"You're just jealous because Hugo Montecue has a new girl."

"Oh, shut up," I say, scowling. "The boy was my ticket to passing mathematics, that's all. He was a good teacher."

Marquis smirks. "I bet he was."

I rummage in my purse for the coins to pay the bookbinder, my cheeks growing warm. My romances—even the insincere ones—must stay as secret as my cousin's.

"You're one to talk," I mutter quietly. "You have as many boyfriends as you do silk scarves."

The bookbinder hands me the portfolio and I murmur a word of thanks. Beneath the expensive leather cover lie my best translations, and I feel a shiver of pride.

Every act of translation requires sacrifice—it is this harsh truth that made me fall in love. There exists no direct correlation between the words of one language and another, and no translation can be entirely faithful to its original. So, while a person can more or less bridge the gap between languages using words, there is always some deeper meaning left unsaid, a secret invisible to those who only have one language with which to navigate the world.

A translator, on the other hand, is a creature that flies with several pairs of wings.

I slip the portfolio under one arm and follow Marquis out of the shop toward home, passing the University of London on the way. We have been students there for two months already, me having skipped my final year at school to attend early. I love it so much that weekends have become a bore. I'm still jealous that Marquis was permitted to take rooms there, on account of him being male, but I know some universities don't allow women to attend at all.

You must see the silver lining of the situation, Uncle Thomas told me.

And I do. The University of London, with its sun-kissed campus, spired buildings, and giant library, is everything I've ever dreamed of.

Dreams . . . I think about the Draconic word from this morning.

6

Mengkhenyass.

It's Komodonese, a dragon tongue not much spoken in Britannia except by the traders traveling to Singapore. Its English translation is on the tip of my tongue, but still I can't remember.

"Slow down," Marquis says suddenly.

A crowd of people is marching down one of the roads that snakes out of Fitzrovia. I glance at the sign they walk past as they flood into the square.

CAMDEN TOWN—THIRD CLASS QUARTER

That's where Sophie's halfway house is.

"The Peace Agreement is corrupt!" shouts a voice.

The disheveled-looking group is interspersed with men in white uniforms and helmets.

Guardians of Peace.

I reach instinctively for my class pass and sense Marquis do the same.

"Free the Third Class!" a woman shouts at the top of her lungs.

She and the people with her are hoisting signs above their heads.

THE HUMAN-DRAGON COALITION OF BRITANNIA
DEMANDS REFORM!
DEFEND DEMOCRACY!
GENERAL ELECTION NOW!

I flinch as she's knocked to the ground and the crowd behind her surges, trampling her.

"Justice for dragons!" screams another voice.

More Guardians appear, all of them holding silver batons, and I jump aside as another group of protesters runs up behind me, one of their signs hitting my cheek. I reach for Marquis's hand as the two groups merge, spilling farther across the square.

"Come on," Marquis says, pulling me toward home.

We hurry across the cobbles and a flash catches my eye. A silver baton is raised high, glinting in the sunlight just a few steps away.

"Down with Wyvernmire!"

The air rings with screams as the baton comes down onto the crowd. Blood splatters across my coat and the cover of my portfolio.

"Oh."

I sway, the stunned noise that escapes my lips immediately silenced by a woman's shrieking. Then the crowd is seething, growing bigger and moving closer in a mass of cascading bodies. I register the horror on Marquis's face and run, then stumble as I realize I'm about to step on someone's head. The girl is lying on the ground, her long hair matted with blood, her eyes dead and staring.

A shot cracks through the air.

"Viv!" Marquis roars.

We break into a sprint. The street-sellers are scattering and Guardian motorcars hurtle down the road toward us. I see home, the tall white house with the blue curtains. I clamber up the steps, tripping as a second shot sounds, followed by a third. I push the key into the lock with shaking hands as Marquis presses urgently against my back.

"I can't—"

We collapse into the foyer and Marquis slams the front door behind us. I stare, breathless, at my cousin's ashen face and blood-stained shoes. My heart beats relentlessly inside my chest, and my hair is drenched in sweat.

"What *was* that?" I say.

"Rebel protesters," Marquis replies.

The dead girl's bloodied hair flashes in front of my eyes and I press my hand to my mouth, stomach churning. I've always imagined the rebels to be an organized political party with official headquarters, its members angry dragons and armed radicals. Not the men and women I see crossing the square each day. Not teenage girls.

I jump as the front door springs open and Mama bursts through, carrying a wailing Ursa.

"Lock the door," she says sharply, setting Ursa down. "And keep away from the windows."

I do as I'm told, exchanging a glance with Marquis as Mama strips Ursa of her coat and boots.

"Bring me your shoes and anything else that has been dirtied, both of you," Mama says, shrugging off her own coat. "And tend to your sister."

"Hush, little bear," I whisper, kneeling down to murmur soothing words in Ursa's ear.

Marquis gets to his feet and stares stubbornly out the window. A few hours from now, Mama will have erased any trace of our accidental presence at the rebel protest. My clothes will appear in my wardrobe, pressed and pristine, and it will be as if I had never crossed paths with a silver baton or the body of a Third Class girl.

This is why.

The thought strikes me suddenly, steady and reassuring.

This is why I can count the few bad grades I've ever received in the line of white scars up my arm.

This is why I let Hugo Montecue slip his hands beneath my dress in exchange for math lessons last year.

This is why I betrayed my best friend.

To pass the Examination. To become a Draconic Translator. To never, ever risk being demoted to Third Class.

Ursa hiccups, stroking the new pale blue ribbon threaded through her class pass.

"Want to play a game?" Marquis says, taking her by the hand.

I wait until they disappear into the parlor before picking up my portfolio off the floor. I wipe the blood from the cover, glad that Mama didn't see it and make me dispose of it, and wander into the dining room where the table has already been set. This evening's meal has been entirely orchestrated by Mama, as we've never had a maid or a cook. That would leave no money for tutors.

I place the portfolio on the seat of my chair—the dark marks on the cover will easily pass for water stains. It will be enough, won't it, to make Rita Hollingsworth consider me for the apprenticeship? And with my letters of recommendation and the professional, smiley demeanor I was taught at school, I'll be as convincing as I was on the day of the Examination. *Fruit ripe for the picking*, Dad called me that day. I still don't understand what he meant, but it's how I see myself now.

I am a bright, ripe fruit: shiny on the surface, but rotten at the core.

The doorbell rings at seven o'clock, just as Mama is placing the last of the flowers in the vase on the table. Wisps of pale hair escape their pins, framing her face, and she gives me an encouraging smile. With my dark curls and freckled skin, I look nothing like her, and that comes as no surprise to me. She is wise, even-tempered, patient. I am fretful, hotheaded, selfish.

Dad plants a kiss on her cheek and pulls out two bottles of wine from behind his back with a flourish.

"I thought we agreed on just one bottle?" Mama says.

"We did," Dad replies, "but with such a distinguished guest gracing our table, I thought we might need more."

Uncle Thomas growls from his seat. Dad started drinking during the wait for my Examination results and didn't stop.

"Give me those," Uncle Thomas says, taking the bottles of Merlot.

He opens them with a pop and sets them by the fire to breathe. Dad leans closer to Mama, points to her research on the mantelpiece, and whispers, "Don't lay all your cards on the table straightaway."

I know enough about Mama's research to understand that tonight is important. I know that she believes that each dragon tongue contains dialects, branches of a language particular to a group or place. Showing the existence and cultural significance of these dialects, Mama says, will remind our society of just how similar dragons and humans are. But the Academy maintains that dragons are too solitary for their tongues to have spread and developed into anything more.

The dining room is bright and warm, the table set with Mama's best pink china. Bookshelves and paintings line every wall, and Mina, our fluffy white cat, is asleep on the chaise longue. This is the room my parents stay up in with Uncle Thomas, night after night. At first, I thought they were discussing work, but Uncle Thomas isn't an anthropologist like Mama and Dad. It's the rebellion they talk about—that and the threat of another war. I heard snatches of their conversation last night on my way to bed.

The penalty for a coup d'état *is death.*

"Dr. Hollingsworth," Mama exclaims. "Welcome to our home!"

We all turn to look at the small silver-haired woman being shown into the room. She has bronzed, weatherworn skin and crow's-feet at the corners of her eyes. She holds a long cigarette holder in one hand and a briefcase in the other. Her fingers glitter with rings and Ursa stares at them greedily.

"Such a delight to be here," says Dr. Hollingsworth, handing her coat to Marquis.

He raises an eyebrow at me and I glare back, urging him to be polite to the woman who potentially holds the key to my future.

"Are you aware, Dr. and Dr. Featherswallow, of the rebel demonstration that took place this afternoon?" Dr. Hollingsworth says as Dad shows her to her seat. "What a violent disturbance to have outside your home."

"We were fortunate to have been able to stay safely indoors," Mama says quickly, shooting me a warning glance. "Dr. Hollingsworth, can I offer you a glass of wine?"

I listen to Rita Hollingsworth talk with my parents over bowls of buttery pierogi, her eyes burning with what I can only describe as brilliance. This is the woman who single-handedly recorded the syntax of three ancient dragon tongues, the chancellor of an institution that has given Dragonese a written form. And here she is, in *my* house, listening to *my* mama.

"As you know, Dr. Hollingsworth, dragons have conversed in hundreds of languages for millennia," Mama says. "And my research shows that their linguistic capabilities stretch even further than that. I believe that small, close-knit groups speak in dialects born from the languages they know. These dialects are clearly distinct from one another, in the same way that the Queen's English is distinct from, for example, Scouse."

"Dr. Featherswallow, if dragons spoke in regional dialects, surely we would have heard them."

"The dialects may not be regional," Mama replies eagerly. "They could be—"

She falters as Dr. Hollingsworth holds out a palm to signal her to stop talking. I almost choke on my pierogi, and across the table Marquis spits his wine back into the glass.

"You are from Bulgaria, Dr. Featherswallow, are you not?"

"I . . . yes," Mama replies.

"And you came to England when?"

"In 1865, as an infant."

"Following the Massacre of Bulgaria, then." Dr. Hollingsworth sets down her fork. "Did you lose many of your family members to the Bulgarian dragons?"

"Several, including my mother," Mama says quietly.

It's all Mama has ever told me about her family. That they fled Bulgaria when the dragon uprising happened, and that only Mama and her father survived. My grandmother perished alongside most of the human population of Bulgaria.

"I must admit that it surprises me that you became a dragon anthropologist, studying the very creatures that caused your family so much suffering," Dr. Hollingsworth says. "Many of the Bulgarians I know carry herbs they believe will protect them against dragons and have vowed never to trust one again."

Mama smiles and Dad reaches for her hand.

"Before the Travel Ban, my wife toured the world for her research, Dr. Hollingsworth," he says. "For every bloodthirsty dragon encountered in Bulgaria, she has met several more who want nothing but peace."

Dr. Hollingsworth meets Dad's gaze. "And aren't we lucky, to have the Peace Agreement to thank for that?"

Dad stiffens and I see Mama press a hand to his back. He pours himself another glass of wine.

"Praise for peace and prosperity!" Mama recites Britannia's national motto in the same singsong voice she uses to help Ursa memorize her lessons, and Dr. Hollingsworth smiles approvingly.

I lay a hand on the portfolio in my lap, thinking of the Draecksum past participle on page nine. Is now a good time to broach the subject of the apprenticeship? I'm looking to Mama for permission when I realize that Dr. Hollingsworth is staring straight at me.

"Vivien Featherswallow," she says, "I understand you're a budding linguist, too?"

My blood burns with a sudden energy and I sit up straighter. This is my chance. I smile the way I've been taught.

"I'm reading Dragon Tongues at the University of London," I say. "It's my first year."

"Wonderful," Dr. Hollingsworth says. "Do you get much practice?"

"Practice?" I say.

"With dragons, dear."

"Oh . . ."

The question makes sense, but I've never given it much thought. Now that I do, I realize I haven't said more than a few words to a dragon since I was Ursa's age.

"The last dragon professor was replaced by a human this year, so—"

14

"How many dragon tongues do you speak?" she asks me in perfect Wyrmerian.

"Six," I reply in the same language. Then I switch to Komodonese, which I've only just started learning. "But I'm not fluent in this last one."

"*Esti tin Drageoir?*" she says in Drageoir. "*Depuise quantem temps scrutes?*"

"As it's the official dragon tongue in France, I began learning it when I was eight," I reply with the perfect Drageoir accent I learned from one of my tutors. "It's among the easier ones, in my opinion."

Dr. Hollingsworth gives me an amused smile before switching back to English. "And how did you find the Examination? You passed with flying colors, or so I heard."

I feel my stomach knot at the mention of the Examination, but maintain my own smile. Where did she hear that?

"Vivien worked extremely hard to pass," Dad says. "Some of her friends were not so lucky."

Dr. Hollingsworth's head snaps toward my father.

"You would say luck comes into it, would you, Dr. Featherswallow?"

"Our friend Sophie worked just as hard as Viv did," Marquis says. "She wasn't expected to fail."

The knot in my stomach pulls tight. Being a year older, Marquis took the Examination before Sophie and me. But her demotion hit him hard.

Ursa stabs loudly at her pierogi with her fork.

"And what do *you* think, Miss Featherswallow?"

I glance nervously at Mama. What does any of this have to do with dragon dialects? All teenagers take the Examination when they turn sixteen. Those who pass remain in their class of birth, except for the Third Class kids, who get promoted to Second Class. Those who fail are demoted by one class, except for the Third Class, who can't go any lower. It's been that way since before I was born.

I think about the months of revision, of the university applications, of Hugo Montecue's wandering hands.

"Failing wasn't an option for me," I reply.

That's why I ruined Sophie's life.

Dr. Hollingsworth winks at me and I lean back in my seat, surprised. Did I say the right thing? Mama gives me the smallest of nods.

"You speak of luck, Dr. Featherswallow, yet you pay for the best books, the best tutors, the best schools for both your daughters, do you not?"

Not the best, I want to argue. *Cheltenham Ladies' College only accepts First Class girls.* But I say nothing. We may have to make a few sacrifices now, but the Featherswallows could be First Class within the next generation.

Dad drains his glass of wine and refills it, his eyes narrowing. It's like the temperature of the room has suddenly dropped.

"I do more than that, ma'am," he says. "Vivien was signed up for St. Saviour's School for Girls before she was even born. Her mother wouldn't let her sleep at night until she knew her books word for word. She has scars on her arms, inflicted by her own father—" Dad's voice breaks and Uncle Thomas lets out a loud cough.

My heart seems to freeze. For a second, I can't bring myself to tear my eyes from Dad's face. How did we get here? I stare from Marquis to Mama to Dad, who takes another deep glug of wine.

Dr. Hollingsworth is smiling. "The actions of any *good* father," she says softly.

"But they wouldn't be necessary, would they, if—"

Mama snatches the wineglass from Dad as he slurs his words.

"—if my daughters didn't have the threat of the Third Class hanging over their heads."

Mama jumps as if scalded and the glass falls from her hand, splattering wine across the wooden floor. It seeps into the cracks and crevices, a flood of crimson. Dr. Hollingsworth stands up. I hold my breath.

"If you'll excuse me," she says, pulling her cigarette holder out of her pocket, "I think I'll retire to the smoking room."

She picks up her briefcase and leaves the dining room. I turn to Marquis, but he's staring at Dad with a look of stunned admiration.

"You've done it now, John," Uncle Thomas murmurs.

Mama is shaking, her mouth set in a hard line. Dad leans back in his chair and stares at me, his lips stained purple from the wine. He has tears in his eyes. I've never heard him say a word against the way of things before, never heard him express regret for how he raised me. Why has he chosen to do it now, in front of a stranger, and an important one at that? He reaches inside his pocket and pulls out a flask, but Mama hits it from his hand before he can unscrew the top.

"Mama," Ursa says. "Why are you so cross?"

Mama pinches the bridge of her nose and Uncle Thomas leans over to whisper something in her ear.

What's got into your dad? Marquis mouths.

Two bottles of wine, I want to say. The flame of excitement I felt has been doused and is replaced by a simmering rage. I glare at my father. My one chance to show Dr. Hollingsworth my translations is lost.

17

"Can *I* go to the smoking room?" Ursa pipes up.

Marquis and I look at each other. We don't have a smoking room.

So where has Rita Hollingsworth gone?

Dad tries to pull Mama into his lap, but she pushes him away.

"I'm sorry, Helina . . . ," he begins.

I snatch up my portfolio and slip out the door.

The foyer is silent except for the ticking of the grandfather clock. Down the hallway is a small sitting room and my parents' study. Could either of those count as a smoking room? I move quietly toward them, my mind still reeling. What possessed Dad to speak in a way that almost made him sound like he's *against* the Class System? The door to the study is ajar and faint lamplight shines through the gap. I rearrange my features into another smile and push the door open.

"I'm sorry for my father's loose tongue, Dr. Hollingsworth."

She is sitting at Dad's desk, a cigarette smoking in the ashtray. Two of the drawers are open. She looks up without so much as flinching.

"Wine makes the best of us argumentative, Vivien," she says indulgently. She waves a small silver box at me. "Cigarette?"

"I don't smoke," I say.

"You will one day if you ever have a career like mine."

I seize my chance. "Dr. Hollingsworth, would you consider me for your summer apprenticeship program?" I slide my portfolio across the desk. "Here's all my best work, as well as a letter of recommendation from one of my professors."

She looks at me thoughtfully, smoke escaping from her mouth and nose.

"Do you wish to become an academic like your parents?"

"No," I reply. "I want to be a translator. I want to discover new dragon languages. Like you."

The brilliant light in Rita Hollingsworth's eyes shines brighter.

"I've heard positive things about you," she says. "You're exactly the type of student I'm looking to recruit."

My heart skips a beat. "It would be an honor—"

There's a loud crash, followed by the sound of breaking glass. I spin round. Has Dad knocked something over? I move toward the door, but Hollingsworth catches me by the sleeve.

"I see a bright future for you, Vivien. But to reach it you may have to look in unexpected places."

I search her face, trying to understand what she means. Among the powdered wrinkles and red lipstick is a look of knowing. My eyes fall on the telephone. It's off the hook.

Mama screams.

"Guardians of Peace!" bellows a voice. "You're under arrest!"

The world slows. I stare at Rita Hollingworth and at the piece of paper she has just pulled from Dad's desk drawer. Realization drops into my mind with a clunk.

"You didn't come to hear my mother's theories, did you?"

She lets go of my sleeve and smiles. And the word from my dream and all its translations come hurtling back to me.

Mengkhenyass.

Serpent.

Enemy.

Imposter.

TWO

Now that I remember the word in one dragon language, I recall it in others, too. The translations roll off my tongue as I run, head spinning, toward the dining room.

Faitour. Slangrieger. Izmamnees.

Two Guardians of Peace stand in the foyer, shards of glass from the smashed front door scattered at their feet. The light of the lamps reflects off their visors, which hide their eyes. I skid to a halt as Dad bursts from the dining room.

"How dare you enter my house—"

More of them come marching through the front door, the glass crunching beneath their heavy boots. They seize Dad by the arms.

"Let go of him!"

I move toward my father, but Uncle Thomas gets there faster. He throws himself between Dad and the Guardians and I hear a sickening crunch as his foot meets someone's knee. He twists one of the Guardians in his grip and slams him to the ground.

"Vivien!"

Mama calls from the doorway. I reach her side at the same time as another Guardian, this one pointing a gun. Ursa is screaming, struggling in Marquis's grip as she tries to run toward Dad. Marquis flings his free arm in front of Mama and me and stares into the Guardian's helmet.

"Don't hurt them!" he says. "Please."

I am frozen to the spot, staring at the barrel of the gun now pressed against Marquis's shoulder. Ursa buries her face into the back of Mama's skirt as the Guardian lowers his weapon.

"Helina Featherswallow, John Featherswallow, Thomas Featherswallow," he says, "you are under arrest on suspicion of civil disobedience."

Civil disobedience?

There are at least ten Guardians standing in the foyer. Dad and Uncle Thomas are pressed to the ground, their hands cuffed behind their backs. I stare at Mama. She is crying silent tears, her hands stroking the top of Ursa's head. Why isn't she explaining that there's been a terrible mistake?

"Tell them, Mama," I plead. "Tell them they have the wrong house."

Mama's blue eyes are electric. "Take your sister and cousin and get out of London," she tells me in Bulgarian. Someone binds her wrists together in front of her. "Get as far away as you can."

My heart plummets.

"Mama!" Ursa is stumbling after Mama as two Guardians push her toward the front door, searching her pockets. Out on the street, a line of sleek black motorcars are waiting. Curtains twitch in the windows of the neighboring houses. The sky is as dark as dragonsmoke.

"Dad, please tell me what's happening!"

I barely notice Marquis clinging to Uncle Thomas's shoulder, shouting at him as the Guardians drag him by the arms. I'm too busy watching my own father being pushed into one of the cars. I get as close as they'll let me.

"Dad?" I say, trying to keep my voice steady.

He swallows loudly and I reach out to touch his face. He leans forward, his eyes red-rimmed. He smells of wine, but the look he gives me is stone-cold sober.

"People shouldn't fear their prime ministers, Vivien," he says. "Prime ministers should fear their people."

They push him into the seat and slam the door closed. I stumble backward, blood rushing in my ears. The cobbled pavement of Fitzroy Square swims in front of me. Somewhere far away, I can hear the banging of fists against glass. A high-pitched cry pierces the air.

"Come on, dear, let go now."

Hollingsworth is kneeling next to a sobbing Ursa, trying to convince her to let go of Mama. It's the sight of my sister, of her tiny fingers clenched tightly round the material of Mama's skirt, that brings me back to myself.

"Don't you dare speak to her!" I say.

I prize Ursa's fist open and lift her bodily from the ground as she howls. Hollingsworth stands up, her lips pursed.

"Remember what I told you," Mama whispers to me in Bulgarian.

There's a hardness in her eyes now. The back of her hand brushes against mine, an invisible gesture of tenderness that says a hundred things at once. Then she kisses Ursa's cheek and steps into the motorcar, disappearing behind a shaded window. I can still smell her perfume. I let out a choked sob as the car drives away and nausea rises in my stomach. Ursa has gone limp in my arms.

"Class pass," a Guardian barks at me. "Let me see it."

I reach for the pass around my neck and offer it to him.

"Second Class. Age seventeen," he says to his superior.

"And this one?"

The superior gestures to Marquis, who is staring at the empty spot the motorcar containing his father has just pulled away from. The other Guardian seizes his class pass.

"Second Class. Age eighteen."

The superior nods and the Guardian grabs Marquis by the shoulder, then handcuffs him.

"No!" I cry. "He did nothing wrong. He's—"

"Vivien Featherswallow, as a minor, you are not currently under arrest. But by order of the law you must remain housebound until your parents undergo trial and your innocence can be proven."

Marquis stares from me to Ursa, a pulse flickering in his jaw.

"The penalty for disobeying this order is immediate imprisonment," the superior continues. "Do you understand?"

"Yes, but my cousin—"

"Is an adult and will be tried as one," the superior snaps.

Ursa hiccups in my arms and reaches out for Marquis, but he is already being pushed into the last remaining motorcar.

"Don't worry, Marquis," I say, throwing myself at the car before they can stop me. "They'll let you go as soon as they realize you're innocent, all of you!"

He gives me a look of utter despair before the door slams in his face and someone pulls me away.

I turn round as another Guardian emerges from the house carrying a box, a knife in a leather sheath hanging from his belt.

"The Prime Minister will want to see this. Found it in a secret cupboard in the office."

A secret cupboard? In our house?

The Guardian sets the box down. "The key was beneath the mother's dress."

Rage seeps through me like a fever. He looks at me and grins.

"Smile, beautiful."

"If you lay a hand on my mother—"

The slap comes out of nowhere. I stumble backward as spots dance before my eyes. Marquis roars inside the locked car and Ursa's hysterical cries ring through the street. The Guardian lifts his visor and looks at me with vague amusement.

"Now, now, Guardian 707," says his superior. "That's no way to treat a Second Class citizen. Miss Featherswallow is simply asking you to treat her mother with the respect her class deserves. Even if she is a Bulgarian leech." He laughs loudly through his helmet and I turn away.

"Hush, Ursa," I soothe, trying to control the sob in my own throat.

"Send that evidence straight to Prime Minister Wyvernmire's office," the superior guardian says. "She'll examine it upon her return from the dragon territories in the morning."

"Be quick about it," says a cool voice. "This is a matter of utmost urgency." Rita Hollingsworth slips the paper she took from Dad's desk inside her pocket. Through my tears, I can see a line of scribbles written in turquoise ink.

"You were never interested in my mother's research," I say. "It was all a ruse to get into our house. You betrayed them—"

"No, Vivien," Hollingsworth replies. "*They* betrayed you. And your sister. And their country."

"That's not true!" I shout. "You've arrested the wrong people!"

One more car pulls up behind the one that holds Marquis.

"Prime Minister Wyvernmire has had people watching your house for months," Hollingsworth says. "People watching *you*. I told you earlier, Vivien, that you will find your future in unexpected places. When you do, you must seize and keep it, no matter the cost." Her brilliant eyes shine as they stare into mine. "I'm sure I'll be meeting you again very soon."

She gets into the car and pulls the door closed. Both the motor-cars drive away and I watch Marquis's silhouette in the back window until it disappears into the distance.

"Come on," I whisper into Ursa's hair. "Let's go inside."

I pick my way across the glittering glass that used to sit in the front door. The dining room has been searched, the contents of every drawer and cupboard upturned. The table lies on its side and the floor is scattered with food and broken china. One of the paintings is crooked, as if someone has looked behind it. And Mina is crouched beneath the chaise longue, hissing.

For an awful moment, I feel the urge to laugh.

I set Ursa down and she stares at the scene with slumped shoulders. Her hair ribbon is gone, her eyelashes wet with tears.

"Let's just clean this up a bit," I say, forcing myself to sound cheerful.

Ursa looks at me with big, solemn eyes.

"I'm sure Mama and Daddy will be back in a few days, and we don't want it to be a mess for them, do we?"

I pick up the table and scrape the pierogi from the floor, trying to keep my hands steady. I straighten the painting and clear away the empty wine bottles. While I sweep the glass from the foyer, Ursa feeds the cat.

"Eat nicely," I hear her tell Mina. "We don't want it to be a mess for Mama and Daddy, do we?"

Afterward, I help Ursa dress for bed.

"I haven't recited my lessons," she says, yawning.

"You can miss them just this once," I reply.

I stroke her hair until she falls asleep, then close the nursery door. Downstairs, the dining room is silent except for the crackle of the fire. I sit on a chair and remember the curl of the Guardian's lip as he pronounced the word *leech*. Are we being targeted, framed somehow, because Mama is Bulgarian? Poor Marquis is locked inside a prison cell on some false charge while I'm here alone in this big, empty house. And my parents . . . I let out a gasp, then a sob.

The penalty for a coup d'état *is death.*

Is that really the reason for all those nights spent talking in the dining room? Have my parents and uncle been planning to join some rebel group and overthrow the government? I can't believe it. I won't. The Featherswallows wear their passes, respect class boundaries, and prepare their children for the Examination. Mama and Dad would never do something so stupid, so selfish.

People shouldn't fear their prime ministers, Vivien. Prime ministers should fear their people.

Wyvernmire is serving her second term as our first female prime minister. She got Britannia through the Great War and has upheld peace between humans and dragons. I've never heard my parents say a word against her. So what did Dad mean?

I stand up so fast that my head spins. The Guardian said something about a secret cupboard. In the study, papers are scattered all over the floor and books have been tossed from the bookcases, their spines cracked open. The window is ajar, letting in the cold, creeping wind. The stub of Hollingsworth's cigarette sits in the ashtray. I feel the tears well up again. This is where Mama and Dad spend most of their time, working to prove their latest theories about dragon behavior and culture. It's a room full of knowledge, of questions, of what-ifs.

Through my tears, I spot something. The side of Dad's desk is . . . open? Heart hammering, I kneel beside it. The wooden panel opens like a door, with a tiny keyhole disguised in the decorative gold stringing. Behind it is a secret compartment, empty except for a penknife. I slip it into my pocket and shake my head in disbelief. They *have* been hiding something. And whatever it was is now sitting in a box inside a Guardian motorcar.

I scan the rest of the room. The worn green sofa looks undisturbed, as does the piano and the cabinet that holds my school trophies. Only the drinks trolley has been moved. It's a painted globe, the top half of which can be lifted to reveal the bottles of wine inside. I used to love tracing the outlines of each country with my finger and learning the names of the different seas. I peer closer at it. There is Rumania, Yugoslavia, and Greece, and nestled between them all is Bulgaria—dragon country. Around the left side of the globe is the United States, the place where Marquis's mother was born, where some states live in peace with dragons and others hunt them like prey.

I frown. Someone has scored a line across the painted surface of the globe with a sharp object, creating an incision that begins in Bulgaria and runs all the way to Britannia. And just next to the line is a tiny version of Wyvernmire's crest, a *W* entangled in a wyvern's tail. It's been drawn in turquoise ink. The same color Dad uses in his fountain pen.

What was he thinking, drawing that on his drinks cabinet? Did the Guardians see it? What does it mean? First the mention of a *coup d'état*, then Mama telling me to flee London, and now this. I lean back against the desk and close my eyes.

It means they're guilty.

If that's true, then whatever the Guardians found in that secret cupboard might prove it. And if the government sees it, or it's used in court . . .

My parents and Uncle Thomas will be sentenced to death.

And what about Marquis? A small moan escapes my lips. How could our parents do this to us? How could they have done everything they told us not to? *Never remove your pass, never socialize below your class, never break the rules.* The thought of my demotion terrifies Dad enough for him to lick a birch rod across my arm . . . so why has he done something that guarantees that Ursa and I will find ourselves in a halfway house before his body turns cold?

The clock on the wall says ten o'clock. Tomorrow morning, Prime Minister Wyvernmire will arrive at her office in Westminster and examine whatever evidence her Guardians have found.

I jump at the loud squawk that comes from the corner of the room. Dad's dracovol—a tiny subspecies of dragon perched inside a hanging cage—is staring at me. He hasn't been out since yesterday, when Mama sent him to deliver a letter. I pick up the cage, set it on the windowsill, and open the door. The dracovol flies off into the night. I pull the window closed and stare at the empty cage.

I need to get rid of the evidence against my parents, but there's no chance I'll get past the security at Westminster. So, unless the box of incriminating papers decides to spontaneously combust during the night, there's no way out of this.

A light flashes on in my brain.

It's a ridiculous idea, probably the worst I've ever had. But what's the alternative? If I don't do something, then my sister will end up in a halfway house, my career will be over before it's begun, and my family . . .

My family will be dead.

Ten minutes later, I carry a sleeping Ursa out of the house. Mina yowls mournfully from inside my sister's schoolbag, which is packed with a change of clothes and a favorite teddy bear. The night air is cold and the street eerily silent. In the sky high above the streetlamps, I see the distant shape of a soaring dragon. I'm lucky that Marylebone is only a short walk away and that I won't have to sneak across any Third Class quarters to get there. A poster stares out at me from a tram stop, the image of a respectable family smiling obliviously while a gun-clad rebel with a dragon's tail snatches their child from behind. The young protesters Marquis and I saw must have been victims of radicalization, but my parents can think for themselves. So how did it come to this?

Sophie's parents live in a modest redbrick house with an apple tree growing outside. The curtains are tightly closed and shadows loom across the lawn. I walk up the stone pathway, my arms aching from the weight of my sister. I rap the brass knocker and wait.

Silence.

I glance nervously over my shoulder. Then a light comes on in the hallway. Abel opens the front door. Sophie's father is gray-haired, his face creased with age, or sleep, or perhaps the trauma of losing his only daughter.

"Vivien?" he whispers into the dark. "Is that you?"

"Yes," I squeak. "Abel, I'm in trouble."

Abel opens the door wider, beckoning me inside, but I shake my head.

"No time," I say, hearing the tremor in my voice. "My parents have been arrested. They're being accused of civil disobedience or something, but I have an idea that might save them. Will you take Ursa?"

Sophie's father blinks.

"Abel?"

His wife appears in the doorway, wrapped in a flannel dressing gown.

"Vivien?"

"I need you to take Ursa," I say, a sob rising in my throat. "I need you to look after her until I get back, which will probably be tomorrow, but if it's not, I need you to keep her safe and I need to know she'll be okay, because otherwise I might—"

My voice cracks. Horror creeps into Alice's face as she looks from me to her husband.

"Vivien," Abel says slowly, "if your parents have been arrested, there's nothing you can do—"

"I can't do nothing," I reply loudly, and Ursa startles. I lower my voice. "My family will die."

"Not if they're innocent."

"*Sophie* was innocent," Alice says fiercely. "And God knows where she is now."

Abel seems to crumple at the mention of his daughter's name.

"Alice, if the Guardians come looking—"

"Then they'll find nothing more than two childless parents caring for a parentless child." Alice reaches out her arms to Ursa. "Give her to me, dear."

I fight down a sob as the weight of the sleeping bundle is lifted from my arms.

"Vivien, going against the law is more dangerous than I think you realize." Abel's blue eyes stare into my own. "Our Sophie—" He pauses, a hand clutching the doorframe. "Sophie tried to come home several times after she was demoted. The Guardians would escort her back to Camden, to her Third Class quarter, but she always returned. And we let her. Alice . . . Alice even tried to hide her. And now she's gone."

My chest tightens. "What do you mean she's gone? Gone where?"

"The council told us she moved to another quarter for work, but she never wrote to us. She *would* write to us if that were true. Wouldn't she?"

He's looking at me as if I might know what Sophie is thinking, or at least where she is. All I can do is nod. Sophie would never abandon her family.

"Now don't you go disappearing, too," Alice says to me, her eyes shining with tears.

I hand Ursa's bag to Abel, and Mina lets out a hiss. "The cat . . . ," I mutter apologetically. "Ursa's class pass is round her neck. I'll be back for her, I promise."

Alice nods, tucking the blanket round Ursa as she turns away. I begin to cry as the little golden head disappears into the house. Abel waits patiently for me to compose myself, and I'm suddenly aware of how much time has passed since I was last inside this house. The memories threaten to overflow, each of them now stained with shame. Sophie's bedroom window fills with light and I know I need to leave. Alice has taken Ursa without a second thought. Would she have done so if she knew Sophie was missing because of me? If she knew how I tore her family apart?

"Be careful, Vivien," Abel says.

31

I nod before slipping back down the pathway and onto the street, pulling the strap of my satchel across my body. I have a long night ahead. I need a dragon, a dragon with a motive.

Luckily for me, I know exactly where to find one.

THREE

The library is located in the University of London's North Tower. Every doorway and window is shrouded in shadow and the grand iron gates stand tall and imposing in the darkness. But I know they're just for show. I slip silently over the wall, my leather shoes sinking softly into the grass. The tower's oak doors are bolted closed so I creep round the side of the building to a small window illuminated by a streetlamp. I run a finger along the edges of the windowpane. Dad's penknife is cold and heavy in my pocket. I flick it open and place the tip in the groove between the window frame and the glass.

I've seen Dad do this before, when Ursa locked herself in the garden shed in protest against starting school. He lifted her out and explained to her that an education would ensure her a good profession that would allow her to stay with the family forever.

The resistance softens as the blade meets the rubber and I begin to cut, dragging the knife down and round the pane of glass. Dad is gentler with Ursa than he used to be with me. I was six when I exchanged my class pass with Vera Malloy from the Third Class quarter across the square. We did it as a joke, but it wasn't funny when a Guardian motorcar pulled up and Vera fled, my pass still round her neck.

The Guardian demanded to know what I, Vera Malloy, was

doing in a Second Class quarter without an authorization badge. My entire body went cold with dread, but instead of arresting me, the Guardian walked me to Vera's quarter and left me in a street I didn't know. So I screamed at him in Wyrmerian, and then in several other dragon tongues, asking how I could speak so many if I attended a Third Class school.

Your languages saved you, Vivien, and they'll save you again, Dad told me.

But he forbade me from playing out in the street after that.

The pane of glass wobbles as I dig my blade beneath it, then comes free. I set it gently on the ground, stick my hand through the gap, and lift the handle on the inside. The window swings open and I heave myself through, scuffing my shoes on the wall in the process. In all my childhood fantasies about the University of London, I never pictured myself breaking into it.

I'm standing behind the receptionist's desk in a small, book-lined nook of the library. I edge my way through the dark, across the worn floorboards to the entrance hall until I find the lift, then step in and close the cage doors. I pull the crank all the way to the left. As the lift begins to rise, I catch flashes of the different floors through the tiny window. It stops with a shudder at the top and I exit at the bottom of the spiral staircase. I've been up here once before, as a dare.

Bet you don't have it in you to go and see that dragon for yourself, Marquis had said.

I had climbed the staircase into the dragon's prison, reveling in my cousin's dismay, before darting back down. Just to prove that I could. Now, with my hand skimming the curved banister, I climb again.

A breeze chills the air and I shiver as I step into the circular room. My eyes dart immediately to the line of bookcases I saw the dragon sprawled across last time, seeking out its shape in the light of the moon. But there's nothing there. A set of steps lead up onto a balcony that allows access to the highest bookshelves. I wonder what sort of books they hold—they can't be of much importance if they've been left up here.

A sweet, rotting smell turns my stomach. I take a step forward and something crunches underfoot. It's the white skull of a small mammal, a cat perhaps. It must have wandered up here in search of mice only to meet its own gory end. Either that or the maintenance workers have started feeding their pets to the dragon.

Anticipation rises in my stomach. I *have* to do this. I have no other choice. The thought makes me feel braver. But where is the dragon?

I walk through the archway ahead. It leads into a second room, larger than the first. I step onto the carpet and it crackles beneath my shoes. It's not a carpet at all. It's a huge shed dragon skin, pale and papery. To the right is an abandoned desk splattered in bird droppings and to the left a faded sign.

Knowledge Requests, it reads.

Older students have told me that the library dragon is a criminal who rebelled against the creation of the Peace Agreement because it refused to be governed by human laws. So it was sent here to serve humans—the worst punishment that could be inflicted on its kind. Its sentence was to provide the scholars with relevant knowledge or history. After all, a creature that has lived for centuries is a hundred times more informative than any book. But the decision backfired when the dragon almost killed a student. I suppose that now it will simply be left here until it dies.

I stare up into the eaves of the tower, but nothing moves except for a nesting pigeon. A gust of wind hits my face as I turn the corner. The wall has been knocked through, opening on to the outer terraces of the tower like a gaping wound made of limestone and jagged metal. I feel the hairs on the back of my neck lift. It's as if the air has been sucked out of the room. Standing with its back to me, its body spanning the whole space, is the dragon.

It is staring out across the parapet walls that overlook the campus below and the city beyond. Its spike-encrusted tail is curled round its body like a cat's and its skin, a deep pink color, is covered in scales that glitter like glass in the moonlight. It's the biggest, most terrifying dragon I've ever seen.

On a research trip with Mama I barely remember, I once slept among friendly wyverns, their bodies giving off heat like snoring suns. During the zeppelin air raids of the Great War, I watched dragons guard their posts on Fitzroy Square, queue in Blackfriars to be armored, deflect bombs above Westminster. But this is something else entirely. This is a criminal dragon.

What the hell was I thinking? I back away slowly, but my foot meets a lump of stone.

Shit.

I wince as the stone skitters across the ground. My heart thumps loudly in my chest. The dragon's tail twitches. How long has it known I'm here?

At least you can't run away now.

I clear my throat and try to keep my voice steady.

"Are you the library dragon?" I sound like a frightened child.

The dragon lets out a purr. "Which other dragon would I be?"

It's speaking English with a Slavic accent—is it Bulgarian? This really is the worst idea I've ever had.

I swallow. "I was wondering—"

"I haven't taken knowledge requests since 1903."

Its voice is hoarse yet soft, and undoubtedly female. The dragon turns suddenly, swinging her huge head toward me. Her face is covered in spikes, too, and there are white rings around her eyes.

"I'm not here for a knowledge request," I say quickly.

She lets out a growl that vibrates beneath my feet. "Well, that is fortunate," she says. "I would have sliced your tongue from your mouth if you were."

I feel my insides shrink. "Is that what you did to the last student who came up here?"

"Alas, I do not recall."

"Dragon memory is capable of recalling over ten times the information retained in a human brain," I say. "And the humans here seem to remember quite well."

Do I have a death wish? The dragon's tail moves as she stares at me with eyes like bright amber globes. Above her giant talons are several rows of silky black feathers. She's beautiful, but there are sores up her legs and a grayish tinge to her skin.

"You're a prisoner," I say, pointing to the tiny silver box I know is attached to the space between the dragon's wings.

It's a detonator, fused to the creature's skin and filled with an explosive.

"How observant," the dragon replies.

"Are you a Bulgarian dragon?" I remember Marquis's sketches of the different species. "A Bolgorith?"

"So what if I am?"

"*Moyava maìka izlydane e v Bolgor,*" I say in Slavidraneishá.

My mother is from Bulgaria.

"The child speaks dragon tongue."

A thrill shoots through me. She understood what I said. For the first time in my life, I'm speaking Dragonese with an actual dragon.

"I speak Slavidraneishá, Wyrmerian, Harpentesa, Drageoir, Draecksum, and a little Komodonese. And some human languages, obviously."

I push my hair behind my ears and take a deep breath.

"What's your name?"

The dragon lets out a deep sigh.

"I'm Vivien," I offer.

"I am Chumana."

"Snake Maiden?" I say. "That's what it means in English, doesn't it?"

"What do you want, human girl?"

I brace myself. This conversation could go either way. Chumana has tried to kill a student once before—who's to say she won't do it again?

"I've come to offer you a deal," I say.

Chumana makes a noise that can only be a laugh.

"What kind of deal could a human girl possibly offer a criminal dragon?"

I hesitate, but only for a second. "Escape," I say. "Freedom. Revenge."

"You are delusional," Chumana breathes, turning away.

"I can get that detonator off you!" I say. "After that, you could simply fly away. But first . . ." I pause. "First, I need you to burn Prime Minister Wyvernmire's office to the ground."

The dragon turns back to look at me. "You require me to serve you?"

"No!" I scowl. "I told you, we'd be making a deal. Between equals."

Chumana laughs again and I feel my face go hot.

"You would dare make a deal with a dragon?"

I think of Marquis's horrified face, of Ursa's cries, of my mother left alone with those Guardians.

"I would."

"Do you know what will happen if you break it?"

Chumana's voice is as seductive as silk on bare skin.

"You'll kill me," I say simply.

The criminal dragon studies me, her amber eyes darkening.

"Burn Wyvernmire's office to the ground?" she hisses. "It would be my pleasure."

My heart leaps out of my chest and back in again, but I nod, trying to look calm.

"The detonator," I say, jerking my head in the direction of Chumana's wings.

Marquis has told me about dragon detonators and how they were somehow negotiated into the Peace Agreement for use on criminal dragons only. The silver box is no bigger than my hand, but packed with—if I remember correctly—mercury fulminate crystals.

"Do you have a blade, human girl?" says Chumana. "We both know we cannot count on your teeth."

I bite back a smile. So dragons do humor as well as sarcasm? I take out Dad's penknife and Chumana snorts through her snout.

"That is no match for my hide," she says. She lifts a claw in the direction of the library. "Above the desk."

I go back inside and Chumana follows, her long tail trailing behind like a serpent. Mounted on the wall above the desk is a sword encased in a glass frame. I climb onto the desk to remove the heavy case from the wall, then set it down on the floor. Chumana watches, a puff of smoke rising from her nostrils.

"Why would they leave this here with a prisoner?" I ask as I search the desk drawers for something heavy.

"Do *you* know of any human willing to cut a dangerous explosive from the body of a murderous dragon?" says Chumana.

I shrug—I bet the Third Class girl I saw killed at the protest would be.

Except her kind rarely gets anywhere near university libraries.

My hand touches something round and cold and I pull a paperweight out of a drawer. I throw it down onto the glass case, smashing it to pieces. Then I carefully pull the sword out. It's heavy and definitely real. The hilt is slightly rusted, but the blade is razor-sharp.

"Right," I say, turning round. Chumana is standing between two bookcases, waiting.

"How do you want to do this?"

"You will have to climb," she says.

I nod, trying to still my shaking hands. I walk round Chumana's left side, close enough to see the calluses on her skin.

"I'll need some light," I say from behind her. "I don't suppose you could . . . set something on fire?"

"No," the dragon growls. "Not unless you want us both to explode."

"I see," I say weakly. "I'll light the lamps, then."

I light the old gas lamps on the wall, then stare up at Chumana's body. Her wings shiver on each side of her back, giant leathery

40

things that I know will span the space of the whole room when unfolded. Dome-shaped scales run up the length of her spine.

I grip the sword tighter in one hand. "So I'll just—"

"Get on with it."

I place a foot at the base of Chumana's tail.

Oh, Marquis, if you could see me now.

The climbing is easier than I expected. Chumana's scales provide holds for my hands and feet—it's somewhat similar to ascending a breathing cliff. My fingertips brush over the skin between the scales and it's warm, almost hot, to the touch. Chumana smells of animal and dragonsmoke and old books.

I stop at the top of her back, my knees on either side of her spine. The detonator is strategically placed at the base of her wings and surrounded by thick scar tissue. How does it feel to have a piece of metal melted into your skin? Does it hurt less for dragons, whose body temperature is already so high? I hope so.

"Chumana," I say suddenly. "How does this detonator work?"

She shifts ever so slightly and I grab hold of her wing so as not to fall off.

"You must take care," Chumana says. "The crystals in the detonator are sensitive to shock, as well as heat. Once you've removed it, do *not* drop it."

I feel my heart race. So I could potentially be about to kill us both?

"But *how* does it work?" I repeat. "How has it stopped you from escaping all this time?"

"Friction," the dragon growls. "If I were to fly, the movement of my wings would set the detonator off. And if that were to fail, the elevation of my body heat caused by my increased heart rate would react with the crystals." Chumana growls. "It is an ingenious human invention."

I stare at the lethal silver box, trying to wrap my mind round the cruelty of binding a dragon's innate need to fly with its certain death.

"Are you ready?" I ask, and Chumana grunts.

I've never used a sword before. I run a finger along the scar tissue. What if I cut too deep and Chumana bleeds out? Then I laugh at myself. As if I, Viv Featherswallow, am capable of accidentally killing a dragon.

I push myself onto my knees and hold the hilt of the sword in both hands. Then I angle the length of the blade against the skin and press hard. Red blood spills from the cut. Chumana doesn't move. I slice deeper. Once I feel the edge of the box against the blade, I slice down beneath it, cutting through the flesh like a knife through butter. Chumana lets out a loud hiss as I catch the bloody box in my left hand.

Do not *drop it.*

I fling the blade to the floor and slide down Chumana's back slowly, my eyes never leaving the detonator. On the desk chair is a soft, moth-bitten cushion and I set the detonator on top of it carefully. I breathe and turn toward Chumana with a smug smile. Her eyes open and settle on me. I wait. I have just freed a criminal dragon who protested the Peace Agreement held between my species and her own. What's to say she'll keep her end of the deal?

"Why do you wish to burn Wyvernmire's office?"

"It contains evidence that my parents are rebels," I reply. "I need it gone."

The whiskers on Chumana's snout twitch. She bows her head.

"Then consider it gone, human girl."

Her wings unfold suddenly, knocking bookcases over like dominoes. The edges are tipped with spikes and as strong as bone, but the membrane looks paper-thin and feather-light.

"Chumana," I say suddenly. "What's your maxim?"

If she hears me, she doesn't show it. I run behind her as she crashes out onto the terrace and, without warning, jolts forward and up into the air. Her talons hit the parapet walls, sending them crumbling to the ground below with a boom that echoes across campus. She nosedives, her body fighting for balance.

Chumana hovers midair, then flies.

I laugh, adrenaline pumping through my body as I watch the dragon shrink into the distance, the shape of her outlined by stars. How long has it been since she last flew? The thought sobers me.

I wipe my bloody hands on my trousers and ride the lift downstairs. I need to be back in Fitzrovia by dawn, but that leaves me enough time to see Chumana keep her side of the deal with my own eyes. Wyvernmire isn't in her office, so she won't be harmed. Then, with the evidence of my family's crimes destroyed, I'll pick up Ursa from Sophie's and wait for them all at home.

I hop back over the wall and walk through the darkness toward Westminster with a soaring heart.

By the time I turn on to Downing Street, rain is plummeting from the sky. I crouch in the shadows, keeping to the opposite side of the road as I watch the Guardians patrolling outside Number 10. Rain drips through my hair and down the back of my neck and I shiver. The sky is full of dark clouds. There is still no sign of Chumana.

She's not coming.

I stare at the Guardians as rain pools in the grass beneath my shoes. I play with the frayed red string around my wrist, the friendship bracelet Sophie gave me, the one I've never been able to bring myself to cut off.

She lied.

I try to distract myself by guessing Chumana's maxim. All dragons have one, a motto they choose for themselves, usually in Latin. A maxim is the one constant they live by. Ten minutes later, my clothes are soaked through and she still isn't here. I sink back on my heels and let out a shaky breath. The sun will rise soon and the evidence of my family's rebellion will be moved again, no doubt to somewhere more secure. I swallow a lump in my throat. I've spent the whole night out here for nothing. I can't save them.

Movement catches my eye. A shadow is gliding through the night. Chumana flies silently over 10 Downing Street and back again, her huge body like a dark paper cutout against the sky. The Guardians continue their patrol, oblivious. Then flames bloom from the clouds. The left side of the building catches alight first and the Guardians jump back in alarm. As they shout for backup and reach for their weapons, Chumana sends more fire licking up the right side. I crouch lower behind the bushes as Guardians come running from several directions, firing shots into the air. Black smoke billows into the sky and the orange flames climb higher and higher, as if reaching for the rain. An alarm sounds and Chumana disappears.

There's a crash as windowpanes burst and people begin rushing from the building. Somewhere far away, a fire engine wails. I once heard that Wyvernmire's ancestors were hunters of wyverns. It's said she has the wyvern heads mounted on her office walls, as a reminder of that dark time when dragons and humans preyed on each other mercilessly. I wonder if they're burning, too. I cough as the smoke fills the bushes I'm hiding in.

Time to go.

Guardians and staff fill the street, fleeing the flames that are spreading at an alarming speed. I saw my fair share of dragonfire during the war, but I forgot how vicious it is.

Please don't let anyone be hurt.

In any case, the incriminating papers have surely burned to ash. I stand up and back away—

A cold hand slides round my neck.

I try to shout as I'm dragged backward, but my breath is crushed in my throat. Pain shoots down my arm as my fist connects with a hard Guardian helmet and the buildings around me seem to spin. The Guardian throws me into the back of a van.

"You're under arrest," he says as he cuffs my hands. "Anything you say from this moment forward could be used against you in court."

No, no, no.

I'm kneeling in the dark and almost fall sideways as the van pulls away.

"Under arrest on what charge?" I gasp.

My wet clothes cling to my skin and my hair smells of dragonsmoke. The van turns sharply and the Guardian catches me as I lurch forward.

"Vivien Featherswallow, you are under arrest for breaking the Peace Agreement."

THE ILLUSTRATED
LONDON NEWS

Saturday, November 24, 1923
The Lives and Deaths of the Royal Heirs—
Portraits and Personal Notes

TODAY MARKS the Silver Jubilee of Queen Beatrice Mary Victoria Feodore, the ninth child of Queen Victoria and Prince Albert, born in 1857. Her Majesty ascended to the throne in 1898 upon the death of her last remaining brother, King Leopold. During her reign, our beloved Queen Beatrice has played a unifying role as figurehead of the Empire, launched the British Association for Bulgarian Refugees, and commissioned the first Dragon Guard at Balmoral Castle, made up of wyverns currently indebted to the Crown. As a child, she raised two dragonlings, who emancipated themselves upon the signing of the Peace Agreement.

LINE OF SUCCESSION (PORTRAITS ON PAGE 8)

King Edward VII † Death by dragon during a hunting accident in
Bechuanaland Protectorate, alongside his sons.

Prince Alfred † Overdose of Reptiliaum
(a now-illegal dragon saliva opioid).

Prince Arthur † Death by dragon during an exhibition
of live dragon eggs at Buckingham Palace

King Leopold † Hemophilia

Queen Beatrice I—Born 1857

Feodora, Princess Royal—Born 1887

FOUR

You are under *arrest for breaking the Peace Agreement.*

The words play over and over in my mind as I lie on the bed in the prison cell. I sit up and swallow, my throat as dry as sandpaper. Why did I take the risk of going to watch Chumana burn Wyvernmire's office? Why didn't I just go straight home? The dawn light filters through the tiny cell window and a sudden pang clutches at my heart. Ursa will be waking up in a strange house with people she barely knows. Will she cry when she realizes I'm gone? Will she think I've left her forever? What will the state do with the abandoned child of rebels?

The guilt crushes my chest, forcing my breath out in short, painful sobs. I thought I'd never do anything worse than what I did to Sophie back in the summer. But now the stain of despair left by that one decision—the stain that always manages to seep into every good thing—has grown bigger. It's like I can't stop making mistakes that hurt the people I love.

I close my eyes and welcome the guilt, more painful than the stinging welts left by the birch rod or the humiliation of being discarded by Hugo Montecue after I gained the courage to push his hands away. I force myself to feel every drop of it.

Don't make mistakes if you're not prepared to live with the consequences, Mama has always told me.

This pain is the consequence of my actions.

I dwell on it all day, my eyes fixed on the patch of sky through the window. I wait as long as I can bear before I'm forced to use the chamber pot in the corner, and as I crouch over it I hear a loud boom that reverberates through the whole building. Outside, people scream. I drift in and out of sleep as the white clouds are replaced by stars. When I wake again, the sun is high in the sky, and a bolt slides loudly across the door.

Stay calm, I tell myself. *They can't prove anything.*

"Stand up!" orders the voice through the Guardian helmet.

I stand.

"Arms out."

"I've been here for a whole day *and* night," I say as the Guardian searches me. "You still haven't read any official charges against me."

"The Prime Minister's office was the target of arson," the Guardian says. "You and a dragon were both seen at the scene of the crime."

"In that case, I think it was most likely the dragon that lit that fire, don't you?" I spit.

My insides twist like snakes. What's wrong with me? If I'm going to get out of here, I need to show the shiny schoolgirl version of Viv Featherswallow—not this new, angry, breaking-into-buildings-with-her-rebel-father's-penknife version.

"Hands behind your back."

The Guardian handcuffs me and pushes me toward the door. The corridor is full of cells identical to my own. Are my parents in one of them? Is Marquis? I'm pushed into a lift, shinier and more modern than the one in the library, and it jolts to a stop several floors up. We emerge onto a carpeted corridor that smells strongly of tea. Photographs of important-looking people line one wall and in the center is a framed copy of the Peace Agreement—signed by the Dragon Queen Ignacia herself in her own blood. The former Prime Minister's ink pen must have seemed embarrassingly pathetic in comparison.

I eye the tiny printed words, lines and lines of promises and clauses negotiated between humans and dragons. The same document that took pride of place in every classroom I've ever sat in. My only chance is to convince whoever runs the prison how much I agree with it.

The Guardian leads me into a small parlor lit by dull electric lamps. Ugly metal filing cabinets stand against the walls and on a table at the far end of the room is a model of what looks like a city in miniature, with paper dragons suspended above.

"Sit," the Guardian says, steering me toward an armchair.

I sit. A teapot is steaming on a small table set for two, with a box of tea leaves beside it.

"This is a mistake," I tell the Guardian, who has positioned himself by the door. "I support the Peace Agreement. It literally stops humans and dragons from killing each other, so why would I—"

A tall woman strides into the room and I bite my cheek so hard I taste blood. Prime Minister Wyvernmire wears a long dark coat and a brooch the shape of a dragon's talon. A symbol of her commitment to the Peace Agreement and to the Dragon Queen. Her red hair is coiffed and set with hair spray so that it resembles a puffy halo round her head. Her face, pale as milk, contains several fine, powdered lines. She's older than I imagined.

"Good morning, Miss Featherswallow."

Her voice sounds exactly the same as it does on the radio—severe and smooth. She takes a seat in the armchair opposite mine. I open my mouth, then close it again. I am meeting the Prime Minister of Britannia. In handcuffs.

"Welcome to Highfall Prison, where the country's most radical rebels are guarded with the highest security levels." Prime Minister Wyvernmire's eyes narrow. "You should feel right at home."

I shrink into my seat.

Rebels are tax-avoiding sloths at best and violent anarchists at worst. I've read the newspaper articles about the acts of vandalism, the bombs in letterboxes, the attempted assassinations.

"No, I don't," is all I manage to say.

"Forgive me," Wyvernmire says, pouring the tea into cups. "I simply thought that, given who your parents are . . ."

"You can't prove anything about my parents," I say, instantly regretting it.

"Unfortunately, you are correct," Wyvernmire replies. "The evidence my Guardians collected was destroyed in a fire that ravaged Ten Downing Street in the early hours of yesterday morning. But of course you know all about that."

My stomach plummets. Any fierceness I was feeling before dissolves on the spot.

"Nevertheless," Wyvernmire continues, "we have eyewitnesses more than happy to give evidence of your parents' crimes. It's ironic how even the most radical insurrectionists are willing to betray their comrades when their own necks are on the line."

I feel the heat rise in my cheeks. "My parents aren't insurrectionists. And neither am I."

Wyvernmire sets a teacup in front of me.

"You released a criminal dragon from its prison at the University of London, somehow convincing it to set fire to my office in a gross act of arson. Or are you going to tell me that the destruction of the evidence linking your parents to the rebellion against my government was a mere coincidence?"

I stare at the ground, my face stinging with shame.

"Do you know what we call an attack on a political building, Vivien?"

"Terrorism," I whisper.

"Clever girl."

The reality of what I asked Chumana to do begins to sink in.

"But what interests me is how you managed to persuade this dragon to do your bidding," Wyvernmire says. "Your actions have only further incriminated your parents, and yourself, in the process. And yet . . . I believe there is something more to you. You made quite an impression on Rita Hollingsworth."

"I never want to see that woman again," I say.

"Top of your class twelve years running. Fluent in nine languages. The apple of your parents' eye."

Wyvernmire gestures to the Guardian to uncuff me. I rub my sore wrists and take a sip of the hot, sweet tea.

"My dear girl," the Prime Minister says, "what on earth possessed you?"

The gentleness in her voice takes me by surprise. My tears mingle with the steam from the teacup. Two days ago, all I wanted was an apprenticeship in the Academy's translation department, but now I'll probably never go back to university.

"My parents are good people, and I wanted to help them," I say slowly.

"They made a choice that ripped your family apart," Wyvernmire says, her voice resuming its slow, austere quality. "They used their influential positions in society to aid the rebel movement. And they deliberately kept you in the dark, leading you to make a decision that has ruined any chance of you achieving your dream career and potentially orphaning yourself *and* your sister."

I suck in a sharp breath. "This is all a mistake," I say, stumbling over the words. "My mother has worked for the Academy; my uncle is part of the military—"

"We've been watching your home for months," Wyvernmire says. "Ever since you applied to university. The people who come in and out of your house are known—"

"I'm sorry," I say. "Did you say ever since I applied to university?"

"We don't let just anyone read for a degree in Dragon Tongues, Vivien."

"You don't?"

"The last few decades have seen a substantial rise in rebellion and dissidence, most commonly found in those whose careers keep them in regular contact with . . . dragons." The Prime Minister closes her eyes as if that last word caused her physical pain. "We have found it wise to discourage the learning of dragon tongues, or at least to entrust it to those citizens we know to be loyal."

She smiles at me, and such a gesture doesn't seem to come naturally to her. "Why else would the university have asked you for so many character references?"

References. I needed five, but only had four by the time application day arrived. That was why I'd gone to see Mistress Morris, who asked me to . . .

No, I can't think about that now.

"The protocol investigations following your application flagged some irregularities regarding your parents and uncle," Wyvernmire says. "They are part of a group of Second Class Coalition sympathizers."

"But that's impossible," I whisper. "My parents were always strict about class boundaries, and we attend the Peace Agreement Celebration every year . . ."

"Vivien," Wyvernmire says patiently, "I am quite convinced that you knew nothing of your parents' crimes. However, my Guardians watched you break your house arrest, drop your sister off at a house in Marylebone, and force entry into the University of London."

They know where Ursa is.

"On Saturday evening, you didn't just release a criminal dragon. You *told it* to commit an act of terrorism on Ten Downing Street, which is a direct breach of the Peace Agreement between the humans and dragons of Britannia."

Prime Minister Wyvernmire sets her tea down and stares at me with unblinking green eyes.

"You started a war."

Blood rushes in my ears. "A war?"

"Surely you must realize that?"

I gaze out the window just as a dragon streaks past, so close to the building that I see the green feathers of its wing. The tea swirls in my empty stomach. I look back at Prime Minister Wyvernmire.

"My military is now poised to attack the dragons in retaliation," she says. "All alliances have been broken. And the chaos you have created has given the rebel groups the opportunity to move against my government."

There is a low, heavy rumble from down the street. The windows rattle. What have I done? The room swims around me. Why didn't I just leave London like Mama told me to?

"I'm sorry," I murmur. "I didn't mean for this to happen. I just wanted my parents home."

"For fifty-seven years, the Peace Agreement has kept us safe," Wyvernmire says. "Fortunately, I have been preparing for the possibility of its dismantling for quite some time."

She pauses. "While the rebels have spent the last twenty-four hours carrying out acts of war across the country, *I* spent them conversing with Queen Ignacia. She takes no responsibility for the act of the dragon who helped you start this war and has ordered it destroyed."

I think of Chumana, finally free only to be murdered midflight.

"And we have come to an understanding."

I'm nodding, but I don't understand a word of what the Prime Minister is saying. All I can think of is how much better things would have been for Ursa if I'd just stayed at home.

"The Peace Agreement will remain in place," Wyvernmire says, "but we will use this attempt to thwart it as an opportunity to come down on rebel humans and dragons alike. The rebel movement is attacking, and we must defend ourselves."

"So . . . this is a civil war?" I say. "With the government and the Dragon Queen on one side, and the rebels on the other?"

"Correct," Wyvernmire says. "The question now, Vivien, is this: Which side will you be on?"

The clock on the wall counts the seconds of silence.

"I don't understand," I say. "I broke the Peace Agreement. My parents are rebels. I'm a criminal now, aren't I?"

Wyvernmire leans forward. "Are you really fluent in nine languages?"

"Yes . . . ," I reply. Why does this matter? "Three human languages and five dragon tongues . . . six if you count Komodonese."

Wyvernmire folds her hands in her lap.

"The War Effort requires the skills of a polyglot," she says simply. "A speaker of dragon tongues. Someone with a unique talent for deciphering . . . meaning."

I blink.

"Your family is currently facing the death penalty," she continues. "Your sister will be orphaned and placed in a Third Class children's home and the people currently caring for her will be punished for harboring the child of rebels—"

"No!" I say. "They're only doing what any decent person would do."

Wyvernmire's expression turns cold.

"I am offering you a once-in-a-lifetime opportunity," she says. "I am offering you a job."

A job?

I suddenly see myself in a labor camp, my life flashing before my eyes in one continuous stream of pain and drudgery.

"Should you accept—and excel—then, and only then, will you and your family be pardoned."

My heart leaps.

Is this real?

"Your parents and uncle will be unable to exercise their current professions. However, they will be permitted to seek work elsewhere," Wyvernmire says. "You will be allowed to return to your studies, having proved your loyalty to the government once and for all."

"And my cousin?" I say. "He's the most innocent of all of us."

"He will also be pardoned."

I let out a shaky breath. I don't know if I'll ever forgive Mama and Dad for what they've done, but at least I can save their lives. At least I can bring them home.

"What is the job?"

"I'm afraid you won't be told until you get there." Wyvernmire glances at the gold watch on her wrist. "Do you accept?"

I force myself to pause, to take a sip of lukewarm tea, to pretend as if I have a choice in the matter.

"Where will my family be in the meantime?"

"At Highfall."

My stomach lurches. So they *are* here.

"And my sister and her . . . caregivers? They'll be safe?"

"Of course," Wyvernmire replies. "Unless you fail to carry out the work given to you."

I nod slowly, hope flooding my body. The sunlight hits the window, surrounding the Prime Minister in a golden glow. Here is the woman I have long admired—fair and dignified, who commands respect like a man. Among the first of Britannia's women to attend university, she has achieved as much for the nation as Hollingsworth has for the Academy. Wyvernmire is just doing her job, I realize. The job that keeps society running. The one that has kept the alliance between the British humans and dragons—hanging by a thread thanks to me—intact. And now she's offering me the opportunity to erase the past two days as if they were just one terrible dream.

Your languages saved you, Vivien, and they'll save you again.

"All right," I say. "But I have one condition."

"You are hardly in a position to bargain."

"My cousin Marquis. He's clever—he studies dragon anatomy. Give him a job, too."

Wyvernmire stares at me. "No."

"He can't stay here; he's done nothing wrong!" I feel braver, buoyed by the realization that the Prime Minister of the United Kingdom has just suggested she *needs* me. "Take us both," I say, "and we'll *both* help you win this war."

She studies my face for a long time, as if seeking out a lie.

"Very well," she says.

I feel weightless, as if I might begin to float at any moment.

"But if you fail, your cousin will meet his end by way of the hangman's noose—just like the rest of your family."

I nod. "I accept your offer."

Wyvernmire reaches into her briefcase and pulls out a handful of typewritten pages.

"You are required to sign the Official Secrets Act before you go anywhere. In doing so, you are taking a lifelong vow never to reveal the details of the job you are about to undertake. Do you understand?"

"Yes," I say, taking the pen being offered to me.

I scan the page quickly and words like *SECRETS* and *DRAG-ONS* and *GOVERNMENT GUIDELINES* jump out at me. But there's no point in reading it. This job is my only hope.

I sign the paperwork and Wyvernmire gives me a satisfied nod. Then she tips her head in the Guardian's direction.

"Get Miss Featherswallow cleaned up."

I suddenly notice the state of my trousers, smeared in dragon blood.

"And release the boy," Wyvernmire says. "They're going to the DDAD."

"Can I ask one question?" I say as the Guardian escorts me to the door, without handcuffs this time.

"One," Wyvernmire says.

"The dragon, the one that burned your office. Has it been destroyed yet?"

Lines crease across the Prime Minister's forehead.

"No," she says. "For now, that particular rebel is still alive.'"

Transcript of an excerpt from "A Natural History of Dragon Tongues," a paper delivered to students at the University of London in 1919, by Dragon Anthropologist Dr. Helina Featherswallow, MA, PhD.

Before one can embark on the proper study of dragon tongues, as all you bright young things are about to do, one must first take into account their origins.

Over the last fifty years of scholarship, it has become widely accepted that dragon tongues did, in fact, develop from human languages. Indeed, had human beings not walked this earth, dragons might never have developed any form of spoken language at all. And yet dragons display a mastery of language that far surpasses our own.

There is no evidence to suggest that dragons ever spoke verbally before the evolution of humans on our planet. When our ancestors, whose first spoken languages began to emerge only once they learned to control their primitive vocalizations, started to migrate throughout the world, interaction with the dragon populations became inevitable. It was at this precise moment in time, when the dragons had grasped the basic foundations of human language, that dragon tongues were born.

This explains why the six known dragon tongues spoken in the anglophone countries of England, Australia, and America bear multiple similarities to English (a Germanic human language) but almost none to Spanish (a Romance human language). Indeed, these six English-related dragon tongues bear in turn similarities to the dragon tongue spoken in Germany, due of course to the fact that both German and English evolved from the same unwritten ancestor, Proto-Germanic.

Furthermore, Wyrmerian, a modern-day tongue spoken by British dragons, and Draecksum, spoken by Dutch dragons, are so close that many words are interchangeable. This is because Holland is one of the main areas from which the Anglo-Saxon settlers in England migrated. Our human languages now even borrow from dragon tongues, with skrit, a common word in English vocabulary meaning fool, originating from Wyrmerian. It is interesting to note that dragon languages contain many words requiring the "s" sound, which comes naturally to dragons due to the forked nature of their tongues.

Only once a linguist has understood the origins of Dragonese as a whole can they hope to study each tongue separately. Indeed, it is this manner of proceeding that will allow one to delve even further into the subject of dragon linguistics, as I know you hope to do, beginning with the fascinating theory of dragon dialects, which—

[Long pause, unintelligible whisperings, recording ends]

FIVE

St. Pancras Station is chaos. The sharp November air slips its frozen hands inside my coat and I shiver. The Guardians let me wash and change into new clothes before climbing into the same type of motorcar that took my parents away. I pull at the jumper and the too-small skirt, trying not to think about who they might have belonged to before. Marquis, I was told, will be following in a separate car. But as I watch people running to catch trains, pulling groaning suitcases and crying children, I see no sign of my cousin.

"Britannia is at war once more!"

The newspaper-seller has parked his stall in front of the ticket office, where a man with a trolley, holding a cello and several other instruments, is gesticulating urgently. The vendor's voice echoes through the station as a train pulls up in a gush of steam. It's small and old and blue. Something tells me I won't be needing a ticket.

"Are you sure this is the right one?" I ask the Guardian closest to me.

He nods, the visor of his helmet hiding his face, and pushes me toward the train. I peer through the window at the empty seats, then step on board. My escorts remain on the platform. My coat, the only thing I was allowed to keep, still smells of dragonsmoke. I find a carriage and sit in a window seat as my stomach fills with dread.

Marquis isn't here. I should have known, shouldn't I? As if the Prime Minister would bargain with a seventeen-year-old criminal. I blink away hot tears—I won't cry with the Guardians watching me. A newspaper is stuffed down the side of my seat and I pull it out, flicking past the Selfridges' ads for ladies' mackintoshes on the front page.

Peace Agreement to be Upheld: A War on Rebels Begins, says the first headline.

A war on rebels.

I think back to my parents' many late-night conversations. All this time, they must have been discussing secret meetings or attacks or whatever it is rebels discuss. How could they do that to me, to Marquis, to Ursa? I read the rest of the headlines, trying to calm my breathing.

LONDON ATTACKED BY HUMAN-DRAGON
COALITION IN *COUP D'ÉTAT*
FROM PROTEST TO PUTSCH—BRITANNIA'S FIRST
INTERSPECIES PARTY DECLARES WAR
MASS BREAKOUT FROM GRANGER'S PRISON

I tap my foot nervously against the floor. It's no wonder Rita Hollingsworth refused to publish Mama's latest papers if the government knew she was a rebel. But the idea of the Academy discouraging the learning of dragon tongues sounds extreme—surely Hollingsworth doesn't agree with that? I crumple the paper into a ball and toss it to the floor. The train shudders suddenly, pulling away from the station. I throw myself at the window.

"My cousin!" I shout at the Guardians. "He's not here!"

A burst of flames hits the platform.

I flinch and stumble backward, hitting my knee on the arm of the seat. The Guardians turn, lifting their guns skyward, as a dragon crashes through the glass roof of the station. People flee in every direction, their screams almost inaudible amid the sound of smashing glass and screeching iron. The dragon's belly, a violent purple, skims the platform as its spiked tail sends a stone pillar crumbling. It turns its head toward the luggage office, its hexagonal scales glistening as though forged from metal, and the horns beneath its chin impale a porter's trolley and lift it into the air. The last thing I see as the train drives through the raining shards is the Guardians who escorted me engulfed in flames.

The door to the carriage opens with a bang and I spin round.

Standing in the doorway, his hair tangled and a bruising cut beneath his eye, is Marquis. I burst into tears. Marquis almost falls across the carriage to get to me and then I am breathing in the sweet, familiar smell of home.

"All right?" he says gruffly, as if we're merely meeting for a lecture. And then, "How the fuck did you get me out of there, Viv?"

"I thought you weren't coming," I say quietly as we break apart. "I thought she lied to me."

"Who?"

"Wyvernmire."

"You met Wyvernmire?"

I nod. We sit down, and for a moment we just stare out at the tall gray buildings flashing by as the train leaves London.

"What happened out there?" Marquis says.

"A dragon attacked the station," I reply. "Set fire to the platform. I think the Guardians escorting me were killed."

"Good riddance," Marquis mutters.

I shudder and point to the cut on his face. "Did they do that to you?"

"Yes, and the next thing I knew they were telling me my cousin had negotiated my release." He runs his fingers through his hair. "Viv, can you please tell me what the bloody hell is going on?"

I tell him everything, from leaving Ursa with Sophie's parents to the meeting with Wyvernmire. He replies with a string of foul language.

"You cut a detonator out of the library dragon?"

"I did worse than that," I croak. "I started a war."

Marquis smiles. "*You* started a war?"

"What Chumana did—what I helped her do—was a direct breach of the Peace Agreement," I say. "The rebels saw it as some sort of green light, and now there's a civil war, and it's all my fault."

Marquis pulls a bag of tobacco out of his boot.

"The rebels have been planning a coup for months," he says, reaching for a rolling paper. "We all knew it was coming. You've read the papers—you've even *seen* one of their protests for yourself."

The dead Third Class girl's face flashes before my eyes.

"But the dragonfire on Downing Street was the tipping point. Wyvernmire said so—"

"Sounds like she's trying to get you to blame yourself," Marquis says, rolling a cigarette between his fingers. "When really she knew just as much as the next person that this war was coming."

"The only reason we still have a Peace Agreement is because she didn't order her army to retaliate," I say bitterly. "What I did . . . it could have created a war between species."

"Seems to me you're giving yourself credit for something

63

much bigger than you are."

I frown. "I don't want any credit for this," I say. "I want nothing to do with the rebels."

We fall silent as my words land heavy in the space between us.

"Did you know?" I say, looking my cousin in the eye. "About our parents?"

Marquis breathes smoke out through his teeth. "Don't be stupid. Did you?"

"No." My lip trembles and I bite it to keep it still.

"How long have they been part of it, do you think?" I say.

"The rebellion? From what I've read, the coalition between rebel humans and rebel dragons is fairly new. And, knowing your mama, it was the dragons that got her involved."

"But why would they be part of it at all?" I say. "Their lives were perfectly fine, good even—"

"I don't think it was about *their* lives," Marquis says. "It's about the lives of the Third Class, about the injustices done to dragons on behalf of the Peace Agreement—"

"Injustices?" I reply. "What are you talking about? The dragons *agreed* to the Peace Agreement. That and the Class System have both worked fine for years."

"It's not all good, though, is it?"

I look at him expectantly.

"The restriction of movement for starters," Marquis says.

I roll my eyes. "The Travel Ban exists to stop overcrowding."

"If it had existed back when the Massacre of Bulgaria happened, your mama would be dead and you wouldn't be here," Marquis replies.

I close my eyes, remembering how the Guardian called Mama a

Bulgarian leech. My cousin is right about that.

"And it doesn't seem fair that there are things we can do, places we can go, that the Third Class can't."

I was twelve when I saw a girl being physically removed from the public library because she was Third Class. They searched her, emptying her pockets of pages ripped from Dickens's *A Christmas Carol*. I was shocked by her vandalism, but even more so by her determination to access literature. The Class System feeds ambition, Uncle Thomas explained later. Would the girl have wanted to read that book so desperately if she'd been allowed to? Would I be such a good student if, like Dad said, I didn't have the threat of the Third Class hanging over my head?

"Doesn't it bother you that you're learning dragon tongues in a country that keeps interaction between humans and dragons to the bare minimum?" Marquis says.

"We *do* interact with dragons," I say indignantly. "We walk past the nest on top of the British Library every day, and there's that silver dragon who counts money at the bank . . ." I pause, trying to remember her name. "Sheba."

"And how many times have you spoken to Sheba?" Marquis replies coolly. "They say that before the Peace Agreement there were dragons everywhere. And, up until a couple of decades ago, they were still treated as humans' equals. My dad told me that he and my mother were *friends* with some of them. With dragons, Viv!"

I stare out at the cow fields flashing by. Marquis's mother, my aunt Florence, died when he was born. Her family is from North Carolina, where human babies and dragonlings share nests. Marquis has only been to see them once, before the Travel Ban.

He blows smoke out of the tiny sliding window. "All I'm saying is that the Peace Agreement and the Class System might not be as wonderful as you think they are."

"I've heard the rumors," I say, thinking of the hushed conversations about secret clauses and a rigged voting system I've heard on campus. "And, quite frankly, I'm surprised you've let the fearmongering get to you."

"And I'm *not* surprised to hear you call something fearmongering just because you don't understand it," Marquis retorts.

I turn away, seething. What is happening to my family? First my dad, now Marquis.

"Prime Minister Wyvernmire and Queen Ignacia will win this war," I say. "And the rebels—our parents—will pay for it with their lives."

"Not if we earn them a fresh start," Marquis says quietly. "That's why we're here, isn't it? We do the job, give the government what they want, and go home."

Home. Marquis is right. The faster I do the job, the faster I'll return to a normal life, a life where my parents aren't rebels. I imagine myself back in my bedroom, being awoken by Ursa jumping on the bed. I let my mind wander through Fitzrovia, across the square beneath my window, overflowing with its colorful mix of artists and immigrants and intellectuals. I sit in the university library full of books, study on the lawn with Marquis, climb the steps to the Bank of London and ask to talk with Sheba . . .

Marquis shakes me awake. "We're here."

The train has come to a stop in the pale afternoon light. I rub the sleep from my eyes and peer out the window. The platform is tiny, built in the shadow of a single broad oak tree with a ticket office the size of a telephone box. The sign reads Bletchley Railway Station.

"Bletchley?" I say.

Marquis shrugs. "Never heard of it."

A Guardian is waiting on the platform, holding his helmet under his arm. I've never seen one without a helmet before. I follow Marquis off the train.

"Vivien and Marquis Featherswallow?" the man says. His accent is Irish and strangely comforting.

"Yes," we both reply together.

"Grand. I'm Guardian 601. Real name Owen."

I've never known a Guardian's name before.

He gestures toward the road and my heart sinks at the sight of yet another sleek Guardian motorcar.

"Weren't sure what time you'd be here," Owen says, climbing into the driver's seat. "You lot have been arriving nonstop since dawn. Government's stepping it up a notch now the war's started."

With that, he falls quiet, and an awkward silence creeps over the car. We drive through a plain town with brick buildings and a deserted playing field. A line of people are gathered outside a greengrocer's and a woman is pushing a pram past a blackened shop that was likely destroyed during the Great War and never rebuilt. This must be a Third Class quarter.

The roads give way to tree-lined lanes, and a lake appears, dark blue beneath the low sun. Beyond it are more trees and a field and, behind that, a manor house. It's built of red brick with tall iron entrance gates that open mechanically. Behind them, a small army of Guardians of Peace parts to let the motorcar through.

"Quite the welcome party you've got," Owen says quietly, and I wonder what he's been told about us.

The motorcar comes to a stop in the manor's white gravel courtyard. I lean over Marquis to stare up at the building. It's grand, that's for certain, but there is something hodgepodge about it, with its cathedral-style porches and Gothic stone lions standing alongside glass sunrooms and suburban bay windows. Its different architectural styles rage against each other—Mama would call it vulgar. But basked in the soft sunlight, it looks reassuringly unpretentious.

I step out of the car. Owen leads the way up the steps and into an entrance hall with a domed roof. Two oak staircases run up either side of the room and onto a wide raised landing above.

"You're expected in the West Wing," Owen says, leading us down a corridor on the left.

We stop in front of a closed door and Owen raps loudly. There's a shuffling noise and then the door creaks open to reveal a large man in a deep purple suit. His eyes bulge as he looks at us and he lifts a pudgy hand to stroke his short beard.

"Ah, Vivien and Marquis," he says. "We were waiting."

I recognize his voice from the radio, too. This man is Deputy Prime Minister Ravensloe. We walk into what looks like an unused university seminar room, everything in it covered in a thick layer of dust and gloom. Blackout curtains have been drawn across the windows and the white daylight presses at their edges, threatening to burst inside. Several people, all about my age, are sitting at desks like students. They stare at us, unsmiling, and I suddenly wish the ground would open up and swallow me whole. Do *they* know why I'm here? Do they know what I've done?

"Please, take your seats," Ravensloe says pleasantly. "Our class is almost complete."

I choose an empty seat between two boys. The first is tall and broad, and glares angrily at me when I look at him. The second has high cheekbones and black skin that shines against the white collar round his neck. He's sitting upright and alert, as if he's about to take an exam. When I slip into the seat next to him, I catch the scent of peppermint and tobacco. Marquis sits a few seats to the right in the row ahead.

Ravensloe is standing by a desk at the front of the room, an armed Guardian behind him.

"Look at you all," Ravensloe says, his piglike eyes gleaming. "Class of 1923."

Nobody speaks and the Deputy Prime Minister shuffles some paperwork. "Straight down to business it is," he says. "Welcome, all of you, to the DDAD."

A hand shoots up. It belongs to a girl with long fiery red hair and glasses.

"Please, sir," she says, "what does DDAD stand for?"

Ravensloe gives her a patronizing smile, as if the question is a stupid one. I feel a wave of revulsion for him.

"Let me rephrase that for you, young lady," he replies. "Welcome, all of you, to the Department for the Defense Against Dragons."

The door opens with a bang and two more Guardians march in. Between them is a girl with singed clothes, her blond hair streaked with dirt.

"Here's the last one, sir."

My heart flutters as I take in the familiar light-footed gait and the red string around the girl's wrist. I feel the blood drain from my face. The girl looks up.

I stare, my whole body erupting in goose bumps.

Our eyes meet and the girl's bottom lip trembles.

"Excellent," Ravensloe says. "Class, let me introduce you to our last recruit. Her name is—"

"Sophie," the girl says. "My name is Sophie."

SIX

I stare straight ahead as Sophie takes the last empty seat. I can sense Marquis trying to get my attention, but I can't move. My mind feels like it's spinning out of control. Sophie's parents told me she'd been missing for weeks. And suddenly she's here. At the Department for the Defense Against Dragons. On the same day as me.

I've barely registered a word of what Ravensloe is saying.

"The DDAD was set up upon the signing of the Peace Agreement, a precautionary measure to preserve us from a tragedy like the one that took place in Bulgaria . . ."

I slowly turn my head to glance at Sophie. She's wearing her favorite blue jumper—the one her mother bought her last Christmas—but the sleeve is blackened and torn. Her fingernails, always so neat and clean, are bitten, and the little silver earrings that used to adorn her ears are gone.

". . . gathering intelligence that could help us in the event that we were forced to combat dragons . . ."

Sophie's fingers run along the string round her wrist. She doesn't look at me.

Where has she been all this time? And why does she look like she's walked through flames? Is she a criminal, too? I jump as Ravensloe's hand slams on my desk.

"Vivien Featherswallow, are you quite with us?"

Sophie doesn't move, but everyone else turns to stare at me. Out of the corner of my eye, I see Marquis roll his eyes.

"Yes, sir," I say as if we're at school.

When Ravensloe continues his speech, I look at Marquis.

What is going on? he mouths.

I shake my head and concentrate on Ravensloe.

"With the government being targeted by rebel dragons and humans alike, the DDAD has suddenly become crucial to the survival of our nation's values and way of life." The Deputy Prime Minister paces the floor. "That is why, for many months now, Prime Minister Wyvernmire has been recruiting diamond-sharp minds—strong, healthy people with a specialized skill set, who work well under pressure." Ravensloe pauses to look at us. "We believe you fit the bill."

I wait for the polite laughter that usually follows a terrible joke, but none comes. I may work well under pressure—the years leading up to the Examination made sure of that—but a diamond-sharp mind? I'm good at languages, that's true, but I'm only seventeen. And Marquis? I practically had to beg for him to be here.

"Each of you have found yourselves in a situation of societal rejection," Ravensloe continues. "You are all, in one way or another, misfits."

I flush, surprised at the sudden shame flooding through me.

Misfit.

It's a sad word, used to describe someone whose behavior is strange or out of place, someone who disregards the rules. I never imagined it would be used to describe *me*.

"However, thanks to the generosity of our nation's leader, you

72

have each been given an opportunity. A chance to be someone else. A chance at redemption."

The silence in the room is palpable. Sophie still hasn't moved. I raise my hand.

"We were told we would be given a job," I say. "What exactly will that involve?"

Finally, Sophie turns her head to look at me. Her gaze is cold and unrecognizable.

"Excellent question," Ravensloe says.

He gestures to the Guardian, who walks over to the door and opens it. Two men and a woman walk in. One man has a long white beard; the other is tall and awkward-looking. The woman is pretty, with dark hair and red glasses that look too big for her face. Ravensloe beams at them as if they are the bearers of great news.

"You will each be assigned one of three categories," he says. "These are your heads of categories: Professor Marcus Lumens, Mr. Rob Knott, and Dr. Dolores Seymour."

The woman, Dr. Dolores Seymour, gives a small wave.

"Among yourselves, there will be no class distinctions," says Ravensloe. "You are all of equal status with equal chances. However, much like in life outside Bletchley Park, contribution is key. Fail to contribute and you will be demoted."

"Demoted? What's lower than *misfit*?" Marquis says jokingly, making the girl behind him giggle.

Ravensloe's eyes swivel toward him, all trace of his smile gone.

"Do you really want to know?" he says softly.

I glare at Marquis, and for a second I wish I could slap that defiant smile off his face. He's going to get us into trouble before we've even started. I know he's thinking about our discussion on the train. The lives of the Third Class, the rumors about the Peace Agreement and the Class System. But *I* feel a strange lightness in my chest, a sense of relief. If all I need to do is work hard, then I—and my family—will be safe. I've been playing this game my whole life, after all. Work, grades, praise . . . these are the things I know.

Ravensloe clears his throat. "Before your arrival, you signed the Official Secrets Act, as did all persons working at the DDAD. You will not discuss your work with anyone except each other—and *only* if necessary. There is no place for petty conversation here. The blackout curtains on the windows are to be in place in every room before nightfall. Allowing the enemy to discover our location would pose a risk to our victory and indeed our lives."

I think of the dragon attack back at St. Pancras, my skin crawling at the memory of the flames licking up the Guardians' legs.

"The townspeople have been fed the pretext that we are here for administrative purposes only," Ravensloe says. "If any visitors to this house ask, you will perpetuate that pretext. You may not send letters or communicate with anyone outside Bletchley."

The boy in the white collar drums his fingers impatiently on his thigh.

"Shifts are seven hours long and you will have Sundays off. You will work with the other members of your category as a team in order to complete your mission as quickly as possible. If you provide us with the information needed to win the war, the members of each successful category will be free to reintegrate into society in the class you belonged to before you accepted this job, *or* at the time of the last census, whichever is higher. Any crimes you may have committed will be pardoned."

I stare at Sophie, the edges of my vision softening.

Or *at the time of the last census.*

Is it fate that we're both here together? Or is it the most outrageous stroke of luck I will ever encounter? The last census was almost a year ago, before the Examination. Before Sophie was demoted. Meaning that if her category succeeds, she'll go back to the Second Class. Back home.

My breath catches in my throat. Will we be put in the same category? If we are, then this is my chance to give her back what I took from her. If we all succeed, Marquis, Sophie, and I will go back to the Second Class *together.*

This is my chance to save her.

"Are there any questions?" Ravensloe says, stroking his beard again.

In my peripheral vision, I see the boy in the white collar raise his hand, but I'm still staring at Sophie, willing her to acknowledge me.

"Just to be clear, Deputy Prime Minister . . . who exactly are we fighting in this war?"

The boy's deep, steady voice makes me turn my head before I can stop myself. He has a Third Class accent, possibly Bristolian, but his tone is as sharp as cut glass. He sees me looking and his lips press into a crooked smile. Ravensloe narrows his eyes.

"Anyone who plots against the state, anyone who collaborates with the rebellion, anyone who harbors the enemy, human or dragon . . . that is who we are fighting. Does that clear things up for you, boy?"

The smile that spread for me widens as the boy holds Ravensloe's gaze.

"Indeed it does. Sir."

I look away, my heart beating faster than it was moments ago.

Ravensloe clicks his fingers and Dr. Dolores Seymour begins distributing files. Mine is covered in brown paper with my name scrawled across the front in black ink.

"You will read your respective files once before they are destroyed," Ravensloe says.

Marquis raises an eyebrow at me as the room fills with the sound of front covers being turned. I flip my file open and begin to read.

NAME: VIVIEN MARIE FEATHERSWALLOW
SHIFT: 5 A.M.–12 P.M.
SHIFT LOCATION: GLASSHOUSE
JOB CATEGORY: CODEBREAKING

Codebreaking? My eyes tear back through the words, looking for any information I might have missed, but there's nothing. My stomach drops. Wyvernmire said she needed someone who speaks dragon tongues, a polyglot. I don't know the first thing about codebreaking. Maybe I've been given the wrong file. Hushed whispers fill the room. I look across at Marquis. He's shaking his head in disbelief. Sophie has closed her file and buried her face in her hands. Only the boy in the white collar seems serene. In fact, he almost looks amused.

"Guardian 601 will help you locate your accommodation," says Ravensloe as Owen reappears at the door. "Shifts begin in the morning. I would advise you to bear in mind that you are undertaking top-secret government business that is to be completed with the utmost urgency. You have three months."

Three months? Three months to win a war?

"Unfortunately, the previous team did not heed my advice."

A cold chill runs down my spine. So we're not the first. I stare at the three category leaders, but their faces betray no emotion. Did they work with the *previous team*, too? How long, exactly, have they been preparing for this war? The other recruits are glancing round at each other, as if looking for reassurance that they simply misheard.

"Remember, recruits, that what you do here will help determine the course of the war."

With that, the Deputy Prime Minister and his Guardian leave the room. The category leaders begin to collect the files and my mind races. Three months. It's not enough time, and yet it's too long to be away from Ursa. I'm suddenly desperate to get to work, to know exactly what this job will entail.

"Well?" Marquis murmurs, checking that the category leaders aren't watching before approaching my desk. "What did you get?"

"We're not supposed to talk about it," I snap.

"Come now, cousin," Marquis says with a wink. "For once in your life, try *not* being teacher's pet."

We've been here five minutes and he already wants to break the rules.

"We signed an Official Secrets Act," I whisper. "Ravensloe said—"

"That we can discuss our work with *each other*," Marquis says, perching on the edge of my desk. "We both know you're going to tell me. So just bloody hell get on with it."

"Fine," I say. "I'm a codebreaker."

"A what?" Marquis says loudly.

"*Shhh!*" I hiss as several heads turn toward us. "Are you not, then?"

"No," Marquis replies. "They've put me in Aviation."

I snort. "As in flying planes?"

"How am I supposed to know?" Marquis replies. "You did tell them I'm studying dragon anatomy, didn't you, Viv?"

But I'm no longer listening. As the recruits begin to file out of the room, Sophie walks past us without so much as a glance.

"Sophie!" Marquis calls.

She ignores him and he turns back to me with a look of outrage.

"So she hates us now?"

My heart races. "Why would she hate us? We haven't seen her in months and it's not like she knows . . ."

I trail off, feeling my face flush with heat.

"Knows what?" Marquis asks. He pulls a prerolled cigarette out of his boot and sticks it behind his ear.

"Nothing," I mutter as we follow the recruits down the corridor.

My stomach twists into tight knots. Sophie doesn't know how I hurt her and I never intend on letting her find out. I'll fix what I did, and everything will go back to the way it was before.

SEVEN

Owen leads us up the staircase to the second floor. An obscene number of signs appear on the walls, all giving instructions or prohibitions. At the entrance to the house's East Wing, there's a circular sign depicting a mouth with a finger pressed to it.

Discretion Not Discussion, the instructions beneath say.

"Girls to the left of the hallway, boys to the right," Owen calls over our heads.

I can see Sophie up ahead, talking to another girl. I feel a pang of sadness. Why will she talk to a stranger but not to me? Marquis reaches for my hand and squeezes.

"If you need me, send the signal," he says.

The signal is a series of low whistles he, Sophie, and I used to find each other as children when we were lost in the overcrowded underground bunkers during the war. It's stuck with us since, a sound guaranteed to bring the others running.

The boy in the white collar is standing by the door to the boys' dormitory, fiddling with something in his pocket. He stops when he catches me watching and grins. I force myself to tear my gaze away.

"Send the signal," I repeat with a nod. "I'll see you later."

The girls' dormitory is large and dully lit by brass wall lamps. Poking out from behind the blackout drapes is a set of frilled pink curtains. There's a tapestry of the alphabet on the wall and a sad-looking rocking horse in the corner. Whose nursery did this used to be? There are six beds, crammed together but neatly made, with uniforms waiting on each one. A shirt and black silk tie, a navy wool skirt and a navy jacket, black stockings and a hat. There's a brooch, too. A dragon flying through a silver circle. It could be a crown.

Or a net.

Sophie has taken the bed next to mine—the only one left. She picks up the sleeve of her jacket and drops it again. Her cheeks are sunken and hollow, and there's a nasty burn on her hand. I stare at her until she's forced to look at me.

"Hello," I say, surprised at how quiet my voice has become. "It's good to see you."

She gives me a withering look. "What are you even doing here?"

"I could ask you the same question."

Around us, the other recruits are introducing themselves.

"I'm a misfit now, remember?" Sophie says, rolling her eyes. "But you and Marquis . . . you should be in Fitzrovia."

"Your parents told me you've been missing for weeks—"

"You've seen my parents?"

"I left Ursa with them," I begin. "So much has happened, Sophie—"

"Ursa?" Sophie says. "Why? Where are your—"

"They've been arrested," I whisper. My chest suddenly aches. "I was told that if I came and worked here, they would be released." I don't mention Chumana or the Peace Agreement. Sophie wouldn't believe me. "Where have you been?"

"Granger's Prison," Sophie replies, visibly satisfied at the look of shock on my face. "The place where they send class evaders."

Granger's Prison is where the people who refuse to be demoted go. I suddenly remember the headlines from this morning.

"I read there was a mass breakout," I say. "Did you . . ."

Sophie shakes her head. "No, I didn't escape like the rest of them. I was recruited. That woman—Dolores Seymour—she came and spoke to loads of us, but she picked me." Sophie shrugs. "I don't know why."

"Your parents said you kept trying to go home, but they don't know you were arrested."

"Of course they don't. How could they?" Sophie picks up the dragon brooch and turns it over in her palm. "And you?" she says, her green eyes fixed on mine. "What's your excuse?"

"My excuse?"

"For abandoning me. For pretending like we were never friends. You never wrote to me, never tried to visit me."

So she does hate me.

"Marquis said we should leave you to settle into your halfway house," I lie.

Sophie lets out a hollow laugh. "You've clearly never set foot inside a halfway house, Viv."

"I . . ."

The truth is, after Sophie was demoted, all I wanted was to forget. How could I visit her in her halfway house, knowing it was my fault she was there?

"After the Examination—"

"Don't you want to know why my parents were arrested?" I say. I'll admit to them being rebels if it means Sophie will stop talking about her demotion. "They—"

"Care to let us join the conversation?" A haughty-looking girl with black skin and hair worn in sleek twists round her face is staring at us. "It seems you both have a lot to discuss."

"Yes, we do," I snap, pulling Sophie by the sleeve.

She shakes me off.

"Sorry," she says to the girl. "Vivien's not accustomed to being interrupted."

The comment smarts like a slap. I stare at Sophie and her bottom lip curls.

The girl grins and shakes Sophie's hand. "Serena Serpentine."

First Class, then. Most First Class families have dragon-descended names, a symbol of power and wealth.

"Sophie Rundell," Sophie says, turning expectantly to me.

"Vivien Featherswallow," I mutter, glaring at Serena.

So much for showing the shiny version of myself.

"I'm Dodie," says the girl with red hair, the one who asked Ravensloe a question. She clutches the pass round her neck and I glimpse the words *Second Class*.

"Katherine," says a pale, pixie-like girl. "Anyone else here a codebreaker?"

My heart leaps. "I am," I say quickly.

Discretion be damned.

"Any idea what kind of code we'll be breaking?"

I shake my head, disappointed that she doesn't know, either. "They told me I'd be working with languages."

"I bloody hope not," Sophie snorts.

I spin round. "You're a—"

"Codebreaker? I'm afraid so," she says. "What's wrong, Vivvy? Did you think you were the only one?"

I turn away, a hollow feeling growing in my stomach. Sophie is in the same category as me, which is exactly what I was hoping for. But she was supposed to study math at university. If she's been chosen to be a codebreaker, then maybe this job has nothing to do with dragon tongues, after all. Maybe Wyvernmire lied to me.

I take a deep breath. This is *good* news. It means that if I save myself, I save Sophie, too.

"They picked me because I'm good at chess," Katherine says. "That Dolores woman recruited me after I beat everyone in my prison, including the prison warden's chess-champion son."

I don't ask Katherine what she was in prison for.

"I'm in Aviation," Serena says, lifting a small leather suitcase onto her bed.

Why was *she* allowed to bring luggage?

"What's the last category?"

"Zoology," Dodie says softly.

"Zoology?" I say. "Like the study of animals?"

"Not animals." Serena laughs. "Dragons, darling!"

We all stare at her.

"Codebreaking, Aviation, Zoology . . . they are all Wyvernmire's attempt to *imitate* dragons." Her voice is warm and smooth, bursting with articulate confidence. "That is how she plans to win the war."

I sit down on my bed. So my codebreaking *is* related to dragons. But how?

"Is that dragonbone?" Dodie asks.

She's looking at the hairbrush Serena has just pulled out of her suitcase. Its handle is pearly white, stark against the black horsehair bristles. Dragonbone has been illegal since the signing of the Peace Agreement.

Serena shrugs. "A family heirloom. My mother gave it to me before sending me here."

"Your mother *sent* you here?" Dodie says.

"Oh yes," Serena replies bitterly. "After I failed the Examination on purpose and refused to marry the man she chose for me to keep me in First Class, she practically begged Ravensloe to take me."

"Why would you fail the Examination on purpose?" asks Sophie.

Serena shrugs. "I was bored—in my class, it's nothing more than a few questions with an examiner over tea. And watching my mother descend into a frenzy is amusing."

"That's it?" I say. "You're here because Deputy Prime Minister Ravensloe did your mother a favor?"

"No," Serena replies, giving me an irritated look. "Ravensloe refused, actually. But my father organized a soirée in our home, to celebrate the engagement I didn't agree to and quell the rumors that his only daughter had been demoted. And Ravensloe was there."

I roll my eyes at the fact that Serena comes from a family that celebrates milestones with the Deputy Prime Minister. She's the type of person who can afford to ruin her education simply to distress her mother—recklessness isn't much of a risk when you're not one mistake away from being demoted to Third. The worst that could happen to Serena is a slightly less privileged life with the Seconds.

"I make . . . contraptions," she continues. "That's what my mother calls them. Model planes and wings, things that fly. It's a hobby. Ravensloe caught me in the hallway, trying to rescue one of my models from the maids my mother had ordered to clear my rooms. And he told her he'd changed his mind. I refused to attend my engagement party, so my mother knew I wasn't going to give in. She thinks I'll take one look at the work expected of me here and run home. But I won't. If I do the job, I'll stay First Class. And then I'll start selling my models—"

"I don't mean to be rude," Dodie says quietly, "but how is making models going to help the war effort?"

Serena is unbuttoning the front of her dress. "More dragons join the rebel movement each day," she says, shrugging her dress off so she's standing in nothing but a silk chemise. She pulls on the black stockings and navy skirt. "And if you want to defeat a dragon, you must fight like a dragon, correct?"

Aviation—the operating of an aircraft—and zoology—the study of animals—could be linked to dragons at a stretch. But code-breaking? There's a loud knock. The boy in the white collar pokes his head round the door just as Serena is closing her shirt.

"Oh—sorry," he says, averting his eyes.

Serena gives him a sweet smile, and I decide I don't like her.

"Sorry to bother you all," the boy begins again when Serena is dressed, "but we've just been called for dinner."

The blue of his uniform makes his brown eyes shine. I notice he's still wearing the white collar, poking out from beneath his jacket.

"Oooh, I *am* hungry," Serena says.

I doubt Serena has ever been hungry a day in her life, but I change into my uniform—stuffing my class pass beneath my pillow—and follow the girls out into the hallway where Marquis is waiting.

"Nice uniform," he smirks, eyeing the brooch on my collar.

"Likewise," I say, straightening his tie.

"Sophie?"

"She despises me, so the same probably goes for you, too."

"Ah."

I watch as she heads toward the staircase with Serena, just

ahead of Katherine and Dodie.

"There's a First Class girl who says Wyvernmire wants us to imitate dragons. That's how she plans to win the war."

Marquis tilts his head, trying to work out if I'm serious.

"Are any of the boys codebreakers?" I ask.

"One," Marquis says. "Gideon. The tall, good-looking one. Apparently, he speaks several languages."

My heart leaps. I remember the boy who glared at me back in the seminar room. If he's a polyglot, too, then maybe this code *does* have something to do with dragon tongues. I run a hand down the thin scars on my arm. The good grades, the awards, the acclamatory teacher-parent meetings . . . they've always been mine. And this dragon code will be, too.

The dining room is full of shadows, candlelight flickering like stars on the molded ceiling. Portraits stare at us through the semidarkness and the long table is set with silver cutlery and steaming dishes. The radio crackles below the noise of polite chatter. Marquis makes a beeline for Sophie and whispers something in her ear. She gives him a reluctant smile and he hugs her, lifting her off her feet. My blood boils. So *he* can get away with not writing to her, but I can't? It's odd seeing them together again, as if no time has passed.

My two best friends.

I take a seat opposite Gideon. He's as handsome as Marquis said—tall with blond curls and a flushed complexion. I help myself to a spoonful of honey-roasted carrots. He gives me a surly nod, and I wonder how to begin a conversation. I decide to get straight to the point.

"I hear you're a codebreaker, too?"

Gideon, who has just taken a bite of chicken, pauses midchew.

He glances nervously at Owen, who is standing by the door with his gun on his shoulder.

"I'm not asking you to break any rules," I say quickly. "I don't want to get into trouble, either. I'm just curious to know if we'll be working together."

He nods again.

"Do you know anything about code?"

"No," Gideon mumbles, staring down at his plate. He takes another bite and doesn't look at me again.

"Oh." I sit back in my chair, disappointed.

At the far end of the table, Katherine and Serena are comparing their class passes, which they clearly haven't been able to bring themselves to remove. While Katherine's hangs round her neck from a piece of string, Serena's is threaded with a delicate gold chain.

"I used to sew dresses for girls like you," Katherine tells her admiringly. "Trust me, it's a lot more pleasant than packing chrysanthemums, although your hands do get stabbed by all the needles."

Serena gives her a puzzled smile and I take a sip of wine. It's rich and warm and makes my lips tingle.

"It's a bit of an extravagant meal for a group of misfits, isn't it?" Dodie says nervously. "Why have they gone to all this trouble? It's not as if anyone outside Bletchley Park knows we're here."

I feel a jolt of unease at her words, but Marquis flashes her his winning smile. "We're doing work that will change the course of the war," he says, imitating Ravensloe's plummy drawl. "We are strong, healthy people with diamond-sharp minds who finally have a chance at . . . what was it? Respectability? Rejuvenation? Romance?"

The room rings with laughter.

"Redemption," Dodie says with a small smile.

The recruits are staring at Marquis in admiration, which of course was his intention all along. Sometimes I wonder if he hopes that by showing people how witty he is, they won't notice how he is different. I wonder if I hope it, too.

"It makes sense for them to feed us up," he tells Dodie, resuming a serious voice. "Although they could at least have lit a fire."

I roll my eyes and take a bite of mashed potato. It's the first thing I've eaten in days and it tastes like heaven. On the other side of Marquis, Sophie is shoveling roast chicken into her mouth as if her life depends on it.

"Of course, darlin', let's set the most secret location in England aglow so that it can be seen from the dragon-infested skies," Katherine says, batting her eyelashes at Marquis, who looks pleased.

Katherine seems to have missed the point of blackout curtains.

"And who are you, *my lady*?" Marquis says.

I help myself to more gravy, ladling it across my chicken as my new roommate laughs. She's about to be seriously disappointed.

"Katherine," she says, eyeing Marquis's bruised cheek. "I've always had a thing for men who can brawl."

Marquis reaches for her hand over the table and kisses it.

"Oh, for goodness' sake," I say as Dodie laughs into her glass. "Katherine, that's not—"

"Not my cup of tea," says Marquis.

"You mean brawling?" Katherine replies.

Marquis doesn't answer, instead gesturing to Gideon. "He's a strapping lad—I'm sure he'd be up for a brawl."

Gideon scowls, but at least the tension in the air has been broken, and easy conversation mingles with the sound of the radio. There are nine of us in total—five girls and four boys. The boy in the white collar is talking to a quiet-looking boy with shaved hair called Karim.

"Made any friends yet?" Marquis says to me.

"No," I reply bluntly. "But it looks like *you* have."

Marquis shrugs. "Better to have friends than enemies."

"Aren't you worried?" I say quietly, taking a sip of water.

"About what?" he replies. "The dragon-infested skies? The fact that we're essentially prisoners disguised as guests? Or the reality that neither of us knows what we're doing?"

"That one," I say.

Marquis's smile falters ever so slightly and he lowers his voice.

"Of course I'm worried," he says. "I've never touched a plane in my life. But we'll learn, won't we? I'll build whatever flying contraption they want building, and you'll break whatever code they want breaking, and then we'll go home."

"And what if we fail?" I say, the glass in my hand shaking. "We'll get sent to prison and our family will never be pardoned. And Ursa . . ." I put my drink down as my voice breaks.

The boy in the white collar presses a napkin to his lips and shoots me a curious glance.

"It will be all right, Viv," Marquis says firmly.

I know the stubborn expression on my cousin's face too well. It's the same look he wore as a child when a group of boys told him he was too much of a *pansy* to make the football team, so he broke his leg trying. Nothing is impossible for Marquis, who eventually became captain of that team. But I'm not like him. I'm . . . realistic. And I still can't see what languages and codebreaking and dragons have to do with each other.

"London has suffered a series of attacks . . ."

The hopeful atmosphere dissipates as we listen to the reports of bombing and dragonfire. We stay silent until the report finishes and the radio lets out an endless crackling. Marquis stands up and turns it off, and then there's just the sound of spoons scraping against bowls. The high that we've all been riding, the one fueled by the promise of another chance, plummets.

"How is your food, Vivien Featherswallow?"

I blink. The boy in the white collar is talking to me, leaning across the table so close that I can see the stubble on his chin. His skin is as smooth as glass.

"It's fine," I say. "How do you know my name?"

"I listened," the boy says pleasantly. "I'm Atlas. Atlas King."

"Nice to meet you, Atlas King," I say. "How is your wine?"

Atlas takes a sip from the glass in front of him and makes a face. "Corked. As to be expected from this place."

I put my spoon down. "Corked?"

"Tainted, spoiled, corrupted," Atlas says. He looks around. "Oh, come on now. You don't really believe anything Ravensloe said about this being our chance at redemption, do you?"

I glance nervously at Owen. This is definitely the kind of talk that could get us demoted.

"Yes, I do," I reply coldly. "What would he gain from not keeping his word?"

"Let me guess," Atlas says with a knowing smile. "You're First Class?"

I raise an eyebrow. "Second."

I can sense both Marquis and Sophie edging closer to the conversation.

Atlas leans back in his chair. "In any case, you're not Third.

Otherwise, you'd understand why I don't trust him."

Sophie lets out a quiet laugh and I blush. So he *is* Third Class. I knew it from the moment I heard him speak with a Bristolian accent, because the city of Bristol is mostly Third. I stare back at him. People get judged on their accents all the time, which is why I speak carefully, elongating my vowels and clipping my tone. I want people to make the right assumptions about me—in other words, the opposite of the kind I've already made about Atlas King.

"So you're suggesting that, even if we win this war, none of us will go free?" says Marquis.

The recruits around us are standing up to leave and a maid appears, collecting our dirty bowls. Atlas smiles an infuriating smile and begins to gather the cutlery, doing the maid's job for her. He hands her the spoons, causing her to turn red and give some sort of awkward curtsy, before turning back to face us.

"That, my friends," he says, "depends entirely on who you mean by *we*."

EIGHT

I awake to the low drone of a siren. It takes me a moment to realize that I'm not in my bed on Fitzroy Square but at Bletchley Park, surrounded by the soft snores of strangers. Or almost strangers. Sophie lights the lamp and nods me a begrudging greeting. We dress in silence, the weight of the task awaiting us suddenly heavier. Nerves flutter in my stomach as I plait my hair and straighten my brooch. What if we fail? Wyvernmire will have no choice but to implement the law. My family will be sentenced to death. I'll be imprisoned. Ursa will grow up an orphan. Today is my sister's third day waking up in Marylebone with Abel and Alice. Does she think I've left her behind?

That's exactly what you did.

I follow the others out into the hall where Marquis is waiting, his face still soft with sleep.

"All right?" he says.

I nod, blinking back tears. I just need to focus. A helmeted Guardian is waiting for us in the entrance hall. He pushes a basket full of buttered rolls at Marquis.

"Share these out, then report for duty."

His voice sounds familiar, but I can't picture where I've heard it before.

"Those of you in the glasshouse, with me," he says. "The rest of you, with Guardians 629 and 311."

I bite into my roll and watch as Atlas disappears through a door behind the staircase. He looks like so many of the boys I knew at school, all good grades and smiles. But last night he spoke in arrogant riddles and made it clear enough that he doesn't care for rules. Obeying the rules is currently the only thing keeping us safe, so I decide to keep my distance from him from now on.

I follow the Guardian down the steps to the courtyard with Sophie and the two other recruits in our category—Katherine, the chess player, and Gideon, the polyglot. The sky is a bruised blue, bleeding lighter around the edges like a watercolor painting. We take a pathway round the side of the manor house into a garden with a perfectly mowed lawn. A flock of chickens peck at the weeds and cluck in alarm as we pass by.

We walk in silence, the morning frost crunching beneath our feet, until Katherine trips and lets out a yelp. I look up. A huge, hulking figure emerges from the trees ahead. The dragon is a vibrant red, the color of autumn. I stare at the black spikes on its face. Its chest glitters with ebony scales and the ridged peaks of its skull are like a crown atop its head. Beside me, Gideon has gone rigid, his hands balled into fists.

"Good morning, Yndrir," the Guardian says.

The dragon nods his head as he walks by, so big that the leaves of the trees trail across his back. His long tail brushes against my boot and Gideon jumps backward. Katherine clutches Sophie's arm.

"It's a Ddraig Goch," I whisper to no one in particular.

A Welsh dragon. He's magnificent.

"Get a move on, all of you," the Guardian calls from up ahead.

Why didn't I expect there to be dragons at Bletchley? The other recruits are still staring at Yndrir in awe. This is probably the closest they've ever been to a dragon in their lives. How many more dragons are working at the DDAD, and what do they *do*? I glance back over my shoulder as the Ddraig Goch rounds the corner of the house, excitement fizzing in my chest. So I *will* be working with dragon tongues. Maybe I'll be talking to *actual dragons*.

I catch up with Sophie, wait until no one's looking, and pull her by the arm.

"Ow, Viv!"

Sophie turns on me angrily, her long hair whipping her face. Now that she's clean and fed, she looks more like the Sophie I know. I close my eyes and try to ignore the surfacing memories of that day. *I'm sorry*, I want to say. But I can't. Because I know that sorry isn't good enough.

"Look," I say, "regardless of what happened last summer, both of us are here now, and both of us need to complete the jobs we've been given to go home. I think we should work together."

Sophie's eyes narrow. "Of course *you're* past what happened in the summer because *your* life went on as normal. But mine . . ." Her lip tremors and the guilt fills me so quickly I almost double over.

"Tell me about it," I plead. "Tell me where you've been."

"I already did," Sophie replies. "Granger's Prison."

"For how long?"

"A few weeks," she says. "It was better than where I was living before."

A hollow carves itself into my stomach. I had hoped—convinced myself even—that the Third Class wouldn't be as bad as the rumors say. That, despite our parents' warnings, being demoted wasn't the end of the world.

"You mean the halfway house?"

Sophie nods. "I don't want to talk about it."

"All right," I say gently. "But suppose we work together? On whatever code we're supposed to be breaking? I don't know anything about it, and I'm sure neither do you. And I want us to get out of here, you, me, and Marquis. Together. Two heads are better than one, right, Soph?"

Sophie looks up at the mention of her childhood nickname.

"They promised me that if I did the job here, I'd be promoted," Sophie says, staring into the trees ahead. "They promised I'd be Second Class again."

I nod. *I* deserve to be here, but Sophie doesn't. She doesn't deserve to have memories so terrible she can't talk about them. She doesn't deserve to have a traitor for a friend. We pick our way across the roots and mounds of earth in the forest, pausing only to look at the tennis court hidden in a clearing to the right of the trees.

"The glasshouse is our most protected location," the Guardian is saying as we catch up with the group. "Several dragons and Guardians guard it, and the forest makes it almost undetectable from the sky."

Almost undetectable from the sky. How many dragons fly over Bletchley each day? From above, the manor and its grounds must look like nothing more than a First Class house. The DDAD is hiding in plain sight and the rebels have no idea. As we walk deeper into the forest, a tall glass building emerges from the trees. Plants and leaves press up against the inside of the windows, making the house look as though it grew from the forest itself. Dotted in the grass around it are several sheets of black rubber, mounted on legs and ribbed like dragon scales. What are they? The Guardian holds the door open and our eyes meet. I jump. Where do I know him from?

"Welcome to the glasshouse!"

Dr. Dolores Seymour smiles at us from behind her oversized glasses, her green dress blending in with the tall potted plants that surround her. Behind her are a patterned rug and an upholstered sofa, as well as two large bookcases and a cupboard that stand in the shade of yet more leaves. The glass ceiling stops among the branches of a neighboring elm tree, so the whole room is lit by a greenish hue. Blackout curtains are gathered in the corners of the walls and the ceiling, and I imagine them cloaking this whole place in darkness at the pull of a string. Wires snake across the floor like twisted black roots, reaching all the way back to a line of machines and two smaller contraptions that stand atop some tables at the very back of the room.

"No time for niceties, Dr. Seymour," the Guardian says. "Your recruits will need strict instruction in order to overcome the innate lack of respect for authority they all no doubt possess." He looks at me and sneers, amusement dancing in his eyes.

I step backward in shock, the ghost of a slap stinging my face. Guardian 707.

This is the man who hit me when my parents were arrested. Who joked about finding a key beneath Mama's dress. I can tell by the way he's staring at me that he recognizes me, too.

"Thank you, Ralph, but these recruits are *my* responsibility, not yours," says Dr. Seymour. "If you could please take your assigned position *outside* the glasshouse, then we'll all be able to get down to work."

Ralph directs his sneer toward Dr. Seymour and for a second I think he might refuse, but he suddenly turns on his heel and leaves, letting the door slam behind him. Dr. Seymour smiles at us.

"Please," she says, gesturing to the back of the room. "Take a seat."

I pull out a chair at one of the tables. The glasshouse looks like someone has built a library amid a jungle. Bulbous lamps made of pretty blue china, plush cushions, and magazines titled *Dragons Daily* sit beneath tumbling vines of ivy and the sharp leaves of some tropical plant the size of a small tree. The machines seem completely out of place.

I peer at the device in front of me. It's a box made of glass shaped a bit like a radio with a tall, retractable aerial and a small gold speaker that looks like it belongs on a gramophone. There are several brass dials, *play* and *pause* buttons, and a large switch.

"My name is Dolores Seymour. I'm a dragon behaviorist, and Head of Codebreaking *and* Recruitment at Bletchley Park. You have each been chosen to join me in the glasshouse because you possess a particular skill set that is well adapted to the work I do here." Dr. Seymour gestures around us. "For example, Katherine: *you* are a previously undiscovered chess champion."

Katherine nods slowly, looking bewildered.

"Your logic, memory, and ability to solve puzzles is exactly the kind of talent we need here." Dr. Seymour turns to Sophie. "And you, Sophie, have strong mathematical abilities *and* you are fluent in Morse code, thanks to your experience sending coded messages via the telegraph system."

That's why Sophie was recruited? Because she helped her mother in the telegraph offices during the war?

"And, of course, we have our polyglots!" Dr. Seymour looks from me to Gideon with a smile. "Gideon speaks several human languages, while Vivien specializes in dragon tongues. Together, you bring a wealth of linguistic knowledge to the table."

I raise my hand. "Excuse me, Dr. Seymour?"

"Yes, Vivien?"

"I can see why chess or Morse might be useful for codebreaking, but languages?" I glance at Gideon. "Are you sure we've been assigned the correct category?"

Dr. Seymour takes a seat on a stool, her hands clasped in her lap. "Well, Vivien, you must already know that dragons are the world's greatest linguists, capable of learning multiple languages at an impressive speed."

I nod.

"But dragons communicate in other ways, too. Do you know what I mean by that?"

I suddenly feel like I'm back at university, surprised by a lecturer's trick question. I shake my head.

"Of course you don't," she says, smiling as if amused by her own joke. "Dragons also communicate via sonar. It's a form of echolocation, the same used by whales and bats."

Whales and bats? Why would dragons need to communicate like animals when they learn several languages in their first year of life alone?

"Dragons communicate via echolocation when separated by long distances, or are underwater. Have any of you ever heard about echolocation and how it works?"

Gideon raises his hand and I feel a pang of jealousy. How does *he* know the answer?

"I've heard of sonar being used in the war, to detect submarines?" he says tentatively.

Dr. Seymour nods. "The first sonar listening device was invented at the beginning of the century, and became the eyes and ears of underwater warships. But nature is the author of the original sonar system. Echolocation was first observed in bats and whales. During the Great War, we realized that dragons—who coordinated attacks during flight with minute precision—were using it, too."

My skin prickles. It's been five years since the war ended—why was I never taught about this in any of my modules on dragon communication?

"Dragons send out sound waves through their mouths, and when the waves hit objects they produce echoes," Dr. Seymour says. "There are two types of echolocation calls—ranging calls, which dragons use to detect objects in the space around them, and social calls. All on a frequency too high for us humans to hear."

I glance at the contraption on my desk again. "Are the rebel dragons communicating via echolocation? Is that why we're here, to read ultrasonic sound waves?"

"You're going to listen to them, not read them," Dr. Seymour says. "And then you'll translate them."

A fly hovers across the room and lands on the speaker of the contraption. Could its buzzes be decoded, too, if we had the right machine?

"We're not sure when or why dragons began communicating via echolocation, but we know it is crucial to how they organize themselves in battle. Deciphering what they're saying—and perhaps one day being able to reproduce the calls ourselves—would give us a huge advantage."

"Why doesn't the Prime Minister just ask the Dragon Queen to tell her how it works?" Katherine asks. "Wouldn't she agree if it means helping us beat the rebels?"

"The dragons do not want humans to know that they possess a natural sonar system. It seems they intend to keep this method of communication a secret."

"How does it work?" Sophie asks. She has tied her hair back and her eyes are shining with determination.

"Dragon echolocation is made up of hundreds of ultrasonic sounds—clicks and calls and pulses—which, when recorded and slowed down, may imitate the rhythm and structure of many dragon tongues," Dr. Seymour says. "And that is where our polyglots come in."

"I translate languages, not code," I say slowly. "I'm not qualified for this."

"Me neither," says Katherine, shaking her head.

"Surely dragon echolocation is more similar to whale or bat echolocation than it is to spoken language?" Gideon says.

"But dragon echolocation *is* a language," Dr. Seymour says patiently. "And it seems to be more sophisticated than the echolocation we have observed in other creatures. While the clicks they send out to locate objects in the air could be likened to the tapping of Morse code, the dragon's ultrasonic *social calls* sound almost verbal, and we believe they have complex meanings. Of course, the *dragon code*, as we refer to it, has nothing to do with human-made Morse, but those who are trained in Morse, those capable of solving complex puzzles, and people with an ear for linguistics have the best chance at translating it successfully."

"So what's my job?" Gideon asks. "You want me to listen to

recordings of dragon echolocation and tell you if they sound any-thing like the languages I know? I don't speak any dragon tongues."

I want to laugh at the ridiculousness of it all.

"You know as well as I do that all dragon tongues originate from human languages," Dr. Seymour says. "And no, we don't want you to simply listen to recordings." She looks up through the glass roof at the sky. "Dragons fly over Bletchley day and night. And since glass is one of the few materials sonar travels through, we want you to listen in live."

So I am to be a spy.

"Around-the-clock surveillance would be ideal, but for now the four of you will take the morning shift and myself the afternoon one," Dr. Seymour says. "We believe you'll work faster together and with a common purpose."

"To learn to speak dragon code," Katherine says with a defeated sigh.

I try to stay calm as the panic rises inside me. At least Sophie has some experience in coded meanings, but me? I speak languages that are made up of grammar and structure and the alphabet. Not clicks and calls. How am I going to translate ultrasonic batlike sounds into words on a page?

"Is this what we'll use?" I ask Dr. Seymour, pointing to the device in front of me and the one next to it.

Dr. Seymour nods. "These two are loquisonus machines—the most recent echolocation detection devices." She points toward the tall black machines that line the wall behind us. "The reperisonus machines over there are used to store the recordings made by their smaller but much more impressive sisters."

Her hand settles on one of the smaller devices. "We have the only loquisonus machines in Britannia here at Bletchley. They're portable, meaning they can detect echolocation anywhere we take them." She reaches for the one in front of me and flicks the switch. "And their functions can be reversed, meaning they can emit sound as well as record it. In other words, they can be used, theoretically, to communicate via echolocation."

I lean closer to the loquisonus machine and feel a jolt of anticipation. If what Dr. Seymour is saying is true, then it could be used to talk to dragons miles away. . . .

"It's all very new technology," Dr. Seymour says, "and, as we haven't been able to decipher many of the dragon echolocation calls yet, we haven't been able to play them back as a means of communication."

"Wouldn't the dragons hear, if you did?" Sophie asks.

I imagine the rebels flying over Bletchley and picking up echolocation calls—it would give our location away immediately.

Dr. Seymour smiles. "That's why we have blockers. You may have seen them outside. They're large rubber sheets that block outgoing sonar, so no echolocation calls can accidentally be emitted from the glasshouse and attract dragon attention. It's a bit like a one-way mirror—we can see out, but they can't see in." Dr. Seymour leans forward on her stool. "It is *crucial* that none of the dragons guarding Bletchley Park learn of the codebreaking going on inside the glasshouse."

I think of Yndrir and the sharp spikes on his face, the strength of his tail. What would he do if he knew what he was protecting?

"Why don't they want us to know about echolocation?" Sophie asks. "If bats and whales use it, it's not like the dragons own it."

"The government believes the dragons want to use it as a war weapon, in the event that humans ever turn against them, but . . ."

"But you don't think so," I say quietly.

Dr. Seymour looks nervously at the door, but doesn't reply.

I sit back, my mind spinning. The DDAD is deciphering dragon echolocation, something the dragons of Britannia—and therefore the Dragon Queen—don't want to happen. So what would they do if they found out? And why is Wyvernmire risking Queen Ignacia's support to get this dragon code? Is it really that important?

"The recordings you make in here will likely be of echolocation calls made by passing dragons," says Dr. Seymour. "But when we take the loquisonus machines with us on field trips throughout Bletchley Park, you'll mostly be recording communication between our patrol dragons. In that case, it's important to note down which patrol dragon you are listening to."

"Why?" I ask. "Isn't the whole point of this to spy on the *rebel* dragons?"

"There's more to it than that," Dr. Seymour replies. "The point is to learn how to speak echolocation—it doesn't matter which dragons we learn it from. As with any area of study, it's always useful to have as much information as possible. It would be interesting to compare, for example, where the particular dragons we hear using echolocation come from."

She holds up a book. "Here is a photograph book of the different dragons you may meet around Bletchley. You'll have to memorize their names."

Dr. Seymour comes to stand between me and Gideon and adjusts something on both our machines. "Let's start by listening to some recordings. The DDAD is mostly interested in the dragons' social calls. We want to know what the rebel dragons are saying to each other, and how they coordinate themselves during an attack. But knowing their ranging sounds could be beneficial as well."

Gideon leans over the other loquisonus machine eagerly.

"What you're about to listen to is a selection of ranging calls emitted by a dragon during a hunt for prey," Dr. Seymour says. "The loquisonus converts them to an audible frequency and slows them down so as to allow us to hear. Listen carefully, please."

She presses a button and a static sound erupts from the gramophone speaker. It's interrupted by a loud chirping, like a bird. A whole sequence of identical sounds follows. I glance nervously at the door. What must these sounds, now on an audible human frequency, sound like to Yndrir? Could he recognize them as echolocation calls, or does it simply sound like a bird is trapped inside the glasshouse?

Dr. Seymour catches me looking. "We usually use headphones."

Then there's a different noise, much longer, like a melody. The chirping sounds resume for a few seconds, and then the recording stops. Dr. Seymour looks at me.

"Did you hear the ranging calls, the identical ones that appear at three-second intervals? Those were helping the dragon locate its prey. But there was another sound right in the middle, a lower but harmonious trilling sound. Did you notice?"

I nod.

"That was a social call," Dr. Seymour continues, "which suggests this dragon was not hunting alone."

A shiver shoots down my spine as I imagine the dragons soaring above us, unaware they're being listened to as they hunt. It's like we're flying with them, invisible.

Dr. Seymour fiddles with the machine again. "Now remember

that when you're listening in real time there will be a short delay between the emission of the calls and what you hear, because the machine needs a few seconds to convert them. Here's another recording."

This time, the chirping sounds come at faster intervals, and get faster and faster until they blend into a high buzz.

"That bit at the end is called a feeding buzz," Dr. Seymour explains. "As the dragon homes in on its prey, it emits several clicks in quick succession for greater accuracy. This allows it to stay updated on the prey's slightest change of direction. You can hear one last buzz at the end just before it catches it."

I place my hands on the loquisonus machine. This is clever, cleverer and more complex than any form of dragon communication I've ever studied. But if dragons don't want humans knowing about echolocation, does that mean they don't want us learning their spoken languages, either? That they're against humans studying dragon tongues?

I think back to Chumana in the library.

The child speaks dragon tongue.

She didn't seem to mind. In fact, I'd like to think she was impressed. But echolocation is different. To be able to understand and imitate it would mean Wyvernmire's government could not only spy on the rebel dragons or apply echolocation techniques to their own means of communication, but potentially emit undercover calls that would lead the rebels astray. It would be groundbreaking. Now I understand why Wyvernmire needs this code. It truly *could* change the course of the war.

"Who designed these machines?" I ask.

"I did," Dr. Seymour replies quietly.

She brushes a strand of loose hair behind her ear and I feel a wave of admiration for her.

"Of course, this is going to take a lot of training. You'll have to listen to hundreds of recordings—and at different speeds—until you can even begin to make sense of them. Vivien and Gideon, you'll then attempt to liken echolocation to any word-based languages you know. Sophie and Katherine, you'll be looking for patterns in phonology and occurrence. I want you all to start by learning the terminology."

She pulls a box out of the cupboard and removes the lid. It's full of alphabetically ordered index cards. "For this to work, you must know the difference between a click and a tick, a rasp and a trill. For us humans to be consistent in our observations, we must use a common lexicon."

"What are these?" Gideon mumbles, pointing to a pile of notebooks on the table.

"Those are our logbooks," Dr. Seymour says. "They must never be removed from the glasshouse. When you begin your shift, you write your name and the date, then record all of your findings and your workings-out beneath. This allows us to keep up with each other's progress and pick up where colleagues have left off. If you believe you've correctly translated a call, you add it to the indexing system." Dr. Seymour points to the box of index cards.

I peer at the last thing written in the logbook in front of me.

Trill-type2 may be used to alert other dragons to something of
interest.

"You have several hours left of your shift," Dr. Seymour says, glancing at her watch. "Grab yourselves a cup of coffee and start getting to grips with the material."

As Gideon reaches for the photograph book of patrol dragons and Sophie and Katherine share some index cards, I read through the logbook. There are so many questions I want to ask, but first I need to read and learn everything there is to know. I feel a familiar thrill of excitement, the exact same one I used to get when my professors set a lengthy piece of translation homework, like a puzzle waiting to be solved. I stare at the different calls and notes marked beneath them:

Trill-type6

Trill-type10

Translation: Do not land.

Call recorded at 9 p.m., rebel dragon over glasshouse, thought
      to be accompanied by two others.

It's like reading the dragons' thoughts. I look over at the loquisonus machines, glinting like gold in the morning sunlight. We're not just translating a language, I realize. We're recording it for the very first time.

I look through the remaining index cards to cross-check the translation. I want to know which of these trills means *land*. I pick up a pencil to make notes, but it's blunt. I go to the cupboard and rummage among the boxes for a sharpener. I can't find one, but there's a tin of fresh pencils. I pick it up and notice an envelope beneath. There's no name or address, but there are two three-pronged claw marks on the front, on the left and the right. I know what that is.

It's dracovol mail.

I glance at Dr. Seymour, but she's busy explaining one of the cards to Katherine. My parents used to send our dracovol to pick up schoolbooks for me, as dracovol mail is quicker than the Royal Mail. It's a private, uncontrolled form of sending and receiving, where letters and parcels are transported by a tiny, long-tailed dragon that's as fast as a falcon and trained to deliver to a few specific locations. Most Second Class families I know have a dracovol. But there's no dracovol cage inside the glasshouse, and I haven't seen any miniature dragons flying around. Besides, Ravensloe said that sending letters isn't allowed at Bletchley. So what's Dr. Seymour up to? I tug half the letter out of the envelope and read the sentence written in neat handwriting at the top.

Canna, Rùm, and Eigg are all

I can't see the rest without unfolding the letter. I glance over my shoulder. Gideon is watching me so I stuff the letter back in the envelope and close the cupboard door. I know that Rùm is an island off the coast of Scotland, officially made dragon territory at the signing of the Peace Agreement. They use it as their hatching grounds. But I've never heard of the others. I sit back down at my desk with my fresh pencil. Why is Dr. Seymour receiving dracovol mail? She must have special permission from Ravensloe, maybe for secret echolocation research.

I glance at the box of index cards. There are hundreds of them, and yet Dr. Seymour seems to think we haven't even scratched the surface of this echolocation language. Despite her enthusiasm, I'm starting to feel like cracking this dragon code in three months will be impossible. No one can learn an entire language that fast.

With my previous translations, I'd spend hours poring over books to research context, reading round the subject until suddenly a new way of using a word jumped out at me, a translation I hadn't considered that gave the text a whole new meaning. That's how I'll have to start this time, too. And for that I'll need a library. Surely Bletchley has one of those?

I begin taking notes, keeping my eyes on the page even when I feel Dr. Seymour watching me. The first thing I'll research are the Scottish Isles. If Dr. Seymour is receiving letters about them, then they must be important to learning echolocation. Perhaps I'll discover something that will give me a head start. I glance at the others and feel a spark of competitiveness. I know it's stupid because we're all in this together. But if anyone is going to crack a code that will win the war and erase my mistakes, I want it to be me.

NINE

"You mean you're secretly listening in on what the rebel dragons are saying to each other so you can translate and pass it on to Wyvernmire?"

I sit with Marquis at the dining table, speaking quietly as the other recruits take their places for lunch. The air hums with discussions about work and the war, and I see Katherine and Gideon talking animatedly over their food.

"Yes," I reply, sipping my soup. "And the Dragon Queen doesn't want Wyvernmire to know about echolocation, even though it could help them *both* defeat the rebels."

"One of my professors mentioned dragon echolocation once," Marquis says, "but he said it was just a theory. The idea that an entire species came up with a secret code inside their heads for the purpose of fighting humans—"

"Dr. Seymour doesn't seem to think it's a weapon. And it's not a code, not really. It's a language."

"Whatever it is, it's basically mind reading," says Marquis excitedly. "Like some crazy primal advantage dragons have."

"No more of an advantage than our ability to talk via wireless." Atlas pulls up a chair next to us and I frown. How long has he been listening?

"Of course it's an advantage," I argue. "*We* don't have a wireless inside our heads."

Serena and Karim join us at the table. Karim gives me a shy smile—I haven't heard him speak yet and he blushes every time someone looks in his direction. Serena is not so discreet.

"I've learned to *fly* planes, of course, but I never thought I'd find myself *designing* them," she says, her elbow grazing Atlas's arm as she reaches for the bread. "And fighter planes at that. Aviation sounds like the most useful of the three categories." She looks pointedly at me.

"Fighter planes?" I say to Marquis, ignoring Serena's stare.

"Hmmm," Marquis replies through a mouthful of potatoes. "Knott has designed wings modeled on dragon flight. I suggested we incorporate a mechanical gizzard into the plane, to make it breathe fire."

"A mechanical what?" says Sophie, sitting down beside me.

I sneak a surprised glance at her—does this mean she agrees to us working together?

"It's how dragons make flames," Marquis says. "They have several stomachs, like cows, and a gizzard, like chickens. When the food they eat ferments, it produces methane."

Atlas raises an eyebrow.

"Dragon gizzards are covered in flint-like scales," Marquis explains. "And dragons eat small rocks for digestion. So, when the rocks strike against the scales in the presence of methane, flames spark. It's all ridiculously clever."

"And you think they'll work?" Atlas says. "These fire-breathing planes?"

Ralph walks into the room, his helmet under his arm, and

everyone falls quiet. I'm shocked at how young he is. He can't be any older than twenty-five. His pale skin shines against his dark hair and his eyes are lined with thick lashes. His prettiness is on a par with his cruelty. We eat in silence as Ralph makes himself a plate of food, eyeing us suspiciously, then leaves.

"What are you doing in Zoology?" Katherine asks Dodie.

Dodie and Atlas exchange a look.

"Looking at reptile growth and development," Dodie says.

"And dragon eugenics," Atlas adds coolly. "Lumens has asked us to research the subject in the library, although I'm thinking of refusing."

"So there *is* a library here?" I say.

"I think I saw one on the third floor," Dodie says, casting Atlas a worried look. "I'll show you if you like—"

"I'll take you, Featherswallow," Atlas interrupts. "I'm actually going there now."

"Oh," I say.

A boy willing to disobey his category leader's orders when his entire future is at stake is bad news. I want to stay as far away from Atlas King as possible.

"Well, actually, I did promise Marquis I'd show him the tennis c—"

"Karim knows where it is," Marquis says quickly. "He'll show me."

I stare from Marquis to Karim, who is turning a deep shade of beetroot. Atlas smiles pleasantly.

So I'm going to be alone with the rule-breaker.

"Soph, do you want to come?"

"Just because we're in the same category doesn't mean we're

friends again," Sophie says dryly.

"Fine," I say, pulling my hair down to hide my burning cheeks.

I glance at Atlas and he jumps up. "After you."

We climb the stairs in silence, and on the landing Atlas beckons me down a hallway.

"You're lucky coming here with two people you know," he says.

The hallway has large windows with a view of the forest. We cross it and climb a second set of stairs hidden behind a door.

"I didn't come here with Sophie," I say. "I just knew her before."

"Did you have an argument?"

"Something like that."

We stop outside a set of double doors.

"Featherswallow. That's a dragon-descended name, isn't it? When I heard it, I thought you were First Class."

I shrug. "My family must have been once. And they must have done something to get demoted. Something cowardly."

"Why cowardly?"

I raise an eyebrow. "You know the legend. Britannia's cowardly dragons, those who betrayed their own, lost their scales in punishment and were turned into swallows. My uncle Thomas said that centuries ago men who went against the king had the word *Swallow* added to their family name, to single them out."

"I read a different tale," Atlas says softly. "Swallows were originally dragons who could speak every language in the world. But it weighed on them, being able to empathize with the stories of so many, so they asked God to relieve their burden and make them light and carefree. He turned them into birds and gave them tails forked like a dragon's tongue, to remind them of what they once were."

Goose bumps rise on my arms. The swallows were *linguists*? I've never heard that version of the legend before. Atlas smiles, holding the door open for me, and when I walk past him into the library I catch that scent again—peppermint and tobacco.

The library is small and dark and cluttered. There's only one window and no one has bothered to lift its blackout blind. We set to work lighting the gas lamps, and when I turn round I see books piled up on the floor, bursting from the shelves and stuffed into alcoves in the walls. There's an upstairs section, accessible by a ladder, and I spot a small, round table and a few chairs up there. The air smells of damp paper.

"What are you looking for?" Atlas asks.

"A book on the Scottish Isles," I say, peering closer at the spines of the books.

"The Scottish Isles? Why?"

There's a piece of paper tacked to the wall. I scan it until I find what I'm looking for:

GEOGRAPHY—UPPER LEVEL

I step onto the ladder. "I just think it will be a good place to begin."

Atlas is right behind me, climbing off the ladder and into the upper section just after I do.

"Do you always do more work than is required?" He smiles at me, his mouth twitching.

"Yes," I say without smiling back. "I like to get a head start."

"But I thought you were translating," Atlas says. "Why do you need a book on the Scottish Isles for that?"

I ignore him and peer up at the wall. It's covered in old maps, framed and mounted in neat rows. My eyes follow the lines that represent islands, the quick pencil marks indicating mountains and rivers, until I see an expanse of land with nothing but three words in the middle.

"Here be dragons," I read out loud.

"They say some cartographers were too afraid to chart certain territories." Atlas comes up behind me. "Whenever they came across an unexplored area, they simply marked a warning on the maps they were drawing. It means they don't know what's there, but there are most definitely dragons."

"How do you know that?" I say.

He grins. "How do you not?"

I turn away and run my hand along the books on the geography shelves. I'm surprised to see they're arranged by country. After the Travel Ban was imposed, many libraries removed the books that focused on foreign countries and replaced them with texts about Britannia instead. But now I'm seeing spines with titles like *Capital Cities of the World* and *Dragon Diaspora in Paris and Its Environs*. This must be someone's private collection. I wonder who lived at Bletchley before the government requisitioned it. I find the section on Britannia and kneel to look at the lowest books.

Britannia, a Kingdom by the Sea
British Territories: A Tale of Two Species
The Book of Welsh Estuaries
A Brief History of the Beginnings of Scotland
The Viking Isles
The Hebrides: Exploring Scotland's Islands

My hand stops. I pull out the last book and bring it to the table. While I flick through the pages, I watch Atlas out of the corner of my eye. He's engrossed in the politics section, his lips moving silently as he reads. His white collar is still poking out from beneath his uniform. Why does he insist on keeping his own clothes?

Something catches my eye on page 265.

The Hebrides comprise more than forty islands extending in an arc off the Atlantic west coast of Scotland. However, most of these islands are uninhabited. The Small Isles, which include Canna, Sanday, Rùm, Eigg, and Muck, used to be home to humans and dragons alike. Rùm has been used as a hatching ground for British dragons since the twelfth century, but officially became dragon-only territory upon the signing of the Peace Agreement in 1866. Dragons claim that hatching season is disturbed by human activity, therefore, plane routes are no longer directed across the islands. When the Peace Agreement was signed, the government requisitioned the neighboring islands of Eigg and Canna for official purposes. A total of 360 inhabitants were moved to the mainland.

If Eigg and Canna are government-owned, then whatever Dr. Seymour has to do with them must have been sanctioned by Ravensloe. But how are those places linked to dragon echolocation?

Rùm has been used as a hatching ground for British dragons since the twelfth century.

I imagine a grassy island covered in dragon nests, eggs the size of bowling balls sheltered by leathery wings.

"Find anything interesting?"

Atlas leans over my shoulder and I jump.

"Not really," I say, slamming the book shut. "But thanks for bringing me here."

"You're welcome."

I turn round to look at him. He smiles, his lips rising on one side to form a dimple in his cheek. This time, I can't help but smile back.

Who is this boy?

"So why were you put in Zoology?" I ask. "I mean, what did you do before?"

"I bred horses," Atlas replies.

I raise an eyebrow. "Horses are quite different to dragons."

Atlas smirks. "They are. And they were never meant to be my career. My mother got me a job working in the stables of a lord, and he decided I had an eye for good bloodstock."

Hugo Montecue's father breeds racehorses for the First Class families of Sandringham. It's a complicated job, requiring the study of genetics and veterinary sciences. To say it's an unusual career for a Third Class boy would be an understatement.

"So you don't mind the genetic selection of desirable characteristics in horses, but you're against it when it comes to dragons?" I say.

I don't know why I want to provoke him, but it works.

His lips purse. "Like you said, horses are quite different to dragons."

Suddenly I can't meet his gaze. I'm being rude, despite the fact that he volunteered to show me the library.

"It was Father David who got me books on equine physiology," he says gently.

And now he's being kind enough to continue the conversation.

"Father David?"

"Lord Lovat had a priest living next to the chapel on his estate. He became a bit like my mentor, I suppose."

I nod. I really want to know how a Third Class horse breeder mentored by a priest came to be at Bletchley, but I can't say that in case he asks me a similar question.

I made a deal with a criminal dragon to save my rebel parents and broke the Peace Agreement in the process, I imagine myself saying.

Perhaps not.

"So you'll go back to the estate, if your category succeeds?"

Atlas shakes his head. "I don't think so. I've been a seminarian for the past year."

"A semi-what?"

"A seminarian. A priest-in-training."

I try to mask my surprise by clearing my throat, but inhale some dust from the book and end up coughing so hard that tears stream down my face.

"Wow," I croak as Atlas's mouth twitches again. "So Father David really got to you."

Atlas lets out a deep laugh. "Why do you look so horrified?"

"I'm not!" I exclaim, trying to appear neutral. "I just didn't expect you to be a priest."

"Priest-in-training," he corrects me. He points to his collar. "Didn't this give it away?"

Of course.

"I just thought you were sentimental about your old clothes," I say weakly.

Atlas laughs again as I brush the rest of the dust from the cover of the book. Aren't priests wrinkled, judgmental old men? Atlas has glowing skin, muscular arms, and a smile that is difficult to look away from. He returns my book to the shelf and I glance at the stubble on his cheek and the dark curl at the nape of his neck.

"I thought priests followed strict rules," I say, instantly regretting it.

"Are you suggesting I don't?" He tilts his head playfully.

Is he flirting with me? Am I being flirted with by a *priest*?

In training, I correct myself.

"What do priests even *do*?"

"Lots of things. But mostly they seek God," Atlas replies. "Isn't that what we're all doing?"

"I don't believe—"

"Recruit Featherswallow!"

I spin round. Ralph is standing in the doorway to the library, his gun slung over his shoulder. When he sees Atlas standing next to me, his eyes narrow.

"Your services are required downstairs, but it looks like you think you have better things to do."

"My services?"

"Do I need to remind you two that you are here to *work*?" He glares at us. "What are you doing up there?"

"Researching," Atlas replies quickly. "Recruit Featherswallow needed some reading material."

"*Featherswallow* should be downstairs making herself available

119

to any superiors who might be in need of her . . . assistance."

He sneers at me and I stand up. I climb down the ladder slowly.

"I was under the impression that the Guardians of Bletchley are here for our protection," Atlas says from the upper level. "So shouldn't it be *you* assisting Featherswallow, Guardian 707?"

My feet touch the floor and my face burns at Atlas's daring. I turn to Ralph.

"Who is asking for me? Is it Dr. Seymour?"

"What were you doing together?" he says instead of answering my question. "You're from different categories."

"Atlas showed me where the library is."

"You're not supposed to be sneaking around—"

"We're not," I say. "He was just helping me—"

"I've a mind to have you punished!" Ralph spits. "Both for interrupting a Guardian *and* for disobeying Bletchley Park protocol."

Atlas jumps off the ladder, his face twisting with anger. "She wasn't disobeying anything—"

"And you'll be going to isolation—once for lying, and again for being a Third Class rat!"

"You can't do that—" I shout, but my words are cut short as Ralph's hand comes down on the back of my neck.

I twist in his grip, but his hand squeezes tighter. He's strong, stronger than I would have imagined.

"Don't give me an excuse to slap you a second time," he whispers in my ear.

My nails scrape against the back of his hand as my vision blurs with rage. "Get off me, you bas—"

His grip loosens suddenly and when I look up, Atlas has

Ralph in a chokehold against the wall. The door to the library slams open and Professor Lumens appears.

"*What* is going on in here?"

Atlas lets go of Ralph and he lunges toward him, pointing his gun.

"Recruits disobeying the rules, Lumens," he spits. "This one"—he jerks his head toward Atlas—"just attacked me."

"You liar," I breathe.

Professor Lumens holds up his hand. The Head of Zoology has a white beard and is carrying a briefcase under one arm. He looks from me to Atlas, whose hands are balled into fists. Two red spots have appeared on his cheeks.

"Did you attack this Guardian, boy?" he growls.

"He put his hands on her—" Atlas begins.

"So you attacked him?"

"He was defending me!" I say, but Lumens ignores me.

"Apologize," he tells Atlas.

"What?" Atlas snarls. "This Guardian just manhandled a woman and he should be fired—"

"Apologize, recruit," Lumens says coldly, "to Ralph Wyvernmire."

I freeze.

Wyvernmire?

Guardian 707 is related to the Prime Minister?

Atlas stares at Lumens for a moment, then turns to Ralph.

"I apologize," he grunts.

Lumens gives a satisfied nod. "Is there a particular reason for which you find yourself in this library, Guardian 707?"

Ralph pulls himself up to his full height.

"Recruit Featherswallow's translation services are required

in the grounds, yet when somebody was sent to get her, she was nowhere to be found."

"Well then, I think you'd best be going, don't you, Miss Featherswallow?"

Professor Lumens winks at me and I nod.

"I'll see to it that she gets to the right place," Ralph says, laying a hand on my shoulder. I shrug him off.

"Actually, Guardian 707, I thought I heard you threatening punishment to these recruits?" says Lumens. "Perhaps we might decide on Mr. King's together?"

I slip out the door and run downstairs before Ralph can catch up. My whole body is shaking. Is Ralph really related to Wyvernmire? No wonder he acts like he owns the place. I remember the force with which Atlas slammed him against the wall. Ralph won't forget that and Atlas . . . he could get into serious trouble. What if he's demoted? A shiver of fear shoots through me as I try to imagine where demoted recruits go. I've only been here for a day and I've already drawn attention to myself. I knew I should have stayed away from that boy.

But he defended you.

Stop it, I tell myself.

My only goal is to crack the dragon code and go home to Ursa, and I'll never do that if I let myself get distracted. Or if Wyvernmire's Guardian relative decides to make my life a living hell. I reach the entrance hall and head for the front door. Ralph said I was needed in the grounds. There's a Guardian motorcar waiting at the bottom of the steps. The Guardian behind the steering wheel winds the window down.

"Vivien Featherswallow?"

I nod.

"We have an unexpected visitor. Get in."

I slip into the back seat and glance up at the third-floor windows of the house. I can't see the library from here, but I hope Atlas isn't in too much trouble. And that Professor Lumens is as diplomatic as he seems.

The car drives through Bletchley Park, past the lake and then onto a dirt road that runs through an expanse of grassy fields. Who is the unexpected visitor and why are they waiting all the way out here? As the car rolls across the grass, three huge shapes come into view through the windscreen. My heart leaps.

Dragons.

Several Guardians are already parked in the field and the dragons—two juveniles and a larger one—are bleeding from their flanks. The smaller ones are blue and purple, and the third is black with horns protruding from its face. It's huge, even bigger than Chumana. I feel a flutter of nerves as I look at the thick blood oozing down the dragons' scales. Something has gone wrong. The car comes to a stop and the Guardian turns round to face me, his face white.

"Out you get, then."

Out you get? I peer through the window. The other Guardians are waiting inside their motorcars, too. I open the door slowly and step out. The grass is so long it almost reaches my knees. A low growl vibrates beneath my feet. Everyone, including the dragons, is staring at me. Finally, the Guardians get out of their cars, clutching their guns tightly. Relief floods through me as I see a familiar face through an open helmet. It's Owen, the Guardian who picked Marquis and me up from the station.

"Hello," he says to me grimly.

I nod at him, my eyes on the dragons. The black one is looking at me through slitted eyes, its mouth slightly open to reveal canines the length of my finger and a red, double-forked tongue. Its talons are crowned with feathers, like Chumana's.

"This dragon flew across the Channel several hours ago and circled over Bletchley," Owen tells me. "Our patrol dragons—Muirgen and Rhydderch—put up a good fight until they realized the guest comes in . . . peace."

I glance at the smaller patrol dragons.

"This Bolgorith seems to have come from Bulgaria," the blue dragon—Muirgen—tells me in English.

I freeze. A dragon from Bulgaria? But those dragons don't have anything to do with humans. Not since they wiped out Mama's entire country in three days. I exchange a horrified glance with Owen.

"We have been unable to communicate with him," Rhydderch says.

"I don't understand," I say slowly. "You're dragons. You speak several languages. . . . How can you not have a single one in common?"

"Bulgarian dragons don't—"

"I know," I interrupt Owen. "Bulgarian dragons haven't taught their young human languages since the Massacre of Bulgaria." I stare up at the Bolgorith. "But you were born before that," I say in Bulgarian. "You must speak Bulgarian, at least."

The dragon's lips pull into a grin.

"The question is," he replies, "why do you?"

"My mother is from Bulgaria," I say coldly. "Her family was murdered there."

"How unfortunate," he says. "I am Borislav."

"How can I help you, Borislav?"

124

I switch to Slavidraneishá, Chumana's mother tongue. Now Bulgaria's official language. Borislav lowers his head until it's level with my face, unable to mask his surprise at me speaking a dragon language, too. His neck is the length of a motorcar, spiked along the top and the bottom.

"It is unusual for a human to speak multiple tongues," he hisses. "Where did you learn?"

"At school," I reply. "In books."

"Of course," he snarls. "You humans insist on recording our tongues in your inky scrawls."

"It's so we can pass them down."

"I had forgotten how bad you are at teaching your offspring to speak," Borislav replies, shaking his head so that several Guardians jump back in alarm. "Dragonlings learn at least three tongues in their first year of life."

"And yet here you are, unable to converse with your own species without a human translator," I reply coolly.

Borislav roars, rearing backward with a terrible screeching sound as his tail hits a tree. The Guardians raise their guns as splinters of wood rain down onto the cars.

"What did you say to him?" Owen bellows as Muirgen and Rhydderch snarl.

"English is a slothful language, one I refuse to speak. And your patrol dragons are juveniles, still unlearned in the tongues of the East," Borislav spits. "It is a weakness akin to their so-called peace with humans."

My heart thumps loudly in my chest. For a moment, I thought the Bulgarian dragon was about to kill me.

"What do you want me to translate?" I ask.

Borislav gnashes his teeth, his tail still swinging from side to side. "Tell Wyvernmire that the dragons of Bulgaria agree."

I relay the words to Owen.

"Agree to what?" Rhydderch growls in English.

I turn to ask Borislav, but Owen speaks first.

"That's all we need, Vivien."

Rhydderch's eyes narrow. I look at him, then up at Borislav. What have the dragons of Bulgaria and Wyvernmire agreed to? And why doesn't Rhydderch—who serves Queen Ignacia—seem to know?

"Tell the dragon that Wyvernmire thanks him for traveling all this way," Owen says. "And remind him that his hunting must be restricted to wild animals until he has crossed British borders."

I translate and Borislav lets out a laugh.

"You tell your superior that I feasted on two of his colleagues when flying over London this daybreak." His eyes swivel in their sockets to look at me. "We don't obey human rules—your Prime Minister knows that."

Borislav's wings unfold suddenly, stretching across the field and knocking the mirror off one of the cars. After a few thundering steps, the dragon launches himself into the air. We watch in silence as he soars upward, circling over the field a few times before disappearing into the clouds above the forest.

"Someone get me Ravensloe," Owen says. "Now!"

Muirgen and Rhydderch have moved closer together and are conversing quietly. They don't seem to understand anything more about this encounter than I do. But why is that? The question circles in my mind as Owen opens the car door for me and the Guardian drives me back to Bletchley Manor. If all dragons speak echolocation, then why weren't the patrol dragons able to communicate with Borislav when they saw him in the sky? I decide to ask Dr. Seymour about it, because there's already an even bigger question pressing on me.

Why is Wyvernmire talking with the Bulgarian dragons, the most ruthless dragons in Europe? And if the Dragon Queen is Wyvernmire's ally, then why did her dragons look so surprised?

TEN

I pull my headphones off and swear. I've spent an entire week listening to the same sequence of echolocation calls on repeat and every time I feel like I'm beginning to understand what they mean, I hear them used in a different context that has me back at square one.

"Trill-type4 seems to mean 'let's hunt,' right?" I say to Gideon. Gideon glances up from the index cards and nods.

"Then why is it being used *here* as a command to follow?"

I hand my headphones to Gideon, hit *rewind* then *play*. He listens for a moment, then gives me a bewildered look.

"See!" I say, throwing my hands up in the air. "It makes no sense."

I glance over my shoulder. Dr. Seymour is working on a reperisonus machine, trying to fix one of the wires, and I wonder how it could possibly have been damaged when it's tucked away against the rear wall. Sophie is at the other loquisonus, attempting to write down the rhythm of a sound pattern with Katherine's help.

The scribbles in my logbook swim in front of my eyes. I've been trying to liken the echolocation calls to the dragon tongues I know, searching for similarities in the lexicon or pace. But the calls I hear through the loquisonus machine are sounds more similar to the song of a bird or the blare of a horn than they are to spoken words.

Languages—even dragon ones—can be transcribed onto paper using letters or symbols that deconstruct each sound or meaning, but echolocation isn't like that. The terminology we're using, like Trill-type13, doesn't *audibly* sound like the noises I hear through the headphones in the way that the letter *s* conveys the hissing of the word *hahriss*, which means *together* in Slavidraneishá. Bulgarian is easier to grasp once one knows that the capital Cyrillic letter *Ve* looks like a capital Romanized *B*. Echolocation, on the other hand, has none of these rules, none of these signposts that could eventually lead to a full translation of the sounds.

Why did Wyvernmire even bother to hire linguists when echolocation is more similar to Sophie's Morse code than it is to any language I've ever known?

"Give it here," Gideon says, nodding toward the loquisonus machine.

"I'm fine—" I begin, but he's already pulling it toward him.

I feel my cheeks flush with irritation, but force a laugh. "What makes you think you'll do any better than me?"

"I'm just . . . better suited," he replies.

"I had no idea boys were better suited to listening to ultrasonic dragon calls than girls," Sophie says before I can spit back my own reply.

"Not because I'm a boy, although the art of codebreaking *is* traditionally a man's domain." Gideon smirks. "But I've been around a lot of dragons."

I swallow down my next retort as my curiosity gets the better of me. "You have?"

"How about a field trip?" Dr. Seymour interrupts.

We load the two loquisonus machines and other tools into a

small pull-along buggy and traipse into the forest. I breathe in the fresh air and lift my face to the sun. Since meeting Muirgen and Rhydderch in the field when translating for Borislav, I've started seeing dragons everywhere. Flying past my window in the morning, patrolling the forest, or landing in the courtyard to converse with Guardians. I can never keep my eyes off them. I haven't seen this many dragons in the same place since the war, and even though they pay absolutely no attention to me, I can't stop myself from hazarding guesses with Marquis about what species they are or which languages they might speak.

"Right," Dr. Seymour says as we stop in a small clearing.

I can see the green of the tennis court through the trees.

"Headphones on and find the right frequency."

I step toward Sophie, hoping to share a loquisonus machine with her, but she glares at me and pairs with Katherine instead. So I kneel over the other machine with Gideon, my stockings soaking up the damp from the forest floor, and twist the dials on our machine until the crackling subsides and I find the ultrasonic frequency that echolocation exists on.

"Remember, there are no blockers here," Dr. Seymour tells us quietly, glancing up above the trees. "So you must under no circumstances play back any of the echolocation calls you record. If you do, the dragons will be able to hear."

I nod, and Gideon glances nervously at the gold, trumpet-like speakers on the machines as if they might suddenly come to life. A clicking sound fills my ears. I pause. Is it a Trill-type13 or a Skrill-type62? I reach for the index cards in the buggy, but suddenly a huge shadow passes over us. I stare upward as sunlight floods over us again and a dragon flies toward the tennis court. The clicks crackle in my ears and I press my headphones closer.

"Can anyone identify that dragon?" Dr. Seymour says softly. She's peering at it through a pair of binoculars.

Gideon flicks through the photograph book.

"It might be Soresten," he says. "A hundred and ten years old, male, a British Sand Dragon."

There is a long sequence of social calls, starting with a Trill-type2. I know what that means. The dragon has seen something of interest.

But who is he talking to?

I squint in the sunlight, staring past the edge of the forest and the tennis court to the fields that lead to the lake. There's a hut there, apparently abandoned since the Great War. Perched on top of it, a hazy, glittering blue shape, is another dragon.

"That one's Muirgen," I say confidently. "She's the only blue Western Drake here."

Soresten hovers above her and a Trill-type10 sounds in my ears. Suddenly Muirgen swoops downward, landing effortlessly in the fields out of my view. Soresten is still airborne, a glint of gold in the sky. Then comes another sequence of social calls, different from the first, but still similar. It begins with what sounds like a Trill-type10, but it's longer, with an inflection at the end, like the intonation humans make at the end of a question. I flick through the index cards, looking for one that describes what I've just heard, but find nothing.

"Let me listen," Gideon murmurs, holding out his hand for a turn at the headphones.

I ignore him as another dragon appears beyond the hut, circling once overhead before landing with Muirgen in the field.

Dr. Seymour is crouching next to Katherine, sharing her headphones. "Did you see what happened there?" she says.

I shake my head, wishing I had the correct answer.

"The dragons both did the same thing, landing in the field. Soresten is a chief patrol dragon, so it's likely they did so on his orders."

"But he said different things to them," I say. "The calls he used were different."

"Maybe Soresten wasn't the only one talking," Katherine offers. "Maybe the first sequence was Soresten's orders, and the second was another dragon's response."

"Nice theory, Katherine," says Dr. Seymour. "That's entirely possible, but the slight similarity between the first Trill-type10 and the second longer one suggests that the same thing is being said, just differently."

"So there are different ways of saying things in echolocation?" I ask. "Like synonyms?"

No wonder this morning's recordings had me confused.

Dr. Seymour smiles. "Perhaps. But remember this is all theoretical. I'm learning just as you are."

"But why bother?" I say. "Why would Soresten waste time saying the same thing two different ways?"

Dr. Seymour gives me an empty shrug.

"Dr. Seymour," I say suddenly. "You know the Bulgarian dragon I translated for last week? Why did they need me? Even though he didn't speak the same tongue as Muirgen and Rhydderch, couldn't they have spoken in echolocation?"

She stands up. "I wondered this, too," she replies. "Perhaps they *did* communicate via echolocation before landing, but hid this from you so as not to bring it to your—and therefore Prime

132

Minister Wyvernmire's—attention. They all want it to remain a secret, remember?"

I nod, but I'm not convinced. If the dragons were truly able to communicate via echolocation, they wouldn't have gone through the trouble of asking for a human translator just to hide the fact that they were doing so. So is it possible there are different types of echolocation, like the synonyms I referred to earlier? And, if so, why doesn't Dr. Seymour—who invented the loquisonus machine—seem interested?

I stay in the glasshouse all day, poring over the index cards in the corner while Dr. Seymour works her own shift. Sophie has offered to take notes for her, and while I initially feel irked at this shameless attempt to get ahead, I remind myself that we're a team—whether Sophie likes it or not.

The idea that echolocation has several ways of saying the same thing fascinates me like the dragon tongue Harpentesa did the first time I heard Mama speak it on an expedition in Norfolk when I was four. I take a fresh index card and describe the second call Soresten made.

Similar to Trill-type10, but with an inflection at the end. Both
    calls seem to indicate an order to land.

Then I give the new call a name.

Trill-type14.

At the end of the day, Sophie hangs back and I see her slip a logbook beneath her jacket.

"Dr. Seymour said we're not supposed to take them out of the glasshouse," I say. "For security—"

"I know that," Sophie snaps. "But a seven-hour shift isn't enough to figure all this out."

She lifts a hand to her mouth and bites her nails. She's worried. Of course she is. Her entire future depends on whether or not we crack this so-called code.

"Come on," I say, holding the door open for her. "I'm sure Dr. Seymour won't notice it's gone."

She steps through without a thank-you.

"It all feels like a waste of time," she says as we walk back through the forest. "I've been comparing echolocation to Morse code, and they're nothing alike."

I kick at a pile of soft, damp leaves and nod. "It's nothing like dragon tongues, either."

"We've got to figure it out, though," Sophie says. "Otherwise, we'll never go home."

"We will," I say fiercely.

I pull my collar up against the cold and plunge my hands into my pockets. We walk in silence, craning our necks to the sky each time a dragon passes over. Sometimes, when I'm lying in bed, I imagine what it would be like if rebel dragons discovered our location and descended on Bletchley. Would they burn us like the dragon burned those Guardians back at the station? Surely it's only a matter of time until they discover us. Sophie's right. We're not progressing fast enough. If only I could ask some of the patrol dragons about echolocation—

Footsteps sound behind us and I shake the image of furious dragons away. Atlas appears at Sophie's side. His hands are full of small pieces of wood, and when Sophie and I glance at each other, he lifts them up to show us, grinning.

"Was just looking for materials," Atlas says. "I do a bit of carpentry in my spare time. You know, for fun."

A horse breeder turned priest-in-training who whittles wood for fun.

"I didn't know you two worked afternoons."

"We don't," Sophie says. "I was helping Dr. Seymour, and Viv was just doing some . . . extra research."

I smile sweetly at him. "I like to do more work than is required, remember?"

He chuckles and looks down at his feet, then back up again.

"Speaking of research . . . that reading you were doing in the library? You should take a look at the books again, just in case there's something you missed."

I stare at him, thinking back to the book on the Scottish Isles. Atlas didn't even know what I was looking for in that book because I didn't tell him. "What are you talking about?"

He gives me an innocent look. "I was just doing a bit of organizing of the shelves after Ralph came to say hello—"

"Organizing?" I say.

Sophie raises an eyebrow.

"Yes," Atlas says, a smile playing on his lips. "Do you have a problem with that?"

"None at all," I reply. "It seems you're a man of many talents, Atlas King."

"You have no idea, Featherswallow."

Sophie clears her throat loudly and Atlas almost drops his sticks. "See you at dinner," he says brightly. "Bye, Sophie."

We both watch in silence as Atlas strides through the gardens toward the house. I feel a strange swooping sensation in my stomach as I watch him go.

Sophie turns to me. "What. Was. That?"

"I have no idea," I reply. "What did he mean about the research—"

"You were flirting with him!" Sophie accuses me.

"I absolutely was not," I say. "I can't believe you'd suggest such a thing."

"Why?" she says. "You've courted Third Class boys before."

"It has nothing to do with his class and everything to do with the fact that I'm here to help us win this war and go home. Nothing more."

"Oh," Sophie says. "Right."

She falls quiet until we reach the garden, then stops walking.

"I can't go back there," she says softly.

"Back where?"

"To the Third Class. To the halfway house."

I swallow. "Was it really that bad?"

"I met some good people," Sophie says slowly. "My friend Nicolas. He lived in the halfway house with me."

"Did he . . . fail the Examination?"

I can't believe I'm pronouncing those words to her, dancing along the knife edge of truth about what I did. Sophie nods. I stare at a spider crawling up the trunk of a tree.

"What was so bad about it?" I say carefully. "I thought it was supposed to be a place that helps you adapt to your new class . . ." I trail off as Sophie shakes her head.

"There was a welfare worker, someone from the government, but she barely ever came. And when she did, she didn't care about what we had to say." Sophie starts walking again and I follow. "She knew that the Camden halfway house was being used as a black-market location, but she never reported it."

136

"Black market?"

"There was a group of adults living on the top floor, selling class passes out of the bedrooms. There was a lot of drinking and fighting and . . ." Sophie takes a deep breath. "It was run by a man, Finley, but he brought other people in, too. Men and women, all from different classes."

We stop in the courtyard and Sophie leans back against the wall of the manor.

"Nicolas and I worked the same shift at the Raven Inn and we . . . well, you know . . ." She gives me a wide-eyed look and I nod, trying not to look surprised at the idea that Sophie had a boyfriend. She always used to insist that boys were a distraction she couldn't indulge in until after the Examination.

"He moved his things into my room and we set up a sort of camp in there, staying away from the third floor and only using the kitchen when everyone else was asleep. One night I woke up to see smoke coming under the door. The whole downstairs was on fire, and so was the staircase. We threw our blankets out the window so we could jump, but Finley and his men came into our room with boxes of stuff, class passes and dragonbone, to get it all out of the window safely. It must have been worth a lot because they wouldn't let us near the window, wouldn't let us out until they'd saved their merchandise. By that time, the flames had spread to our door so Nicolas pushed Finley out of the way and then—" Sophie lets out a yelp and my blood runs cold. "Then they were fighting and Nicolas screamed at me to jump."

Sophie's breath comes in ragged sobs and I take her hand. "I thought he was right behind me. But just after I hit the ground, there was this explosion." Her eyes stare past me into the trees. "When they pulled Nicolas out, his whole body was covered in burns. I took him to the hospital, but they didn't have the right equipment or medication. None of the Third Class hospitals do. His injuries were so bad and . . ."

I close my eyes.

"He died."

"Soph," I whisper. "I'm so, so sorry."

"I tried to go home after that." Sophie wipes her nose on her sleeve. "But the government wanted to relocate the survivors to another halfway house. They kept finding me. My mum tried to hide me, but that just got her in trouble. So I decided I didn't want to be part of it anymore."

The words tumble out of her mouth as if she can't stop them, and all I can do is listen in horror.

"It's not fair," she says hoarsely, "that Nicolas died when other hospitals—Second Class hospitals—had everything that could have saved him."

I imagine Sophie in a Camden hospital, crying over the body of the boyfriend who died protecting her.

Protecting her from the place *I* sent her to.

"I went into Marylebone, to the greengrocer, the library, the park. Just like I used to," Sophie says. "I waited three hours for a Guardian to ask for my class pass and then arrest me. I told him I wouldn't go to any halfway house and ripped up my class pass in front of him. It felt good, you know?" She looks at me as if I might be able to understand what it felt like. "It felt good to show him, to show anyone, what I think of Wyvernmire's stupid Class System." She spits out the last words. "In the end, they sent me to Granger's Prison. Viv, are you all right?"

My eyes are full of tears. I nod silently as I let them fall. I can't bring myself to look at her. I can't even breathe. Sophie was demoted because of me. She was caught in that fire because of me. She could have died, and if she hadn't been there in the first place then maybe Nicolas wouldn't be——

"Viv?"

The shame makes me want to curl into a ball and stop existing.

I've done so many terrible, unforgivable things. Sophie's face softens. She raises a hand and wipes away my tears.

Stop! I want to scream. *Stop being kind to me.*

"Come on," she says gently, taking my hand.

I let her lead me into the common room where the rest of the recruits are crowded round the radio, arguing about which way to turn the dial. Atlas is sitting on the window seat, whittling a piece of wood with a small knife. I avoid his gaze and slump into an armchair.

"What's wrong, Featherswallow?" Katherine says. "You look like someone died."

Someone did, I want to say as Sophie winces. *So shut up and leave me alone.*

The common room is furnished with old, worn furniture and ugly green curtains with pink flowers. A bookcase that holds some long-forgotten, prewar children's stories stands in a corner and the walls are bare expect for some of Marquis's dragon sketches, which Katherine and Dodie insisted he give them to *spruce things up*. That explains why there's a diagram titled *Dragon Abdominal Anatomy* stuck above the fireplace.

The recruits are the only ones ever in here. We work, eat, and sleep together, barely seeing another human except for our category leaders and the Guardians on shift.

"Have you seen Marquis?" I ask Katherine.

She folds up the sheet of paper she's holding, but not before I see the list of echolocation calls scribbled across it. "He's with Karim." She smirks. "Again."

It comes as no surprise to me that my cousin has found himself a boyfriend in the middle of a civil war. He is, after all, the biggest flirt I have ever known.

"Everyone shut up!" Serena shouts as she finds the right station and the radio crackles to life.

She turns the volume up and music fills the room. I close my eyes, playing the horror of Sophie's story over and over in my mind. If we don't crack this code and win the war, Sophie will live at Granger's Prison forever. A lifetime as a class evader. There's no way I can let that happen, no way I can let what I did to Sophie hurt her any more than it already has—

"Dance with me?"

Marquis slips through the door, grinning, and holds out his hand. I shake my head, but he insists, pulling me out of my seat and spinning me into the center of the room as Dodie claps. The music is a jazz song, one we used to play at home, and Serena twirls Katherine toward us. Gideon and Karim laugh, and when Atlas and Sophie prance across the rug with the setting sunlight in their hair, I forget about who we are, forget about the dark secrets that shroud each of our lives.

And for a moment, just a moment, we are golden.

"This is London. You will now hear a statement from the Prime Minister."

I look up as Wyvernmire's voice replaces the music.

"I am speaking to you from the Cabinet Room of Ten Downing Street.

After a week of war, and courageous battle on the part of our army and volunteering countrymen, the Human-Dragon Coalition launched this afternoon a brutal attack on the innocent people of Central London."

I drop back into the armchair as everyone breaks apart. Atlas pulls the blackout curtains closed.

"We, as a nation, have a clear conscience. We have done all that any country could do to establish peace between humans and dragons. And yet the rebels insist on betraying the Peace Agreement, on betraying Parliament, on betraying democracy. Reports have so far confirmed that this attack has taken the lives of over two thousand First, Second, and Third Class citizens since midday in the quarters of Soho, Camden, Mayfair, Fitzrovia, Bloomsbury, and Marylebone."

I jump to my feet.

"We are a country whose soul has known the iron of adversity and defeat. But we shall know it no more! The assurance of support we have received from Queen Ignacia, as well as from the independent wyvern community of the Mendip Hills, has been reiterated . . ."

A deep, sickening horror rises in my stomach. I stare back at the shocked faces around me and my eyes land on Sophie.

"You, the British people, must report for duty in accordance with the instructions you receive . . ."

Marylebone.

Wyvernmire said Marylebone, the one place I thought Ursa might be safe. I grasp the arm of the chair as my legs go weak.

". . . together we will put an end to the unjust persecution of our countrymen and countrydragons . . ."

I stumble from the room and grip the banister tightly as I half walk, half trip down the stairs. Two thousand people dead. I moan. Why did I leave her? *How* could I? The front doors are locked. I try the doors of the passages that lead out of the entrance hall. One of them opens into a corridor and through to the kitchen. I stumble through the dark, beneath the rows of pots and pans hanging from the ceiling, as Ursa's crying face flashes before my eyes. I turn the key to the back door of the kitchen and stumble out into the dark walled garden, taking deep gasps of cold air.

If Ursa is dead, then I have nothing left to live for.

I sink to my knees.

Please not her. Anyone but her.

My chest tightens and I double over.

"Recruit? Do you need a doctor?"

Guardian boots crunch across the gravel and someone pulls me to my feet. Ralph takes one look at my tearstained face.

"Featherswallow. You've heard the news, then."

I stare at him.

"Fitzrovia, that's where you lived, wasn't it?" He lets go of me and lights a cigarette. "Lose someone, did you?"

"I shouldn't be here," I say. "I'll go back inside."

"No, you won't." He taps the end of his cigarette and looks at me. "But I *should* report you for being out after hours." He nods toward the kitchen door. "You could have let some light out."

I don't answer. I imagine Abel and Alice trying to shield Ursa as the ceiling comes down around them.

"Ravensloe would be interested to know how you willingly compromised our location, don't you think?"

I nod and turn toward the door. Ralph grabs me by the arm.

"I said you weren't going inside," he growls. He flings the half-smoked cigarette to the ground. "Do you by any chance know where Dr. Seymour keeps the key to the glasshouse?"

"What?" *What is he talking about?* "No."

"Are you sure?"

His hand is still squeezing my arm. The wool of my jacket is thick, but I can feel the skin bruising beneath.

"I'm sure," I say. "I've never seen a key."

Ralph licks his lips. "I don't believe you."

I stare at him, the salt from my tears drying on my face. He laughs quietly and shakes his head.

"You think you've got it bad?"

Why is he even talking to me? I try to pull my arm away, but he grips it tighter.

"I'm only here because my aunt kept me from returning to Germany when this war started."

Aunt.

"I was training in dragon combat with the Freikorps, and rising to the top. I came home on leave, working as a temporary Guardian, but when the Peace Agreement was compromised I wasn't allowed to go back. It wouldn't do for the Prime Minister's nephew to fail to defend his own country." Ralph sneers and takes a step closer to me. "I lost friends, connections, opportunities. All to be stationed here to babysit a bunch of would-be criminals. I lost my fucking chance!"

I stare straight ahead into the dark garden. "Guardian 707, you're hurting me."

"And it's because of *you*."

My head snaps back toward him.

"Your new friends might not know why you're here," Ralph says, "but *I* do."

An invisible vise grips my heart. Ralph just smiles.

"Vivien Featherswallow, the girl who collaborated with a

criminal dragon," he says loudly. "The girl who started the war. The girl who left her sister behind to save a group of rebels."

"Stop it!" I whisper hoarsely, covering my ears. "Please, stop."

"Why is it," Ralph says, "that young women, of perfectly docile appearance, think they can come here and do men's work? Do you think you know more about dragons than I do?"

He twists my arm and I shriek, a sob rising in my throat until the pain cuts my breath short.

"I should break your arm," he says. "You deserve it, don't you?" His mouth is against my cheek. "Tell me you don't deserve it and I'll stop."

I try to reach my free arm out to push him away, but my body is locked against his.

I don't say a word. Ursa is dead. Two thousand people are dead. And Sophie lost everything because of me. All because of my selfish choices. Pain clouds my vision.

Of course I deserve it.

I gasp as Ralph's hand slips beneath the collar of my shirt, his fingers grazing the top of my breastbone.

Searching for a key.

"Nothing there?" he says in mock surprise, his hands still on my skin. "Perhaps you're not as cunning as your mama—"

I ram my elbow into his gut.

He sucks in a sharp breath. "You little bitch."

Ralph lunges forward, pinning me between his body and the wall. I scream as white-hot pain shoots through my wrist.

There's a crunch.

A popping sound.

The snap of bone as Ralph breaks my arm.

ELEVEN

I wake up in a darkness shot through by candlelight. I'm lying in a bed, a blanket pulled up to my chin. My head feels heavy and when I move I realize my left arm is bound to my chest. I can hear a scratching sound. I sit up slowly, and it takes all my effort to reach for the candle on my bedside table and lift it up. My arm is in a sling. There are empty beds on either side of me and a shelf lined with bottles full of liquids and pills. A nurse is sitting at a desk in a corner, her pen scratching against paper.

"Recruit Featherswallow," she says sternly, "go back to sleep."

"Where am I?" I ask.

"The sanatorium," the nurse says. She stands up, lifting her own candle.

"What's a sanatorium?"

"The hospital ward." The nurse nods at my arm. "That's what you get for trying to abandon your post."

A sharp pain shoots through my arm, followed by a heavy throbbing.

"I didn't abandon my post," I say. "I was . . ."

I was trying to get away from Ralph. But what happened after?

"Guardian 707 said you put up quite a struggle." The nurse takes a bottle from the shelf and pours a deep red liquid onto a spoon. "He accidentally broke your arm trying to prevent you from endangering yourself."

Accidentally?

"I wasn't endangering myself—"

"There are dragons everywhere, child! And rebel ones at that." The nurse tuts. "You young ones have grown up thinking dragons are just the stuff of fairy tales. Back in my day, you were lucky if you could walk down the street without seeing one."

She spoons the medicine into my mouth and I gag. It's as thick as syrup and tastes of smoke and metal. I force myself to swallow it and my eyes instantly feel heavier.

"What was that?" I say.

"Fireblod," she says, her mouth pursed as if daring me to say any more.

I've just swallowed an illegal medicine made from the blood of dragons, only available on the black market. I've heard rumors the First Class have access to it, and now I know they're true.

"That'll heat your veins and have your bones fixed in no time," she says. "You fainted from the pain of the break, of course, and it's a good thing you did." She screws the cap onto the medicine bottle and gives me a pitying look. "We all have our part to play in the war, dear. Be brave, do your duty, and all will be well."

I sink back into the pillows as my vision clouds.

When I wake again, the sanatorium is filled with light. The nurse is standing with her back to me by the washbasin, rinsing some cloths. A breeze comes in through the open window next to my bed. I peer out of it and see the tops of the forest trees, two dragons soaring above them.

There's a knock at the door.

"Yes?" the nurse calls.

Marquis steps into the room, followed by Sophie.

"Ten minutes only, please," the nurse warns.

Marquis kneels at my bedside and takes my hand, his eyes full of concern.

"That bastard!" he spits.

"Watch your language, recruit, or I'll have you removed!" the nurse snaps.

Marquis pulls up a chair and Sophie lingers behind him. I do my best to smile.

"What happened?" I say. "I don't remember my arm breaking, or fainting, or—"

"Ralph told Ravensloe that it was an accident, that you were running away, but—"

"We *saw* him break your arm," Sophie says. "And he enjoyed it."

I remember Ralph talking about Germany, his hand searching for the key, a hot pain . . . I feel a sudden burst of horror. The radio report. Two thousand people. Ursa.

"Have you heard anything about home—"

Marquis is already shaking his head and a tear runs down his nose. The despair floods through me again, twisting in my chest like an aching knot. I let out a shaky breath.

I'd rather suffer a hundred broken arms than this.

Sophie lays a hand on Marquis's shoulder, but her face betrays no emotion at the fact that her parents might be dead. Perhaps she's suffered so much pain that it no longer has an effect on her.

"There *are* survivors," she says. "The hospitals are full and the dragons are lifting the rubble."

I nod. "Who found me?"

"Atlas, Marquis, and I followed you downstairs," Sophie says. "We saw Ralph snap your arm up against that wall—"

"I carried you inside," Marquis says, "but you were unconscious—"

"And Atlas?" I say.

Why hasn't he come to visit?

Marquis and Sophie glance at each other.

"Atlas . . . hit Ralph," Sophie says. "More than once."

"A lot more than once, actually," Marquis says weakly.

"Luckily, Gideon and Serena appeared and stopped him from doing any real damage."

I wait as an awkward silence creeps over the room.

"He's been in isolation since last night," Marquis says, and I close my eyes.

"Dr. Seymour said we should prepare ourselves for his demotion," says Sophie.

The words hang in the air as we all wonder what Atlas, a Third Class *misfit*, could possibly be demoted to.

"But apparently Lumens is negotiating with Ravensloe," Marquis says. "He says he and Dodie can't run the Zoology Department without Atlas."

"Five minutes left," the nurse calls, and Marquis glares at her. He takes my hand.

"Don't worry about Ursa," he says. "Wyvernmire knows that without her, she has less of a hold over you. She'll have protected her."

"And we won't let Ralph get anywhere near you again," Sophie says. "We'll stay together. We'll—"

I shake my head, my eyes filling with tears at their attempt to comfort me. Neither of them know what I know.

That I let Ralph break my arm because I deserve it.

That I changed our friendship with one selfish choice.

That I ruined Sophie's life.

"Time's up," the nurse says. She looks at me. "You'll be discharged tomorrow. The Deputy Prime Minister wants you back at work."

My grip tightens on Marquis's hand as he stands up. I think of the last time I spoke to Atlas, walking back through the forest with Sophie.

"Can you bring me some books from the library?" I say quietly. I scribble down a few titles on a piece of paper and hand it to him. "And can you ask Dr. Seymour to come and see me?"

"No more visitors—" the nurse begins.

"Please," I say. "It's for work purposes."

The nurse tuts again and Marquis nods.

"See you tomorrow."

I wave at Sophie, who gives me a sad smile, then lie back in bed and wait.

Dr. Seymour arrives an hour later. Her mouth is set in a hard line and she winces when she sees my arm.

"That was no accident," she says.

"No."

"What did he want?"

"To feel powerful, I suppose," I say. "And the key to the glasshouse."

Dr. Seymour nods, unsurprised.

"I believe Ralph requested to work in Codebreaking when he

arrived at Bletchley," she says. "He felt his time in Germany had given him the competency to do so, and it must have been a personal offense to him when Prime Minister Wyvernmire insisted he remain a Guardian instead."

"Why is he interested in codebreaking?" I ask.

"It's not the codebreaking that excites him," Dr. Seymour says. "It's the dragons."

"Dr. Seymour," I say, "I need to ask you a favor."

"Of course. What is it?"

I wait until the nurse carries a pile of laundry out of the room.

"I need to borrow your dracovol."

Dr. Seymour freezes. Horror creeps into her face, followed by confusion.

"It's okay," I whisper. "I know you're using it for secret government purposes. But listen. I need to find out if my sister is alive. I need to know whether or not she survived . . ."

Dr. Seymour is shaking her head.

"It's all I can think about," I whimper. "I won't be able to do anything until I know. Dr. Seymour, please—"

"I don't know what you're talking about," she says, standing up.

"I saw some dracovol mail in your cupboard," I say. "I didn't mean to—"

"So you've been looking through my personal things?"

Dr. Seymour's cheeks flush an angry red.

"I was looking for a pencil . . ."

"Who have you mentioned this to?"

"No one!" I say. "I just want to send a message. I won't even sign it. I'll—"

"No, Vivien!" She glances over her shoulder and lowers her

voice. "If you get caught, you'll be demoted and I'll be . . ."

She closes and opens her mouth as if the rest of the sentence might be too terrible to say out loud.

"My sister is only five years old," I say. "Our parents are in prison. She doesn't have anyone in the world except me."

"I'm sorry—"

"I'll never crack that code," I say, my eyes filling with tears again. "Not if she's dead. Not if there's no one to fight for."

"There's a whole country to fight for," Dr. Seymour says.

"Please," I say. "I have to know."

Dr. Seymour glances at the door, then back at me. She sits down. "I'll need something for it to scent," she says slowly. "My dracovol is only trained to fly to a few specific locations and, besides, I'm afraid that if your sister is in Central London then there's no guarantee that her address exists anymore."

"My coat," I say weakly. "In the wardrobe in my dorm."

It smells of dragonsmoke, but it might still have the scent of home on it.

Ursa's scent.

Dr. Seymour nods. "You can't tell anyone about this." Her eyes stare into mine as the nurse comes back into the room. "*Especially* not Ravensloe," she whispers.

I nod. "Thank you."

My library books are delivered that afternoon and among them is *The Hebrides: Exploring Scotland's Islands*. I flip through to page 265 and a piece of paper falls out onto the bedcovers. I check that the nurse isn't looking before I unfold it, heart thumping.

Hello, Featherswallow. Ralph Wyvernmire's irritating interruptions won't bother us here. I want to get to know you.

May I?

I smile and for a split second a weight lifts off my chest. Talking to this boy is a terrible idea and everything about him is infuriatingly puzzling. But I haven't yet encountered a puzzle I can't solve. He's a liability . . . and so damn convincing. I scribble back a reply.

> *Hello, Atlas King. Since leaving me this message, you have attacked the Prime Minister's nephew and got yourself sent to isolation. It was rather unpriestly of you, but I appreciate the sentiment so . . . consider the getting to know me commenced. Perhaps you might oblige me by answering this question: Where, for the love of dragons, is the fun in whittling wood? Leave your reply in C. Amsterton's novel,* Searching for Swallows.

The nurse discharges me on Sunday afternoon, my arm wrapped in a fresh sling. I stop by the library and slot the book back into place, my reply tucked safely inside. Then I go straight to the common room where I'm greeted by a weak cheering that dies out almost as soon as it's begun. Music is playing, and by the fire, Karim is embroidering a length of cloth. The atmosphere feels forced, as if we're all avoiding the elephant in the room. I sit down, noting Atlas's absence, and see a wicker picnic basket on the table.

"Gideon made some progress in the glasshouse yesterday," Katherine sings.

I turn to Gideon, who is half hidden behind the open picnic-basket lid. "What sort of progress?"

"Certain echolocation calls have different meanings depending on the dragon emitting them," Gideon says, closing the lid. "Echolocation is even more complex than we thought."

Different ways of saying things . . . like synonyms.

"We found that out days ago," I say. "When we heard Soresten say the same thing two different ways."

"But Dr. Seymour and I have *confirmed* the theory through further observation of the patrol dragons," Gideon says with a smug smile. "We don't know how the various meanings differ from each other yet—it might be a question of tone or register—but we'll soon find out."

I glance out of the window so Gideon can't see the fury in my face. Wasn't I the one to suggest the theory to Dr. Seymour in the first place? Now Gideon is getting all the credit, while I'm being accused of trying to desert my post.

"Is Atlas out yet?" I ask Marquis.

He's perched on the arm of the sofa Karim is sitting on. He shakes his head.

"I've seen Ralph, though," Marquis says, a slow smile spreading across his face. "It looks like he won't be removing his helmet for a while."

Did Atlas really do that? I thought priests were supposed to be calm, restrained, peaceful.

Rain begins to splatter across the windows, gradually getting heavier until it becomes hard to hear each other talk. I hope it's raining in London and that it puts out the rest of the dragonfire. Sophie is staring into the fog. She must be thinking of her parents, and I can't think of anything to say to her. I feel a surge of anger for my own parents and Uncle Thomas. Was this what they wanted when they decided to join the rebels? For London to burn? For their children to live through another war?

Gideon loads wood onto the fire and Katherine pulls sandwiches and a chocolate cake out of the basket.

"They say picnics are good for convalescing," she says to me with a wink.

I want to tell her that I don't give a dragon's arse about her picnic because my sister might be dead, but then she smiles at me so genuinely that I say nothing. I sit on the rug and lean back against the side of the sofa, kicking off my shoes. Dodie hands me a glass of lime cordial and Serena nods toward my bandaged arm, her eyebrows raised.

"You're even more stubborn than I thought," she says. "Couldn't you have just done as you were told? If you had, Atlas wouldn't be in isolation."

I glare at her, trying to decide which part of this absurd suggestion to argue with first.

"She's not stubborn," Dodie says with a frown. "She's dragon-hearted."

Dragon-hearted.

Brave.

The compliment sends a warm feeling through me, and I give Dodie a surprised smile.

"How long until you can use it again?" she asks.

"A few days," I reply. "The nurse gave me fireblod."

The chatter falls silent as everyone turns to look at me.

"Fireblod?" Gideon says. "But that type of medicine is banned in Britannia."

I shrug and take a bite of the salty chicken sandwich in front of me.

"Not for the First Class," Sophie says. "They buy it by the gallon off the black market. I've seen it with my own eyes."

"Don't be ridiculous," Gideon says, his eyes narrowing. "My family never—"

"Perhaps your family sees the evil in harvesting blood from captive juvenile dragons," Sophie says dryly. "But that's not the case for everyone."

I steal a glance at Serena. She doesn't look as defensive as Gideon.

"I was told it was only harvested from dragons who died of natural causes," Serena says.

"Impossible," says Marquis. "The proteins would need to be taken from a live donor."

Serena swallows. "In any case, fireblod has saved lives—"

"Not everyone's lives," Sophie spits. "The Third Class has never seen so much as a vial of it, or any other medicine, even though it could have—"

She stops, her voice tremoring, and I know she's thinking of Nicolas.

We eat in awkward silence and my mind fills with the image of live dragons being emptied of their blood. I put my sandwich down.

"Sophie," Dodie says carefully, "what else doesn't the Third Class have?"

I glance at Sophie, waiting. She only spent six months as Third Class, yet I can tell she has so many things to list she doesn't know where to start.

"Meat," she says, taking another bite of chicken. "The butcher shops are all in the Second Class quarters."

"We had one come door to door, selling ham and beef bones sometimes," Katherine says. "But they were always this awful gray color."

I glance at Marquis—the food in Second was never gray—but

he doesn't look the least bit surprised.

"The shelves in my local greengrocer's were always empty," Sophie says. "Nothing but wilted greens and the occasional bag of potatoes."

"Maybe you had a bad supplier," I say. "Mama says . . ."

I trail off as they all stare at me.

"It's not a supply problem," Karim says gently. "The Third Class shops are only stocked with what the Second and First Classes don't buy."

My cheeks burn. Why didn't I know that? Why had I assumed that the shops were all stocked the same? Sophie gives me a despairing shake of her head, and suddenly I feel like a naive child.

"Our schoolbooks had pages missing and someone else's name in them," Katherine says. "And the clothes were either stained or torn."

"Hot water," Sophie says. "No matter how careful we were, our baths were always cold."

"Couldn't you have heated it on a stove?" Serena asks.

"Yes," Sophie says, eyeing Serena coolly. "Except there was never any coal."

"Because you couldn't afford it?"

"Because the higher classes like to keep a fire burning in every room."

Serena takes a sip of her cordial and says nothing.

"But the Class System exists to give everyone a fair chance," I say.

I look to Marquis for reassurance. We were both taught the same thing, at school and on the radio at home. The result of its dismantling would be social chaos.

"It means that no one is left on the streets, that every child goes to school. That's why Wyvernmire was reelected . . . because she ensured it stayed in place. People *want* the Class System."

"Living between four walls doesn't mean you're warm or fed," Sophie says. "Going to school doesn't mean you learn. And who are you to say what *people* want?"

I keep my back straight, trying not to wither beneath Sophie's cold glare.

"We had a dragon keep our house warm," Karim says. "There was no coal, so he just breathed flames straight onto the walls from the outside. The house—and our shop—was all made of stone. Just as well, really."

"A dragon?" I say.

Karim nods. "There are so many more in Scotland than there are here. My parents paid him in lace—my mam's a lacemaker."

"Lace?" Dodie asks. "What would a dragon need lace for?"

"Aye, lace is worth a lot. Even the scraps my parents can't use."

"I thought dragons only worked for humans if they were forced to," I say, thinking of Chumana. "Like a punishment."

"Some don't have a choice," Karim says. "The ones who have hoards don't need to work, but the ones who don't, well . . ."

Hoards. Like piles of gold or money. Why do dragons need money? They don't shop for groceries or pay bills. It hits me that, in all my years learning dragon tongues, I've never questioned how dragons fit into our human society.

Just like I've never questioned where the Third Class get their food.

"Let's play a game," Katherine says in an obvious attempt to ease the tension. "Does everyone know Two Truths and a Lie?"

"One of my favorites," Marquis says with a smirk. "You first, Kath."

Katherine sits up on her knees and grins.

"One, I'm Third Class but my aunt is Second. Two, I've been playing chess since I was six years old. Three, I killed a Guardian of Peace."

I lean back against the sofa. It's entirely possible for Katherine to be Third Class and her aunt Second. And if she's an undiscovered chess champion then it makes sense that she's been playing since she was six.

"Three is the lie," Gideon says, biting into a slice of chocolate cake.

Katherine gives him a wry smile and shakes her head. The bite of cake falls out of Gideon's mouth and onto the rug.

"I started playing chess when I was seven," she says.

I search her face for a trace of humor, but find only resigned weariness. Katherine is the smallest one of us here. How could she possibly kill a Guardian of Peace?

She did say she was recruited from prison.

"Gideon's turn!" Katherine says.

Gideon frowns, his cheeks blushing. I lean in, eager to know where he's from and why he thinks himself some sort of dragon expert.

"One, my father was an important government official. Two, I wish he wasn't my father. Three, I know someone who is in love with a dragon."

Marquis laughs loudly and Gideon blushes an even deeper shade of red.

"No one could be in love with a dragon—" I begin.

"Actually, the King of Egypt is currently *married* to a dragon," Dodie says. "Didn't you know that?"

"I . . . no?" I say.

Marquis whispers something into Karim's ear and they both erupt into laughter.

"Three is the lie," Serena says.

Gideon scowls. "That was too easy."

I wonder who his father is and whether it was his job that put Gideon in contact with dragons. What made me think that I ever knew my fellow recruits at all?

"Viv's turn," Gideon says.

I freeze, feeling the panic creep over me. All *my* truths are too unbearable to say.

I abandoned my sister. I helped a criminal dragon break the Peace Agreement. I betrayed my best friend.

The door to the common room creaks open and Dr. Seymour appears.

"Do you mind if I join you?" she asks shyly. "The glasshouse is being inspected."

"Inspected?" Sophie and I say in unison.

"It's a common protocol," Dr. Seymour says with a smile that doesn't reach her eyes. "To make sure everything's working and to ensure the Official Secrets Act is being respected."

"We're playing Two Truths and a Lie," Marquis says lazily.

He's now sprawled out on the rug next to me, rolling a cigarette. I wonder which Guardian he has buying him tobacco.

"Maybe we shouldn't," Gideon murmurs.

The mention of the Official Secrets Act, and the fact that Ravensloe has Guardians checking it's being respected, has suddenly turned the room cold. As if the attack on London and the conversation about class differences weren't enough.

Dr. Seymour comes and sits beside me, smoothing her skirt over her knees. As Karim hands out a tray of biscuits, Dr. Seymour pulls a piece of paper from her pocket and shoves it into my hand. I unfold it in my lap. The words have been scrawled by a hurried hand, with a smear of ink across the top.

Alive.

My breath catches in my throat. Ursa and Sophie's parents are alive. Joy bursts inside me.

She will become a ward of the state tomorrow.

My heart plummets.

Ward of the state? Are Abel and Alice giving Ursa up? Or has Wyvernmire sent Guardians to remove her? Didn't she say she'd leave Ursa with her caregivers until I'd finished at Bletchley? Dr. Seymour gives me a questioning look and I force myself to smile.

It's good news, I tell myself.

Twenty-four hours ago, I would have given anything to read these words. But now all I can think about is Ursa being torn from Alice's arms, just like she was torn from our mother's.

We don't resume the game and for the rest of the evening I sit by the fire, clutching the dracovol note.

"Now you have something to fight for," Dr. Seymour whispers to me when we all go to bed.

I wait until everyone's sleeping before I let myself cry. I wish I could turn back time and stay under house arrest with Ursa. Then we would never have been separated.

But Marquis would still be in prison, or worse. Mama and Dad would be dead.

I press my face into the pillow and let out a sob. Someone slips into bed beside me and I jump.

"It's me," Sophie whispers. "Are you all right?"

I turn round to face her in the dark as she lays her head next to mine. This is how we used to sleep when we were children. Not top and tail, like Mama made Marquis and I do, but hands interlaced, cheeks pressed together so we could whisper through the night.

I reach under my pillow and hand her the note. I should have shown it to her earlier, but my thoughts were consumed with my sister. She lifts it to the crack of light shining in from under the door.

"That's my dad's handwriting," she says breathlessly. "How did you—"

"Never mind that," I say, blinking back tears. "Where do you think they'll take her?"

"To an orphanage probably," Sophie says. "But don't worry, Viv, they won't lose her, not while they need you."

"I wish we could go home," I say. "Both of us. Back to Fitzrovia and Marylebone. I wish we could go back to before."

Sophie nods and grasps my hand.

"We still can," she says. "But you have to focus, Viv. Ursa is alive, but the only way you'll ever see her again is if we can learn echolocation."

I close my eyes, but the tears seep through.

How are we going to crack a code that is actually a language, one that's dizzyingly complicated?

We don't know how the various meanings differ from each other yet—it might be a question of tone or register.

Gideon and Dr. Seymour have no idea what they're doing. And neither do I.

"Do you remember when we were children and you'd make up those silly little languages for us?" Sophie whispers. "We'd pretend to everyone at school that we understood what the other was saying."

I smile. "We even had my dad convinced. He thought there was a new dragon tongue on the curriculum."

Sophie laughs into my hair. "Didn't he get really angry when he found out the truth?"

I nod. "He said it was a waste of time to be making up languages when I already had so many to learn. He made me stay up half the night just to prove that I knew all my French verbs."

"Do you think they were too hard on us?" Sophie whispers. "Our parents?"

She reaches a hand to the inside of her arm and I know she's feeling for the line of scars along the skin, identical to my own. The use of a birch rod is a common practice among Second Class families, and perhaps the only pain we suffer that the Third Class don't.

"I don't think parents can afford to be soft when their children are only one class away from a life of poverty," I say.

We're silent for a moment as memories surface. My family used to be supporters of the Class System. So what made them change their minds?

"When you were demoted," I whisper, surprised at the words coming out of my mouth, "I didn't think I'd ever be happy again."

Sophie doesn't say anything and for a minute I just listen to her soft breathing.

I want to say sorry. I want to beg her forgiveness for all of it— the bits she knows about and the bits she doesn't. But I know it's too late for that. She squeezes my hand and we lie in silence, enveloped in each other's warmth. Everything about her is familiar—the mole on the back of her hand, the smell of her skin, the slight wheeze in her chest from a childhood illness. Eventually, Sophie falls asleep.

"I'll never hurt you again," I whisper into the dark. "I'll make sure you go home, Soph. I promise you that."

Very slowly, I climb out of bed. I slip my boots on and pull my coat over my nightdress, draping it round my shoulders because of the sling. Ralph told Ravensloe I tried to abandon my post, and that's why Wyvernmire has taken Ursa. To make sure she has something I want. I can't let her think I'm not taking this seriously. If I'm going to keep my promise to Sophie, if I'm going to be reunited with Ursa and save our family from execution, then I need to give the Prime Minister the dragon code.

I sneak downstairs and across the hallway. I know the way to the kitchen now and it's only a few seconds before I'm through the back door once again. There's no Guardian patrolling here, but that only means Ravensloe has extra dragons guarding the perimeter of Bletchley Park. I keep my eyes on the sky as I traipse through the moonlit garden, then take a dirt path into the fields. I don't need a car to reach the spot where I translated for Borislav.

I remember the disgust he showed Muirgen and Rhydderch when he realized they couldn't speak his tongue. They hadn't been able to communicate by echolocation, either, meaning the patrol dragons had thought they were under attack. And no one, not even Dr. Seymour, can tell me why that is.

I push through the long grass, my head full of questions I *know* there are answers to. My eyes search the star-studded sky for the only way of obtaining those answers, no matter how forbidden it might be. I stop in my tracks when I spot what I'm looking for in the fields just beyond.

The dark silhouettes of two dragons.

TWELVE

The dragons are standing side by side, watching me as I walk toward them. My body is already stiff with cold and I plunge my free hand into my pocket. The blue and purple scales of the dragons' hides are difficult to see in the dark, and if it wasn't for their size they would blend into the shadows.

"I don't recall summoning a translator," Rhydderch growls as I approach.

I stop a few feet away and wonder how to begin.

"I don't believe you should be out at this hour," Muirgen says, licking her lips. "Shouldn't you be in the glasshouse? I've seen you run in and out so often during my patrols with Soresten and Addax that we've started to believe Ravensloe has you working on something that might actually help us *win* the war."

Both dragons laugh—a low, guttural sound—and I fake a smile. So the dragon I saw with Soresten and Muirgen in the field the other day was Addax.

"I've come to ask you a question." My voice comes out quieter than I intended.

The dragons' huge yellow eyes stare at me and I see the movement of a tail in the dark.

"Go on," Rhydderch says.

"The Bulgarian dragon that landed here," I say. "Borislav."

"Yes?"

"Why did you need a translator to understand him?"

"You already know this," Muirgen says lazily. "We do not speak the dragon tongues of the East—"

"But don't dragons have other ways of talking to each other?" I interrupt.

Muirgen cocks her head, her eyes unblinking.

It is crucial *that none of the dragons guarding Bletchley Park learn of the codebreaking going on inside the glasshouse.*

Dr. Seymour would kill me if she knew I was here. But if we want to crack the code in three months then surely she must realize that we can't keep playing this guessing game. I have to ask the question I came here to ask.

"Can you communicate using a . . . sixth sense? One that humans don't have?"

A field mouse scurries across my shoe, and before I can recoil, Muirgen skewers it on the end of a long black claw. She lifts it to her face and watches as it jerks several times, then dies. She swallows it whole.

"What exactly are you referring to?"

"Something a dragon told me about a long time ago," I lie. "He said that dragons can speak to each other in a . . . in a sort of code." I try to look innocent. "Is that right?"

A low growling sound comes from Rhydderch's chest. Black smoke is rising from Muirgen's nostrils and, as she takes a step closer to me, the moon illuminates the spikes along her back.

"A code?" she purrs. "Is *that* what you think it is?"

"Quiet, Muirgen," Rhydderch snaps. He bares his teeth at me.

"What has your Prime Minister been telling you?"

"Nothing," I say quickly. "I told you, it was a dragon. Was he telling the truth? Can dragons read each other's minds?"

"How dare you come here seeking knowledge that is not yours to possess," Muirgen snarls.

"I'm a translator," I say calmly, even as my body grows hot with fear. "Of course I'm interested in knowing all the ways dragons can communicate—"

"The Koinamens belongs to dragons and dragons alone!" Muirgen roars.

She rears backward and stamps her two front feet on the ground. The impact sends me flying and I wince as I land on my bad arm six feet away. I scramble to my feet, ignoring the burning pain in my wrist.

"Please," I say, glancing back toward the manor house. "You'll wake everyone up. I just want to know why you and Borislav didn't speak the same . . . Koinamens."

"The dragon who told you of it betrayed his own kind," Rhydderch says. "It is a mystery that must remain among dragons."

His tail flicks in Muirgen's direction and she takes a step backward. They're communicating, I realize.

They're talking in echolocation.

"But why?" I ask. "Why must it stay a mystery?"

"It is sacred," Muirgen hisses. "It is the only thing we dragons have that you humans cannot take for your own."

Sacred? As far as I know, dragons don't have a religion. What could be sacred about a language?

"Are there different types of Koinamens?" I say. "Different . . . sequences?"

"I'm about to skin this human alive, Rhydderch—"

Muirgen thrusts her huge head toward me, but Rhydderch snaps at her face. She roars in pain and I stumble backward. Rhydderch brings his head close to mine, so close that I can see a line of downy fur on his snout.

"You are making the surviving Peace Agreement very difficult to uphold," he snarls. "I suggest you leave, before I let my sister murder you."

I nod. They have no intention of telling me anything. I take a few steps backward, edging away slowly, then stop. Rhydderch turns toward Muirgen and brings his snout close to hers. Blood is dripping from a wound made by his teeth, just beneath her left eye. The two dragons remain motionless and then slowly the wound begins to shrink. I squint in the moonlight. Am I seeing what I think I'm seeing? The edges of the wound are pulling together like a thread sewing two corners of a cloth, and suddenly there's only a spot of blood where the injury was.

"How did you do that?" I ask Muirgen.

I run through everything Marquis has ever told me about dragon anatomy, but I can't remember anything about self-healing wounds.

"The Koinamens is sacred," Muirgen repeats. "Never ask about it again."

I shrink back into the darkness and hurry across the field, my heart thumping in my chest. Did Rhydderch just heal Muirgen using echolocation?

I have a horrible feeling in my stomach.

I've learned nothing about echolocation except that dragons call it the Koinamens and consider it sacred. But neither of those two pieces of information will get me any closer to deciphering it. I reach the garden and glance up at Bletchley Manor. It's still and silent and almost invisible in the dark.

I think of the things considered sacred to humans. Knowledge, religious texts, traditions. Those have all definitely been used as weapons by weak and power-hungry humans, but most dragons are neither of those things. Perhaps they view the Koinamens the same way humans see nature, or children, or love. Sacred not for what it can *do* but for what it *is*, with a deeper, more intrinsic meaning than anything we can hope to understand. The kind of sacredness that must never be corrupted or abused. Perhaps it's something instinctive, something that's a part of the dragons' common identity.

A twig snaps behind me.

I freeze and turn my head toward the forest. Someone is walking through it, leaves and frost crunching underfoot. The figure of a man emerges from between the trees and crosses the lawn toward me.

My breath catches in my throat. What if it's Ralph? The man hesitates when he sees me, then walks faster. It's too late to hide now. I cradle my broken arm against me and wait.

"Featherswallow?"

"Atlas?"

"What are you doing out here?"

I breathe a sigh of relief. "What are *you* doing? I thought you were in isolation."

Atlas catches my hand and pulls me into the shadow of the house. He pockets a string of prayer beads, a tiny cross dangling from the end.

"They let me out a few hours ago," he says.

"So . . . why were you in the forest?"

There's nothing out there except for trees and the glasshouse.

He smirks in the moonlight. "Why were you in the fields?"

Shit.

He lowers his voice. "How about we agree not to discuss what the other was doing outside in the middle of the night?"

I nod, then shiver. The freezing air fills my open coat, which is still draped awkwardly across my shoulders and sling. Atlas has noticed it, and for a second he eyes the thin material of my nightdress against my thigh. Then he pulls the coat around me and fastens the buttons.

I stare at his hands, which are covered in red cuts, and at the shadow of a bruise across his cheekbone.

"Thank you," I say. "For what you did."

Atlas shakes his head. "Nothing to be proud of."

"You were just trying to stop him—"

"I broke the man's nose," Atlas says.

"You did him a favor, then."

Atlas grins and we both burst into laughter.

"*Shhh!*" he says, pushing me into the bushes. "I think Ravensloe's window is somewhere around here."

I'm suddenly very aware of his hands on my waist.

"What did they do to you in isolation?" I whisper.

We're standing between two bushes, our backs to the wall of the house. The moon has disappeared behind a cloud and it's so dark I can't see Atlas's face.

"Questioned me, reprimanded me, left me there for a while," he says quietly. "Apparently, Lumens negotiated my release."

I nod. "You'll have to be on your best behavior from now on. No more saving me from Ralph."

His hand finds mine in the dark.

"We should go in," I say, although that's the last thing I want to do. "You could do with some sleep."

Atlas is rummaging inside his jacket pocket. "All I need is ice, a whisky, and a good confessor."

"Confessor?"

A flame springs to life between us and Atlas's face is illuminated by a fizzing matchstick.

"For my sins," he says with a grin.

"Can't you just confess your sins to yourself or something?" I say.

A cockerel crows somewhere far away. It must be nearly dawn.

"That's not how it works, I'm afraid," he says. "And I'm not a priest yet anyway, remember?"

"Sorry," I say. "Priest-in-training."

We're grinning again.

"Speaking of sins," he says casually, "why do you hate yourself so much for yours?"

"What?"

Atlas shrugs. "You would rather let Ralph break your bones than give him the satisfaction of forcing words out of your mouth, and I admire you for it. But he told you that you deserved it, and it seemed like you agreed. You went limp just before he broke your arm. You let him do it. And you let Sophie talk to you like you're—"

"She's just angry with me," I say.

And rightfully so.

"Yes, well, whatever you two argued about, it seems to me like you're beating yourself up for it a lot."

"So?" I say. "When you do something wrong, isn't it normal to punish yourself for it?"

"To spend your whole life punishing yourself for something you can never take back?" Atlas shakes his head. "No way."

"What makes you think I'm going to spend my whole life doing it?"

"Marquis told me it's been six months since you and Sophie argued."

Marquis has been talking about me behind my back? With Atlas?

"He had no right—"

"I asked him," Atlas says quickly. He has the decency to look apologetic. "I was curious, but he didn't give me any details."

I can't decide whether to be flattered or annoyed.

"Can't you just forgive each other?" he says. "Forgive yourselves?"

He smiles. I find the whole situation—receiving unsolicited advice from a boy who just risked demotion by beating up a Guardian—strangely hilarious.

"Well, maybe that's possible for you," I say, eyeing his ever-present collar. "But some things are unforgivable."

"You're wrong," Atlas says. All trace of his smile has disappeared. "Nothing is unforgivable. Not if you're truly sorry."

"So you're saying that people can go around committing horrible crimes, just for them to be forgotten when they say they're sorry?"

"Yes, that's about the gist of it."

I snort. "In that case, I could murder you right now and get away with it, as long as I sit in a little box and apologize afterwards?"

"*Would* you be sorry, though?" he says, grinning again. "It looks like you really want to kill me right now."

I glare at him. "*You're* a bloody saint when you're not punching people," I say. "What I did to get here, what I did to Sophie, it's all so much worse."

Why am I telling him this?

"She'd never forgive me if she knew the whole story. She'd be so hurt that she'd hate me forever—and I wouldn't blame her."

Tears prick my eyes and suddenly I want to scream. This is none of Atlas's business and yet here I am, revealing the innermost details of my past.

He just shrugs. "That's her right. She doesn't *have* to forgive you, and you can't make her. But *you* can't hate *you* forever. Otherwise, how will you ever learn from your mistakes?"

"Learn?"

"My mum says it's never too late to change."

"Mine says we must live with the consequences of our actions."

Atlas nods slowly. "Sounds like we have a different understanding of what *sorry* means."

Of course we have. We're chalk and cheese. A Third Class boy and a Second Class girl. A priest and a criminal.

The match dies and I speak into the dark.

"Sometimes, Atlas, sorry just isn't good enough."

THIRTEEN

In the glasshouse, the clicks and calls coming from the loquisonus machine threaten to put me to sleep. I stifle a yawn, and when Dr. Seymour asks if I slept poorly I blame it on my arm, which is sort of true. As it turns out, healing broken bones with fireblod is excruciating. I keep last night's events to myself. Revealing that echolocation's true name is the Koinamens would be admitting to discussing it with Muirgen and Rhydderch—and risking immediate demotion.

Dr. Seymour has added an hourly lesson to our shifts, which she teaches with the loquisonus machines on high volume in case of live activity. We look at the theory of sonar waves and at dragon biology, and she bombards us with rhetorical questions: Are dragon horns necessary for the transmission of echolocation? Why is the tongue of the Bolgorith double-forked? Are particular dragon species better suited to particular languages?

We study semantic shifts in relation to dragon-migration patterns, and I learn that there are twenty Arctic Indigenous dragon languages that have almost three hundred different words for *cold*, made up of synonyms, metaphors, and metonymy. Could the same be said of echolocation? she asks us. Only after this drilling session does she allow us to take our stations at the loquisonus machines.

Today I pore over the logbook until my eyes hurt, determined to catch up on everything I missed when I was in the sanatorium. There are two days' worth of recordings containing several calls that sound different, but have the same meaning. The recordings in which the words *unidentified noise* are communicated by a Skrill-type54 are always of conversations between Muirgen and Rhydderch. But they're also said using a Skrill-type64, in a communication between the two Sand Dragons, Soresten and Addax.

So what if Muirgen and Rhydderch speak one version of echolocation and Soresten and Addax another? Both versions could be similar with subtle variations. That might explain what we observed in the fields: how Soresten used a particular echolocation call to give an order to Muirgen, but a slightly different one when talking to Addax. My heart races as I scribble my thoughts across the pages of the logbook.

I make three lists: calls unique to Muirgen and Rhydderch; calls unique to Soresten and Addax; and calls shared between them all. There are more calls in the first two lists than the third. And the calls used by the four dragons communicating *all together* have more simple meanings: *come, go, wait, stop* . . .

I rub my eyes and force myself to think. I can feel an idea forming on the very edge of my mind, glittering in the corner of my vision. It grows like a bubble filling with air, then bursts.

Echolocation isn't simply a language.

It's a language with even more languages inside it.

Mama has been pushing the theory of the existence of dialects within *spoken* dragon tongues for years and nobody ever believed her. What if she was right, and echolocation is a language with dialects, too, just inaudible to the human ear? My hand shakes as I press hard on the pen, unable to keep up with my own thoughts. Across the table, Gideon is deep in concentration, unsuspecting.

What if the universal echolocation language—the Koinamens—used by the entire dragon species is simple? Limited in its vocabulary and less developed than the dialects that exist within it. That's why Muirgen and Rhydderch couldn't speak in great detail with Borislav and ended up fighting him. Had they spoken the same dialect, Borislav could have alerted them to the fact that he was not an intruder but a messenger.

But how did these dialects develop in the first place? Why don't all dragons just speak one form of echolocation that communicates both simple and complex meanings? I should have listened more to what Mama was telling Dr. Hollingsworth about dragon dialects, instead of obsessing over my portfolio and potential apprenticeship.

Dr. Featherswallow, if dragons spoke in regional dialects, surely we would have heard them.

That's what Hollingsworth said. Well, she was wrong and Mama was right. I stare at my scribbles.

My heart seems to stop and start. Are the echolocation dialects regional, too? Rhydderch said last night that Muirgen is his sister, meaning they were hatched and likely reared in the same place. So maybe echolocation dialects vary depending on the location in which a dragonling learns to echolocate. And if Soresten and Addax are both Sand Dragons, perhaps they come from the same region—

"Vivien!"

Dr. Seymour is staring at me, a bemused smile on her face.

"Are you sure you're all right?" she says. "I've said your name three times."

"Sorry," I say, closing my logbook abruptly. "I was . . . concentrating."

"Have you made any progress?" Dr. Seymour says, adjusting her glasses.

I shake my head. Last time I made progress, Gideon managed to take the credit for it. This time, if this theory can be proved, I want Wyvernmire to know it's mine.

"Come on," Dr. Seymour says. "We're going on another trip."

We drag the buggy full of loquisonus machines past Yndrir—on the morning guard shift—and deep into the forest. I remember how Atlas appeared from it last night, like a light in the dark, and feel a sudden feverish curiosity about the reply I hope is waiting for me in the library.

"I reckon the dragons have several types of code to stop humans from deciphering echolocation," Gideon says as we walk.

"Why would they go to all that trouble?" I say. "The war is between the government and the rebels, not humans and dragons."

"Well, they probably created the code *before* the Peace Agreement, didn't they?" he replies with a withering look. "And anyway, not all dragons want peace."

They didn't create the code, idiot, is what I want to tell him.

"Even the rebel dragons are collaborating with humans," I say instead. "I don't think dragons everywhere woke up one day and said, *Let's create a code with the mind-reading skills we coincidentally have, just in case things get bad with the humans.*"

I laugh, pleased with myself, and Gideon glares at me.

"Maybe they were preparing for the day they wouldn't be able to speak without humans like *you* understanding their every word."

"Says you, Bletchley's other polyglot," I reply shrilly.

"I limit myself to the languages of my own species, in case you haven't noticed," Gideon mutters. He looks at Dr. Seymour. "My bet is that these rebel dragons will use the rebel humans while they need them, then turn on us all once they've won the war, just like the Bulgarian dragons—"

"*Shhh!*" Katherine whispers. "Look."

She's staring through the trees up ahead. I follow her gaze. There's a movement in the giant oak straight in front of us. A dracovol flies from branch to branch, perching and then hovering again, a dead mouse between its jaws.

"A dragon messenger," Gideon whispers.

I glance at Dr. Seymour. Her face has turned pale.

"Those aren't allowed at Bletchley," Gideon says, running toward the tree. "It might be carrying a rebel message."

"Gideon, wait!" I call as I follow him through the forest.

We stop at the bottom of the tree and stare up at the creature. It surveys us with black, unblinking eyes. It has a short, rounded snout, and two of its lower teeth are poking up through its nose. Long, scaled tendrils rise up from its head, like whiskers. It's the size of a cat. While dracovols don't have the level of dragon or human intelligence, they're said to be as clever as dolphins. The dracovol gulps down the mouse, then crawls along the tree trunk and into a large crevice.

"Leave it, Gideon," Dr. Seymour says sharply as Gideon peers inside. "Dracovols are known to live in the wild, too, so there's nothing to suggest this one is carrying a message—"

"She has eggs," Gideon says.

"Let me see," I say, pushing him out of the way.

The crevice is at eye level and has been lined with small rocks and stones. Heat rises from them, warming my face, and when the dracovol breathes a flame across their surface they turn red, then white. Nestled in between the hot stones are three small black eggs. The dracovol curls her tail round them and lets out a small warning hiss. Behind me, Gideon has taken one of the loquisonus machines from the buggy and is setting it up on the ground.

"Maybe she's not carrying a written message, but an echolocation one," he says excitedly as he puts on the headphones.

"She's not carrying a message, Gideon," Sophie says, rolling her eyes. "She's parenting."

But Gideon is twisting the dials on the loquisonus machine, searching for the right frequency. Dr. Seymour stares helplessly at him and an awful thought shatters my good mood. Is this *Dr. Seymour's* dracovol? I feel a prick of terror as she sits down on the forest floor with her head in her hands.

This isn't a wild dracovol at all.

"I'm right," Gideon says with a grin. "She's echolocating."

Can dracovols echolocate like dragons? Dr. Seymour never mentioned that.

She never mentioned her secret messenger, either.

"Who is she talking to?" I ask as my stomach fills with dread.

Could there be several dracovols in the area? And if so, who owns the other ones? Does someone at Bletchley know Dr. Seymour sent this one to look for Ursa?

I stare into the crevice again. The dracovol is pressing her snout to one of the eggs, her eyes still on me.

"It doesn't sound anything like dragon echolocation," Gideon says, concentrating on the live transmission.

I hold my hand out. "Can I listen?"

He hesitates, then gives me the headphones. I press them to my ears. I hear two simultaneous sounds: a low humming and a twitching, scratching sort of noise. This echolocation call is continuous. There's no pause, no opportunity for a response. I hand the headphones to Dr. Seymour, who takes them reluctantly, and look back inside the tree crevice. The dracovol's eyes are closed now, her head still on top of the eggs. Suddenly one of them shivers.

"Oh my God," I say quietly. "I think . . . she's talking to *them*."

"To who?" Sophie says, peering in beside me.

"To the eggs."

"Impossible," Gideon says.

I turn round to face Dr. Seymour.

"*Is* it impossible?" I say. "Or could she be communicating with the dracovolets inside the eggs?"

Dr. Seymour snaps into life again, standing up and looking inside the tree. When the dracovol sees Dr. Seymour, she gives a high, throaty chirp.

"It might not be female," Dr. Seymour says. "Sometimes the female dracovol abandons the eggs and the male hatches them instead."

Gideon, I notice, is writing all this down in a notebook he has produced from his pocket.

"But is it possible?" I say.

She sighs. "Yes, I suppose it is."

"Then dragons probably do the same, right?"

Dr. Seymour nods.

"Well then, this is proof," I say, raising an eyebrow at Gideon. "If dragons and dracovols echolocate with their young inside the eggs, then echolocation was never intended as a weapon."

"Viv's right," Katherine says. "Echolocation must come naturally to them, like an in— What's the word?"

"Instinct," Sophie finishes.

"Doesn't mean they can't *use* it as a weapon," Gideon argues.

"Stay focused, all of you," Dr. Seymour says. "Weapon or not, our job is simply to decipher it."

"Maybe dragon eggs *depend* on echolocation to be able to hatch!" I say. "Maybe, without it, the dragonlings can't grow. That would explain why dragon echolocation is so much more complex than whale or bat echolocation. Because the species depends on it to survive."

"It's a possible theory, Vivien," Dr. Seymour says. "We'll explore it further, of course, but remember that for now it's just that. A theory."

I stare at her. This makes so much sense. This is *progress*. Why isn't she celebrating?

"Time to pack up, Gideon, please."

Gideon loads the loquisonus machine back into the buggy. I peer into the crevice again.

"Leave it, Vivien," Dr. Seymour says sharply, and I recoil.

She's never spoken to me like this before. She's restless, moving from one foot to another, biting her nails. What's wrong with her? Is she worried Ravensloe will find out she let me use the dracovol?

On the way back to the glasshouse, she strides ahead of us. I hurry to catch up and check that the others are still a few feet behind before I lower my voice.

"Is it the message I sent?" I ask. "Is that what's bothering you?"

"I told you never to mention it," she says.

Back in the glasshouse, I return to my logbook. I know what I saw. The dracovol was echolocating to its eggs. I understand now why the Koinamens is sacred. It has meaning and purpose beyond winning any war.

I drop my pen. What would Wyvernmire do with a secret like this? With an insight into a species beyond anything any scientist or zoologist has ever had? She'll win the war, that's certain. But will she use her knowledge of echolocation for other things? I think of the wyvern heads that supposedly used to be mounted on her wall. What if she used echolocation as a weapon *against* the dragons?

The thought makes my skin crawl. Suddenly I see why Muirgen was so angry with me for asking about echolocation. If dragons use it to hatch their eggs and heal each other, what else can it do?

That's not your concern, I tell myself. *Your concern is saving your family, saving Ursa. And now you have the tools to do just that.*

Now that I know that echolocation is a language that very possibly contains dialects, the key to winning the war is to learn to speak them. I've learned nine languages already—what are a few more?

Dr. Seymour doesn't speak to me for the rest of the shift and Gideon simply glowers every time I look up from my logbook.

"You realize we're supposed to be working together, don't you?" he says. "I could check your findings if you want—"

"No thanks." I smile so hard my cheeks hurt. "After all, the art of languages *is* traditionally a woman's domain."

As soon as the siren sounds, I go to the library. It only takes me a few moments to find *Searching for Swallows* in the fiction section and I feel a swoop of nerves as I lift the front cover and spot a loose scrap of paper.

Atlas has replied.

I don't let myself read it straightaway. Instead, I take it downstairs to the dormitory, where I kick off my boots and sit on my bed with my legs folded beneath me. With a glance at the closed door, I retrieve the note.

Featherswallow, I wish I could express to you in a few short words the joys of carpentry, but the task is an impossible one. Instead, I'll say this: there is an exhilarating feeling in creating something that has never existed before.

I smile as a warmth creeps into my cheeks. Why do I feel so energized? Is it simply the novelty of this secret conversation, of the clandestine passing of notes? Or is it the fact that I'm speaking with a boy who actually has something clever to say, whose choice of words is more poetic than Hugo Montecue could ever hope to be? I reach for a pencil, intending to think carefully before writing my reply, but it comes on its own.

Atlas, languages are like that. You can say the same thing a hundred different ways, and occasionally one of those ways is so unique to the translator that it is impossible to reproduce. No other translator will use the same words, the same rhythm, the same turn of phrase ever again. Translating is creating, too.

I slip my note beneath the book's cover and hide it under the others piled high on my bedside table. I'll return it to the library before dinner.

I run my hand along the spines of my current reads, the pages dog-eared from my late-night research. Every section of the library is stocked with an array of dragon-related books, so I'm now reading about a ridiculous amount of topics, from dragon dens to the hatching process. And although I know none of them will mention dialects, some might give me some information about dragon languages in relation to different regions or locations.

I lie on my front and flick through *Whispering with Wyrms: The Dragon Tongues of the Modern World* in the vague hope of making sense of everything I learned today. I scan the list of dragon species at the back, from the Frilled Baikia to the Silver Drake, then turn to page 189.

> *The British Sand Dragon (*Draco arenicolus*) is brown, green, or beige in color. The underbellies of fertile females turn yellow during the mating season. Nests contain one to two eggs and are made of hot sand. The first tongue learned by the dragonlings is usually Wyrmerian.*
>
> *The British Sand Dragon is native to the sandy heathlands of Dorset and Kent in the South of England.*

So Soresten and Addax, both Sand Dragons, are very possibly from the same region of England. Which further backs up my theory that echolocation dialects could be regional. My chest flutters. It's all coming together and—

I drop the book. There's a box on the floor at the end of my bed, with an envelope stuck to the top. How did I not notice it before? I pick up the envelope and turn it over. The paper is thick and expensive and sealed with red wax. My name is written on the front in purple ink. There's a box by every bed, I realize. I tear the envelope open.

YOUR PRESENCE IS REQUESTED AT PRIME MINISTER
WYVERNMIRE'S CHRISTMAS BALL

THIS FRIDAY EVENING AT SEVEN O'CLOCK.

FORMAL DRESS ONLY.

PLEASE BE ADVISED THAT LEAVING THE BUILDING AFTER

BLACKOUT IS STRICTLY FORBIDDEN.

P.S. ATTENDANCE FOR RECRUITS IS MANDATORY.

I untie the string around the box and lift the top. My fingers brush against tissue paper, which I pull away, and then something like satin. I lift out a rose-colored dress made of silk marocain. The material shimmers as it slips between my fingers. It's sleeveless and dripping with beads, the most beautiful item of clothing I've ever seen. The door to the dormitory bangs open.

"Have you seen this?" Marquis says incredulously.

He's holding a green suit and a pair of leather shoes. Atlas appears behind him, a red smoking jacket and a black tie in his hands.

"Nice to see you keeping daylight hours, Featherswallow," he says with a wink. "Any idea what's going on?"

I stare from my dress to the silver heels neatly packaged at the bottom of my box. Then I look back at the boys, all thoughts of Sand Dragons gone.

"It seems," I say, "that we're going to a ball."

FROM THE PRIVATE PAPERS OF DR. DOLORES SEYMOUR
Excursion to Rùm—June 1919

6 June—Day 1

I am here at last. The necessary permissions weren't granted until late last night, so I arrived on Rùm in the early hours of this morning. The Isle of Rùm, one of the Small Isles of the Inner Hebrides, is a rocky, mountainous landscape with scarcely an acre of level land. The smallest Scottish island to possess a summit above 2,500 feet, Rùm is an ideal hatching ground for British dragons. From its coast, one can see the Isles of Eigg and Canna, both property of the government. While trespassing on Eigg would result in a prison sentence of up to ten years, permission has been granted to the dragons to hunt on Canna, which, by the sounds of the screams, may be inhabited by wild pigs. Traveling to Rùm by any form of advanced transport that may disrupt the nesting space is illegal, as stipulated by the Peace Agreement. Therefore, I accessed the island by way of the most primitive of rowing boats from the mainland. My camp for the next few days is composed of a tent and a cave, which—my colleagues have assured me—remains uninhabited.

7 June—Day 2

The spring mating season has given way to a time of nest-building and egg-laying. The dragons do not inhabit Rùm all year round, nor do they use it to mate.

Extraordinarily, Rùm is used solely as a hatching ground and, even more incredibly, by <u>all</u> species of dragons. None are discriminated against. Since my arrival yesterday, I have spotted several species, including the Western Drake (*Draco occidentalis*), the Green-spotted Wyvern (*Draco bipes viridi*), and the Wyrm (*Hydrus volatilis*), one of the rarer, non-fire-breathing breeds that lays its eggs in the shallows.

8 June—Day 3

Oh, the exhilaration my work induces! Today I had the opportunity to observe, from a safe distance, a female Western Drake with her egg. The latter was purple in color, and the shell was covered in calcium peaks that formed jagged edges not unlike the spikes along the ridge of the mother's snout. She has chosen a precarious location for her nest, on the very edge of a cliff—so precarious, in fact, that I did much of my observing from a tree. Although more and more dragons land on Rùm each day in search of a nesting spot, the island is far from overcrowded. This female's decision therefore remains a mystery to me.

9 June—Day 4

The Western Drake left her nest long enough for me to see it up close. It is lined with stones, which she keeps smoldering hot, and dry ferns that occasionally catch alight. She has only one egg, which, I believe, is not unusual for a young first-time mother. The reason for her absence was to converse with another Western Drake, in the process of building her nest on a neighboring cliff. While I couldn't hear much of their conversation, I was able to establish they were speaking Wyrmerian—the one and only dragon tongue whose basic grammar I can grasp. I wish I could attempt communication with them, but I don't dare. My presence here, I have no doubt, will only be tolerated for so long.

10 June—Day 5

The crash of waves against rocks, the screeches of the gulls, and the cacophony of hundreds of dragon voices—these are the sounds I fall asleep to. I fear the noisiness of the hatching season—almost a social event—may suggest that the Royal Observatory's speculation about dragons' ability to communicate via ultrasonic sound waves is incorrect. If the dragons could do so, why would they deign to use their voices at all? There are both males and females present on Rùm—some share the egg-nurturing duties while other single parents are merely visited by their flightier mates. I have been watching two British Sand Dragons tending to their nest on one of the beaches near my camp. Both are female. I have seen them both turn the eggs over with their talons before burying them once more. There is no sign of a male partner in the vicinity.

11 June—Day 6

The Western Drake's egg is moving. If one watches very closely, one can see it tremble for just a second before standing still. This phenomenon only occurs when the mother approaches the nest. It's almost as though the tiny creature inside can sense her presence. And yet she rarely touches it, except to turn it over or bathe it in flame.

12 June—Day 7

Today I observed some peculiar behavior. The Western Drake brought her head down to the top of her egg, as if smelling it. And again I saw the egg move, more visibly this time. It shook almost violently, then toppled over onto its side. The mother raised her head, satisfied, and left to hunt. It is almost as if she had instructed the creature inside the egg to move. I have had a tentative, outrageous thought. What if dragons <u>do</u> possess a means of communication that is not the spoken word? It is a theory we considered during the war, then further explored last year through the observation of a small, isolated dragon clan on Guernsey, a highly unusual group because they spoke only one singular tongue. Might it be possible that these dragons had decided they had no use for multiple tongues, seeing as they could read each other's minds?

13 June—Day 8

Something truly horrific has happened. The Western Drake is dead! Last night she returned to the nest foaming at the mouth, and despite my attempts to help her, she succumbed. Following this catastrophe, I did something reckless. I took her egg, as well as the contents of the nest, and brought it into my cave. I have built a small fire beneath the nest in an attempt to keep it hot.

14 June—Day 9

I rise every two hours during the night to stoke the fire. My cave is full of smoke. I know little about how hot the egg should be, or if the heat it receives should be constant or sporadic. The dragons who came to eat the body of the dead mother have left it untouched. I fear this means she was poisoned. I depart for the mainland in two days.

15 June—Day 10

No movement from the egg. Its surface has begun to crack. Today I walked three miles to observe the nest of the other Western Drake. The stones beneath her two eggs seem to be constantly smoldering. I therefore dare to hope that I am doing things right. I found the courage to approach her and ask her—in English—if she might adopt the egg. "No," she replied, nodding toward her own two eggs. "I do not have enough flame for three."

16 June—Day 11

The egg is dead. The shell has begun to disintegrate and smell. I leave for the mainland in the morning. What does a dragon egg need to survive and hatch, apart from heat? What was it about the mother's presence that made her egg tremble in response? I am determined to make this the topic of my next research project.

FOURTEEN

On the evening of the ball, dusk falls earlier than it has since we arrived at Bletchley. It's cold outside—too cold for snow—and in the grounds around the manor house, frozen dragon tracks are entrenched deep in the dirt. A fire burns in the grate of the girls' dormitory, and we dress in its flickering orange light.

"Which one of you has taken my hairbrush?" Serena calls from the bathroom.

In the reflection of the mirror, I see Katherine pretend not to hear as she pulls the dragonbone brush through her unruly hair. Gravel crunches outside—cars have been arriving all afternoon. My dress fits me like a glove and the rose-colored satin warms my complexion. The fireblod has entirely healed my arm and the sling is gone. Behind me, Dodie reaches up to coil my hair round a long pin.

"You look beautiful," she says.

She's dressed in a blue chiffon the color of her eyes. Serena comes out of the bathroom, her hair freed of its twists and rising in thick dark waves above her head. She wraps a length of silk round her temples and the effect is a regality only she could achieve.

"I wore something almost as lovely when I was a deb last year," she says, gazing at herself in the mirror.

"What's a deb?" Katherine asks.

"A debutante," says Dodie, reaching to untangle the brush from Katherine's hair.

Beside them, Sophie is swathed in a deep green silk and I'm reminded of the dress she bought for her Examination Award Ceremony, the one she never got to wear.

"Here," Dodie says, handing me a folded piece of cloth with a shy smile. "An early Christmas gift. I made one for each of us."

It's a cotton handkerchief, the edges embroidered with tiny red dragon tongues.

"Dodie, it's beautiful."

I embrace her, finding myself enveloped in a sweet almond smell, and when I let go I notice her fingers are covered in bloody pinpricks.

"Karim had to help me," she says, blushing.

I nod, stunned that she would go to such an effort out of kindness. The other girls descend on her, squealing their thank-yous, and I sit down on my bed to fasten my shoes. The radio blares loudly from the common room down the hall.

"The rebel movement strikes again in an attack on London's West End that has killed several Guardians of Peace," the nasal voice of the reporter says. *"An estimated one hundred rebels descended on a conference at the Academy for Draconic Linguistics this afternoon in a raid that resulted in the theft of hundreds of language-related documents. There were no civilian casualties and several arrests were made. However, most of the perpetrators were seen escaping on dragonback—"*

The voice is cut off and followed by a long crackling sound. I'm already halfway down the hallway by the time it springs back to life. Except the voice is different this time, deep and smooth.

"This is a message to the citizens of Britannia from the Human-Dragon Coalition."

Marquis and Gideon, both in suits, look up from their armchairs in shock.

"We have infiltrated this radio broadcast in an attempt to set the record straight. It has just been reported that the Coalition launched an attack on the Academy for Draconic Linguistics in London today. This is a lie."

I place both hands on the mantelpiece and stare at the radio.

"Coalition members carried out a series of protests this afternoon outside the Academy in response to the new government guidelines concerning the study of dragon tongues. As of tomorrow, only First Class citizens who have undergone an intense government vetting process will be permitted to study dragon tongues. Citizens are hereby banned from speaking Dragonese in public spaces. This is an act of species segregation not seen in Britannia since the signing of the Peace Agreement and instatement of the Class System, which divided our society into an array of cruel and unnatural opposites: human versus dragon, native versus immigrant, rich versus poor.

"In retaliation, the Coalition seized a number of linguistic documents in order to ensure that access to dragon tongues cannot be further hoarded by the ruling class. The Coalition will continue to fight until Britannia is liberated from the tyranny of a leader who rules in the name of peace, yet commits injustice upon injustice against humans and dragons alike. We would like to remind our fellow countrymen that it was never our party's intention to overthrow the system. After the Great War, we asked for a new general election, for reform to come from inside the government itself. We did not want a coup, but democracy! But that is a word our leadership no longer knows. Wyvernmire's party continually blames the Coalition for the deaths caused by this war, but fails to take responsibility for its own part in this. People of Britannia,

your Prime Minister is lying to you. Dragons of Britannia, your Queen is lying to you. Down with the Peace Agreement! Down with the Class System! Long live the Coalition!"

The voice gives way to more crackles, then nothing.

"Species segregation?" I say slowly.

I've never heard the term before. I imagine the rebels swooping into London on dragonback and stealing documents from the Academy. Is the government really so afraid of rebellion that it would limit the study of dragon tongues in this way? Fear clutches at my heart. What will happen when I go home? Will the university refuse to reenroll me because I'm not First Class?

"She did that quietly, didn't she?" Marquis says grimly.

He's referring to Wyvernmire—and he's not wrong. The vetting process my family and I underwent after I applied to study dragon tongues was kept secret, and now Wyvernmire has sprung these further restrictions on the country without a word of warning. Banning the speaking of Dragonese? Why would the very woman who seemed so impressed by my knowledge of dragon tongues make such a law?

"One of the most important steps in a coup is to gain control of the media," Gideon says, leaning forward in his chair. "Those rebels are just trying to make people believe they haven't committed any crimes."

"So you *don't* think Wyvernmire's gatekeeping dragon tongues?" I say hopefully.

Gideon shrugs. "The more the rebel humans and dragons can communicate, the better chance they have of winning the war. So maybe she is." He glances at me. "Like I said, I bet the rebel dragons don't mind the humans learning their languages for now, if they're going to wipe us all out when—"

"Talking nonsense again, are you, Gideon?"

Atlas is leaning against the doorframe, wearing a red suit and black tie. The stubble on his jaw is darker, and it's the first time I've seen him without the white collar. He winks at me, his eyes lingering on my dress. My hands reach up to smooth my hair before I can stop them.

"It's not nonsense," Gideon says angrily. "Why do you think Wyvernmire's fighting them so hard? She's protecting us from the bestial nature of dragons, from what happened in Bulgaria—"

"What happened in Bulgaria was the revenge of hundreds of angry dragons, fueled by the response to the colonization of the wyvern community, the dragon fighting rings, and the mass kidnapping of eggs and dragonlings."

"You're saying the Bulgarian humans deserved to get murdered?" Gideon says, his eyes narrowing.

My gaze flits to Atlas.

"I'm saying," Atlas says pointedly, "that when you oppress a community for centuries you can't exactly be surprised when it rises up against you."

"But *we're* not oppressing any dragons," I say. "They *agreed* to the Peace Agreement. The Dragon Queen signed it herself. She—"

"The Dragon Queen signed it," Atlas says, "but the thousands of dragons of Britannia did not. That's the same as saying that Wyvernmire speaks for every individual in this country." He stares at me. "I don't know about you, but I don't remember giving my consent for this so-called Peace Agreement."

Marquis gives me an uncomfortable glance and I realize they're waiting for me to reply. I think of what Wyvernmire said when I met

194

her at Highfall Prison, about entrusting the study of dragon tongues only to citizens the government knows to be loyal. My heart sinks. Of course the rebel report must be true. Wyvernmire said herself that she fears languages will allow the rebel dragons and humans to collaborate further. They're probably what got my parents involved in the first place.

"It must be part of her strategy," I say quickly. "And once we've won the war, everything will go back to normal and people will be able to study and speak dragon tongues again."

Atlas gives me a glance that resembles pity.

When the others join us, Owen escorts us through the dark hallways to a wing I haven't been in before. Laughing voices ring along a corridor and we follow it to a door with light pouring out from beneath it. Owen pushes it open and the noise explodes.

The ballroom stretches out in front of us, a sea of glittering bodies gathered beneath crystal chandeliers. Molded ceilings rise high above the marble fireplaces and a vast mirror reflects the scene of more people than I've laid eyes on in months. Women in beaded dresses gasp as a butler on a stepladder pours a rush of champagne into a pyramid of glasses, then ooh as it cascades down into the coupes below. There's a huge Christmas tree decked with candles and beads, a small orchestra, and a singer with a harp. Her voice fills every corner of the space, languid and dizzying. Heads turn as we edge into the room and I feel Marquis move closer to me.

Dr. Seymour is walking toward us in a long red dress. She looks dazzling. The other category leaders join her in ushering us into the room, and Lumens whisks Atlas and Dodie away to meet a tall, important-looking man.

"Don't be shy," Dr. Seymour says to Marquis and me. "All these people are desperate to meet you."

I glance at my cousin, whose face mirrors my own confusion. Desperate to meet *us*? I follow Dr. Seymour, horribly aware of my every movement, and when I'm offered a glass of champagne I almost grab it from the tray, just to have something to do.

"Who are all these people?" I say to Dr. Seymour, taking a sip of my drink.

I watch as Sophie and Serena are beckoned away by a group of smiling young men, and Karim is pulled into the twinkling light of the Christmas tree by an elderly woman who bears him like a trophy to her friends.

"Supporters of the war effort," Dr. Seymour says after some hesitation. "That man with the mustache, the one talking to Knott, is the German Secretary of Defense. Next to him, the woman in the silver silk, is our Minister for Education." Dr. Seymour pauses. "And that woman there is the Chancellor of the Academy for Draconic Linguistics."

I smother a gasp and look where Dr. Seymour is pointing. Standing next to the baby grand piano, her silver hair coiffed into a neat bob and rings glittering on every finger, is Dr. Hollingsworth. I lay a hand on Marquis's arm as his face turns red.

"You can't," I say to him because I already know what he's thinking.

That's the woman who got our parents arrested. The woman who pretended to be their friend before sentencing them to death. Dr. Seymour gives us both a confused look.

"Do you know her?" she says.

"We've met her," I say grimly. "Dr. Seymour, did you hear the—"

"The radio interference?" Dr. Seymour lowers her voice as she nods. "If what the Coalition said is true, then that woman must be at the top of the order to ban dragon tongues."

Part of me wants to march over there and ask her why she has gone against everything she worked so long to build. The learning of languages—and translation in particular—is about giving a voice to people, to species and countries who have yet to be heard by the world. To learn nothing but human tongues would be to turn in on ourselves, would be like erasing the dragons and their history.

Ravensloe walks past us, accompanied by a pasty-faced young man.

"One doesn't have much time to keep up with the news at Oxford, especially with mods being next term," the man drawls. "But that damn Coalition is the talk of the quad."

"You'll know the ouroboros, of course?" Ravensloe replies. "The Ancient Greek symbol depicting a dragon eating its own tail? If only those rebel dragons would do the same thing. If instead of fighting their neighbor's tail, they turned round and bit their own, we should finally have peace."

Both of them dissolve into fits of loud laughter.

"Marquis Featherswallow?"

We turn round. A man with long dark curls and a black cane is smiling at us.

"You are working in Aviation, yes?"

The man has an accent identical to Mama's.

"I'm afraid I'm not allowed to talk about it—" Marquis begins, but the man just laughs and beckons him closer.

"I, too, am party to the Prime Minister's secrets," he says with a wink. "Now, I am interested to know more about your work . . ."

Marquis gives me a helpless look as the man puts an arm round his shoulder and steers him toward the bar. I'm left alone with Dr. Seymour and suddenly I remember every moment of our last conversation. My insistence on discussing the dracovol seems rude now, more humiliating without the heady excitement of progress that accompanied it.

"Dr. Seymour," I begin, "I'm sorry about—"

"Ah, Dolores," says a voice. "How delightful to see you here."

A man approaches us, a woman hanging off each arm.

"I haven't seen you since our university years. Let me introduce you to my wife, Iris, and my sister, Penelope."

The women both have upturned noses and pale skin. I can't guess which one is which.

"How do you do," Dr. Seymour says. "Vivien, this is Lord Rushby, the Earl of Fife. Rushby, this is one of my most talented recruits, Vivien Featherswallow."

I give them all a polite nod and notice Gideon watching me from the next group over. As Dr. Seymour continues to sing my praises, his ears slowly turn red. I take another gulp of champagne. My glass is almost empty.

Lord Rushby eyes me curiously. "Everyone is so *interested* in the work you do here at Bletchley, and yet it seems you are only at liberty to discuss it with a select few?"

He's young and handsome and smooth.

"A necessary precaution," I recite with a smile, "to protect the war effort."

His head snaps toward the woman on his right. "Dolores and I studied in the Dragon Department at university, dearest. She was always a few marks ahead of me, a true teacher's pet."

Everyone laughs and I see something like amusement flicker in Dr. Seymour's eyes as Lord Rushby disregards her intelligence as mere favoritism.

"Well, you have rather a good turnout," he says, clearly bored. "So many people crossing the country to be here in the spirit of . . . Christmas."

His eyes glint as he gives me a sideways glance, as if he's expecting me to grasp the hidden meaning behind his words. Why does it seem like every guest here knows *exactly* what's happening at Bletchley Park?

"To be honest," I say, because I know I should say something, "I'd forgotten all about Christmas."

"Of course you did," Rushby says good-naturedly, taking another glass of champagne from a tray and handing it to me. "You've been so *busy*. But one must keep one's spirits up, even in the midst of a war. The presence of the German Secretary of Defense, and of that Bulgarian refugee—"

"The last surviving member of the Bulgarian royal family!" Penelope says.

"—is, of course, mere coincidence."

"I heard," Iris whispers, "that the German Peace Agreement is on its last legs."

I glance at Dr. Seymour, but she wears an expression of perfect indifference. Violins sing from across the room and I take another sip of champagne. My body is starting to feel deliciously light and warm. I stare at the golden bubbles rising in the glass.

"Isn't it tedious," Iris says to Dr. Seymour, "to have to watch all these people talk about the boring war and the way it affects their boring lives?"

"Your husband will entertain us, I'm sure," Penelope says. She tugs on Rushby's arm like a child. "Tell us one of your riveting stories."

I withhold a sigh and notice that Dr. Seymour's attention is also drifting. She glances round the room, perhaps looking for someone—anyone—more interesting to talk to. I hope she spots them soon.

"Here's one," Rushby says. "The rebels have officially taken Eigg."

Dr. Seymour's gaze snaps back toward our group.

"Are you quite sure?" she says. "I've heard no reports."

"It's not something the government wants shouted from the rooftops, Dolores dear," the earl says lazily. "But they've seized it with their dragon power, and the word is they're aiming for Canna next."

Eigg. Canna. The islands mentioned in Dr. Seymour's dracovol letter. If they're government-owned, and they're related to the echolocation research Ravensloe has Dr. Seymour doing, then why doesn't she know about this?

"What would they want with Canna?" Iris says. "It's a ghastly place."

"Ghastly?" I say when Dr. Seymour doesn't speak. "Why?"

"For us perhaps, but not so much for the dragons." Lord Rushby laughs loudly and takes a fat cigar out of his pocket.

"Oh dear, brother," Penelope says, twisting a curl round her finger. "I don't think Vivien gets your meaning."

"You don't?" Rushby says, bemused. He glances at Dr. Seymour. "I thought the knowledge was common in these circles."

Dr. Seymour shakes her head and Lord Rushby's smile grows wider.

"Canna is—for the dragons of Britannia—a silver platter of human flesh."

I stare at him as my mind takes his words and tries to turn them into something that makes sense.

"Now, now, dear, you'll alarm the girl," says Iris.

Rushby ignores her and lights his cigar. "This is why it is such a mystery to me that there are dragons among the rebels. Those creatures have everything they could possibly need, and yet still they complain."

Penelope tuts and shakes her head. I feel like a fool, but I don't care. I have to ask.

"Lord Rushby, what do you mean by human flesh?"

"Canna is where they send the criminal youths," Rushby says. He puffs on the cigar. "With the law stating that minors cannot be executed, and the overcrowding due to the influx of immigrants from Bulgaria after the massacre, the government needed to put them *somewhere*."

The noise around me dulls as I concentrate on Rushby's voice.

"So, instead of filling up the prisons, our former Prime Minister found a better way to deal with crime."

"Lawbreakers below the age of eighteen are sent to Canna as *food* for the dragons," Penelope says. She lets out an outraged gasp. "Isn't it *gory*?"

"It worked for a time," Rushby says, unbothered by my stunned silence. "But now the buggers are finding ways to survive." He snorts. "Just imagine: children as young as seven getting the best of dragons."

"Predators fooled by prey," Iris says with a sigh.

"But . . . but how is that allowed?" I say.

"It's in the Peace Agreement, darling!" Penelope says. "A clause added to appease the dragons for having to share their skies with our planes."

I set my glass down as the room swims in front of me. The protest in Fitzrovia flashes through my mind, the blood on my portfolio, the dead girl's face. My stomach churns. I can almost hear the protesters' voices screaming above the quiver of the violins.

The Peace Agreement is corrupt!

"Now look, you've frightened her," Iris says.

Dr. Seymour reaches a hand out to me, but I take a step backward, bumping into someone. Lips press against my ear.

"Let's get some air, shall we?" Atlas says.

He steers me across the room and out into the hallway, closing the door on the noise behind us. My voice explodes into the silence of the corridor.

"An island full of children!" I say. "Sent to be food for dragons. The Earl of Fife just told me about it. And he was laughing!"

Owen, guarding the door, turns away as if he can't hear us.

"The whole point of the Peace Agreement is that humans and dragons can't kill each other," I say, pacing the floor.

My cheeks are on fire and I feel like I might be sick if I stand still.

"But if there's a clause, it means Wyvernmire knows about it. That she condones it! And Dr. Seymour . . ." I whip round to stare at the closed ballroom door. "*She* must know, too."

Atlas is watching me, his hands in his pockets.

I choke on my words. "Did *you* know?"

"Yes," he says quietly. "But only because I've heard the rumors. The clause isn't included in the version of the Peace Agreement

202

available to the public—it's only written in the government's copies."

"It's there in black and white, is it?" I say furiously. "Dragons are allowed to eat human children in exchange for sharing the sky?"

Atlas shakes his head. "I think it says something along the lines of: *At the discretion of the government, extraordinary hunting rights will be granted to the dragons of Britannia on the Isle of Canna only.*"

"Extraordinary hunting rights," I scoff. "Now that's a code if ever I heard one."

He smothers a smile.

"It's not funny!" I say. "Atlas, this means that the rebels are right on one thing . . ." My head spins. "The Peace Agreement *is* corrupt. I thought dragons were good—"

"It's not all dragons," Atlas says. "The Coalition wants *true* peace between the species, not this self-serving fake agreement invented by the elite."

He's been radicalized, I realize. His mind filled with the rebels' lies.

"It's not peace the rebels want," I say. "It's lawlessness."

"Come on," Atlas says, glancing at Owen. "Let's go somewhere more private."

I nod and follow him down the hall. My head aches and the champagne has left a dry tang in my mouth. What would have happened to me after I set Chumana free if Wyvernmire hadn't offered me a job at Bletchley? Would I have been sent to Canna like a pig to slaughter? We wander through the unexplored wing whose walls are lined with old portraits and tapestries.

"Look at the Class System," I say, determined to prove him wrong. "It might *seem* strict, but its opportunity for promotion allows for the self-improvement of the British people. Except the rebels aren't interested in that. Instead, they've declared war and they're killing innocent people."

Atlas sighs. "The Coalition didn't have a choice. Wyvernmire has been spreading propaganda about them for years, and just look who she has on her side. The German Minister for Defense, a right-wing nationalist, the last Prince of Bulgaria, proudly pro-dragon rings, and some old English lords who would rather kill criminal kids than rewrite the Peace Agreement."

"That's exactly why the rebels should surrender!" I say. "All *they* have are deluded insurgents, a mysterious voice on the radio, and a few dragons who somehow think they're victims of injustice—" I put up my hand as Atlas opens his mouth to argue. "Don't talk to me about dragon fighting rings," I say shrilly. "They're banned in Britannia *thanks to* the Peace Agreement."

"But dragons are still suffering," Atlas says. "Industrialization is pushing them from the land *and* from the skies, their hoards are being taxed and looted, and they're not even considered members of society anymore. People either hate dragons, or they're afraid of them. But before the Peace Agreement the dragons lived *among* us. They were academics, politicians, landowners. Now, dragons only work as manual laborers or as punishment for their crimes."

I slow beneath a tapestry of a wyvern being pulled from the sky by rope-wrangling men below.

"Britannia—and that means Wyvernmire—is the only place in Europe to have continuously held an alliance with its dragons," I say. "We've always listened to them, negotiated with them. . . . That's why our Peace Agreement is so famous in the first place. Of course the Prime Minister wants to uphold that, because she wants the best for us—"

"Northern Ireland *and* the Irish Free State both have their own Peace Agreements," Atlas says. "There's a reason they don't want ours."

I blink and he sighs again.

"When I was little, my cousins lived in one of East Anglia's steel-making quarters," he says.

I lean against the wall and he comes to a stop beside me, careful not to step on the hem of my dress.

"They all spoke Harpentesa before they spoke English, just from being around all the dragons who worked in the foundries. Their first language was a dragon tongue, but now they'll have to resort to English to talk with the dragons."

I've never met a Third Class person who could speak a dragon tongue.

A few weeks ago, I would have thought nothing of dragon tongues being banned among the Third Class because they can't study them at university anyway. Yet Atlas's Third Class cousins could speak Harpentesa before I even knew what it was. And it's only now, when the study of dragon tongues is being banned for the Second Class, for people like me, that I care.

"I traveled once, with the lord I worked for," Atlas says. "We had special post–Travel Ban permission. We went to a horse show in France, just outside Paris. Our guide was a dragon. He taught me some Drageoir, showed me how to light a fire with a piece of flint and a spark. When we went for breakfast and coffee, he sat on the roof of a *boulangerie* and ordered a bowl of cognac. And no one batted an eyelid. Tell me that's not a better world to live in. A world where humans and dragons live together and—"

A door swings open down the hall and a Guardian steps out. My heart stops.

It's Ralph.

He's holding his helmet under one arm and I notice a cut across the bridge of his nose. He turns in the opposite direction to us and walks back toward the ballroom. We both stare as his footsteps echo through the hall and he turns a corner. I edge toward the nearest door and feel for the handle. I twist it, grab Atlas by the back of his jacket, and pull him inside.

"I bet he's furious he wasn't invited to the ball," Atlas smirks as I close the door as quietly as I can.

We're standing at the bottom of a narrow staircase. I follow Atlas up it into another hallway, with tall windows covered in blackout curtains. Lines of white statues stand on slabs of stone on either side and miniature marble dragon heads stare out from the windowsills. I'm still thinking of the cognac-drinking dragon.

"Say, Featherswallow?" he says.

I peer at a statue of two amorous dragons, their bodies entwined. "Hmm?"

"I got your last note . . . and I left my reply."

He looks at me through his eyelashes and I feel my body warm. "I'll be sure to read it, then."

"In the meantime, can I give you something else?"

The solemn look on his face makes me grin.

"What sort of something?" I tease.

He opens his palm. A tiny wooden swallow sits at the center of it, hanging from a plaited ribbon. Two metal claps are attached at either end. I suddenly remember him whittling a piece of wood in the common room.

"I . . . Did you make this?"

Atlas nods. "May I?"

I turn round, lifting my hair, as Atlas fastens the ribbon round my neck. The swallow sits at the same level as my class pass used to, except it's so small it drops between my breasts, hidden from view.

"To remind you of *who* you are," Atlas whispers in my ear.

Swallows were originally dragons who could speak every language in the world. But it weighed on them, being able to empathize with the stories of so many.

I don't know what to say. The gesture is so mind-bogglingly sweet that I feel my face growing red and—to my horror—my eyes well with tears.

I suck in a breath. "Atlas, I—"

"Race you to that giant egg up there."

I peer through the gloom of the badly lit hall, grateful for the interjection. At the end is a tall silver egg.

"You've been here before, haven't you?" I say.

Atlas shrugs. "Wyvernmire's office is nearby, and I like to see what she gets up to."

Then, without warning, he tears off down the hall. Laughter bubbles up inside me as I watch him run. I want to follow him, but my silver heels are dangerously high.

Oh, to hell with the shoes.

I run after him as fast as I dare. As he stretches out his arm to touch the egg, I catch him by the back of his jacket and he jerks backward, tripping over my foot. I lose my balance and we both fall to the ground, breathless, noses pressed up to the silver feet of the egg.

"You cheat!" he wheezes, rubbing his knee.

I sit up, see the laughter in his eyes, and cackle as I fall back

207

down. The ceiling spins above me and suddenly I'm laughing so hard I can't breathe.

"You got a head start," I splutter.

My pin has come loose and I pull it out so that my hair falls down over my shoulders. Atlas rolls over to look at me, propping his head up on his elbow.

"You know what I think?" he says, his mouth twitching.

"What?"

"I think this is the first time I've seen you laugh."

"And I think this is the first time I've seen you lose," I say with a smug smile.

He snorts. "I didn't lose. I would have got there first if you hadn't resorted to sabotage."

"I'm faster than you," I reply. "You knew that dragon egg was there before we walked through the door, so really the only cheat here is you."

There's a piece of wool from his suit caught in his stubble. I pull it away and his eyes linger on my fingers, then on the ribbon around my neck.

"Why have you always wanted to be a Draconic Translator?" he says.

The question is sudden, but I can tell he's been wanting to ask it for a while.

"My mother speaks to me in Bulgarian," I say. "And I think, once you've learned two languages, you want to know them all." I stare up at the ceiling again, trying to ignore how his face is only a few inches from mine. "Dragon tongues—and dragons—have always fascinated me. I started preparing for university when I was twelve."

"I heard the universities are becoming stricter on who they let in. You must have worked really hard."

I nod again. "We studied constantly."

"We?"

"Sophie and I."

"Sophie told me she failed her Examination," he says. "So did I."

I already know that. If Atlas had passed, he would have been promoted to Second Class.

"They didn't give *us* any time to study," Atlas says. "We just arrived at school one day and they sprang the Examination on us."

"What?" I say. "Why?"

Atlas shrugs. "We never had enough teachers to go around and they had to do it on a day when they could get enough examiners in, so they had no time to let us know." He frowns and lays his head down beside mine. "Or so they said."

"Well then, it's no wonder you failed," I say angrily.

I think of the months of studying I did, how my desk was piled high with textbooks. I complained at the time, but at least I had the chance to prepare myself.

"Oh, I don't know," he says. "I'd probably have failed anyway. I'm not like you, Featherswallow."

"Like me?"

"You know . . . academic."

I roll my eyes and laugh. "If only I could see myself the way you see me. 'Empathetic,' 'academic'—"

"Unbelievably beautiful?" Atlas says innocently.

I keep my eyes on the ceiling as I feel my cheeks blush. How much champagne has he had? I want to look at him, but I suddenly feel slightly terrified.

Atlas clears his throat. "Sorry," he says. "That was—"

"No!" I say, a little too loudly. I turn onto my side to face him. "That was . . . fine."

We're so close I can count the tiny moles beneath his eye. His breath tickles my cheek and his lips are parting as if he's about to whisper something. His hand finds my hip as he leans over me. I feel his warmth through my dress. Our faces draw closer and his mouth is above mine. . . .

Atlas sits up. "I'm sorry," he says. "I can't."

My heart races as I fight the urge to pull him back down. A dark expression crosses his face. He looks confused, angry even.

"What's wrong?" I whisper.

I sit up. Why didn't he kiss me?

"It's not that I don't want to," he says.

I try to smile, but my mouth just twists into an awful, pained grin.

"But my . . . vocation," he says awkwardly.

His what?

"To the priesthood."

Oh.

"Priests don't . . . they're not supposed to . . ."

"It's fine," I say, my face burning. "I know."

How could I have been so stupid? Priests are celibate—everyone knows that.

"I always forget," I say, "that you're a priest."

"In training," he says.

This time, the correction doesn't make me smile.

"So you can't even . . . kiss?"

I can't believe I'm asking this. How desperate I must sound. I wish I could take the words back.

"Not if this is truly what I'm called to," Atlas says.

I stare at the dragon egg behind him. We could be kissing beneath it, but instead it's witnessing the most humiliating moment of my existence.

"And you truly believe that God's telling you to be a priest and to never fall in love?" I blurt without thinking.

"Of course He wants me to fall in love," Atlas says. "Just not in that way. We all love in different ways, I'd say. For some, it might be another person. Or it could be teaching, or healing, or art or"—he nods at me—"languages. But for me it's the priesthood."

I love languages, but I've never thought of them as being a *way* to love. They're practical, quantifiable, translatable. Everything love is not.

"But how can you be sure?" I say. "That this is what you're called to?"

He brushes his hand through his hair and hesitates.

"I . . . I don't know," he says quietly.

I stand up, wishing I'd never asked the question. "We should go back. Before they notice we're missing."

Atlas nods. He gives me a long, sad look and suddenly I want to be as far away from him as possible. I jump as a loud thump sounds behind me. One of the heavy blackout curtains has fallen away from the window.

"We should put it back up," I say. The hallway is gloomy, but the lights of the gas lamps could still be seen from the sky. "Help me."

I climb up onto the windowsill and Atlas holds the curtain up toward me. I find the clip that held it up and reattach it. What if this happens somewhere else in the house? What if the rebels fly over and spot—

I pause. In the courtyard below is a tiny orange light. Someone is out there smoking.

"Have you done it?" Atlas asks.

I press my face up against the window. We're only one story high and the moonlight is bright. I can make out the shape of a woman wrapped in a fur coat, silver glittering on her fingers as she smokes.

Dr. Hollingsworth.

The sight of her fills me with anger. Smoking was the excuse she made to go and rifle through Mama and Dad's study until she found evidence that could incriminate them.

Evidence that I ensured was burned.

I bet you weren't expecting that, were you, you old hag?

"What are you doing?" Atlas says from behind me.

My mind rushes back to that awful night when we sat eating our pierogi, oblivious to the fact that life as we knew it was about to come to an end.

Dr. Featherswallow, if dragons spoke in regional dialects, surely we would have heard them.

And what had Mama said?

The dialects may not be regional. They could be—

Hollingsworth hadn't let her finish her sentence. I watch the smoke rise up above her head. Mama had been desperate to explain her theory about dragon dialects. So desperate that she had sent her research to the Academy several times, with no response. Hollingsworth must have read that research herself. She knew exactly what Mama was trying to prove, but the government already suspected her of being a rebel. And if the Academy and Wyvernmire were planning to restrict the learning of dragon tongues, then of course they weren't going to publish Mama's work.

212

But if Hollingsworth has a copy of Mama's research, I could ask her to let me see it. Mama's study of dragon dialects might help me with my own theory that echolocation contains dialects, too.

Mama could help me crack the code.

I attach the last curtain clip and step backward. The heel of my shoe meets with thin air and I flail, falling off the windowsill and into Atlas. He grasps me round the waist, as the back of my head almost hits his nose, and sets me down. We stand for a moment, his arms wrapped round me, my back against his chest.

"Those shoes are more dangerous than dragonfire," he breathes into my hair.

I shrug him off. We walk back to the ballroom in silence, and when Atlas tries to take my hand I pretend not to notice. I slip through the door and Marquis immediately locks eyes on me from across the room. When he sees my loose hair and Atlas appear in the doorway behind me, his mouth spreads into a smirk. I ignore him and scan the room. Hollingsworth has also returned and is talking to a small man by the drinks table. I make a beeline for her and Marquis's smile falters.

"I'm sorry to interrupt," I say loudly.

The man looks at me in surprise and Hollingsworth turns round.

"Vivien," she says, smiling. "How delightful to see you again."

I glower at her.

"Would you excuse me, Henry?" she says to her friend.

The man bows his head and, with a curious glance in my direction, scurries away. Hollingsworth looks at me expectantly.

"So?" she says. "How have you been enjoying life at Bletchley?"

"Do you mean how am I enjoying life since you got my parents arrested and ruined my future?"

Hollingsworth clicks her tongue and takes a sip of champagne, leaving a smattering of red lipstick on the rim of the glass.

"We've already discussed this, Vivien. Your parents have no one to blame for their arrest but themselves. And, if I'm not mistaken, you ruined your own future by breaking your house arrest to free a criminal dragon. Am I wrong?"

I feel my cheeks warm. She's not wrong. I could have stayed home with Ursa. Had I done that, I would simply be the unfortunate daughter of criminals. Not a criminal myself.

"You were never interested in my mother's work," I say. "When my university application flagged my parents as a potential threat, Wyvernmire sent *you* undercover to find out if they were rebels."

"Yes, I admit that is true," Hollingsworth says. "*But* I also had my own intentions. Your mother is interesting, of course, but it was you who intrigued me. Universities send the applications they receive to study Dragonese to the Academy, and yours impressed me. I've yet to meet another person your age who speaks so many dragon tongues."

I try to keep my expression hostile, but the shock shines through.

"I fully intended to invite you to join my apprenticeship program," Hollingsworth says. "But our Prime Minister had other ideas. She decided *she* was going to have you. I was sent to recruit you, not for myself, but for the DDAD."

I glance around nervously. So Hollingsworth must have signed the Official Secrets Act, too.

"So Wyvernmire was always going to offer me a job?" I say, thinking of the day I met her in handcuffs. I lower my voice. "Even if I hadn't freed that dragon?"

Hollingsworth nods. "The DDAD operated a cross-country, cross-class recruitment program, but the university application process gave them some of the finest selections to choose from. They spotted you just like I did. Of course, if you hadn't broken your house arrest, then you wouldn't be a criminal like most of the recruits here, but Wyvernmire had plenty of offers up her sleeve to entice you."

"She has me working with . . . languages," I say hesitantly. There's no way I can be sure about what exactly Hollingsworth knows.

"Of course she has," she replies. "Language is as crucial to war as any weapon."

"Then how can you let her gatekeep them?" I say suddenly. "You're the *Chancellor* of the Academy for Draconic Linguistics—your job is to preserve and promote dragon tongues!"

She leans in closer to me, still gripping her now-empty glass. "That Academy is *government*-funded, Vivien." Her eyes dart once round the room. "And government-controlled."

I look at her as understanding dawns on me. How long exactly has the government been controlling the learning of dragon tongues?

"Over the years our funding has become smaller and smaller, our access to new languages more restricted," Hollingsworth says quietly. "Two-thirds of our departments have been shut down."

"But why?" I say. "War or no war, we still need to be able to communicate with the dragons. Dragon tongues are part of our society, part of our country's heritage—"

"Did you know that the Academy was the first institution to record the dragon tongues of Bulgaria in writing?" Hollingsworth says. "We created their written form using the Latin alphabet, instead of Bulgaria's natural Cyrillic. Do you know why?" She peers at me closely and her voice becomes almost urgent. "Few people in

Britannia's government read Cyrillic, and one must be able to understand a language in order to manipulate it."

Why would the British government want to manipulate Bulgaria's dragon tongues?

"To control languages, to control words, is to control what people know."

Then Hollingsworth lets out a laugh, so fake that I almost recoil. But I understand what it means. Someone is watching us. I force a smile, try to act natural.

"I need to read my mother's research proposal," I say quickly. "The one on dragon dialects. It could help us bring an end to the war."

Hollingsworth frowns and gives me a long, curious look. I can tell that she's bursting to ask me more, but the Official Secrets Act binds us both.

"You told me I have a bright future and to seize it," I say. "Well, that's what I'm doing. Send me my mother's research. Please."

"Excuse me."

I spin round. Marquis is standing there, eyeing Hollingsworth coldly. She gives him a courteous nod, but then turns back to me, a hundred questions on her lips.

"We've been summoned to a meeting," Marquis says. "Recruits only."

Is he lying? I glance around at all the guests, who are being invited to take seats at the dining tables.

"Now?" I say.

"Now," Marquis replies.

I nod goodbye to Hollingsworth and follow Marquis.

"Why the hell are you talking to her?" he says.

I follow him out of the ballroom and see the other recruits queuing outside a door to the right of the hall.

"What are we doing here?" I ask, ignoring his question.

"Wyvernmire wants to speak to us before making her grand entrance," Atlas says from the queue, rolling his eyes.

Beside him, Dodie fidgets nervously. "Do you think we're in trouble?"

"Of course not," Atlas replies, giving her a reassuring smile. "She probably wants an update on our progress, to give her something to boast about."

We file into what seems to be an unused parlor. White sheets cover the furniture and above us a dusty chandelier flickers with pale yellow light. Prime Minister Wyvernmire is sitting on an uncovered armchair upholstered in red velvet. Both Ralph and Owen are standing behind her. I want to ask her where Ursa is, and why she took her when she promised she wouldn't. But I can't do that without admitting to the dracovol.

"Good evening," she says, "I trust you are enjoying the celebrations?"

We all nod and murmur an agreement as we try to guess what might be about to happen. Two more Guardians enter the room behind us.

"I wanted to greet you all personally before making my appearance at tonight's Christmas Ball," she says. "We have a lot of distinguished guests this evening, but none are quite as important as you."

Atlas lets out a loud cough.

"You have had almost a month to settle into your roles at

217

Bletchley Park," she continues. "And in that time the rebels have grown bolder. I am sure you were as disturbed as I was to learn about the recent attacks on civilians in the country's capital."

I think of the two very different radio reports on the conflict at the Academy. How did Wyvernmire react to the rebel radio infiltration?

"I'm afraid I bring to you some even more unsettling news. It seems that the Scots feel more sympathetic toward the rebel groups than we previously suspected. While the British Army put up a good fight, many Scottish citizens have turned their coats, so to speak. As of tonight, the rebels occupy most of Scotland."

Loud whispers fill the room. I stare at Marquis, who is standing close to Karim. A whole country under rebel control? How can the rebels be making so much progress when *we* seem to be making none at all? I've barely heard any reports of government victories—how can that be possible with an entire army at its disposition? I thought the rebel movement was supposed to be small.

"My parents," Karim croaks. "They live in Aberdeenshire, and they're loyal to the government, I swear—"

"Not to worry, Karim," Wyvernmire says. "We extracted your parents from Scotland last week."

I look at her in surprise.

"Why?" Karim says.

"All of you have seen what the work within your respective categories entails. You understand how your particular skills are suited to the task given to you, and know what is required of you in order for my government to win the war." Wyvernmire smoothes her skirt. "However, it seems that many of you are failing to meet our expectations."

Atlas takes my hand and I don't pull away.

"There has not been a single breakthrough, a single piece of information unearthed by you, that has allowed us to make progress when it comes to fighting rebel dragons. And dragons, it appears, are the rebels' strength."

You're wrong, I want to tell her. *I'm on the very edge of a breakthrough*. But I can't divulge what I've learned about echolocation dialects yet, not until I'm certain that they're regional. Giving Wyvernmire the wrong information could have consequences far worse than giving her nothing at all.

"Therefore, as leader of the nation, I find myself duty bound to speed things up."

Ralph tightens his grip on his gun. He stares at me, his mouth twisting into a smirk. The sound of the music wafting out of the ballroom has suddenly increased in volume.

"From tonight onwards, you are all taking part in a race," the Prime Minister says softly. "In each of the categories—Aviation, Zoology, and Codebreaking—only the first person to achieve what is being asked of them will be pardoned. The rest of you—as well as any imprisoned or extracted family members you might have—will be punished in accordance with the severity of your crimes."

I feel my forehead crease into a frown. The ground sways beneath me. The saxophones toll like frantic sirens, their brassy vibrations filling my head. Atlas's hand drops from mine as he lunges toward Wyvernmire only to meet the barrel of Owen's gun. They stare at each other, daring the other to move, as strangled sobs fill the room. Beside me, Dodie is hyperventilating.

"From now on, you will no longer work in teams," Wyvernmire says above the noise. "You will continue to attend the same shifts, under the guidance of your category leaders, but you will each work alone."

Marquis takes two steps forward and Ralph lifts his own weapon. Behind us, more Guardians come in through the door.

"You can't do this," Marquis snarls. "You said that if we came here and did the work that was asked of us, we and our families would be free."

"I said that you would be released if you did the work required to help me *win* the war." Wyvernmire stares into Marquis's face, her nostrils flaring. "But I. Am. Losing."

"So only the one of us who cracks the dragon code will go free?" Gideon is staring between me, Katherine, and Sophie.

"I'm glad you understand, Gideon," Wyvernmire replies.

No.

This can't be happening. The Prime Minister stands for justice, for peace and prosperity. She wouldn't do this to us.

This was my chance to save myself *and* Sophie. Through my tears, I see her staring at me, her face like stone. Only one of us will return to London.

Only one of us will get our life back.

Karim sinks to the floor, sobbing. What crime has he committed? What will happen to him and his parents if he doesn't win his category? If he doesn't compete against Serena, against *Marquis*? I stare round at my friends and realize I don't know what *punished in accordance with the severity of your crimes* means for them. I lock eyes with Marquis. He gives me a long, desperate look as he tries to keep Karim upright. I know what it means for my cousin if he loses. For myself if I end up getting sent to Canna. For our parents.

Death.

220

BABEL DECREE

Article One. English must be the only method of instruction in public, private, and denominational schools. Dragon tongues will no longer be taught.

Article Two. Conversations in public places, on public transport, and over the telephone should be in the English language.

Article Three. All public addresses should and must be in the English language.

Article Four. Degrees in Dragon Tongues may only be undertaken by the First Class and with special government permission.

Article Five. English is the only language permissible when conversing with dragons.

At this time, when dragons are involved in a direct rebellion against the government, the Academy for Draconic Linguistics has advised that the speaking of dragon tongues be restricted, to bring peace to our people and to strengthen the nation in battle. Bilingual education must be abolished in order to rapidly curb unpatriotic influences.

Dragonese is the language of the Human-Dragon Coalition and therefore the language of treason. By virtue of my authority as Head of Government, I, Adrienne P. Wyvernmire, urge that henceforth the within outlined rules be adhered to by all and that, united as one people with one purpose and one language, we fight shoulder to shoulder for the good of mankind.

London, this twentieth day of December 1923
A.P. Wyvernmire

FIFTEEN

No one returns to the ball. Instead, we each find our way back to the common room, Marquis leading a wordless Karim by the hand, Gideon clutching an open bottle of champagne. We sit by the fire as Marquis rolls several cigarettes, the silence interrupted only by the sound of Katherine vomiting in the bathroom. There's a deep, anxious hollow in my stomach. This doesn't feel real and yet here we all are, sitting in some sort of meeting circle like we're merely indulging in a nightcap before bed.

Everything feels numb, as if at some time during the evening a veil was dropped between me and the rest of the world. And still I know, with absolute certainty, that in a few weeks' time I and all the people I love could be dead. I suddenly long for Mama.

Sophie is sitting in the window seat as Dodie unbraids her hair. She won't look at me. *Good.* I don't want to see the hope in her eyes. Hope that we might still both make it out together. Hope that I have a plan. Because I don't. There is no hope when you're going to have to betray your best friend a second time.

I hold out my hand to Gideon and he gives me the bottle of champagne without a word. I swig down three big gulps of it and cough as the bubbles fill my throat and nose. A bit of extra numbness can't hurt. But my brain is already spinning, calculating, trying to fit the echolocation calls I've learned into a pattern that makes sense. That code *has* to be cracked and it *has* to be me who does it.

I won't let my family die.

"Tonight was all just some twisted performance," Serena says, her gold shoes dangling from her hand. "Dress us all up, show us off and for what?" Tears suddenly well in her eyes. "To give us one last taste of freedom?"

"To give the impression that the DDAD is making progress," Marquis says. "To remind us all of what we have to lose."

A snort comes from across the room. Atlas is staring into the fire, his jacket discarded, tie flung over his shoulder.

"And what's that?" he says. The reflection of the flames dances in his eyes as he glares at Marquis. "Overindulging in mince pies with some First Class white men?"

"Redemption," Sophie says icily before Marquis can reply. "This is our one chance to be someone else."

The room turns cold as the reminder of Ravensloe's welcome speech rings awkwardly in the air. Who is the weakest Aviation recruit? I wonder. It's certainly not Marquis—thank God. So is it Serena or Karim?

"I don't need to be someone else," Atlas says quietly. "And neither do any of you."

I want to believe him, but Sophie's right. There's no future for Viv the criminal, the girl who betrayed her friend, the girl who broke the Peace Agreement. But for Viv who cracked the dragon code, ended the war, and saved her family? There might still be some way forward for her.

"I lied," Serena says suddenly, sinking down onto a pile of

cushions on the floor. "I didn't fail the Examination on purpose. I'm just stupid."

"You're not stupid, Serena," Karim says.

"I am. Because now, if I fail Aviation, I'll be married to the Earl of Pembroke. A friend of my parents, owner of the London offices used by the Promotion and Demotion Department." She grimaces in disgust. "He's wanted me for years. And he made it clear that if I choose the Second Class over him, he'll make sure I get demoted to Third."

"Oh, how the tables have turned," Sophie says curtly.

"Shut up, Sophie," Marquis snaps.

Sophie gives him an injured look, then stands up abruptly and flounces off to bed. The rest of us sit in the common room, passing round the champagne and the cigarettes as we listen to the music echo eerily from the ballroom. Atlas broods by the fire and doesn't speak again. He suddenly feels like a stranger. Karim falls asleep with his head in Marquis's lap and slowly, once the bottle is empty, people wander off to the dormitories.

I curl up in an armchair with a shawl round me and kick off my shoes. My cheeks are hot and my head lolls heavily as I suppress a yawn.

"Goodnight, then," Atlas mumbles. He's speaking to everyone, but looking in my direction.

"Goodnight," I say.

There's no smile or gesture as he walks by, nothing to acknowledge that a few hours ago we almost kissed. Gideon suddenly comes to life, too, and staggers off in the direction of the boys' dormitory. There's only me, Marquis, and a sleeping Karim left.

"What's his problem?" Marquis says, nodding toward the spot where Atlas was.

I shrug. "Same problem as everyone else."

"But why's he acting like it's your fault?"

Is he?

"I defended her earlier. Maybe that's it."

"Wyvernmire?"

I nod. "I said she wanted the best for us, for Britannia, but now . . ."

I tell him about Canna and how Hollingsworth all but admitted to me that the government has taken control of the Academy.

Marquis grimaces. "It's almost like Wyvernmire's expecting Britannia's dragons to turn on her, and wants to beat them at their own game."

"But why?" I say. "She's got Queen Ignacia, and therefore the majority of the dragons of Britannia, on her side."

"Do you think she's just bluffing?" Marquis says. "Trying to scare us so that we'll work faster?"

I think of Wyvernmire as I've always seen her in the papers, the woman I believed to be firm but fair. Tonight she was someone different. What if her shininess is just an act, like mine? What if she's rotten on the inside, too?

"I don't—"

Karim stirs in his sleep and we both fall silent. Marquis strokes his short, shaved hair. In the light of the fire, I see his mouth tug into a smile.

"You have real feelings for him," I say.

My cousin rolls his eyes. "I've known him for a month."

"You've never looked at any of them like that before."

"Well, there haven't been that many—"

"Liar."

Marquis lets out a splutter of laughter that makes Karim wake with a jolt. I cover my grin with my hands as he sits up, bleary-eyed.

"Was goin' on?" he mumbles.

"Nothing," Marquis says, his eyes still laughing. "We're going to bed. Come on."

He hugs me goodnight and I stare into the fire, reluctant to leave the warmth of the common room. I close my eyes and try to imagine a scenario in which we all walk out of Bletchley Park together.

When I wake, the embers in the grate are cold. The common room is dark and my legs, curled up beneath me, have gone numb. I sit up. Behind me, a floorboard creaks.

"Who's there?" I whisper.

Hands slide round my neck. I gasp as they pull me back against the chair cushions, crushing my throat. I reach for the arms on either side of my head and sink my nails into them, straining my bare feet against the rug and trying to twist round to see who wants to kill me.

Is it Ralph come to finish off what he started? I lift a fist and ram it, hard, into his face. Teeth graze my knuckles and the grip around my neck becomes vise-tight, crushing the ribbon of Atlas's necklace. I catch a reflection in the metal side of the radio above the fireplace, see my own purple face, and, above it, two strong arms, covered in blond hair, and the face of—

"*Gideon*," I wheeze as my head swims. "*Please . . .*"

Beneath the shawl, my hand meets with something hard.

Those shoes are more dangerous than dragonfire.

I grip my fingers round it and ram the heel into Gideon's cheek. He screams and lets go, and I fall forward onto the rug, choking on air.

Help! I call, but no sound comes out.

Gideon staggers toward me, a deep, bloody hole under his left eye. I lunge for the poker by the fireplace.

"Somebody help!" I manage to shout.

I gasp as he comes toward me, his face contorted, and presses his stomach up against the poker. He seizes the metal rod in both hands and flings it against the wall. I realize with a jolt that the Guardians are all patrolling the North Wing, where the ballroom and the guest suites are. I scrabble backward, burning my elbows on the rug, but he grabs me by the throat and lifts me to my feet—and the common room fills with light.

"You bastard!" Marquis charges at Gideon and aims a blow at his head that knocks him to the floor.

I fall to the ground again, my head spinning, and then Karim is behind me, grasping me under the arms and pulling me to my feet.

Marquis and Gideon roll across the floor, and as Gideon's head hits the edge of the fireplace, his hand finds a log. He raises it above Marquis's head in a shower of wood and ashes, but I kick it from his hand and he lets out a scream.

"What's going on?" Sophie flies into the room, followed by Dodie and Katherine. Marquis has Gideon in a chokehold, his head in the cold ash.

"If the fire was lit, I think I'd burn your face off," Marquis snarls.

"Marquis, let him go," Sophie says sharply.

"He just tried to kill Viv!" Marquis shouts. His hands tighten round Gideon's neck.

"Well, he's outnumbered now." Serena is perched on the side of an armchair with her hair in a silk wrap, looking vaguely amused. Behind her, Katherine stares at the scene in horror, something silver glinting in her hand.

I rub my throat and look around. Everyone's here except Atlas. Karim goes to Marquis's side, whispering something in his ear, and reluctantly he lets go.

"Are you all right?" Marquis says, striding toward me.

He's wearing nothing but a pair of striped pajama bottoms and there's a long, bloody scratch across his face.

"I'm fine," I say.

I raise my hands to my neck, but he bats them away to look at it.

Serena rolls her eyes. "She'll survive, I'm sure—"

"Nobody asked you," Marquis says. He rounds on Gideon, who is still lying with his head in the grate.

"Get up," he spits.

Gideon staggers to his feet, his neck sporting the same red welts I can feel rising on my own and his nose pouring with blood. His left eye is swollen and closed.

"Explain yourself."

The room falls silent as we stare at Gideon. His jaw tremors, and when he speaks, his voice is barely a whisper.

"I can't go back."

"Back where?"

"To my old life." Gideon shakes his head. "I have to win my category, and she's . . ."

He casts a disgusted look in my direction.

"Your fiercest competition," Sophie finishes bitterly.

Of course she's understood Gideon's motives before the rest of us have. Sophie the mathematician, always calculating the potential possibilities before they've happened. Did she even sleep at all? Or did she lie awake, waiting for someone to start a murder spree?

"You tried to *kill* Viv because you're scared she'll crack the code before you do?" Marquis says in disbelief.

Why didn't it occur to me before? Why did I think we'd all just wake up in the morning and carry on as usual, when Wyvernmire has just told us that we must either be rivals or be ruined?

"Katherine," I say slowly, "what's in your hand?"

Katherine hesitates, then opens a trembling fist to reveal a short, thin knife.

"Were you planning on killing me, too?" I spit.

"No," Katherine replies. She looks at Gideon. "But I knew I might need a means of self-defense."

God, I really am naive.

The door creaks open and Atlas walks in, still dressed in his suit. He hasn't been to bed.

"And where the fuck were you?" Marquis says.

His accusatory glare is like ice. Atlas takes one look at the knife in Katherine's hand and the blotches across my neck and launches toward her, grabbing her arm and twisting the weapon from her grip.

The room erupts into shouts as Serena jumps in front of Katherine and Marquis pulls Atlas away.

"Back off, you idiot!" Serena shouts. "She's not your girlfriend's attempted murderer—*he* is."

I tense at the word *girlfriend* and see Sophie raise an eyebrow. As Serena points toward Gideon, he backs away slowly, holding his arms out in front of him.

"Too late to play the knight in shining armor," Marquis mutters, shoving Atlas toward me.

"He tried to kill you?" Atlas breathes heavily.

"He's drunk," I say. "Not thinking straight."

I don't know why I'm defending Gideon, except that I know desperation when I see it. I, too, have done desperate things.

"Does anyone else intend to attempt murder tonight?" Serena sighs as she plucks a cigarette from Gideon's breast pocket.

The room is quiet except for his sobbing.

"In that case, I suggest we all go back to bed."

Nobody moves.

"Go!" she shrieks.

Dodie and Sophie spring toward the dormitory and I wonder if Serena's drunk or just disturbed by tonight's events. She eyes me lazily as she lights her cigarette, then follows.

"You'll sleep here," Marquis snarls at Gideon, pointing to the rug.

Atlas moves closer to me. "Lock your door," he whispers in my ear as we walk out into the hallway. "And take this." He slips Katherine's knife into my hand.

"The girls aren't going to hurt me," I protest, but he grips my elbow urgently.

"No?" he says. He eyes Katherine through the doorway to the girls' dormitory as she climbs into bed. "Then why did she sleep with a weapon? I bet she's got more stashed somewhere."

"Like she said," I say as I spin round to face him, "self-defense. At least she had the sense to realize she might be in danger."

Atlas glares at me. "Maybe that only occurred to her because she plans on committing the same crime she wants to protect herself against."

"And where were you, might I ask?" I whisper, my hand on the doorknob.

"Visiting the chapel," he says quickly.

There's a chapel at Bletchley?

I reach up on tiptoes as if I'm about to kiss him, and he doesn't pull away.

My lips brush against his ear. "Lying is a sin, *Father.*"

I lock the door on his stunned face and sleep with the knife beneath my pillow.

SIXTEEN

In my dreams, Guardians of Peace pull Ursa from Mama's embrace as she begs a cognac-drinking dragon to read her research proposal. Atlas presses me against a giant egg, his lips on mine. "Hollingsworth said I'll pass my Examination if I kiss you," he whispers. Hands slide round my neck and when I look up, the face hovering above me is Sophie's.

I wake with a start. The siren is droning and Katherine lets out a disgruntled groan. I sit up and feel for the knife under my pillow. It's still there, and we're all still alive.

Silver linings.

I dress quickly and traipse across the frozen forest floor to the glasshouse alone, glancing over my shoulder every few minutes. The wind is picking up, moving the treetops and blowing my hair round my face.

"Morning, Soresten," I say to the Sand Dragon on guard outside the glasshouse.

He bows his head in response. "Good morning, recruit."

He's a warm tawny color with a long snout and fine-tendriled whiskers. His eyes are set so wide apart I'm not exactly sure where he's looking. I think of the book I was reading before I found my invitation to the ball, then glance around. No one else is out here.

"Soresten, do you mind me asking where you come from?"

The dragon blinks. "Lyme Regis," he replies. "I was hatched on the Blue Lias rocks in 1813."

Lyme Regis is on the Jurassic Coast in Dorset, where hundreds of dragon fossils are found each year.

"And Addax," I say hesitantly. "She's also a Sand Dragon, isn't she? Does she come from there, too?"

"Of course," Soresten replies. His voice is gentle, almost soft. "Our mother hatched her several years later, but on Rùm that time, as there is less human disturbance there."

Soresten and Addax are siblings, just like Rhydderch and Muirgen. So they *do* come from the same region.

"My maxim," he continues, "reflects an encounter we had back then with a group of local humans who thought they might be able to catch and tame one of us dragonlings."

"What is it?" I ask politely.

Soresten's chest seems to inflate. "*Nullam dominum nisi arenam et mare.* No master but sand and sea."

"That's beautiful. And the encounter with those humans? How did that end?"

"My mother ate them," Soresten replies. "One could resolve one's problems rather quickly, you see, before the Peace Agreement."

I nod, speechless, and pull the door to the glasshouse open. Soresten is still monologuing about relations between dragons and humans when I step into the warm, pulling off my gloves to stretch my cold-bitten fingers. Behind a wall of foliage created by Dr. Seymour's ever-growing plant collection, she's talking to someone.

"I have experience in these matters, as you know. The Freikorps posted me to the dragon battle behavior regiment during my time in Germany."

My stomach drops. It's Ralph. What's he doing here?

"I have a degree in Dragon Behavior and Biology, Guardian 707," Dr. Seymour says, "and another in Firedrake Fight or Flight Theory. And, in case you weren't aware, the latest version of the loquisonus machine is *my* invention."

I peer through the leaves. Dr. Seymour is standing at the make-shift coffee-making station, washing up yesterday's dirty mugs. Ralph is sitting on the plush sofa, his gun slung lazily across his knees.

"Of course, how could I forget Dolores Seymour's brilliant career?" he mocks. "How many men did you invite into your bed to get here?"

There's the tinkling of smashing china in the sink. Dr. Seymour's shoulders tense as she turns round slowly, her lip curling in disgust.

"Tell me, 707, why it is that you're here at dawn, begging for my job, when we both know you're too much of a liability for the Prime Minister to ever trust you with *any* of her combat strategies, least of all this one?"

Ralph jumps to his feet, seizing his gun, and I open the door to the glasshouse and slam it, hard.

"Morning, Dr. Seymour," I call airily. "Is there any coffee ready?"

"Vivien?" Dr. Seymour says. I can hear the relief in her voice. "Guardian 707 is here to give us a bit of extra . . . assistance."

I step through the leaves.

"I heard you were almost murdered last night," Ralph jeers. He stares at my healed arm. "Don't you seem to be in the wars?"

"Not as much as you," I mutter quietly, eyeing the cut on his nose.

How did word of Gideon's attack get around so quickly?

"That idiot went to Ravensloe in the middle of the night and told him what he'd done," Ralph says. "Said that you have *rebel leanings* and should be removed from the program." He takes a step toward me. "Is that true?"

I stare up at him, trying to ignore the fear palpitating in my heart. The memory of the pain of my arm snapping still takes my breath away.

"Gideon is a frightened little boy who feels threatened by the intelligence of the women he finds himself surrounded by." I look from Ralph to Dr. Seymour. "We've met his kind before."

The corners of Dr. Seymour's mouth twitch. The door swings open again and Gideon walks in, followed by Sophie and Katherine. He takes one look at us and bows his head, then sits down in front of a loquisonus machine. There's a bandage round his head, holding a piece of gauze to the wound beneath his eye. *He's* the one who should be removed from the program for trying to kill another recruit. If he's still here, then Ravensloe must be getting desperate.

I take a seat opposite him and pretend to be engrossed in my logbook. My throat aches. The bruises on my neck look worse this morning, but I've concealed them by turning up the collar of my jacket. I hide my face behind my hair and stare at Gideon, at his red cheeks and freckled nose. Physically, he's stronger than I would have given him credit for. But I know that mentally he's barely keeping it together. Last night was his own stupid attempt at surviving. Did he plan on killing Katherine and Sophie after he got rid of me?

Sophie.

She's talking in a low voice to Katherine, both of them casting nervous glances at Gideon. If I crack the dragon code, I'll be leaving her behind. She doesn't know it's my fault she's here in the first place. Is this the world's way of telling me that it's too late to make up for what I did in the summer? Is Atlas's God up there laughing at me for thinking I could somehow avoid the consequences of that one reckless choice?

I slam my logbook shut, but Gideon doesn't even look up. If I decipher echolocation, Sophie will spend her life at Granger's Prison and Gideon and Katherine will go back to whatever hell Wyvernmire plucked them from. If I don't, my family and I will die and Ursa will be orphaned. Whatever happens, I'll have lost something I can never get back.

"I need a break," I call across the room.

I don't wait for a reply. I grab my coat and shrug it on as I walk back to the manor. I find a bathroom, splash my face with cold water, and pull my collar down. My neck is a bluish purple, with half-moon nail marks tracked across the skin. Will Gideon try to kill me again?

I wander through the corridors, walking in circles as last night's events flash through my mind. What if I crack the code and win my category, but Marquis loses his? The thought fills me with dread. Is there no way to convince Wyvernmire to let us all go home, as long as we give her what she wants?

"Featherswallow!"

I spin round. Atlas's head is poking out from a doorway beneath the staircase.

"Why aren't you on shift?" he hisses across the entrance hall.

"I stepped out," I say. "The atmosphere in the glasshouse is . . . strained."

"I wonder why," he replies darkly.

He gestures to me and I glance around for any Guardians before crossing the hall and slipping through the door beside him. We're standing at the top of a narrow staircase that leads down into a poorly lit basement.

"Dodie and Dr. Lumens are on a field trip," Atlas says. "He can only take us out separately now."

The air is stiflingly hot and sweat beads down his forehead.

"Look," he says, "I'm sorry I wasn't there last night when Gideon—when you—"

"It wouldn't have made any difference if you were." I smile. "Are you going to tell me what you were doing?"

He takes my hand and leads me down the stairs without a reply. The basement is huge, even bigger than the ballroom, and sectioned into different areas by the type of screens used for office cubicles. A metallic smell hits me, so strong I can almost taste it.

"Gideon told Ravensloe that I have rebel leanings," I say as I stare around at the mess of old books and scattered paperwork.

"You? Rebel leanings?" Atlas snorts. "You're the biggest rule-follower I know."

"Says the boy who won't even kiss a girl because of some *rule*."

He falls silent and I bite my tongue. Why did I have to bring up that humiliating incident again?

"What do you do down here?" I ask. "And why is it so bloody warm?"

The different sections run all the way to the other side of the room. I walk down the aisle between them, peering round each screen. Some cubicles are filled with desks and books, others with glass cases full of artifacts—a fossil, a large yellow canine, and something that looks suspiciously like dragon dung. One has a cabinet filled with row upon row of tiny wooden drawers, each with strange labels like Marigold Balm—Use For Burns. There's a box next to it with several tiny wooden dragons poking out of the top. I recognize the craftsmanship immediately, my hand rising to touch the swallow beneath my shirt.

"Where did you learn carpentry?" I ask Atlas as he follows me down the aisle.

"My dad taught me before he died."

"I'm sorry."

I pick up a dragon and pretend to study it closely, in case he needs time to compose himself. But when I turn to face him again, he's looking at me intently.

"You're holding that little piece of wood in your hand almost as lovingly as you do all those books you read."

"I'm admiring a miniature masterpiece!" I retort.

Atlas smiles. "So am I."

The air is suddenly so hot I can barely breathe. I put the dragon down.

"Don't say things like that," I say bluntly. "Not if you can't act on them."

His eyes drop to the floor. "You're right. Sorry."

I keep walking. As I near the opposite side of the room, the metallic smell gets stronger.

"What *is* that?" I say, covering my mouth and nose.

Atlas has stopped inside another cubicle and is shoveling coal into one of several small coal-burners. He's rolled up the sleeves of his shirt and the dark hair of his forearms glistens with the humidity. My neck prickles with heat, and I pull off my jacket and tie my hair up. I keep walking until I reach the final cubicle that spans the whole width of the room. A platform has been mounted across it, covered in grass and rocks and sand. It looks like someone has dumped the contents of a beach here. Scattered across the sand are several mounds of dried ferns, feathers, and some loose bits of charred gray coal.

"Atlas," I call over my shoulder. "What's this—"

Something moves inside one of the mounds. I take a step backward. Is it a rat? The ferns shake vigorously, sending feathers flying into the air. It's too big to be a rodent. The movement stops and a long green tail pokes out of the mound. I turn to look at Atlas as he comes up behind.

"I hope that's not what I think it is."

He doesn't joke or say something clever. His face is sober and unsmiling. The tail disappears and a small snout takes its place. The dragonling creeps toward me with its belly to the floor. Spikes run along the length of its back, and when it lifts its head to sniff the air, I see two horns protruding from under its chin. I stare, barely daring to breathe. This Western Drake is only a few days old.

"That shouldn't be here," I say, my voice shaking.

Atlas lifts the lid off a barrel and reaches inside. The smell fills my nostrils, overpowering. The barrel is full of raw meat. He throws a piece onto the platform and the dragonling lets out a squawk and pounces on it, its wings lifting it momentarily into the air. Two more dragonlings appear out of nowhere and jump onto the first one, shrieking as they fight over the piece of meat.

"Why not?" Atlas says.

Is he really asking that question? I stare at him as he tosses more meat, cut up into chunks, and then some tiny stones that the dragonlings lick up off the floor. He opens one of the burners and shovels a spadeful of hot coal onto the platform. The first dragonling sniffs it once, then collapses onto the smoking heap and curls up, resting its snout beneath its wing.

I crouch down to look at it. I've never seen one this small. Its scales are as tiny as fingernails, shimmering with different shades of green and blue and brown as if they haven't yet decided what color they'll be. The horns beneath its chin means it's a male. Where did he come from and where are his parents? The other two snap at one another, their pronged red tongues slick with blood.

"Are they orphans?" I ask.

Atlas shrugs. "Doubt it."

I feel my face flush with anger. "If they're not orphans, then were they stolen?"

"Wyvernmire had them delivered last night by someone attending the ball," Atlas says. His eyes darken as he watches the coals smolder, white-hot, beneath the body of the sleeping dragonling. "I was here settling them in when Gideon attacked you."

"Who delivered them?"

Could it have been the German Secretary of Defense, or Lord Rushby, or that Bulgarian prince?

Atlas just shrugs again.

"You seem . . . unconcerned," I say.

"Doesn't matter what I think," he replies callously. "If these dragonlings help Wyvernmire win the war, then who cares where they're from?"

I suck in a breath through my teeth.

"But who do they belong to?" I ask. "Rebel dragons?"

Atlas nods once. "Taken from some nests in Scotland before the rebels drove the army out."

241

"They'll come looking for them," I say. "The parents."

"Perhaps." His indifference is unnerving.

"What are you going to do with them?" I ask.

"Gain their trust," Atlas says. "Study them and record how fast they grow."

"But they won't grow!" I explode. "Not the way they're supposed to. This isn't their natural habitat, for one, and dragonlings need their parents to learn how to fly, to breathe fire, to speak! Surely you haven't agreed to this?"

When he looks at me, his gaze is cold.

"Do you think I have a choice? We have to win the war, don't we? Isn't that what *you've* agreed to?" He shakes his head and slams the door to the coal-burner closed. "You'll crack the code and give it to Wyvernmire. And for what? So she can fly like a dragon, hunt like a dragon, talk like a dragon? Why do you think she wants to do those things? It's so she can control them, so she can control us!"

So he doesn't agree with all this. He's just trying to provoke me, to get me to admit that Wyvernmire isn't who I thought she was.

"You shouldn't have shown me this," I say bitterly.

Atlas stands up straighter. "Why not? It's made you angry, just like I thought it would."

"Oh, so I'm one of your experiments, too, am I?" I say furiously. "Tell me, Atlas, was my reaction to your satisfaction? Does my anger meet your expectations?"

"Featherswallow," he says, "you knew what we were doing down here, didn't you? My category's called Zoology, dammit!"

"I didn't expect Wyvernmire to have you doing things that go against the Peace Agreement," I hiss.

"The bloody Peace Agreement again," he says, folding his arms across his chest. "Was finding out that Wyvernmire feeds children to dragons not enough for you? Here you are, blaming me because you can't bear the thought that you were wrong about *her*. That your whole life has been built on a false belief system."

I let out a hollow laugh. "A false belief system? That's hilarious coming from someone whose faith is as prehistoric as the dragons he studies. You stand there, acting all pious, but you go around breaking Guardian's noses and . . . and—"

"And what?"

I dare myself to say it. "I saw the way you looked at me when I wore that dress. You're a hotheaded, impulsive hypocrite!"

The silence between us burns.

He looks at me out of the corner of his eye. "If I was as impulsive as you say, Featherswallow, I'd have kissed you ten times already."

I freeze, swallowing my next retort. I feel so furious I could breathe fire. But to my utter disgust, something inside me softens.

"And now that you mention it," he says, "I've always thought of my faith as dragonlike. Thanks for reminding me."

"You . . . I . . . You're not making sense," I splutter.

He shakes his head and wipes his brow with the sleeve of his shirt. "You're right," he says. "I *am* hotheaded, angry—livid, actually. And I'm glad you are, too. Honestly, sometimes I feel like nothing gets to you. You're always so . . . unreadable."

I take a deep breath. "Unreadable?"

I all but begged you to kiss me yesterday. How more readable can a girl get?

"Last night someone tried to kill you and you barely said a word."

I let out a nervous laugh.

"And when Ralph broke your arm I don't think I even saw you cry."

I shrug, remembering the sound of bone snapping.

"I should have known it would take something like dragons to get you fired up."

He's right about that. Taking dragonlings from their parents goes against everything the Peace Agreement is supposed to stand for. Against the whole reason we're fighting this war in the first place.

"What do you mean," I say softly, "about your faith being dragonlike?"

Atlas clears his throat awkwardly. "It feels . . . prehistoric sometimes. It's resilient, like dragons are, and people are often scared of it." His hand slides into his pocket, and I know he's feeling for his prayer beads. "But somehow it's always been there, even when I've tried to cast it aside. And then there's my church back in Bristol. It's got spires like horns and stones like scales, and inside there's this burning sacred heart . . ."

I run my finger along the scaly head of the sleeping dragonling as Atlas's cheeks turn pink.

"It's all part of some older creation, one that most people have moved on from. I *know* that—I'm not blind. And yet here I am, studying the Church *and* dragons, both dinosaurs still very much alive."

The dragonling splutters a tiny flame.

"Ow!" I wince.

The flame has burned my finger and it immediately starts to blister. The two other dragonlings, still playing, pause. The first cocks its head. They both turn to look at us with their bright black eyes and then they stare at each other again. One of them gives a little shiver that vibrates up its wings.

"I think they're communicating," I whisper as I crouch down.

"What?" Atlas says. "You mean . . . telepathically?"

"Sort of."

The third dragonling opens his eyes, looks at the others, then rolls over and goes back to sleep.

"The first two are closer," Atlas says, bending down beside me. "Taken from the same nest. But the other one keeps to himself."

The nest-mates peer at the sleeping dragonling, getting so close that their snouts almost touch his hide, but he doesn't stir again. I wonder if they're trying to talk to him, but surely he would react if they were? Wouldn't it be impossible to sleep if someone was speaking to you inside your own head?

"Would their nests have been close by?" I say. "In the same area?"

"Oh yeah," Atlas says. "They came from the same hatching ground in Inverness. They might even have been neighbors."

So, if the three dragonlings come from the same region and learned whatever echolocation dialect their parents spoke to them before they were hatched, surely all three should understand each other? Unless my theory is wrong and the dialects aren't regional . . .

I stare at the two nest-mates—siblings—and Mama's face flashes through my mind.

The dialects may not be regional. They could be—

Understanding dawns on me slowly, like the sun rising.

"I've got to go," I say, standing up.

"Oh . . . okay."

Atlas follows me as I stride back toward the stairs, my mind connecting the dots so fast I can barely keep up. I pass by one of the open burners and pause. Inside, nestled among the hot coals, is a dragon's egg.

Atlas's face falls. "It came with the dragonlings. I don't think it's going to hatch."

"Of course it's not," I say, my hand on the banister. "It needs something only a dragon can give."

Atlas frowns. "What's that?"

I turn round at the top of the stairs and look down at him. His shoulders are slumped and his face tight, as if simply being here weighs on his every bone.

"Echolocation," I say. "A dragonling won't hatch from its egg unless it hears its parents' calls."

And the truth, the missing piece of the puzzle, is suddenly there before my eyes. I know what Mama was trying to say before Hollingsworth cut her off. She wanted to prove that each dragon *family* speaks its own dialect. And the same is true for echolocation. The Koinamens isn't a war weapon and it's certainly not a dragon-made code. It's a language containing thousands of others, each one sacred, each one unique to a different dragon family. The reason that Soresten and Addax, and Muirgen and Rhydderch, speak their own dialects isn't because they're from the same region. It's because they're related.

The echolocation dialects aren't regional.

They're familial.

DAILY MAIL

DAUGHTERS OR DRAGONLETTES? THE RISE OF HARPENTESA AMONG THIRD CLASS GIRLS

London. Friday, December 20, 1923
BY W. H. HARRIS

A RECENT STUDY by the Academy for Draconic Linguistics shows the alarming speed at which the Third Class, particularly young girls, are acquiring Harpentesa. This dragon tongue, originating from Anglo-Frisian dialects of the West Germanic languages, developed alongside the English we speak today. East Anglia and its steel-making towns are its particular home, as men and dragons have worked there together, melting and casting metal, since the eighteenth century.

Harpentesa is the second most spoken language in East Anglia, more widespread even than its human dialects and the languages of the Fens. Unexpected, though, is the acquisition of this language by the daughters of foundry workers, who, unlike most civilized children, find themselves in close daily contact with the metallurgist dragons that inhabit their towns and villages.

Mr. Moseley, concerned owner of Moseley Iron and Steel Founders, asked me if I thought it appropriate for young girls to be able to converse with creatures of such size. Can their impressionable minds and delicate senses, he asked me, withstand corruption of such bestial nature? Indeed, many educationalists nowadays are questioning whether children, even those born to the upper classes, should be taught dragon tongues at all. Better they learn after the

Examination, if necessary for their profession, when their minds are fully formed and protected against the unrefined instincts of the more carnal members of society.

Of course, dragons hold a natural place in our world as creatures God has ordained with intelligence on a par with that of men. But have these fathers never heard of the Lyminster knucker, who dragged young maidens into its waters? Others question the intentions of the Third Class entirely—is this dragon-human integration attempt merely a reflection of the debasement of our society? Or are their motives intentionally unsavory and perhaps even rebellious?

One must ask: What possible good can come from daughters who converse with dragons?

SEVENTEEN

Back in the glasshouse, Ralph is waiting for me.

"What took you so long?" he barks.

"Burned myself on the hot water in the bathroom and had to go to the sanatorium," I say, holding up my red finger with a sigh.

I take my seat and pull the loquisonus machine toward me. All this time, I've been talking about echolocation as if it's just one singular language that varies slightly according to the region. How can I—a translator—have been so blind? Humans have languages, dialects, and even particular ways of speaking among families: their own accents, words, inside jokes. Why wouldn't dragons—who only developed spoken language because of humans—be the same?

Mama wanted to prove that, like human languages, dragon tongues include dialects. And now it's up to me to prove the same of echolocation, of the Koinamens. It's a language full of family dialects that are not only used to communicate and to hunt, but that have the power to heal, to make dragonlings grow inside their eggs. . . .

Dragons may have only learned to speak orally due to the presence of humans, but language has been woven into their very being since the beginning of time.

"Vivien, a Guardian of Peace just delivered this for you," Dr.

Seymour says. "He claims to have come all the way from London."

I see Sophie flinch at the mention of home. Dr. Seymour glances nervously at Ralph and hands me a parcel. I peer at the words stamped on the back and almost recoil in shock: Academy for Draconic Linguistics.

Did Hollingsworth grant my request?

"Recruits are forbidden from using the postal system, as you well know!" Ralph spits.

"But this was sent by car—"

He snatches the parcel from me and tears it open as everyone stares.

"Dolores, I'll be reporting you for enabling disobedience in your recruits."

Dr. Seymour pales. Beneath the parcel wrapping is a thick pile of bound papers.

"This has been sent to me by Dr. Hollingsworth, the Chancellor of the Academy for Draconic Linguistics, to help me with my research," I say calmly. "Special permission was granted by Prime Minister Wyvernmire, who needed our work in the glasshouse completed yesterday. You can check with her, of course, but I'm not sure she'd appreciate your meddling."

If Ralph sees through my lie, he doesn't show it. He flicks through Mama's research proposal before handing it back to me, visibly annoyed that there's nothing to suggest that I should be excluded from the DDAD on the spot. Dr. Seymour gives me a perplexed glance. I'll explain things to her later, when Ralph isn't around.

Gideon has buried his face in his hands. What will happen to him if I decipher echolocation before he does? I don't want to think about it and I can't afford to. But part of me still hopes that if I can give Wyvernmire the so-called code she desperately wants, maybe I'll be able to negotiate everyone's release.

I look down at the research paper in my hands.

"The Evolution of Dragon Tongues: A Case for Familial Dialects."

My heart flutters as I race through the abstract, hearing Mama's voice in the words she has written. Every thought is carefully presented and meticulously backed up with a study or a citation, and for a second it feels like she's with me. It would be evident to anyone reading this that the author genuinely cares about the welfare of dragons and their place in society. The realization hits me like a ton of bricks. Whatever reason Mama had for joining the rebels, it must have been a good one.

When Gideon goes out for a cigarette break, I listen to some of yesterday's recordings. All this time, we've been adding calls to the indexing system as if they belong to one single language, when in reality they could belong to any one of the family dialects that exist. Soresten used the more simple, universal echolocation calls to talk to Muirgen, but a family dialect to talk to his sister Addax. But why would Soresten go through the trouble of speaking in dialect to Addax if she, too, understands the universal echolocation language he used with Muirgen?

I already know the answer to that question. It's the same reason I speak to Mama in Bulgarian, and not English. Because it's the language I know her through, the one we learned to love each other in. To speak to her in a different one would feel wrong. I lean back in my chair. If I can prove my theory that Muirgen and Rhydderch speak a version of echolocation different to the one Soresten and Addax speak, then I'll be able to take my breakthrough to Wyvernmire.

Dr. Seymour steps outside with Ralph, and I hear her threatening to make a formal complaint if he doesn't let her do her job. Katherine is tapping her fingers nervously on the table, watching me with tired, bloodshot eyes. I do my best to give her a reassuring smile as Sophie appears beside me.

"You're on speaking terms with the Chancellor of the Academy?" she hisses.

"I ran into her at the ball," I reply.

"See?" Katherine tells Sophie darkly. "I told you."

Sophie frowns.

"Told her what?" I say.

"That you're cheating." I'm surprised at the venom in Katherine's usually cheerful voice. "You're using your Second Class status to grovel for help."

I raise an eyebrow and put the headphones on. "That's ridiculous," I say as clicks fill my ears.

I check the loquisonus machine, surprised. I haven't selected a recording yet, but the calls are definitely playing. That means they're happening now. I glance up through the roof, but there's no sign of a dragon in the patches of the sky I can see through the tree branches. Maybe it's Soresten communicating with the dragon due to take over his shift. I write down the calls I can identify, scrawling them across a page of the logbook as they come. It seems to be just one dragon, speaking alone and receiving no response. Some of the calls I don't recognize and I have to reach for the index cards to see if they've previously been recorded. I take notes as fast as I can as the calls become quicker and more erratic, writing down any possible translations.

Pitch-type3 (girl)
Pitch-type4 (female)
Trill-type15 (human)
UNKNOWN CALL
Trill-type15 (human)
Pitch-type3 (girl)

Trill-type15 (human)
Pitch-type4 (female)
UNKNOWN CALL
Trill-type15 (human)
UNKNOWN CALL
Pitch-type3 (girl)
UNKNOWN CALL

I've never seen echolocation used like this before. The dragon seems to be reciting a sequence of words that have no connection to one another. And it's constantly repeating itself. The last call, the one I don't recognize, is similar to Echo-576, which in the indexing system means *break* or *betray*. But it's different, shorter and louder than Echo-576. And, I realize, it's followed by a quiet whistle, so fast it's barely audible. Sophie suggested what it could mean last week: a quiet whistle at the end of a call could denote a noun or a name for someone or something. I decide to go with the closest translation I have.

"Someone who breaks or betrays," I mutter to myself. I go to the cupboard for a dictionary and rifle through the pages until I land on the word I want.

betrayal noun *DECEPTION, corruption, infraction, misdeed, break, delinquency, crime.*

I underline the word that seems to sum up all the others: *crime*. I could be wrong, but I can always go back and pick another definition later.

Sound fills my ears again. The calls have changed now. There are two new ones, repeating one after the other in a constant alternation. The first is a friendly trill I recognize, and there are several different meanings for it in the index system. Trill-type93 has been translated several times as a verb: *to slide* or *slither*. But I've also heard it used by patrol dragons to mean *snake*. I search for a translation for the second call, a Sweep-type3. It's been defined on an index card to signify something new, like a new human or a new patrol.

So I have two more potential words: *snake* and *new*.

This makes no sense, but the *snake new* pattern continues, as persistent as it is confusing. I rub my eyes, staring unseeingly at the word *snake* in the dictionary. I should probably give up on this call and move on to testing my dialect theory. But what if this is a rebel communication? I can't just pretend I haven't heard it. Out of boredom more than anything else, I flick back through the dictionary until I find the definition of the word *new*. I know that in Wyrmerian, the translation—*fersc*—is only used in relation to offspring. A young hatchling, or a human baby, can be *fersc*, for example, but a new building, or a young plant, or a newcomer cannot.

I sigh. What if *new* isn't the right word at all? What if the index card is wrong and the calls all mean something else? I read back through my logbook, looking for an account of the use of Sweep-type3, but there's nothing there.

Gideon's still outside smoking, talking to Dr. Seymour. I can hear his low voice and Dr. Seymour's consoling one. Quickly, I reach for the other logbook, the one Gideon has been using. There it is, a mention of the Sweep-type3 from four months ago in handwriting I don't recognize. But it's been translated not as *new*, like in earlier entries, but as *first*. So could it be a mistranslation? I stare at the word *first*.

It was used between three dragons discussing a first flight, in a recording dated 1 September.

I put the words together with the others I managed to translate, discarding *female*, which seems to be a synonym.

> *Human.*
> *Girl.*
> *Crime.*
> *Snake.*
> *First.*

Human girl who committed a crime? A shiver runs down my spine. That could be said of most of the female recruits, but . . . Suddenly I'm rem embering the words uttered by a voice that set my hair on end.

Do you have a blade, human girl? We both know we cannot count on your teeth.

I seize the dictionary and find the word *first*.

> **first** ordinal number *Coming before all others in time or order; earliest; initial; original; basic*
> OR
> *Before doing something else; first and foremost; in the first place; now*
> OR

The first occurrence of something notable; novelty; new experience; maiden voyage

I feel a jolt of recognition. I take a pencil and circle the first word of the last synonym. Then, barely breathing, I amend my list.

Human.
Girl.
Crime.
Snake.
Maiden.

I've heard those words together before.
Snake Maiden? That's what it means in English, doesn't it?
Chumana.
Chumana is at Bletchley Park, calling to the human girl who committed a crime.
Chumana is calling to me.

EIGHTEEN

I wait for the lunchtime lull to steal a loquisonus machine. At the end of the shift, Sophie seems to want to say something to me, but decides against it, following Dr. Seymour and the others to lunch. Only Soresten is left guarding the glasshouse and he barely glances at me as I walk past the spot where he's basking in a patch of sun.

"I'm taking this for maintenance," I say, shifting the bag onto my shoulder.

Soresten lifts his head as if to sniff it and my heart flutters. It's unlikely he could guess what it's for, but the trumpet-shaped speaker sticking out of the top of the bag hints that it's something used for listening. Still, it's a risk I'm willing to take.

I stumble into the thick forest of trees. What if I'm too late and Chumana is gone? How long has she been calling for me? What if one of the patrol dragons heard her calls and decides to investigate?

I pull the loquisonus machine out and turn it on, listening as I walk deeper. I hear nothing but the occasional ranging call. If I'm outside the blocking range created by Dr. Seymour's rubber sonar blockers, that means I can emit calls through the loquisonus machine. What if I play Chumana's calls back to her? She'll know it's me, and follow the sound until she finds me. It's dangerous, of course. One of the patrol dragons could hear, and then witness me speaking the Koinamens through a machine in the forest.

Do you have a better idea?

I kneel at the foot of a tree and set the loquisonus machine on the hard ground. I take off my gloves, pull the headphones out of the machine, and flick the switch from *input* to *output*. I've never done this before. I don't think even Dr. Seymour has, either. The point of the machine isn't to play back entire recorded calls, but snippets of them, the different calls cut up and stuck together again to say whatever it is we want to say. But there's no time for that.

I press *play* on Chumana's recording.

I can't hear the calls as the loquisonus machine is converting them back to their original frequency. But I can tell they're playing, thanks to a tiny flashing green light. What have I done? I cast a nervous look up at the sky. Any minute now, Muirgen or Yndrir or Soresten are going to swoop down on me and demand to know how and why I'm using their secret ultrasonic language, and then they'll report to their Queen and she'll abandon Wyvernmire and we'll lose the war—

"You dare play that abomination to me, human girl?"

I spin round. A huge pink dragon approaches. How does she tread so quietly with feet the size of boulders? She peers at me with those amber eyes ringed with white circles, and nods her head toward me in greeting.

"Chumana," I breathe. "You came."

Her left shoulder is caked in blood, which oozes from a wound so deep I can see the white glint of bone.

"*You* came," she says in Slavidraneishá.

"You called to me, didn't you?" I say. I glance at the loquisonus machine.

"Yes. I had to use all manner of calls, as I did not know which ones you would recognize." She growls again.

"How did you know I was listening to echolocation?"

"I know a lot about what occurs inside the glasshouse," Chumana replies.

What? But how?

"What are you doing here?" I ask. "You should be in hiding, somewhere far away where Queen Ignacia can't find you."

Chumana lets out a laugh. "I am the least of Ignacia's worries." Her tail twitches. "We cannot stay here. The patrol dragons are on their way—I can hear them calling to each other."

Panic rises in me. Playing Chumana's calls back was a stupid idea. I can't let them find me here.

"Well, come along!" Chumana says, nodding toward her back. "Just like last time."

I hesitate. "No offense, but I don't think either of us is too keen on the idea of me riding you."

Chumana snarls. "Riding is for horses. I am permitting you to take refuge on my back. Now hurry up before I change my mind."

I stuff the loquisonus machine back into the bag. Then I walk round to her side, just like I did in the library, and lay a hand on the base of her spine. Chumana smells different, I realize as I climb. She smells of fresh air and pine trees and warm blood.

"What happened to your shoulder?" I ask.

"It is a mere battle wound," she replies.

I don't ask Chumana what battle she was fighting in. I reach the spot between her wings where the detonator used to be. The scar is neat and smooth.

"Hold on to something," she murmurs.

Then, before I can prepare myself, we lift into the air. The wind steals my shocked gasp, and the bases of Chumana's wings move so vigorously beneath my thighs that I fall forward, clutching on to whatever scale I can find. I press my face to her hide as I cling on for dear life, not daring to move as I feel us rise, the air growing colder around us. I can hear nothing, nothing but rushing wind and the whooshing of wings. My eyes are screwed tightly shut, the loquisonus machine dangling precariously from my shoulder. I open them and peer over Chumana's wing.

The forest is below me, the tops of the pines a sea of green and brown. There's no sign of the glasshouse, perfectly hidden as it is, but beyond the forest is Bletchley Park, the manor as much of a hodge-podge as it looks from below, surrounded by black cars and tiny white Guardians. And dragons. I see them everywhere, patrolling by the lake, perched on top of the manor, and as distant shapes in the sky. Chumana sees them, too, and I scream as she swoops sideways, tilting us at an angle that almost dislodges my feet from their foothold between spikes and scales. We plunge downward, hurtling like a missile toward the ground, and the wind slips between our bodies and almost lifts me from her back, the speed of it stealing the breath from me.

Chumana's giant feet land almost softly in the grass, but the impact still reverberates through her body with a jolt that sends me flying to the ground. I gasp as the air is knocked from my lungs and stare up at her from the grass. Her lips stretch into a grin that reveals pointed yellow teeth.

"I do hope your machine is not broken," she says.

I sit up and pull the loquisonus machine toward me. It seems to have survived the crash landing, thank goodness.

"Where are we?" I ask.

We've landed in a dip in the ground, like a deep ditch. The sides are so steep that I can't see over the top.

"Beyond the forest," Chumana says, pressing a nose to her wound. "An unused field."

It's the first time I've been out of Bletchley since I stepped off that train. The thought occurs to me immediately, of course.

You could go home.

But go home to what? Ursa has been taken by the government and my parents are still at Highfall. If I leave Bletchley, my one chance at saving them will be gone. And besides, I can't go without Marquis.

I stare around at the ditch. The earth is scorched and there's a pile of bones in one corner, as well as a skull that looks like it may have belonged to an unfortunate cow. There's a huge imprint in the ground to the left side, the shape of a heavy body. And a giant papery dragon skin, dead and dry.

"How long have you been sleeping here?" I ask Chumana.

"Several days."

"But why? I thought you escaped after you set fire to Wyvern-mire's office. I expected you to get as far away as possible—"

"Oh, I did," Chumana replies. "But I had to come back."

"You had to come to Bletchley Park specifically?" I say, rolling my eyes.

What does she want?

"I must speak with you."

Her huge head looms above me, the air from her nostrils hot on my face. I stare into her eyes and see my face reflected back in them. She lets out a puff of smoke and shoots a disgusted look at the loquisonus machine.

"Do you have any idea of what you're doing by meddling in affairs that are not your own?"

"How do you know what this is?" I say. "How did you know you could contact me through echolocation—"

"That is not what it is called!" Chumana roars.

I stumble backward as she stamps and the ground shakes beneath us.

"I know," I say, holding up my hands. "I'm sorry. It's the Koinamens. Right?"

Curiosity burns in her eyes. "How do you know its true name?" she snarls.

"It's complicated," I say.

She stares at me and I glare back.

"Earlier, you said you had to use all manner of calls to contact me," I say. "So . . . does each dragon have their own recognizable calls? Did you call to me using the universal calls, instead of . . ."

I trail off as Chumana gives me a long, calculating look.

"If you think I'm going to aid you in the obliteration of my entire species," she says, "you are mistaken."

"The obliteration of your species?" I say. "What are you talking about?"

"I have come to tell you to stop what you're doing in the glasshouse," Chumana says. "The rebels know all about it, and it's only a matter of time before Queen Ignacia learns of it, too."

So Chumana never went into hiding. She's with the Coalition. And if she knows what we're doing with the loquisonus machines, that means someone in the glasshouse must be a rebel spy. The truth hits me as fast as the sea fills sand.

Dr. Seymour.

Her dracovol mail had nothing to do with Ravensloe or her research. She's communicating with the Human-Dragon Coalition.

"Tell me?" I say, unable to keep the indignation out of my voice. "I'm working for Prime Minister Wyvernmire, who has the entire British Army at her command. You can't tell me anything."

"Ah yes, the woman who is threatening to kill your entire family." Chumana sneers. "I didn't know you were such a coward, human girl."

"I'm not," I spit. "I don't have a choice. I'm doing what I'm doing in the glasshouse to save them."

"Do you have *any* idea of the harm you are causing?" Chumana says.

"I'm just doing what I'm told," I reply. "Why would it be so bad if humans spoke the Koinamens? We already speak dragon tongue."

"Because the Koinamens is not part of human nature," Chumana hisses. "That is why you have to resort to using that unnatural, human-made tongue, distorting the sound of my calls and divorcing them from their true essence."

Her eyes land on the loquisonus machine again.

"I know it's not," I say quietly. "I know it can do things that other languages can't. It can heal, and it can make dragonlings grow . . ."

"Which dragon gave you this knowledge?" Chumana says.

"No one. I figured it out for myself. I know the Koinamens isn't a code, and it's not a weapon. You were born with it. It's part of you. And different dragons speak different versions of it, like . . . dialects," I say slowly.

Chumana lets out a deep growl.

"I'm right, aren't I?" I say. And Mama was right, too.

"You are dealing with something that is beyond your

comprehension," Chumana says. "You give our calls names, just like you attempt to categorize the differences in our outward appearances, yet you do not understand how each one fits together to make a whole."

"But I *want* to understand, to know the ways dragons converse—"

"The Koinamens is not *meant* for conversation—we have tongues for that. Yet you continue to probe it in the hope that it is subject to some grammatical rule, because then you might bend it to your will! What you do not see is that while the Koinamens says less than other languages, it *means* more. It is deeper than intellect, faster than light. It is a mother's whisper inside her dragonling's mind, to bring him comfort while he awaits her return to the nest. Tell me, human girl: Can the meaning of a handshake be translated? A child's laugh? A dying breath?"

I stare at a blade of trampled grass. How can a language be faster than light?

"Do you know why the Coalition opposes the Peace Agreement?" Chumana says.

"They think it's corrupt," I say. "They think it ostracizes dragons and oppresses the Third Class."

"And do you believe that?"

I think of the children on Canna, of the ban on dragon tongues, of the dead Third Class girl.

"I think the Peace Agreement was intended for good," I say feebly.

"Many a nation exists without a Peace Agreement, human girl," Chumana says. "But ours? It has reduced dragons to tolerated subcitizens and enabled a class system that suppresses some of the worthiest of your kind simply because of their economic situation. It is a facade, one that allows Prime Minister Wyvernmire to grant favors to her friends and keep the power within her own circle."

"And Queen Ignacia?" I say. "Didn't she sign the Peace Agreement herself?"

"She is just as corrupt," Chumana hisses.

"But what do the rebels suggest?" I say. "Without a Peace Agreement, dragons and humans will fight for land, for resources, and there'll be another war—"

"A different Peace Agreement," Chumana says. "One written by the public, with no hidden clauses or built-in class systems."

I shake my head. "I have no interest in political debates—"

"Only because you are privileged enough not to be concerned by them."

"The sole reason I'm here is to save my parents and—"

"Your parents are truer than you are—"

"My parents are as good as dead!" I shout at the dragon. "Unless I tell Wyvernmire that the dragon code is not a code, but a language with dialects, familial dialects—"

Chumana lets out a deafening roar.

"You play with dragon secrets hidden from humans since the beginning of time! What do you think your Prime Minister will do once she has the ability to imitate the dragons' Koinamens? Will she use it to lure and entrap our family members? Will she kidnap eggs and raise her own army of enslaved dragons? Or will she murder a generation of dragonlings before they are hatched, using the calls that only a desperate mother would send to her own egg?"

I stutter and Chumana laughs a low, dangerous laugh.

"Of course you didn't know that the Koinamens can kill, just as it can heal and grow. You know nothing of its intricacies, nothing of its ancestral power, nothing of the danger it poses in the wrong hands."

"I'm sorry, Chumana," I say. I walk over to the loquisonus machine and pick it up. "But if I don't give Wyvernmire what she wants, my family will die."

"Give it to her and she will win the war," Chumana growls. "Do you really think she'll release your rebel parents after that? Do you think she will let them live? You are on the wrong side of history, human girl."

"My sister," I say, "is innocent. And if my parents die she'll need me even more. This is the only way."

"You would choose your sister over the entire dragon race? Over your fellow humans who are treated no better than animals simply for being born Third Class?"

"I would," I say. "That probably makes me a terrible person. But trust me, that's not news to me."

There's a long pause, silent except for the annoying chirping of a bird. Then Chumana speaks again.

"Dragons are skin-shedders," she says. "Do you know why that matters?"

I glance at the dead skin on the ground and shake my head.

"Every time we shed, we leave an old self behind. Every time we shed, it is a chance to be someone new. A chance to change our minds."

"How convenient for you," I reply dryly.

Her wound is bleeding again, blood dripping down her front leg in a river of red.

"I could heal it, you know," I say. "None of the dragons around here will do it for you, a rebel, but I could record some healing calls.

I could—"

"I would rather die," Chumana snarls.

I nod and start the climb up the side of the ditch.

"I could kill you, human girl," Chumana whispers as I reach the top. "I could burn you to ash where you stand. Better still, I could eat your flesh and hide your bones among the others."

My blood runs cold, but I meet her eyes.

"Why don't you?" I ask. "Kill me, destroy the loquisonus machine, and everyone will think I ran away with it. My parents will be executed, of course, so you'd essentially be sentencing members of your own side to death, but what's two more human deaths if you're already willing to cause one? And here I was thinking the rebels believe humans and dragons are one big happy family."

Her lips pull back slowly to reveal long canines.

"Someone requested I keep my teeth to myself. Otherwise, human girl, you might already be rotting at my feet."

NINETEEN

By the time I get back to Bletchley Park my hands are numb with cold. All I want is to curl up by the fire and fall asleep, but instead I take the loquisonus machine to the glasshouse. Dr. Seymour is in there, her head in a book. She snaps it closed when I walk in.

"Where have you been? Soresten said you'd taken the loquisonus machine for maintenance." She lets out an outraged laugh. "Do you have any idea of the risk you posed to the program today? I've covered for you once, Vivien, but I won't do it again—"

"It's me who's covering for you currently," I say.

Dr. Seymour takes a step backward. "I beg your pardon?"

"I know you're a spy," I say. "That's where I've been today. With one of your *colleagues*."

I spit out the last word and Dr. Seymour pales.

"Chumana?"

I nod.

She closes her eyes. "It's true. The Coalition must have sent Chumana after they received my last message—"

"What was in the message?" I say coldly. "The exact location of Bletchley Park?"

"Don't be silly. They already know that," Dr. Seymour replies. She looks up at the trees around us. "I told them that you were making too much progress, despite the fact that you're trying to hide it from me, and that you'll soon be speaking echolocation yourself."

I falter in surprise. "So you told them to send Chumana to see if she could convince me to stop?" I say, trying to hide my shock. "How do you even know her?"

"Your encounter with the criminal dragon at the University of London didn't exactly go unnoticed by the DDAD *or* the rebels," Dr. Seymour says. "And when you freed her, she joined the Coalition."

"But . . . if you agree with Chumana that humans shouldn't know how to speak echolocation, why did you invent the loquisonus machine?"

"I invented it before I knew the damage it could cause," she says. "And I bitterly regret it."

"Yet you teach us about echolocation every day."

"I have to have a realistic cover," Dr. Seymour says.

"A cover so you can spy on us," I retort. "No wonder we hardly ever pick up rebel calls—they know not to fly over here! And now that they know where we're located, they could attack at any minute—"

"They've known where we are for months," Dr. Seymour says. "They won't attack, not yet."

"Not yet?" I choke. "If the rebels know where we are, why didn't they try to get to Wyvernmire when she was here on the night of the ball?"

"Contrary to what you've been told, the Coalition's goal isn't war, Vivien. It's change." Dr. Seymour gives me a sad look. "Are you going to report me?"

Am I going to report her? If I hand Dr. Seymour over to Ravensloe, she'll be arrested. The rebels might take that as a sign to attack and then all hell will break loose. I've made the most progress anyone has so far with echolocation, and all that's left to do now is to explain to Wyvernmire that it's not a code but a language with dialects, dialects that will need to be learned. It may not be the news she was expecting, but it's the progress she asked for. And then I'll be out of here, back with Ursa and my parents—and maybe, just maybe, everyone else will be released, too.

My eyes linger on the cupboard where I found the dracovol mail. Dr. Seymour used it to communicate with the rebels, but she also lent it to me to find out where Ursa was. Who is this woman?

"I know what's on Canna, thanks to Lord Rushby," I say. "But what's on Eigg?"

"I can't tell you that," Dr. Seymour replies.

Something important, then.

"If the rebel dragons know Bletchley Park is trying to decipher echolocation, why don't they just tell Queen Ignacia, to turn her against Wyvernmire?"

"Because we don't want a bigger war than we already have." Dr. Seymour pauses. "Why did you need your mother's research?"

"Echolocation isn't just one singular language," I say. "But you already knew that, didn't you?"

"But your mother, she—"

"She's a dragon anthropologist," I say. "She discovered that dragon tongues have dialects that aren't regional, but familial."

Dr. Seymour leans closer. "Familial?"

"Each dragon family or group speaks its own dialect. I think echolocation is the same." I pause. "Surely you know this, Dr. Seymour? Surely the Coalition's dragons have told you?"

"They won't discuss echolocation with humans, not even their fellow rebels. And they're right not to. Human nature is fickle. We change sides like we change our clothes. What you said about familial dialects . . . it reminds me of whale pods. Each pod has its own distinct calls; that's how they're able to differentiate between their own members and those of other pods."

How can Dr. Seymour be so knowledgeable and yet . . .

"You're risking everything," I say. "Your career, your research, your life. I heard Ralph the other day. Do you really want to give him the satisfaction of seeing you fired and arrested?"

"I'm risking it all for the people I love," Dr. Seymour says fiercely. "For the Third Class, for the dragons we're losing touch with. For my child." Her hands settle on her stomach and I feel my eyes grow wide. "I want them to grow up in a world that is equal. I want to repair the damage I caused. I was working at the Foreign Office in International Dragon Relations when Ravensloe invited me and my machines to Bletchley. And I accepted because I knew that I could undo some of my mistakes from the inside. The loquisonus machines—"

"Are incredible," I say softly.

"They're dangerous," Dr. Seymour says, her voice hardening. "There's a reason we don't possess the same capabilities as dragons, Vivien. We are far too evil to merit them."

"But think of the progress—a whole new language just waiting to be deciphered. It's the discovery of the century."

"But think of the cost. Did Chumana not tell you? Do you not understand why it's so crucial to the dragons—"

"I understand," I say. "And if my parents weren't at Highfall then maybe . . ." I shake my head. "It will take Wyvernmire years to learn echolocation before she can master it anyway. Maybe, by that time, someone else will be in government. Maybe the rebels will have won the war."

I don't care anymore as long as I can go home.

Dr. Seymour shakes her head bitterly, her hand still resting on her stomach.

"Wyvernmire is one secret short of making dragons subservient to humans," she says. "What do you think happened in Bulgaria? That the dragons massacred an entire population for no reason?"

My heart sinks. "The Bulgarian government discovered echolocation?"

Dr. Seymour nods and looks at the loquisonus still on my shoulder. "What we thought we discovered during the war was already known to Dr. Todorov, thanks to a machine that harnessed the piezoelectric effect of quartz crystals. It was a primitive device, far less developed than its successor—my own loquisonus machine. But it was a beginning. He called it reading the dragons' thoughts. The Bulgarian humans forced dragons into fighting rings, kidnapped their young, and used echolocation to experiment on them. They did terrible things."

"So . . . all this time you've been pretending to know less about dragon echolocation than you do? You knew, from the start, what it is?"

"Yes," Dr. Seymour says. "I've always known it's a language, one the dragons clearly value deeply."

I stare at the loquisonus machine. All along I thought it was the key to saving my family and finding Ursa, but I've been taken for a fool. "So we've just been wasting time," I say bitterly, "learning a language you already know—"

"No, Vivien," Dr. Seymour says. "You forget that I am no translator. The deciphering of echolocation, the meaning of each call, the

272

existence of these dialects . . . that was all you."

"And the previous team?" I say. "Did you recruit them just to sabotage their efforts? Where are they now, Dr. Seymour?"

She has the decency to hang her head in shame.

"The reperisonus wires weren't accidentally broken," I continue. "You cut them. All this time, you've been trying to stop us from learning the very thing you've been teaching us."

"I have," Dr. Seymour admits. "When you suggested that the dracovol was speaking to its eggs through echolocation, I was terrified. Terrified that I could no longer stop you from deciphering it, when you were realizing things it took me years to understand. Terrified that you'd give the information to Dodie or Atlas, who might in turn give Professor Lumens the key to hatching dragon eggs. You were too fast for me to keep up with. It's near impossible to sabotage the work of a skilled translator when one barely speaks the language they're translating."

"So the previous recruits . . . what happened to them?"

"They were simply sent back to the places I recruited them from."

"Are you sure about that?" I say softly.

Dr. Seymour's eyes fill with tears. "I had to keep my position as an informant here. The alternative was—"

I shake my head. I don't want to hear any more. I just want to go home.

"You should understand why I have to give the translated echolocation to Wyvernmire," I say. "You have something too precious to lose, too—"

"Your mother's entire family was murdered in Bulgaria, weren't they?"

I nod.

"If Wyvernmire learns to speak echolocation, the dragons of Britannia *will* rise up," Dr. Seymour says. "History will repeat itself." She gives me a hard, cold stare. "And then we'll both lose what we love."

At dinner, Marquis greets me with a glare.

"Where have you been all afternoon?" he says urgently. "Dr. Seymour said you were getting a machine serviced? You weren't in the workshops, so—"

"Thought you'd spend the afternoon trying to crack the code, did you?" Katherine says. She sits down opposite me, her face hardened with malice. "You weren't getting the loquisonus serviced, you were just hoarding it for yourself, and Dr. Seymour covered for you. We all know she wants you to win the category. She—"

"I had Knott fix one of the dials on it," I lie. "And then . . ."

Better to take the fall for something I didn't do rather than tell everyone I left Bletchley Park with a rebel dragon.

"And then I used it to listen to some of the patrol dragons."

"So Katherine's right," Sophie says coldly. "You wanted it for yourself, despite having had all morning to use it."

Karim passes her a plate of pie, but she doesn't move.

"Typical Viv," she says slowly. "Always intent on winning, no matter the cost to everyone else."

My face burns. I can't deny it. Instead, I pick up my fork and begin eating.

Katherine lets out a forced laugh. "From what I've heard, it's not the first time you've betrayed your own."

What's that supposed to mean?

She glares at me. "Maybe Gideon was right—"

"That's enough!" Marquis snaps.

I can sense Atlas staring at me, but I don't look at him. Now he thinks I stole the loquisonus machine to get ahead of everyone else, when just this morning we were talking about what Wyvernmire will do once she has the code. The room is silent except for the sound of our cutlery scraping against the china plates. Owen is standing by the door as usual, and I see him watching us with a frown. He's counting us. On the mantelpiece, the radio drones the news.

"The British Army suffered yet more losses this morning in an ambush that a rebel battalion seemed ominously prepared for. Now over to John Seymour, wartime correspondent. John, how is it possible that the rebels seem to know the government's every move?"

I take a sip of water and wonder how many spies like Dr. Seymour are hidden within the military.

"Where did you run off to earlier?" Atlas whispers.

Both of his hands are bandaged and smell suspiciously of marigold balm.

"I wish everyone would just stop asking me where I've been," I snap.

"Has anyone seen Dodie?" Karim says.

Atlas tears his eyes away from my face. "I saw her about an hour ago. She said she was going for a walk."

"She's never late," Karim says. "Maybe we should look for—"

An earsplitting siren fills the air. I raise my hands to my ears as a light, so bright it shines through the blackout curtains, begins to flash. Atlas and I both run to the window and wrench away the curtain.

"Oi, you can't do that!" Owen says.

Outside, Guardians are running across the courtyard toward the entrance gates, shouting to each other. A dragon circles above, but the sky is too black to make out who. Then I see it, the thing causing the chaos—a figure scaling the tall fence. Guardians run toward it, and the figure is almost at the top when—

BANG.

The figure sways for a moment, still clinging to the fence. Then it falls backward into the dark.

"Fuck," Marquis says, standing up. "Was that a gunshot?"

Serena pushes Owen out of the way as we run into the entrance hall, but the front doors are barred by more Guardians. Suddenly they burst open. A Guardian strides through with someone in his arms—long red hair, a uniform, and a pair of smashed glasses crooked on her nose . . .

The Guardian lays the broken body on the ground and Sophie lets out a scream, sinking to the floor.

"Atlas?" I say, my voice catching in my throat.

He takes my hand, pushes the others out of the way until we're standing at the front. Horror erupts from the pit of my stomach.

Lying in the middle of the hallway, blood blooming at her breast, is Dodie.

TWENTY

The world slows, then springs into movement.

"You killed her!" Atlas screams.

He charges at the Guardian who was carrying Dodie, and Marquis follows, but both of them are overpowered within seconds.

"Let them go!" I shout at the Guardians pinning them to the floor. "Haven't you done enough?"

Behind us, Sophie is sobbing over Dodie's body, shrugging off Serena's attempt to soothe her. How can someone who was moving, scaling a fence just moments ago, suddenly be so still? I stare at Dodie's body, half expecting her to stand up and smile. I resist the urge to kneel and unbutton her jacket, to see if the blood all over the floor is really coming from her. A Guardian pulls Atlas roughly to his feet, and when I catch a glimpse of his face it's wet with tears. Gideon and Karim are frozen, stricken with panic, and when more Guardians burst into the hall and lift their guns, they raise their hands.

"You killed our friend," Atlas stutters, his face crumpling in disbelief.

I go to him, ignoring the Guardian holding his hands behind his back, and wrap my arms round him.

"Friend?" says a loud voice.

I turn round. Ravensloe is walking down one of the staircases. His eyes harden as he takes in the scene, flicking over Dodie's still body. "This girl was not your friend. Just look at yourselves." He reaches the bottom step and gestures around. "Just look at where you are. This is not some sort of privileged boarding school. You are not here to make *friends*. You're criminals. And you're here to pay for your crimes."

I see Marquis's lip curl as he struggles against the Guardian holding him.

"Tonight Dodie decided to abandon her duties," Ravensloe says quietly. "She was offered a second chance and she refused it. She has paid for her ungratefulness with her life."

"You didn't give her a choice!" Marquis shouts. "You gave her an impossible task and told her that even if she succeeded Atlas would fail."

Atlas lets out a choked cry and I hold on to him, glaring at the Guardian behind him until he looks away.

"This won't stand," Serena tells Ravensloe in a quivering voice. "The First Class won't—I won't—"

"You, Serena Serpentine, should consider yourself lucky you're here at all," Ravensloe says with a sneer. He nods at a Guardian, who steps forward and pulls Sophie away from Dodie's body.

"Let go of me, you bastard!" she screams.

Katherine moves to defend her, but a Guardian blocks her path, lifting his visor. It's Ralph. A wave of hatred courses through me.

"You are to forget any ideas of friendship," Ravensloe says. "You are all here for one sole purpose, a purpose you have so far failed to fulfill. Let Dodie be an example to those entertaining any ideas of shirking their responsibility or submitting to cowardice."

"The only coward here is you," I spit.

The words come out of my mouth before I can stop them and Ralph's lips spread into a delighted grin. Ravensloe's eyes narrow as they settle on me.

"Now seems like a wise time to remind you that if you test me, you *will* be demoted and replaced," he snarls.

As if you have time to teach a new person echolocation, I want to say. Would Ravensloe really risk losing us all now? Or is this demotion talk just an empty threat to scare us into submission?

"Some of you," Ravensloe says as he stares at Atlas, "are closer to demotion than others."

"Demote me, then," Atlas snarls. "Or, better, kill me like you just killed Dodie. Except you can't do that now, can you? If you murder both your Zoology recruits, who is going to grow you an army of dragons?"

Ravensloe's face turns purple as he stares round at the ten Guardians who have just heard information supposed to be kept classified by the Official Secrets Act. My heart thumps in my chest and cold sweat runs down my back. I look up into Atlas's face and he gives me a calm smile.

"Put him in isolation," Ravensloe barks. "The rest of you, to your dormitories."

"Isolation, again?" I say as the Guardians pull Atlas toward the front door and someone jerks me sharply away.

"Atlas!" I call. "Where are they taking you?" But he's already being dragged across the courtyard.

"Lock your door, Featherswallow!" I hear him shout.

The other recruits are already walking up the stairs, Sophie supported by Serena. Marquis waits for me, tears streaming down his face. We follow the others and I feel Ravensloe's eyes on our backs.

Dodie is *dead*. The finality of the word sends my mind reeling. All I can think about is that I will be, too, if I don't give Wyvernmire the code. And so will Marquis if he doesn't figure out how to finish building Knott's plane. I feel nauseous, and the feeling worsens when Katherine's sobbing drifts out onto the landing. Marquis glances over my shoulder into the girls' dormitory.

"Listen, Viv," he says, "you can't trust anyone anymore."

"I know," I say hoarsely.

"Seeing someone die can do crazy things to a person. What just happened . . . it's a reality check for everyone. And Sophie and Katherine can't afford for you to crack the code."

I stare at him. Sophie wouldn't try to kill me. *Would she?*

"You be careful, too," I whisper. "Karim . . ."

"Isn't a threat," Marquis says firmly.

"You barely know him!" I retort. "And Wyvernmire has his parents. She said so."

"He won't hurt me," Marquis repeats.

"But what if he does?" I say. "What if he feels he has no other choice?"

"Then I'll—"

He stops and we both look away. What was he about to say? That he'd kill his boyfriend if it came to it?

I let out a shaky breath. "Who even are we, Marquis?"

He shakes his head. "Two kids with a family to save, that's who. Have you still got that knife Atlas gave you?"

I nod. "It's under my pillow."

"Good," Marquis says. "Signal if you need me."

"Be careful," I whisper.

In the dormitory, we undress in silence. I glance at Sophie, but she shakes her head at me, her eyes swollen from crying. I climb into bed and prop my pillows up, to give me a better view of the room. When I slip the knife out from under my pillow, I find the handkerchief Dodie made me with it. I hold them both tightly in my hand. I always saw Dodie as shy. Gentle. Soft. When really she was brave. She refused to be here anymore, refused to compete with Atlas, refused to work with those kidnapped dragonlings.

Yeah, and look where her bravery got her.

The room doesn't fill with the sound of sleeping breaths like it usually does, and I lie awake for hours, wondering how many of the girls around me believe I might try to sneak up on them in the night. There are Guardian voices outside, still full of urgency and adrenaline, their boots crunching across the gravel. What will they do with Dodie's body? My eyes are heavy and I squeeze the handle of the knife in an attempt to stay awake, staring at the still shapes of the others in their beds.

No one's coming to kill you, Viv.

But how do you know? I argue with myself. *What if someone else here has a reason even bigger than mine for cracking the code? What if they, too, have a family and a sister to lose?*

In the early hours of the morning, as my eyes give way to sleep, I hear two sounds. The whirring of a helicopter and the loud roars of several dragons. They're not calling, or warning or announcing, I decide as my mind drifts. They're commemorating. The roaring is for Dodie, the most dragon-hearted of us all.

We work the morning shift in silence, except for Dr. Seymour's sniffling and the wailing of the wind outside. I ask her where

Dodie's body is and where Atlas has been taken, but she shakes her head and presses a finger to her lips. Are we being listened to? All she'll say is that Wyvernmire is back, that she arrived by helicopter last night.

I stare at the loquisonus machine for hours. Gideon is currently looking for similarities between echolocation and French while Katherine works on her theory that the calls within echolocation structures are strategically placed according to which species of dragon is being addressed. It's so pointless I almost feel sorry for them. Now that I know about the dialects, I know that each one will have to be studied and compared in order to determine which calls are unique to them, and which are used universally by all dragons. It's no longer a case of cracking one code, of learning one language.

We have to learn hundreds.

It will be months, perhaps years, before Wyvernmire has a team of fluent translators. She might never even get the opportunity to use the dragons' Koinamens against them. I feel a sense of relief— maybe what I'm doing isn't as terrible as Chumana and Dr. Seymour think.

I take a large gulp of coffee. The siren rang this morning just after I fell asleep, and my eyes feel like they're full of sand. I think of Dodie and of how desperate she must have felt to scale that fence. The memory of her body falling from the top makes me shiver.

I write down the basics of what I know.

Echolocation is a universal language used by all dragons.
Different dragon groups speak different familial dialects of echolocation.
Possible familial dialects present for study at Bletchley Park:

Dialect A: Muirgen and Rhydderch
Dialect B: Soresten and Addax.

~~Echolocation can heal, grow, and kill. Without it, eggs cannot hatch.~~

No.

I draw a line through the last two sentences. That's a secret I won't give Wyvernmire. I'm not going to let her experiment on innocent dragonlings, no matter how good it might be for the war effort.

But if you don't tell Atlas, those eggs will never hatch and he'll fail his category.

Dread fills my stomach and I feel a sudden yearning for his touch. How must he be feeling, locked up in isolation with nothing to do but relive Dodie's last moments? I think of the tenderness with which he fastened the wooden swallow round my neck, the tears on his face as I held him last night. For all his rebelliousness, Atlas is gentle and good. Will Bletchley Park break him, like it broke Dodie?

I stare back down at my writing and a hot feeling comes over me. The skin on the back of my neck begins to prickle. I've done it, I realize. This is the progress Wyvernmire asked for. Three months was never enough, but thanks to me we know that the key to deciphering echolocation is to learn its dialects.

And I've already started doing that.

When the shift is over, I walk through the empty hallways. Bletchley seems quieter than usual and I wonder where all the Guardians are.

"Marquis?"

He's sitting on one of the tables in the dimly lit seminar room we were brought to when we first arrived.

"What are you doing in the dark all alone?"

He gives me a solemn look. "Ravensloe didn't like you two standing up to him. And Knott keeps threatening Karim with demotion for *lack of contribution*. He's too petrified to share any of his ideas, especially now he knows what will happen to me if he wins."

"You told him you're facing the death penalty?"

"I wish I never had," Marquis says miserably.

"Something happened today—"

"I've got to tell you something, Viv."

We both speak at the same time.

Marquis swivels round to face me. I'm about to tell him that I've done it. The thing I was brought here to do. I've cracked the code, or at least uncovered the key to learning echolocation. He pauses, studying my face, and I realize he looks afraid.

"What?" I say quietly. "Oh God. What have you done?"

"I can't do this anymore," he says, his voice barely a whisper.

"Do what?" I say. "Build planes?"

"I can't work for Wyvernmire. I can't be on her side."

"Marquis, what do you mean? You're not on a side. You're here to save our parents."

"I am on a side, and so are you! We've got to stop acting like we have no responsibility in this. I'm here building planes for the woman who is threatening to execute our parents. The woman who would rather go to war than change the corrupt Peace Agreement. Who had Dodie killed!"

"*Ravensloe* had Dodie killed," I say.

But suddenly all I can think of is what Chumana said to me.

You are on the wrong side of history, human girl.

"What if this whole thing is bigger than saving our family?"

Marquis says. "What if we can save them *and* help the rebels win?"

I shake my head. "If we don't give Wyvernmire what she wants, we'll never see them again. We have too much at stake to be helping anyone but ourselves."

"And then what?" Marquis says. "We go back to the Class System, the Examination, to treating dragons like fourth-class citizens?"

"We go back to peace—"

"What peace, Viv?" he shouts. "We're at war!"

I glare at him. "Wyvernmire will end the war. But the rebels will prolong it for years, trying to get what they want. And if we help them we'll lose everything we're fighting for."

"The rebels are fighting for the people they love, too, Viv." The look he gives me makes me want to cry. "Why save Ursa just to send her back to a life where she could be demoted for failing her schoolwork, where we could lose her overnight—" His voice breaks.

I remember the silver batons and what Sophie told me about how Nicolas died, about the lack of food and medicine.

"I want to help the Third Class, Marquis. And I wish there were dragons on every street corner, just like when our parents were young. But I can't offer Mama and Dad and Uncle Thomas up as a sacrifice to achieve that. I love them too much—"

"And you think I don't?" Marquis says. Tears stream down his face. "But how can we choose a good life for ourselves and not for everyone else?"

I shake my head. It sounds so evil, what I'm suggesting we do, but I don't have another answer. When I think of Ursa and of my parents, fire fills my bones. I am incapable of *not* choosing them. Slowly, Marquis rolls up his sleeves to reveal the scars on his arm.

"What are you doing?"

"Don't you think it's cruel that these scars were given to a child simply because he sometimes failed to follow a set of arbitrary rules?" he says. "How many do *you* have, Viv? Seven? Eight?"

I clutch my own arm. "You're being difficult—"

"Our parents were so terrified of us ending up Third Class," he says. "I like to think they're ashamed of it now."

I lean back against a desk. Where is this conversation going?

"What about Atlas?" Marquis says, his voice harder now. "Did you think you'd both win your categories and run off into the sunset?"

"Stop it," I say sharply. "Don't try to use him against me."

Marquis doesn't roll down his sleeve. "Let's pretend the rebels have won. There's no Peace Agreement, Class System, or Examination. People can live, work, and buy where and what they want. Everyone's equal, right?"

I stare at him. "I suppose, yes—"

"Wrong. You still have your parents' house in Fitzrovia, which you and Ursa will inherit when they die. But your boyfriend? He owns no property because his parents and grandparents were all Third Class until now." He runs a finger down his arm, caressing the white welts on the skin. "He's not as educated as you because his Third Class schools had no allocated resources, so he'll always be picked last for any job he applies for. He has no impressive professional experience because his parents couldn't afford to buy him apprenticeships every summer."

"Stop," I say, heat rising in my cheeks. "I see what you're getting at."

"He has no family to rely on because his mother couldn't afford to feed him *and* the baby in her belly."

I suddenly feel sick. When did Atlas tell him this?

"And then there's the fact that he isn't white."

"Serena isn't white—"

"Serena is First Class, with a dragon-descended name that gets the color of her skin overlooked. It's different for Atlas."

I stare out the window.

"You're right that what the rebels are trying to achieve will take years, because inequality is so deeply entrenched in the foundations of our society that it's going to need to be dug out, rock by prejudiced rock."

He pulls the sleeve down over his scars. "You and Atlas won't be treated as equal, even after the Class System is abolished. That's why we need to act *now*, not when we're cozied up back home. As for the dragons? Since the massacre in Bulgaria, everyone has been terrified of them. They've lost their positions in society and are only tolerated because of their sheer power. Imagine a Fitzrovia where humans and dragons walk London together, where you and Sheba from the bank can actually have a conversation, where the library dragon isn't a prisoner."

I'm suddenly reminded of our childhood during the Great War, when humans and dragons fought together, when the dragon stationed outside our bunker would blow smoke rings to make us laugh.

"Peace isn't peace if it's only given to some," Marquis says. "And I know you know it."

His audacity stops me in my tracks and for a second I *almost* feel proud . . . but I shake the feeling away.

"Did Karim get you into this?" I say quietly. "Or have you been a rebel just as long as our parents have?"

Marquis rolls his eyes. "Do you hear yourself? Stop trying to blame someone else and for once just *listen*."

But I don't need to listen. I already know that what my cousin is saying is true. That what Chumana told me is true. How many times have I imagined, alone in my bed at night, what it might be like to know Atlas outside Bletchley? I want to laugh at myself now. Did I think I'd win the war and then be free to have a relationship with a Third Class boy? Everything about our society is designed to keep us separate. But no matter the truth, it all comes back to one thing.

"I refuse to live without Ursa," I say. "And if I don't give up the code, that's what will happen—if Wyvernmire doesn't decide to have me executed first."

"You want Ursa back, but you don't want to give her any sort of world to come back to," Marquis says. "Well, fine. Go home to your big house in Fitzrovia, where Ursa will get the switch whenever her school performance is anything but outstanding. Better that than be demoted, right?" He glares at me. "But after this is over, I'm going with Karim. I'm going to help the Third Class, the dragons, the—"

"The rebels," I finish for him.

He nods.

"You know both you and Karim can't walk out of here together," I say softly. "Think logically. You can't win against her—you can only help her."

We stare at each other and I feel a sharp pain in my chest, one that takes my breath away.

"Our parents are part of the Coalition," he says. "Do you really think this is what they'd want us to do? Help destroy the cause they were willing to give their lives for? If they were here now, what do you think they'd say?"

Get out of London, Mama told me. She knew all along how dangerous Wyvernmire is.

"The rebels will never win, Marquis. Wyvernmire has an entire army at her command."

"And what if I told you that they *can* win? What if joining the Coalition is *how* we save our family?"

I smile sadly. "You always were a dreamer," I say. "But it's time to be realistic, cousin."

He seems to deflate, as if the last spark of hope in him has suddenly been extinguished by my words.

"There won't be an after for you." My voice quivers as Marquis stands up and walks toward the door. "Not for you and not for Karim. Not if you don't help Wyvernmire win. She'll crush the rebels eventually—it's only a matter of time. And we need to make sure that we—and Ursa—survive."

He gives me a look of deep disgust.

"You know what your problem is, Viv? You're too much of a coward to put your neck on the line. You'd rather continue in your destructive ways than change them. You're just like her."

My eyes fill with hot tears, but I wait as my cousin stares at me, trying to figure out what happened to us. It's only when he's gone, the door slamming behind him, that I let the tears fall. I drop into a chair and weep like a child. I want to call to him to come back, to beg him not to leave me.

Marquis is right. I am a coward. But the prospect of living without my parents, without Ursa, is something I can't let myself imagine. Either I save our family by giving Wyvernmire the code, or I lose them forever. I stand up and wipe my eyes. Maybe I was born bad, or maybe badness takes root once it's been planted and just keeps on growing. I've been making selfish decisions to get what I want since last summer. And now it's just part of who I am. How do you change who you are?

And in the face of all those selfish decisions, what's one more?

PARLIAMENT OF BEATRICE

HANSARD'S
PARLIAMENTARY DEBATES
THIRTY-SECOND PARLIAMENT
OF GREAT BRITANNIA
1922–1923
HOUSE OF LORDS

21 December 1923

EARL of PEMBROKE: *My Lords, in Public Affairs the subject that naturally occupies first place today is the issue of dragon rights, which one is never permitted to forget due to the relentless campaigning of the Human-Dragon Coalition. Their radical position, which permeates London and society at large, is what brings me to the proposal I present to you this morning. Mr. Speaker, while the Human-Dragon Coalition drags our United Kingdom through a series of violent protests, debates, dragonfires, and now war, we, the Humanist Party, are ambitious for the revival of our nation.*

Under Her Majesty's Peace Agreement, it is illegal to kill a dragon. They hunt at will in the fields and forests of Britannia, and when the year's yield is poor, we provide them with our own livestock for consumption. They have a dedicated island for hatching purposes and their own paths through the sky. They fly freely over our cities, hold careers to which they are suited, such as manual labor and glass-making. We purchase from them fire and flint, and in return tax their wealth at only a slightly higher percentage than we tax Britannia's men.

And yet they want more. They accuse us of driving them from their former places of work, and I quote the speakers of the Human-Dragon Coalition here, in the arts, the universities, medicine, and law. They complain that we tax their hoards, which contain gold mined by men and not seen since the reign of King Richard the Lionheart! They claim we make no space for them in our cities, and blame us—us, gentlemen!—for the rising disappearance of their young. They even go so far as to suggest that they are being exploited on the black market, which we know is only used by immoral members of the Third Class.

Tell me, My Lords, do you see any dragons in the House today? No? Is this not because they have a nature different to that of us men, one that yearns for the outdoors, for the great expanse of the natural world, and not the confines of Parliament's walls? Is it really we who have shunned the dragons, or did they not choose to leave?

The emergence of the Human-Dragon Coalition, mere decades after the Massacre of Bulgaria, has shown us just how dangerous, how gluttonous dragons are. Surely it is only the presence of our armies and planes that have kept their gigantesque power in check. Would you feel comfortable sending your sons to be educated by a dragon who has a taste for human blood? How many of you feel concern when letting your small daughters stroll through the park, with only their nursemaids *for protection? Think of your wives, My Lords! We have all heard the distasteful yet true stories of dragon bulls seducing women. My proposal is this: the permanent segregation of humans and dragons.*

What do dragons bring to society that men do not? Who should come first, My Lords? The honorable gentlemen and ladies of Britannia, set on this earth by the hand of God? Or wild beasts? As the scripture says: "Be fruitful, and multiply, and replenish the earth, and subdue it: and have dominion over the fish of the sea, and over the fowl of the air, and over every living thing that moveth upon the earth."

TWENTY-ONE

I find Wyvernmire's office by returning to the hallway with the giant egg statue. It feels like years since I was racing Atlas down to the bottom in heels. I slip through the door behind the egg and into a short, narrow corridor. There's another door at the end. Is this where Atlas comes to spy on the Prime Minister? I gather myself, feeling the tears dry on my face. I meant what I said to Marquis—it's time to be realistic. It's time to give Wyvernmire the code.

I knock.

"Yes?"

The room is large and brightly lit. A fire is burning in the grate and Wyvernmire's briefcase sits neatly on an armchair in front of it. On the coffee table is a chessboard, each piece a different species of dragon carved from marble. The woman herself is sitting behind a wide desk, a soft expression of surprise on her face.

"Vivien," she says smoothly. "How lovely to see you here."

I clear my throat. "Good afternoon, Prime Minister. How was your . . . flight?"

"Rather tumultuous with all this wind," she says, her mouth turning up into a lipsticked smile.

You should try riding a dragon in it.

Wyvernmire looks back down to the paper she's reading and

adds a note with her pen. "To what do I owe the pleasure, Vivien?"

I take a step forward.

Careful, a voice inside my head says.

I stop.

Don't lay all your cards on the table straightaway.

Dad's voice.

"I came to inform you of my progress," I say. "In the glasshouse."

The Prime Minister drops her pen and looks up.

"Come and sit down," she says immediately, gesturing to the chair on the other side of the desk. "What have you discovered?"

I sit down on the hard chair and run a finger across the claw-shaped arms. I feel her gaze on me, expectant.

"Why do you call it a dragon code?" I ask. "When you know that it's a language? That's why you recruited me, a polyglot, isn't it? To learn the language?"

She smiles. "What a wise question. We weren't sure what it was to begin with. And echolocation certainly doesn't behave like any languages we know."

"But you've known for a while that it *is* a language," I insist. "Because Dr. Hollingsworth told you so. That's why you sent *her* to my house to recruit me, and not Dolores Seymour."

Wyvernmire raises an eyebrow.

"Only someone fluent in a language is qualified to vouch for another person's fluency," I say. "Just because someone can attempt some convincing Wyrmerian sentences doesn't mean they have the correct accent, the understanding of the nuances and implications linked to the culture of that language. There was no way Dolores Seymour could have judged my mastery of dragon tongues when she doesn't speak any herself."

Does Wyvernmire know that Hollingsworth sent me my mother's work?

"The Bulgarians referred to it as a code, so that is how it became known," Wyvernmire says.

"The Bulgarians?" I say.

I'm not going to let her know that Dr. Seymour told me about the Bulgarian humans' study of echolocation, the one that got them all murdered. My guess is that she was never supposed to reveal that particular knowledge to her recruits.

"I'm afraid it was their great progress in learning echolocation that drove their fellow countrydragons to massacre them," Wyvernmire says. She watches me closely and I try to feign surprise. "Hence why we are so very careful about keeping your work in the glasshouse a secret."

"But *you* know echolocation is a language that comes as naturally to the dragons as breathing. So why do you still call it a code? Is it to make it sound more dangerous?"

"It might as well be a code, seeing how far we are from understanding it," Wyvernmire says coldly, her peaceful demeanor suddenly gone. "Now, are you here to tell me that might have changed?"

"I'm starting to understand its . . . variations," I say. "But it's going to take longer to learn than we thought. It's not just learning one language. It's more like learning several."

"There are several echolocation languages?" Wyvernmire says.

"I believe so, yes."

"And how different are they from each other?" She sits back in her chair, her forehead suddenly creased.

I pause. If I tell her, then there's no going back.

"Well?" she says. "Are they as different as French and Dutch?"

"No," I say quickly. "They're similar. They all stem from one universal language, like . . ."

"Yes?"

"Like dialects."

Wyvernmire stands up and begins pacing the floor.

"Hollingsworth, Seymour, they must have known this—"

"No!" I say. "They didn't. I only discovered it because my mother was studying dragon dialects related to spoken tongues, and I realized echolocation could work similarly."

"We don't have time to learn several echolocation dialects."

"Prime Minister," I say, "you have the entire Academy for Draconic Linguistics at your disposal. If you recruit some of its linguists, I'm sure they'll decipher the dialects in no time."

Wyvernmire shakes her head. Two bright red splotches have appeared on the soft skin of her neck.

"Three months was never going to be enough," I say. "But five years could be—"

"Five years?" Wyvernmire spins round to face me, her expression dark with fury. "We barely have five days."

Five days?

"The situation has become urgent," Wyvernmire says. "An increasing number of Queen Ignacia's dragons are abandoning her to join the rebellion. I have already made contact with Borislav."

"Borislav? The Bulgarian dragon I translated for?"

"Any good leader has a contingency plan, Vivien. And when the last team failed to crack the code, or indeed provide me with any progress to build up our defense and win the war I knew was coming, I decided that depending entirely on human effort was unwise."

I listen to the quiet ticking of the clock, trying to remember anything from that conversation with the dragon.

Tell Wyvernmire that the dragons of Bulgaria agree.

My breath catches in my throat. I shake my head, hardly believing what I'm hearing.

"You've allied with Bulgaria," I say slowly. "You're going to betray Queen Ignacia, aren't you?"

"Yes," Wyvernmire says without hesitation. "Unless one of you recruits can translate echolocation, build me a squadron fit for fighting dragons, or find a way to breed the blighters themselves, I will be forced to confirm my alliance with Bulgaria in five days' time." She sighs. "It wasn't my preferred plan of action, but you have left me no choice—"

"You're going to get us all killed!" I shout, jumping up from my chair. "Queen Ignacia will want revenge—she'll take out the whole country! It will be worse than this war and the one before it."

"Not with the Bulgarian dragons on our side," Wyvernmire says.

I remember it, then. That turquoise line of ink across Dad's globe, the one linking Britannia to Bulgaria, marked with Wyvernmire's crest. My parents knew all along.

I stare at Wyvernmire.

How did I ever admire this woman?

"On your side?" I say. "The Bulgarian dragons have no respect for humans—as soon as you've given them what they want, they'll eradicate the British people, just like they did in Bulgaria."

"You're wrong," Wyvernmire replies. "Bulgaria was always a threat, of course, even before the massacre. Simply due to the sheer size of its Bolgorith dragons. That is why Britannia always sought to have the upper hand, to be well versed in Bulgaria's dragon tongues, to have ambassadors of both species on its soil. And, in the end, we made sure those dragons were in our debt."

"You mean they're only willing to help you because they owe you a favor?" I splutter. "All this time, you've been waiting for the Peace Agreement to be broken, haven't you? Your agreement with Queen Ignacia was only temporary, to help you fight the rebels until the bigger, better Bulgarian dragons came along."

My head spins with the madness of it all.

"You must have promised them something," I say. "Bulgarian dragons don't give a damn about debt. What could you possibly have promised them to make them ally with you?"

"I'm a politician with over twenty years' experience negotiating with dragons. You leave that side of the business to me. Please compose yourself, and tell me how many of these dialects you can speak so far. What do you need in order to help you learn faster? Name it, and you shall have it."

I laugh. "Of course you're dependent on a criminal teenager, because no one at the Academy will help you, will they? They all know, of course, all those experts in dragon tongues, about echolocation. And none of them will touch it with a barge pole, not even Hollingsworth herself, because they know what happened when the Bulgarian humans did. So am I really the only polyglot you've got?"

I see a flicker of fear in the Prime Minister's eyes.

"My mother ran for her life when the Bulgarian dragons torched her village," I say. "She watched her mother and her uncle and her cousins be eaten. It was a miracle she made it out of Bulgaria alive. They'll do the same to your people, rebels and loyalists alike. But you don't care about them, do you?" I collapse back into my chair and glare at her. "You haven't even said Dodie's name."

"Dodie's story is tragic, I'll agree with you there. But she broke her end of the deal by trying to escape. My Guardians did what was necessary."

"Killing a defenseless girl is never necessary."

"Oh, Vivien," says Wyvernmire with a sigh. "You are trying to be honorable. I admire that, truly I do. But the truth is you're like me. You do what's best for *you*."

I shake my head. "The only reason I'm here is to save my family. I don't care what happens to me anymore."

"Oh, but you do," Wyvernmire says softly. "Of course you *want* to save your family. But you also *want* to be the girl who cracks the dragon code." She lets out a throaty laugh. "Doing what is necessary to achieve your ambitions is not an unknown concept to you, is it?"

My face begins to burn as a knowing smile creeps across Wyvernmire's face.

"You've done it once before, with your friend Sophie."

My throat tightens.

"Oh yes, I know all about that." She speaks slowly, her eyes locked on mine. "I got my information from that teacher who was so desperate for a place for her daughter at the University of London. Tell me, Vivien. Can you still replicate Sophie's handwriting?"

The room spins round me and I feel my entire soul burn with shame.

"If you hadn't done what you did, Sophie would be studying at the University of London with you, instead of that teacher's daughter."

I blink away the threat of more tears. I know more than Wyvernmire does how a split-second decision can alter a life forever. How, somehow, it's always those we love most that we end up hurting.

"It's okay," Wyvernmire soothes. "You did what you needed to do. To get a place at university. To work in Dragon Tongues. To guarantee yourself a high-paying job before the census of your graduation year." The Prime Minister's voice is sweet now, almost maternal. "And look at you now. What will you do once you've cracked the dragon code? You could take a job at the Academy for Draconic Linguistics, of course, the youngest person ever to do so. But why stop there? Why not build a bigger, better loquisonus machine than Dr. Seymour could even begin to envision? Why not spend a lifetime reading dragons' minds?"

Wyvernmire leans forward. "You are like me, Vivien. You are like the Dragon Queen. Ruthlessly ambitious."

I feel like I've been punched in the gut.

"But I don't want to be," I croak.

"You don't have a choice. This is who you are," Wyvernmire says. "So own it."

The light catches the talon-shaped brooch on the Prime Minister's chest. Has she really stood face-to-face with Queen Ignacia? If she has, then she must know that the trinket she wears is a poor imitation of the talons of a Western Drake.

"Is it true that you feed criminal children to the dragons?" I say. "Is that what you've promised the Bulgarian dragons? People to eat?"

"Politics always requires a forfeit of some sort," Wyvernmire says quietly. "And criminals choose to be criminals, do they not? Therefore they must accept the consequences of their actions."

The familiar words drive my brain into dizziness.

"You're everything the rebels say you are," I spit. "All you see is what people can or cannot *do*, instead of who they *are*."

"And what of you, Vivien Featherswallow? Teacher's pet, star pupil, always simpering and desperate to please. Your whole life has been built on what you can do. So much so that you have no idea who you are."

I reel backward as if I've been slapped and Wyvernmire's mouth twists into a tight-lipped smile.

"Now tell me about the dialects."

I stand up and take a step backward. The only dialect I can grasp some meaning of so far is the one used by Rhydderch and Muirgen.

"I don't understand any of them yet," I lie. "I need more time. If you could just give us all some more time—"

"Five days," Wyvernmire interjects. She picks up her pen and turns her eyes back to her paper, suddenly bored of me. "That's all I can give you. In the meantime, I must make a short trip to London. One dialect is all I'll ask of you. Give me one, and you'll have won your category."

"And what about the other recruits?" I say. "If I give you a dialect, will you pardon them, too?"

"Don't be ridiculous," she snaps. "The rules apply to all. Besides, any progress they make will only be a bonus now. It is the echolocation I need. Only echolocation might make me reconsider this alliance. So don't leave it too long, Vivien." I watch as she begins to write in purple ink. "Bulgaria is only a short flight away."

Christmas Eve creeps into the common room by way of a wonky tree, begrudgingly set up by one of the staff. I sink into an armchair, my head throbbing from another day learning Rhydderch and Muirgen's dialect. The house is quiet, and I wonder how many of the

Guardians have been allowed to return home to spend Christmas with their families.

Music is playing on the radio and the fire is piled high with logs, throwing off heat. Outside, snow is falling. Marquis is engrossed in a game of chess with Katherine, his sketchbook sticking out of his pocket. Everyone else is watching, or reading or talking quietly. Nobody is in a festive mood and Dodie's absence fills the room. All I can think of is how there are now only three days left until the Bulgarian dragons get here, unless I tell Wyvernmire everything I know.

Atlas slides onto the sofa beside me. His notes have become more frequent since he was released from isolation the night of my meeting with Wyvernmire. Scraps of paper have appeared in between the pages of my library books, in the pocket of my jacket, and even beneath my dinner plate. I find myself answering them with embarrassing enthusiasm, hesitating for hours over each word.

"What do you usually do for Christmas with your family?" Atlas asks me, reaching over to pull a pine needle from my hair.

I feel a twinge in my chest. Ursa will be spending Christmas with strangers. Will they even buy her a gift?

"We eat and drink and play games," I say, forcing myself to sound cheerful. "Roast goose and Mama's sauerkraut, sherry and charades. Just the six of us." I glance over at Marquis, who has just surrendered his king to Katherine. "And you?"

"Midnight Mass with my mum on Christmas Eve," Atlas says. "Plum pudding, if we can get the plums. And caroling—me and my mum do it to raise money for the Third Class children's hospital."

"Atlas King, you're extraordinary."

Surprise flickers in his eyes and he lets out a low laugh.

"That's the first time I've heard my name and a word like that used in the same sentence," he says with a wry smile.

I lean closer so that our shoulders are touching. He twirls the brass button of his sleeve, his fingers long and calloused.

"What words have you heard used to describe you?"

Atlas shrugs. "Poor. Angry. Misfit."

My stomach lurches. He concentrates on the button and suddenly the desire to kiss him is hard to resist. But there's no comfort I can offer him. Not for this, and not for what will happen in three days' time if I don't give Wyvernmire what she wants. I look around at the other recruits. They have no idea what's coming.

The door opens and two Guardians walk in, followed by Ravensloe.

Marquis and Katherine get to their feet, and I feel Atlas tense beside me. Ravensloe is carrying a decanter of orange liquid and beaming from ear to ear.

"Where is he?" he says impatiently. "Ah yes. Marquis Featherswallow."

Marquis turns a chess piece over in his hands and glares at the Deputy Prime Minister. I sit up straighter as fear burns in my chest. What does he want with my cousin?

"I've just been informed that Mr. Featherswallow's contribution of knowledge concerning the invention of a mechanical gizzard has allowed us to design and build the most dragonlike plane in Britannia." His eyes glitter as he stares round at us. "The Aviation Department is hereby closed."

My eyes meet Marquis's. His face is a deep red, and his fist, now closed tightly round the chess piece, is turning white.

"Congratulations, recruit," Ravensloe says. "You fulfilled your mission." He sticks out his hand, and when Marquis doesn't take it he thrusts the decanter of liquid at him instead. "Some apricot wine as a Christmas reward. Prime Minister Wyvernmire will be thrilled."

The music continues to blare into the otherwise silent room, and Ravensloe gives my cousin another nod before striding away. Everyone stares at Marquis.

"I—I . . . I didn't mean to. I explained to Knott how dragon gizzards work weeks ago, just because I thought it was interesting. I didn't know he would . . ." He looks from me to Karim and his eyes fill with tears.

I'm by his side in an instant. "It doesn't matter," I soothe. "We'll—we'll . . ."

Atlas is staring at me, his brow furrowed.

"Serena and Karim," he says. "We need to get you out of here. Tonight."

The blood drains from Serena's face. "Did you not see what happened to Dodie? I can't—"

"Oh, for God's sake, Serena!" Marquis roars. "The plane is finished—I've gone and won the bloody race! And when Wyvernmire finds out, she's not going to let you and Karim just walk out of here."

He sinks to his knees, dropping the decanter of apricot wine. The stopper falls off and the sweet-smelling liquid seeps into the rug. Panic floods through me. Marquis isn't wrong. Dodie was killed for trying to escape and Wyvernmire has made a deal with the Bulgarian dragons. She's capable of more than I ever expected.

"What will happen to you?" Gideon says. He looks from Serena to Karim. "What did you do to get yourselves here?"

It's the question everyone avoids.

"Fraud," Karim says. "I changed my parents' tax declarations to

304

make sure we could get by. But for the Third Class fraud is punishable by . . ."

"Death," Gideon finishes.

Karim begins to cry.

"You all know my situation," Serena says quietly. "Trust me, I'd rather die than be forced to marry an old man."

My head throbs. Surely there's some way out of Bletchley Park? *Oh.*

"I know someone who might be able to help," I say.

They all stare at me and Marquis raises his head. Atlas stands up abruptly, looking at me as if he's never seen me before.

"Viv?" says Marquis.

"I—I can't tell you anything more," I stammer. "You just have to trust me."

"Trust you?" Sophie says. "How can we trust you? You took the loquisonus machine for yourself, and I saw you coming back from Wyvernmire's office the other day. How do we know you're not going to take Serena and Karim straight to her?"

"How could you think that, Soph?" I swallow as the tension in the air grows tighter. "What would I gain from hurting them? They're not even in my category—"

"But you wouldn't hesitate to hurt *us*—is that what you mean?" Gideon says.

Katherine's eyes narrow.

"That's not what I said." I stare round at the hostile expressions and jump as Atlas slips a warm hand into mine.

"Everyone's getting paranoid," he says. "Let's all just sit down and make a rational plan."

Karim picks up the empty decanter as we all sit back down.

Sophie turns the radio off and I grip the arms of my armchair. I have to tell them. I have to tell them that if I don't give Wyvernmire at least one of the echolocation dialects, then the Bulgarian dragons will enter Britannia.

"Gingerbread?" Katherine says, pushing a plate of cinnamon biscuits at us. "Ralph had the kitchens make them for me."

"Ralph as in the Guardian who broke Viv's arm?" Sophie says blankly.

Katherine shoots her a dark look. "That was a misunderstanding."

She hands me a gingerbread in the shape of a star and her eyes almost dare me to refuse. I swallow an angry retort and accept it, then take a bite. She smiles and begins to nibble on her own, also star-shaped.

"Viv," Serena says with a rare tremor in her voice, "how many of us can this friend of yours help?"

Friend is a bit of an overstatement, I want to say. But Chumana *could* carry several people. What if we try to get Sophie, Gideon, Katherine, and Atlas out, too? Then I could give Wyvernmire the code, stop the Bulgarians, and everyone would be—

Katherine lets out a strangled cry. I jump up as she falls forward onto the rug, her hands round her throat. White foam froths from her mouth.

"Kath!" Sophie screams.

I drop down beside her, pulling her hands away as Atlas thumps her on the back. She lets out another gurgling sound, staring at me with bloodshot eyes. Then she goes limp. Marquis lifts her, holding her upright as Atlas continues to hit between her shoulder blades.

Serena sinks to the floor, her hands covering her face.

"She's not choking," she sobs. "She's been poisoned."

TWENTY-TWO

Marquis lowers Katherine to the floor, his eyes wide. I peer at her gray face. She's dead.

"Poisoned?" Sophie whispers. Slowly, she turns to look at Gideon.

"I didn't do anything, I swear!" Gideon shouts.

Marquis grabs him by the collar of his shirt.

"Stop!" Serena cries. "It wasn't him."

"Then who was it?" Atlas bellows.

I stare at Serena, my heart thumping against my rib cage.

"It was Katherine's poison," Serena says. "I saw her come out of the sanatorium with a bottle of something. She said it was to help her sleep, but later I heard her and Ralph talking about essence of hemlock . . ."

"You think she took too much—" I start to say.

"No, Viv." Serena looks at me through her fingers. "Even a drop of hemlock is deadly. I think . . . I think the gingerbread she ate was meant for you."

I let the rest of the biscuit in my hand drop to the floor.

"Why didn't you say something?" Atlas says.

Serena shakes her head. "I didn't think she would actually use it—"

She freezes and I follow her gaze. Gideon has one hand on the door handle and the other on a gun. And he's pointing it at me.

"Put it down, Gideon," Atlas says.

I stare at Gideon, at his twisted, angry face and his shaking hands. It's a small revolver, the kind some Guardians carry in their belts. I don't dare move, don't dare make him more panicked than he already seems.

"You can get out of here tonight, mate," Marquis says slowly. "No one else needs to die—"

"Sophie's right," Gideon says in a high voice. He nods toward me. "We can't trust her. For all we know, she's already cracked the code and given it to Wyvernmire."

"I haven't," I say quickly. "Gideon, echolocation is made up of dialects, which is why—"

BANG.

Gideon's bullet skitters off the side of the mantelpiece and shoots through the wall, missing me by a mile. Atlas charges at him, but Gideon raises the gun again.

"Atlas, no!" I scream.

Atlas stops as Owen bursts into the room, his own gun raised. Gideon turns round, fumbles with the gun, then fires. The second bullet hits Owen in the chest and he falls backward, a stunned look on his face.

"Owen!" I gasp, falling down beside him as Gideon flees the room.

"Get up," Marquis says, pulling me by the arm. "He's dead."

I stare at the blood spilling from Owen's mouth.

"We have to—"

"I know," I say, cutting Marquis off. I look for Sophie, who seems to be hyperventilating. "Gideon will come back for us. We have to hide."

Serena darts forward, grabs Owen's gun, and runs down the corridor without looking back. I feel a surge of horror.

"Come on," Atlas says, pulling me out into the hallway. "Before more Guardians turn up."

We run up the stairs to the top floor and I scan the hallway, searching for a room.

"The library!"

The five of us flood through the door as Guardian shouts sound below, and I turn the key in the lock. Karim leans against a bookcase, gasping for breath, and Sophie swears. We all stand in the dark, listening to the sound of each other's breathing. Sophie rummages around by one of the tables, then strikes a match and lifts it to a lamp. Light fills the room as I urge myself to tell them what I know. Atlas has his ear pressed up against the door, listening.

I take a deep breath. "The Bulgarian dragons will invade Britannia in less than three days' time."

His eyes lock on to mine and he steps away from the door.

"Say that again?" Marquis says.

I tell them about Wyvernmire's alliance with Bulgaria. That she plans to betray Queen Ignacia. That the Bulgarian dragons will land at Bletchley if I don't give her a way to understand echolocation. Atlas sinks into a chair and Sophie turns toward me.

"Was Gideon right?" she says. "Have you cracked the code?"

I look from her to Marquis, then close my eyes.

"Oh my God," she whispers. "You have."

"It's not as simple as that—" I begin.

"Did you give it to her?" Atlas says sharply. "To Wyvernmire?"

I frown. "No. Soph, the dragon code isn't a weapon. It's a language called the Koinamens, sacred to dragons because they use it to heal and hatch their eggs."

I glance at Atlas and see understanding dawn in his eyes.

"And that's not all," I say. "I discovered the Koinamens contains dialects and that each dragon family has their own. Muirgen and Rhydderch speak one, and Soresten and Addax speak another. That's what I tried to tell Gideon earlier—"

"How long have you known?" Sophie says bitterly.

"A while," I say. "But I wanted to be sure."

"So the other day, when you were in Wyvernmire's office—"

"I told her I needed more time," I say. "After she revealed her alliance with the Bulgarians, I couldn't bring myself to give it to her. Not now that I know what she's capable of. But if I don't give her a dialect she'll confirm the alliance and put the whole of Britannia in danger of another massacre like the one that happened in Bulgaria."

Guardians run past the library and we fall silent. I hear Gideon's name mentioned.

"They'll be looking for *us* soon," Marquis says quietly. "Wyvernmire will want to talk to me about the plane, and I bet she'll pull the rest of the aviators from the program at the same time. Serena obviously thinks she has a better chance at hiding alone."

I look at Karim. "You're not safe here. We'll have to get you out to—"

"You and Sophie can't go anywhere," Atlas tells me. "Not with Gideon on the loose." He looks at me intently. "Who is this person you say will help us?"

"Marquis, do you have the plans for your plane?" I say, ignoring the question.

A pulse flicks in Atlas's jaw.

Marquis pulls his sketchbook out of his pocket.

"If Wyvernmire finds you, use them to stall her. Lie—tell her you have more ideas. Anything that might buy Karim some time."

"If they find us in here, they'll not let us out of their sights," Karim says. "Especially not you, Viv."

"He's right," Atlas says. "Wyvernmire will want to guard you, to keep you safe from any other potential killers. And you should let her."

"But what about—"

"Marquis and I will get Karim out."

"Not tonight you won't," Sophie says. "Do it tomorrow, after your shift. He can stay hidden until then."

"You go with him," I tell her. I glance at Atlas. "And you. This is your chance to escape."

"You still don't get it, do you, Viv?" Sophie says. "Even if I escape here, I'll never be able to go home. I'll never get a class pass again—the system will flag me as a wanted criminal."

"Or," I say, avoiding Atlas's gaze, "we could give Wyvernmire the code together. We tell her we worked on it as a team, that we couldn't have done it without each other. And we stop this insane alliance."

Hope flickers in Sophie's face. "You would do that?" she says.

"Of course I would. I'm not leaving here without you, without any of you—"

Atlas explodes. "None of this is going to matter!"

I whip round to face him.

"If you give Wyvernmire the code, it won't matter who does and doesn't escape. If she wins the war, then everything will go back to the way it was before." He gives me an anguished look. "Of course, that will be all right for some of you, but what about the rest of us?"

"Viv has just told you that eggs need echolocation to hatch," Sophie says. "If you tell Wyvernmire, you'll win your category, too—"

Atlas lets out a low, almost manic laugh.

"You people are unbelievable. Always looking out for your own arses."

"You have no idea what I've been through," Sophie spits.

"Yes, I do!" Atlas shouts. "That's the whole bloody point. You were demoted, Sophie, which means you've seen how the Third Class live. And if Wyvernmire wins the war, those people will keep on suffering in silence. Wyvernmire and Queen Ignacia will continue writing self-serving clauses into the Peace Agreement, and *we* will be responsible for having given the government the perfect methods to exploit and control dragons." His voice is hoarse from shouting. "And yet all you lot can think about is who's going to be the one to doom us all."

"What do you suggest, Atlas?" I say angrily. "That we let her execute us instead? Because that's what will happen to Karim, and possibly to me, if we don't do what she says."

Atlas frowns and shakes his head as if he doesn't believe me.

"My parents are rebels," I continue, my voice shaking. "I released a criminal dragon to try and get rid of the evidence, and somehow the Coalition took that as a sign to start a war. So if we don't win . . . then we die."

"The Coalition can hide you," he says urgently. "If you choose to side with them, they'll keep you safe. They're coming. They're going to attack Bletchley as soon as Wyvernmire returns from her trip."

I gape at him. "How did you get that information?"

Except I already know. Deep down, I've always known.

"Because I'm part of it," he says softly. "I'm a rebel."

I blink. First Dr. Seymour and now him.

"So you've been spying on us?" I say, my voice shaking. "All this time you've been pretending to be *with* us when actually you're an informant?"

"Who's *us* exactly? You and Wyvernmire? You and the Bulgarians? You need to just bloody decide. Are you with them?" Atlas spits. "Or are you with me?"

I shake my head in disbelief. How dare he? He's been lying to me this whole time, pretending to be someone he's not.

Not really, a quiet voice in my head says. *You saw he was a rule-breaker from the start. Maybe he's been honest all along.*

I look round at the others, all of them staring at Atlas in silent shock. Then Marquis gives me a pleading look. I shake my head at him. *We can't,* I try to tell him with my eyes. *If we join the rebels, our family will die.* I know I'm right. The government has our parents and Ursa. There's no way the rebels could ever protect them, no matter how many dragons they have.

Sophie puts a shaky hand on my arm. "If you say the Bulgarians are coming, and Atlas is right that the rebels are going to attack, then there's about to be a fight here."

I nod.

"So . . . how *do* we get out of Bletchley?" Karim asks.

I put a hand on the ladder that leads to the floor above, suddenly desperate to be away from them all.

"Dragonback," I say as I climb.

I lie down to sleep between two bookcases, stuffing my jacket behind my head. I can hear the others sorting out sleeping arrangements as I stare at the ceiling, and then the lamp goes out. Moments later, the ladder creaks.

"Mind if I camp up here?" Atlas says, standing at the opposite end of the row of bookcases.

"As long as you don't mind sleeping with the enemy," I reply.

Atlas throws his own jacket down on the floor and then I hear the rustling of pages.

"What are you doing?" I say in a low voice.

"Reading."

"It's pitch-black, Atlas."

I hear him close the book and we lie quietly, listening to the sound of everyone breathing.

"Featherswallow?" Atlas whispers.

"What?"

"I'm sorry for not telling you I'm with the Coalition."

I don't say anything until I hear him sigh.

"Forget about it," I say. "Now I think about it, it was pretty obvious."

How didn't I suspect him straightaway?

"So how did you get here?" I say quietly. "Did you commit a crime on purpose to get yourself sent to the DDAD?"

"No," Atlas replies. "Father David and I were smuggling wanted rebels to hideaways in the countryside. Some Guardians found one of them hidden in our church, and I was arrested."

"What about Father David?"

"The Guardians killed him."

Horror prickles at my scalp.

Atlas clears his throat. "I managed to send a message to the Coalition before I was arrested, and the next thing I knew Dr. Seymour was in my prison cell, recruiting me for a government program."

"Did you know who she was?" I ask.

"No. But she told me, discreetly, during the interview. To have two rebels inside Bletchley was a once-in-a-lifetime opportunity, so the Coalition jumped at the chance."

So Dr. Seymour and Atlas have been working together all this time.

"What about you?" Atlas whispers. "Did you really release . . . a criminal dragon?"

"To save my parents, yes."

"Did you know that they were with the Coalition?"

I shake my head, then realize he can't see me in the dark. "No. They were undercover, I suppose. Like you."

"And now . . . don't you want to help them?"

"I *am* helping them," I say. "If I give Wyvernmire the code, she'll pardon them."

"And you believe that?"

I don't reply. A few days ago, I would have said yes. But since our meeting in her office I'm not so sure.

"I'm tired of making decisions, Atlas," I whisper. "Tired of making the wrong ones."

Tears fill my eyes and I blink them away. I know what Atlas wants me to say. That I'll follow in my parents' footsteps and become a rebel, that I'll never give Wyvernmire the code. My throat aches with the sudden tears.

"I've hurt people I love before," I say slowly. "I never want to do that again."

"What do you mean?" Atlas says, his voice softening. "What did you do?"

My face burns and I'm glad he can't see it. The floor creaks as he moves closer to me, shuffling into the space between me and the bookcases.

"I'm a seminarian, Featherswallow," he says. "One day it will be my job to hear people's confessions."

I hear the smirk in his voice and turn to face him.

"There's nothing you can say that will shock me," he says in my ear.

So I tell him. I whisper the truth, so nobody but him can hear. I can't believe the words are coming out of my mouth, the words I've never spoken to another soul. But they are. He listens silently as the shame floods through me.

"Do you see why I can't abandon everything to join your Coalition?" I say. "My selfishness already cost Sophie everything. But if I give Wyvernmire the code and tell her Sophie helped me crack it, I can save my family and give Sophie her life back."

I wait for him to say something, but he doesn't speak. He's too disgusted to react. I bury my face in my jacket.

"Do you think, maybe, I was born bad?" I say, my voice muffled.

"No," Atlas says quietly. "I don't think anyone is born bad. I think we've all got good and bad inside us, don't you?"

I turn my face to look at him. I can see the outline of his jaw and the curl of his hair.

316

"This is the way I see it," he says. "If you were *all* bad, if you didn't have any goodness in you, then how would you even know what badness is? Without goodness, there'd be nothing to measure badness against. Badness wouldn't be bad—it would just be a normal state of being. I think you have to have both good and bad inside you to know the difference, Featherswallow. To know which side you want to act on. So, if you feel guilty for what you did, that's a sure sign there's goodness in you."

I turn away, but he pulls me back. "We live in a world that permits everything but forgives nothing. I think Sophie could forgive you, one day. You should tell her the truth."

"Sometimes I wake up in the night and it's there, beside me in bed, the guilt. Like a dark void waiting to suck me in."

Atlas takes my hand. "Then tell it to go away," he whispers fiercely. He presses his lips to my ear. "Banish it, like a dragon banishes the dark."

I go still. My hand is on his wrist, and I feel the soft hair on his arm. I turn my face up to his. Then he moves toward me, slipping an arm beneath my waist, and pulls my body against his. His mouth finds mine. Something inside me explodes. My lips burn as they move, tingling with tiny flames. His mouth is the softest I've ever kissed, and suddenly it's on my neck, my face, my eyes wet with tears. We move almost instinctively, our bodies melting together, and suddenly I'm on top of him, one hand intertwined in his, the other in his hair as I kiss him again and will him not to stop.

Why did this take us so long? I think as his fingers slip beneath my shirt to dance along my spine.

He pulls away, breathing hard. "Featherswallow, I—"

317

I silence him with another kiss, feeling his laugh before I hear it. He turns his head away.

"Viv," he whispers into my hair. My name in his mouth is like velvet.

"What, Atlas?" I say almost impatiently.

"I don't think I want to be a priest anymore."

I go still. "But you've been religious your whole life. You believe in God, and you said He was calling you to the priesthood, so why wouldn't you—"

"But what if He's calling me to something else?" Atlas says.

My heart races, but it's not so much from the kissing as it is the hope that he's about to say the very words I realize I've been longing to hear. A car rolls up on the gravel outside and a tiny sliver of headlight slips through the crack between the blackout curtains, just enough to give me a glimpse of Atlas's face. His eyes are wide and shining.

"Viv," he says again. "What if God's calling me to you?"

TWENTY-THREE

"This is your Deputy Prime Minister! Open the door!"

I wake up with Atlas's arm round me and my face pressed up against the cover of a book.

"Should we open it?" Marquis says groggily from below.

"Wait," I say, sitting up. "Karim, you need to hide."

I climb down the ladder and Karim squeezes into an alcove that serves as a bookshelf.

"Here," Atlas says, passing down the biggest of the framed maps from the upper level.

We hang it over the alcove and Marquis opens the library door. Ravensloe is waiting with a group of Guardians.

"Those of you on shift this morning will be escorted to your places of work," Ravensloe says. "The rest of you"—he glances at Marquis—"will return to your dormitories immediately. The fun is over."

"Oh yeah, because spending the night trying to avoid getting murdered was really fun," Marquis says.

"Where *were* you?" Atlas says to Ravensloe. "Where were your Guardians last night when two people were killed?"

I'm surprised at the uncomfortable look that flickers across Ravensloe's face, but it's soon replaced by a sneer.

"We were unaware we were dealing with a group of uncivilized animals."

"Have you even found Gideon?" I ask. "Or . . . any of the other recruits?"

"We assumed they would be with you," Ravensloe says, peering into the room.

The four of us shake our heads.

"Miss Featherswallow, Miss Rundell, you will be escorted to the glasshouse by these Guardians, for your own safety. And you," he says, looking at Marquis. "Prime Minister Wyvernmire wishes to congratulate you."

When Sophie and I walk into the glasshouse, Dr. Seymour is sipping a steaming cup of coffee at the loquisonus machine. She stands up when she sees us, her eyes red. Tinsel hangs from the ceiling, a half-hearted attempt at celebrating a Christmas Day no one will care to remember.

"Girls, I heard what happened last night, and about Katherine. Are you all right?"

"I . . ."

I've been forcing myself not to think about it. Katherine, who grew up Third Class yet never hesitated in becoming friends with Serena, who flirted shamelessly with Marquis, who beat us endlessly at chess.

I can't believe she tried to kill me. I can't believe she's dead.

Dr. Seymour begins to cry. "It was never meant to happen like this."

"Atlas told me everything," I say. "Do you know about the Bulgarian dragons?"

"The Bulgarian dragons?" she says. "What do you mean?"

"Wyvernmire is set to confirm an alliance with them two days from now, if we haven't cracked the dragon code."

Dr. Seymour sits down again, like a puppet with her strings cut. "I had no idea," she says. "Are you sure?"

I nod. "Wyvernmire told me herself. Dr. Seymour . . . if I give Wyvernmire one of the dialects, the one used by Rhydderch and Muirgen, she'll call off her alliance with the Bulgarians. But if I don't—"

"They'll invade the country," Sophie says grimly.

Dr. Seymour goes to the cupboard without a word and begins scribbling on a piece of paper. A warning to the rebels.

"Your dracovol," I say, thinking of the miniature dragon nesting in the forest. "Will you be able to get to it without anyone seeing?"

She nods, her eyes still on the paper. Of course she will. She's been doing this for months. She seals the envelope.

"Vivien, I have to ask you. Do you intend on giving Wyvernmire this first dialect?"

"I . . . I don't know," I say, hearing the panic rise in my voice. "If I don't give it to her, then she'll ally with the Bulgarians and I'll never see my family again. But—"

Dr. Seymour nods once. "I'm going to find the dracovol."

She disappears behind one of the tall reperisonus machines and I follow her. Behind the machine and the mess of wires, one of the panels of the glasshouse is open like a window. Dr. Seymour steps out of it, the envelope clutched to her chest. Then she closes the panel and disappears into the forest. I meet Sophie's gaze. She has one hand on the loquisonus, the other pulling nervously at her brooch. A dragon in a net. If I told Wyvernmire that Sophie helped me crack the code, would she even believe me?

"I'm going out there, too," I say. "To find the library dragon and ask her to help us."

She nods.

I run past the sonar blockers, deeper into the forest, past where Chumana found me last time. The ground gets steeper here and suddenly I'm climbing uphill, tripping over broken branches and piles of leaves. Dr. Seymour's question plays in my mind on repeat.

Do you intend on giving Wyvernmire this first dialect?

I stop, snatching a breath, before slipping through the barbed-wire fencing separating Bletchley Park territory from the farming fields beyond, so far deep in the forest that it's not even patrolled. My feet trip on something heavy, sending it rolling loudly across the frozen dirt. A Guardian helmet. I stop. Just beyond the felled trunk of a tree is a pile of bodies, their uniforms glinting beneath the packed snow. The Guardians who heard Atlas break the Official Secrets Act after Dodie was killed. They didn't go home for Christmas. I stifle a sob and clench my eyes shut, terrified that I might see a lock of long red hair.

I keep climbing, pushing through the forest, until I come out the other side into a grassy field. There it is, the ditch Chumana brought me to. I peer over the edge. It's empty, save for the dragon skin and several puddles of water from the melted snow. Chumana is gone.

Of course she is, idiot. You all but told her to get lost.

I slide down into the ditch anyway, plastering my boots and trousers with mud. The air smells of fresh earth and chimney smoke. I crouch next to the dragon skin and sob. I can't bear to lose Ursa or the rest of my family. And the only way to save them is to give up

Atlas and Sophie, the rebels, and possibly the whole United Kingdom. So that's what I'm going to do.

Atlas is wrong. I *was* born bad. No matter how hard I try, I can't bring myself to make the *right* decision. Not if it comes at a personal cost. I'm not brave enough, not selfless enough. And I've made too many mistakes to go back now.

"To what do I owe the pleasure, human girl?"

Chumana towers over the ditch, her tail extending halfway round it. She crawls down toward me.

I sniff. "You're still here."

"I had a feeling you would be back."

I brush the tears from my face. "I need your help getting some people out of Bletchley Park."

"You need *my* help?" she purrs. "Again?"

"It's not too much to ask, is it?" I say dryly. "You and Dr. Seymour must be used to working together now."

"Indeed we are," Chumana says. "And you should be glad of it—I might possibly have killed you if it wasn't for that boy."

"Boy?"

"Atlas," she hisses gently.

"You've met Atlas?"

"Yes. He must have known you would aggravate me. His patience with you is astounding."

My mind races. Atlas has been visiting Chumana? He never mentioned her, even after he admitted to being a rebel, even after I told him I freed a criminal dragon who broke the Peace Agreement. He must know Chumana *is* that dragon.

He doesn't trust me. My heart sinks and the truth appears before my eyes with such clarity that I can't believe I didn't see it.

323

Last night's promises that Sophie would one day forgive me, that stuff about God calling him, the kissing . . . It was all an act to make sure I don't give Wyvernmire the code. I blink away more burning tears. How could I have believed Atlas could actually have feelings for someone like me? How could I have dared hope to be forgiven for the unforgivable?

"Have you given Wyvernmire the secrets to my ancestral language yet?"

I will myself not to cry. "Not yet."

"Even though the Bulgarian dragons are set to arrive?"

I look up. "How do you know?"

"I've been listening."

"Dr. Seymour just sent word to the rest of your . . . to the rebels." Chumana gives a slow nod.

"Wyvernmire has no idea there are rebel spies at Bletchley," I say. "No idea that the Coalition knows of the Bulgarian arrival. If you want to stop her from strengthening her army, then the time to attack is now, before she sends the Bulgarians to posts across the country."

"You have this well thought out, human girl. You would make a fine rebel."

"But if I give her the code, the Koinamens," I say slowly, "she might call off the alliance. Then no one would have to deal with the Bulgarian dragons."

"Such an act would be catastrophic to dragons," Chumana says. "With sophisticated loquisonus machines and expert translators to reproduce Koinamens calls, Wyvernmire might extort and infiltrate dragon communities, indoctrinate dragonlings, subjugate or even destroy entire species."

I let out a deep sigh. "I did want to do the right thing, all right? I thought I could change but I can't. And why would I now that Atlas has turned out to be a liar?" I feel my tongue lace with fury. "I can't help you, or the rebels, or the Third Class because that's not the type of person I am."

"What type of person are you?" Chumana says calmly.

"The bad type," I whisper. "Wyvernmire's type. The type that makes the ruthless, necessary decisions, no matter the cost, no matter how many people they hurt."

"Hmmm." Chumana lets out a throaty growl.

It's a boring response. Not the one I wanted. But what *do* I want exactly? I feel anger wash over me and suddenly I want to humiliate Atlas as much as he has humiliated me, to see Dr. Seymour's face as I turn her over to Wyvernmire, to watch Chumana fly away, defeated. Why do I hate them so much?

It's not them you hate, I tell myself. *It's you.*

I press my knuckles to my eyeballs as I see Sophie sinking to the ground with her Examination results in her hand. I see her alone in the halfway house with nothing to eat. I see her lying on top of Nicolas's dead body in a Third Class hospital.

I take a deep, shaky breath. A drop of rain falls on my face.

"Why did you come here?" Chumana says softly.

"To beg for your help," I say, glaring at her. "Is that what you want to hear?"

"I think you came for a different reason."

"Of course you do," I say.

"I've met too many humans with tortured souls."

I snort. "I'm not sure I have a soul."

I'm a bright shiny apple, rotten at the core.

"Oh?" Chumana murmurs. "I feel the same about myself."

"You've been shut away alone in the library for years, and all because of a student you didn't even eat. Why wouldn't you have a soul?"

"You misremember," Chumana says. "I wasn't imprisoned for hurting a student. I was imprisoned for protesting against the Peace Agreement."

I shrug, thinking of how I asked her to break that very Peace Agreement by burning down a human-owned political building. "Aren't we both guilty of that?"

"And, fifty-eight years ago, I fought in the Massacre of Bulgaria."

I stare at Chumana. "No, you didn't."

"I am a Bolgorith, am I not?"

"But . . . I thought you were hatched in Britannia."

"Yes," Chumana replies. "My egg was laid in Bulgaria and then flown across the sea in my mother's pouch. I was hatched on Rùm, like most dragons of Britannia."

"So then, how . . ."

"The British government asked Queen Ignacia to send aid over to Bulgaria."

"To help the human population when they wired us a plea for support," I say, recalling my history lessons.

"No," Chumana growls. "That was a lie. The aid was for the Bulgarian dragons, to ensure their operation was successful."

For a moment, my heart seems to stop.

"They sent British dragons over there to help *kill* the humans?"

"Yes, human girl. To ensure that the most powerful dragons in Europe would forever owe Britannia. Do you really think Wyvernmire convinced the Bulgarians to ally with her on promises alone?"

I shake my head. That can't be possible. Britannia wouldn't betray its fellow humans, and its dragons wouldn't agree to help kill them. Our national motto is *Praise for peace and prosperity!*

I remember what Wyvernmire told me.

And, in the end, we made sure those dragons were in our debt.

"A few important people protested, of course," Chumana says. She curls her spiked tail round her body, and it circles the spot I'm sitting in. "Especially the few who knew it would mean the end of the Bulgarian humans' effort to decipher the Koinamens. The British government didn't understand what the so-called *dragon code* was then, or how much they would come to covet it." She snorts a puff of dark, angry smoke.

Revulsion rises inside me. "Chumana . . . you killed the Bulgarian humans?"

"Yes."

"My mother's family died in that massacre," I spit. "She barely made it out alive. She still has nightmares."

Chumana bows her head, revealing a small row of horns along its crown. "Yes. You told me she was Bulgarian in the library."

I stand up. "Why? Why did you do it?"

"I was following my Queen's orders," Chumana says calmly.

"But . . . but her orders were wrong! She's evil to have ordered such a thing."

Honorable Queen Ignacia is what the dragons call her. Her reign stretches back to before my grandparents were born.

"Evil is not a strong enough word." Chumana meets my gaze and sparks fizz from her mouth. "My first return to my motherland was done in bloodshed. I killed, burned, and destroyed. I chased humans from their homes and demolished the boats they tried to escape on. The flames I breathed did not discriminate between old and young."

"You're lying," I say, my whole body trembling. "You wouldn't."

"Oh, but I did. And after it was over, Britannia's government began talking about a Peace Agreement." She snorts again. "The irony. They saw how easily we slaughtered the Bulgarian people and were suddenly afraid for their own country. The Peace Agreement was written only to ensure that British humans would never suffer the same fate as the Bulgarians they helped murder, and to portray dragons as creatures to be feared. Fear breeds hatred, the kind that oppresses dragons and humans alike."

I think of the detonator I cut from Chumana's skin, of Nicolas's untreated burns, of Dodie and Katherine and Owen.

"Queen Ignacia agreed to it after she was offered . . . special privileges." Chumana stamps the ground, leaving a claw mark the size of my head in the dirt. "I hated myself for what I had done. The horrors committed in Bulgaria were too much to bear, even for a dragon. And I continued to witness the corruption that had always existed between a string of prime ministers and the Dragon Queen. So, on the eve of the signing of the Peace Agreement, I protested its creation. I attempted to kill Queen Ignacia."

Chumana is a Bolgorith, one of the largest dragons in Europe. But the Dragon Queen is rumored to be even stronger, the biggest Western Drake ever recorded, with jaws powerful enough to crush stone.

"Kill?"

She nods. "I consider her a traitor to dragonkind."

My stomach churns.

"I failed, obviously," Chumana says, and her tail twitches

irritably. "I wasn't granted the privilege of a dragon's execution—you have seen the prison they sent me to."

I nod.

"I lived there, haunted by the evil of my own memories, for years. I was considering flying out over the walls of the university to set that detonator off when a human girl appeared and offered to remove it for me."

My heart quickens and Chumana's eyes bore into mine.

"She gave me an opportunity. The opportunity to fly straight to the Coalition and attempt to make up for my crimes. An opportunity to atone for my sins and seek forgiveness. Now tell me, human girl, why don't you extend yourself the same courtesy?"

More rain droplets fall onto my face, one after another. They drip into my hair and down the neck of my shirt as I stare at the Bulgarian dragon in front of me, Chumana the murderer.

"I don't deserve forgiveness," I say. "And neither do you."

"Few of us deserve forgiveness, child," says Chumana. "But answer me this. Where would I be more useful: in that library, rotting into the mulch of my own guilt? Dead from a purposely exploded detonator? Or flying free, helping to bring victory to the rebels?"

I shiver and stare at the rapidly expanding puddles at my feet, wondering how many battles Chumana has helped the rebels win since she joined them. How many documents did she salvage from the Academy for Draconic Linguistics before Wyvernmire took power there? How many lives has she saved?

If she had refused to leave that library when I asked her to, or used that detonator to kill herself, fewer people would be alive right now. My parents certainly wouldn't be. And the rebel movement would have one less dragon.

But who is she to claim forgiveness for herself? She's not the one who lost her country, her family, her life.

"What are you suggesting?" I explode. "That Sophie just forgets what I did to her? That the Bulgarian survivors forget the role you played in history? It can't be as easy as just saying sorry, Chumana!"

"No, it can't," Chumana replies. "But *showing* you're sorry and spending a lifetime proving it? Now that's another thing entirely."

I shake my head. This is just Atlas's spew of holy half-truths all over again. And I know what showing I'm sorry means. It means keeping the Koinamens a secret from Wyvernmire. Only that might give the rebels a chance at winning, free the Third Class from the suffering that pushed Katherine, Dodie, and Gideon to desperate measures, and keep Wyvernmire from enslaving Britannia's dragons.

But what if I help the rebels, and then they fail? I'll never be the most famous dragon linguist in the world, that's for sure. My parents will both be dead. And I will have lost all chance of finding Ursa.

To keep the code a secret would be a noble, selfless choice. But I am neither of those things. Why would I risk losing everything I love for the rebels?

Because you're good, I imagine Atlas saying. *Because if you feel guilty that's a sure sign there's more good than bad in you.*

Can that be true? In the face of everything I've done—sending Sophie to the Third Class where she had her heart shattered over and over, leaving Ursa, almost handing over the code to Wyvernmire—can there still be goodness in me?

"You have fought for your family admirably," Chumana says. "You refused to turn Dr. Seymour in. You offered to heal me, a rebel dragon, with that unsightly machine. Those are not the choices of *Wyvernmire's type of person.*"

I warm at the memory of Dr. Seymour's compassion, of Atlas's lips on mine, of Sophie asleep in my bed, of that spark of pride I refused to let myself feel when Marquis told me that he wanted to be a rebel.

Chumana isn't lying. These are not the choices and memories of a bad person, but of a good one who refuses to forgive herself for the bad things she has done.

Because it's easier to betray your best friend for your career, to sacrifice the entire Third Class for your family, to give Wyvernmire the means to experiment on dragon eggs when you believe you were simply born bad.

But if you're good? Then your goodness and those choices are not compatible.

I blink, staring at my reflection in the puddle at my feet.

But if you're good, I tell myself slowly, *then the people and the dragons you're about to hurt will be harmed because you choose to hurt them. Not because hurting them is an unavoidable part of your nature, but because you've decided they don't matter.*

The thought takes my breath away. I chose to betray Sophie out of my own selfishness. Surely that makes me just as evil as Wyvernmire and Queen Ignacia?

I look up at Chumana, the gray clouds pale against her dark, wet scales.

"I don't think I could ever forgive myself for what I did," I whisper, feeling hot tears overflow again.

"You don't have to forgive yourself," Chumana growls. "Not yet. But you can offer yourself a second chance."

A second chance.

"If you don't, then all your suffering, and all the suffering you caused others, will be for nothing."

I let out a shaky breath and shiver, my clothes as wet as the muddy water now trickling down the sides of the ditch. I can't forgive myself for how I hurt Sophie. And Sophie might never forgive me, which I'll never, ever blame her for. But if I can offer myself a second chance then maybe I can do things differently. I can choose to live a life where what's important isn't what I can achieve—grades, social class, career—but the type of person I can be.

"I do want to prove that I'm sorry," I say to Chumana, raising my voice above the sound of the rain. "Even though I don't believe that any amount of sorry will make up for the pain I caused Sophie."

The dragon's eyes burn brightly.

"But if you say it's possible, if you say it was possible for you . . . then I want to try."

Chumana bows her head down to mine until she's so close that her breath warms my cold skin.

"Do you remember, back in the library, when you asked me for my maxim?" she says.

"Yes?" I reply as the rain begins to slow.

"I refused to tell you because I was ashamed of what it was. But I have discarded it now, like I shed my old skin. I have a new maxim."

I move closer to her, my shoulder brushing against her hot hide, and place a hand on the scales of her flank.

"What is it?" I ask.

"*Remissio dolor redemptus est*," Chumana says. "Forgiveness is suffering redeemed."

TWENTY-FOUR

Chumana brings me back to the forest, and when I slip through the panel of the glasshouse, Dr. Seymour has returned, too. She doesn't ask me where I was. Sophie and I are escorted to the dining room for Christmas lunch, where Atlas and Marquis are whispering over their turkey. There's still no sign of Serena or Gideon.

"Soph?" I say.

I know this is probably the last time she'll let me use that nickname.

"Can I talk to you? Privately?"

Sophie blinks. "All right."

Atlas smiles at me, but I glare back. He doesn't look away. Instead, when Sophie walks back out into the hall, he gives me an almost imperceptible nod.

Who does he think he is?

I glance at the Guardian by the door, who isn't paying much attention, then back at Marquis.

He leaves tonight, I mouth, thinking of Karim still hidden in the library. Then I follow Sophie out of the room.

"Recruits, where are you going?" the Guardian asks.

I've never seen him before and come to the sickening realization that he must be one of the replacements for the Guardians in the forest.

"I need to clean up for lunch," Sophie says, holding out her ink-stained hands. "Deputy Prime Minister Ravensloe says it's better to travel in twos."

"I've been ordered not to let anyone move without an escort."

"Escort us to the dormitory, then?" I say.

The Guardian hesitates, glancing back at Marquis and Atlas, then decides we're more valuable. He follows us up the stairs and stands outside the dormitory door, which I close.

"What's going on, Viv?"

Sophie looks exhausted as she casts a wistful look in the direction of the empty beds. It's hard to believe that all of our dorm-mates are now either dead or in hiding.

"Is this about Chumana? About the code?"

"No," I say. "I'm not giving Wyvernmire the Koinamens. She'll use it to control dragons and win the war, and I know what that will mean for the Third Class. I know what it will mean for you."

She grabs my hand and squeezes. "Atlas was right," she says. "Back in the library, we were only thinking about ourselves. But *this* is how we make sure what happened to Nicolas never happens again. And it means that maybe, one day, we can go home. Together."

Shame prickles my skin. "That's what I want to talk to you about."

With my hand in hers, I feel like a fraud.

She frowns. "Home?"

I let go and sit down on the bed beside her. My heart is thumping in my chest and my face is slowly burning up. How can I bring myself to say the words out loud? I want to be sick.

"I did something terrible," I say.

She eyes me curiously.

"Last summer."

I pause, trying to dredge up every ounce of courage from within me.

"Do you remember when I went to see Mistress Morris about my university application?"

Sophie nods. "We all did. She wrote our recommendation letters."

"Her daughter was also applying to study Mathematics at the University of London," I say.

"I remember," Sophie says. "Lily."

I nod. "Morris was worried Lily wouldn't get in. So she asked me to do something."

"What could you possibly have done to help Lily get into university?"

I close my eyes and remember. Despite Sophie and I being on the Fast Track Program to attend university early, Morris warned me that the universities were becoming even more selective.

"Morris said you were Lily's main competition. And . . ." I take a deep breath and force the words out. "She asked me to imitate your handwriting to change some of your responses to the Examination."

Sophie shakes her head slightly, as if she's misheard me. Then she goes as still as solid rock.

"She said that if I refused, she'd remove me from Fast Track and have me stay on at school for another year. But if I helped her she'd personally speak to the Dragon Tongues admissions team about me."

I wish I could shrink into nothing, but I force myself to look into Sophie's eyes because it's the least she deserves. I can feel my face turning bright red, hot like a fever. "It's my fault you failed the Examination, Sophie. You were never ill-prepared or not clever enough. I changed your results so that you would fail and Lily could get the university place instead of you."

Sophie sways. "B-but . . . why?"

"I wanted to go to university earlier, to be the first to graduate at age twenty as a qualified Draconic Translator," I say, tears streaming down my face. "I was scared that if I didn't do it, she'd write me a bad reference and I'd never get in. But Sophie, listen to me. I promise you that I regretted it as soon as I'd done it. I regret it still. And after you told me what happened to you, to Nicolas . . . I had no idea what life would be like for you."

Sophie's eyes are screwed shut. "But . . . you knew you'd never see me again. That I'd have to leave my parents. That I'd never be able to study."

"I . . . yes," I sob. "I'm so sorry. I hate myself for it. And I don't deserve your forgiveness, I know that. I ruined your life out of self-ishness and ambition. I betrayed you. But please . . . please don't hate me forever."

Sophie is standing up now and when I reach out a hand, she tenses and backs away. Her eyes are still closed, but there's a look of absolute disgust on her face. My chest tightens and my head spins at the sight of it. Then her eyes fly open.

"Hate you?" she says, and her voice is almost a whisper. "I don't even recognize you." Her mouth twists into a pained smile. "But you'll pay for what you did to me."

I can barely breathe, as if I'm about to suffocate within my own body.

"I'm so sorry, Sophie."

It's all I can say, over and over.

"I'm so sorry."

She stares at me, her eyes flashing with fury. For a moment, it looks like she might kill me. I feel drunk, like I've descended into the deepest depths of oblivion with no way out.

"I'll spend my life making it up to you," I say.

Sophie backs away, opens the door with a bang, and runs.

"Oi!" the Guardian shouts.

I slip off the bed onto my knees as the sobs rack my body.

Now she knows, will always know, who I truly am. A liar, a fraud, a shiny fake rotting beneath the surface. Exhaustion washes over me as I climb into Sophie's bed and lay my head against the pillow. I'm enveloped in her smell, the smell of my childhood. I'll never be this close to her again. I try desperately to grasp on to Chumana's words, to remember what she said before my mind spins back into that awful pit of anxiety and hatred it's permanently been in, ever since last summer.

You don't have to forgive yourself. . . . But you can offer yourself a second chance.

A floorboard creaks and suddenly there are familiar arms round me and a voice in my ear. "Care to tell me what's going on, cousin?"

I sit up.

"Viv?" he says, his voice finding a touch of unusual seriousness. "What's happened?"

I tell him.

"I always knew there was more than you were letting on."

"I understand if you don't want anything to do with me anymore."

He scoffs and ruffles my hair. "You're my family. There's nothing you could do to make me not want to have anything to do with you." He pauses. "You did an awful thing. But I know you well enough to know that you regretted it immediately. And I trust you to do the right thing now."

He hugs me and for a moment I just savor the feeling. The feeling of being loved in spite of my mistake.

"Did . . . Atlas say anything?" I ask casually. "Earlier?"

He rolls his eyes. "He wanted to come up here when we saw Sophie run past, but I told him to bugger off. I've barely had a look in your life since he's been around."

I snort. "As if you haven't spent your every waking moment with Karim."

He grins. "What did you mean, yesterday, about Karim escaping on dragonback?"

"The dragon I freed from the library is up in a field behind the forest," I say. "If we can get Karim out during the night, Chumana will take him to safety. Has anyone been found?"

"No," Marquis says grimly. "But the Guardian staff room is just below the library, and Karim has been listening through the floorboards all morning. They think Gideon or Serena might have escaped into the town, so they're widening their search."

"What about Wyvernmire?"

"She congratulated me on winning my category and told me I'd soon be able to return home," he scoffs.

"And our family?"

Marquis shakes his head. "They won't be freed unless you win your category, too. She said I'm only here because of you."

"That's not fair," I seethe. "They're your family, too, and you kept your end of the deal—"

"It was never a real deal, though, was it, Viv?"

I look at him.

"She doesn't care what promises she made. If she did, she would never have made us compete in the first place. And now, because of her, we might have to face Bulgarian dragons. This war is about to get bigger."

I take a deep breath. "If it comes to that . . . we know what side we'll be on. Don't we?"

"Viv . . . I already told you that—"

"And I agree," I say. "You were right about everything you said. I've been wrong my whole life. I want us to join the Coalition, Marquis."

"Is that because your boyfriend's part of it?" he jokes weakly.

"No!" I say. "I can't give Wyvernmire the code. I can't hand the dragons, the Third Class, our friends over to her."

"And if the Bulgarians turn against her?"

"We'll fight them," I say fiercely. "If it comes to that, there will be no government versus rebels anymore. If Wyvernmire's new friends take over, it will be Britannia versus Bulgaria."

Marquis slips his hand into mine. "And we'll get Ursa back," he reassures me. "If the Coalition can seize Bletchley before the Bulgarians get here, we'll make Wyvernmire tell us where she is."

I nod, hope buoying inside me.

"The Coalition could already be on their way, but they're going to need inside help. I've got an idea, but it's risky."

Marquis looks at me expectantly.

"We have to recruit more dragons."

I scribble a last note for Atlas and fold it into four.

>   *Atlas, last night was a mistake. Please don't write to me again.*

I know he prays in the boys' dormitory after lunch, so I slip the note brazenly under the door. Marquis raises his eyebrows.

"Don't ask," I tell him.

Downstairs is empty except for the Guardian at the door, a different one from earlier.

"Viv—" Marquis hisses as we walk toward him.

"It's fine." I nod at the Guardian. "Afternoon," I say brightly.

He stares at me through his helmet.

"We need to get out, please."

He doesn't move.

"I'm the translator," I say in a bored voice, as if he should already know this. "I have orders to meet with some patrol dragons in the grounds, to help prepare for the . . . arrival."

"The grounds of Bletchley Park are now out of bounds to recruits," the Guardian barks.

"Well, not to *all* recruits," I say sweetly. "Did the Prime Minister not inform you?"

The Guardian blinks and I see a hint of hesitation in his eyes.

I lean closer to him. "How are we to welcome our allies if no one here speaks Bulgarian?"

His eyes widen and he stands aside. As we jump down the steps, Marquis turns and gives him a cheerful wave.

"The Bulgarian dragons speak Slavidraneishá, not Bulgarian," I say, shaking my head. "How does nobody know that?"

It doesn't take us long to find Rhydderch. He's patrolling the left side of the park, by the lake. Muirgen is flying above, circling us as we approach her brother. Rhydderch swings his huge head toward us and bares his teeth.

"You again?" he says gruffly. "I thought my sister scared you off when we last met."

Better to get straight to the point this time.

"Hello, Rhydderch," I say. "We've come to warn you."

The dragon lets out a huff that sends smoke streaming out of his nostrils.

"Warn us?" he says.

The reflection of Muirgen's blue tail flashes on the water of the lake. She's listening.

"Prime Minister Wyvernmire is planning an alliance with the dragons of Bulgaria," I say. "They'll be here in two days, to crush the Coalition and force your Queen into submission."

Rhydderch lets out a deep laugh. "The Bulgarians are the very reason the Peace Agreement exists," he says. "Why would Wyvernmire betray it, especially after she deliberately upheld it when that criminal dragon burned Downing Street?"

I shrug. "The Prime Minister grows impatient. She still hasn't won the war, despite having the Queen and all her dragons on her side. She's resorting to other means of victory."

Above us, Muirgen lets out a screech.

"The Dragon Queen and the Prime Minister came together to fight the rebels when they could have fought each other," says Rhydderch. "I don't believe such an arrangement could be—"

"The Bulgarian dragons owe Britannia, remember?"

Marquis grabs my wrist and squeezes it in warning. I know why. I've just interrupted a dragon. Rhydderch growls. Is he surprised that I know of Britannia's role in the Massacre of Bulgaria?

"Yes, the dragons of Bulgaria are in Britannia's debt. In the debt of the human government *and* Queen Ignacia."

"Except Queen Ignacia can't make the promises Wyvernmire can. If she can promise your old, senile Queen the flesh of human children in exchange for peace, what do you think she'll pay the Bulgarian dragons for their strength?"

Rhydderch roars and the ground beneath our feet shakes. Marquis stumbles backward as the dragon's eyes flash.

"Are you angry because I insulted your Queen?" I say. "Or because I know of the secret clauses she had written into the Peace Agreement? It seems Queen Ignacia is not as honorable as the stories say."

"Shut up, Viv," Marquis says from behind me, but I ignore him.

"Why would you betray your leader to me?" Rhydderch says. "If what you say is true, my Queen will have this place burned to the ground."

"She's not my leader anymore," I say. "And I'm telling you because . . ." I hesitate. "Because we need your help."

"We?"

"The Human-Dragon Coalition," Marquis says.

"You are with the enemy," Rhydderch hisses.

"The Coalition isn't your enemy, not anymore!" I say. "Not if Wyvernmire is going to betray Ignacia the same way she's betraying Britannia's humans."

Muirgen's shadow momentarily blocks out the sun as she continues to circle.

"You have joined the cause that seeks to destroy the Peace

Agreement!" Rhydderch roars. "You are spies!"

He steps backward, swinging his head from side to side, and then his eyes dart up to Muirgen in the sky. In a split second, she lands beside him and lets out a scream in our direction, so loud that it lifts the jacket off my back. Marquis grabs me and pulls me away, but I shake him off.

I look at Rhydderch. "You asked Muirgen to land. With the Koinamens."

"I will kill you this time, human traitor," Muirgen spits.

"I lied to you before," I say quickly. "It wasn't a dragon who told me about the Koinamens. It was Wyvernmire. That's why I was recruited by Bletchley Park. To use special machines to decipher the Koinamens. We call it echolocation."

Muirgen breathes inward and her chest inflates, buoying her body upward until she's towering over me, the lingering smell of blood on her breath. There's a blast of heat and suddenly the tree next to us bursts into flames.

"Viv!" Marquis shouts. "We're leaving."

We both stumble backward, tripping, as Rhydderch shoots his own flames at another tree.

"I'm telling the truth!" I shout. "Wyvernmire ordered us to listen to the Koinamens to help her spy on the rebel dragons."

Rhydderch's tail sways violently, sending two trees behind him crashing down.

"But we've been trying to stop her!" I shout desperately.

"For fuck's sake, Viv!" Marquis screams.

"I'm going to make sure she can never understand the Koinamens. But the fact that I know about it, that I understand some of it, is proof that Wyvernmire is against you, not with you."

The two dragons stop, and for a moment, there's no sound except for the crackling of flames. Marquis has pulled me behind a tree, and we peer round the trunk.

"The Bulgarian dragons will be here soon," I say breathlessly. "If you tell your Queen, then she'll declare war not only on the rebels but on every human in Britannia. The losses will be tremendous on both sides. But if you stay here and fight with us, fight with the Coalition, perhaps we can stop the whole thing from happening. We defeat Wyvernmire and drive the Bulgarian dragons out, and then maybe . . ." I wheeze as black smoke fills my chest. "Maybe humans and dragons can reach an agreement again."

"We are done with your bastardly agreements," says Muirgen, sneering.

"Wait," Rhydderch snarls.

I stare as the dragons face each other, communicating silently. Part of me wishes I had the loquisonus machine with me. Marquis, his cheeks bright red from the heat of the flames, looks at me as if I've just sprouted wings. Then Muirgen bows her head to her brother.

"Go," Rhydderch tells us. "Before your lungs explode."

My heart sinks. If the dragons decide to go to their Queen now, Wyvernmire will know I've told them. She'll make sure I never see my parents or Ursa again. And when Queen Ignacia arrives, she won't stop to ask who's on what side.

"Will you help us?" I say. "Will you tell the other dragons— Soresten and Addax and Yndrir—"

"We will consider your request," Rhydderch growls.

Marquis squeezes my hand, a gentle way of telling me that he'll kill me if I antagonize these dragons anymore.

"Thank you," I say.

We back away slowly, and it's only when we reach the cover of several empty cars that Marquis begins to swear.

"*Senile Queen?*" he says incredulously. "*Force your Queen into submission?* You said those things to not one but two dragons, you bloody lunatic."

All I can do is grin like an idiot.

We duck as several Guardians come down the steps of the manor and turn toward the fields.

"What now?" Marquis says quietly as we watch them go.

"Tell Karim to be ready to escape tonight," I say. "I've got to find Atlas—he and Dr. Seymour might have heard from the Coalition."

"Dr. Seymour?" Marquis says incredulously.

I nod and he rubs his forehead in disbelief. Then he stares up at the sky.

"Do you think the rebels will get here in time?"

I imagine the Bulgarian Bolgoriths swooping down over Bletchley and a hollow feeling fills my stomach. "They have to," I say. "Otherwise, we've lost the war."

TWENTY-FIVE

We part ways in the entrance hall, now empty of Guardians, Marquis heading up to the library and me to the basement. I open the door quietly and the heat hits my face as I peer down the stairs. I hear low voices and descend as quietly as I can. Atlas is here, even though his shift is over. I had a feeling he would be. He and Professor Lumens are crouched down by one of the log burners, peering inside.

"I wonder if perhaps we could try putting the eggs together, see if that will start the hatching process?" Professor Lumens says. "There's usually more than one egg in a nest."

"I've tried that, Professor," Atlas replies.

"Well, what about turning them counterclockwise every full moon?"

"I've tried that, too, sir. I've also bathed them in salt water, like you suggested."

He's a good liar.

"Very well," Lumens says. "In that case, I believe we have no choice but to have them fostered."

"Fostered, sir?"

"By a dragon," says Lumens.

Atlas stands up. "What dragon will agree to foster eggs that Prime Minister Wyvernmire has . . . that were stolen?"

"The Prime Minister seems to think that a criminal dragon, one that is imprisoned, might be convinced—"

"That won't work, either," I say, and they both spin round.

"Recruit Featherswallow?" Professor Lumens's eyes widen in surprise. "What are you doing down here?"

"You can't threaten a dragon into caring for those eggs," I say. "Trust me."

To do so, Wyvernmire would have to force the dragon to echolocate to the eggs to make them hatch. And to ensure that happened, she'd have to have someone sit day and night with the dragon. Someone with a loquisonus machine. Someone fluent in that particular dragon's Koinamens dialect, someone who could understand the exact calls needed to hatch a dragonling, who could raise the alarm if the dragon echolocated something different. Or refused to echolocate at all.

The odds of that happening in the next two days are zero to none.

"I must insist you leave," Lumens says sharply. "This is highly unusual—"

"Actually, Professor," Atlas says, "Vivien has been down here before."

Vivien.

I startle at the sound of my full name, the one used only by teachers and my parents. What happened to *Viv*, to *Featherswallow*? Atlas looks at me, his eyes full of hurt.

He got my note, then.

"Down here before?" Lumens looks from Atlas to me, aghast. "The confidentiality of the program must be respected, even among yourselves—"

There's a squawk from the far end of the room. I peer down into the dimness and see the shapes of three young dragons, now slightly larger than dracovols.

"How long have you been studying dragons, Professor Lumens?" I say.

"Thirty years, a number entirely irrelevant to this conversation," Lumens replies.

"I assume your studies took you all round the world, before the Travel Ban?" I say. "My parents' research took them to Europe, to the Americas, to Albania—"

"Your parents?"

I nod. "John and Helina Featherswallow."

Surprise shines in his eyes. "I had no idea," he says. "Your parents are hugely respected dragon anthropologists, experts in their fields. I was shocked to read in the papers about their—"

"Rebellion?" I say.

Lumens looks uncomfortable.

"So was I."

Atlas is watching me curiously.

"But I understand now," I say to Lumens. "I understand why they were—are—rebels. It wasn't just the terrible way this country treats the Third Class, which I refused to admit until recently. It was their love of dragons, you see. What you're doing down there . . ." I gesture toward the shadowy prison of the dragonlings. "They would never have permitted it. In fact, they would have vehemently opposed it. So why haven't you?"

"I . . ." Lumens frowns. "I'm doing what my government—"

"Your government is allying with the Bulgarian dragons," I say. "They'll arrive at Bletchley Park the day after tomorrow and turn the Dragon Queen against us all. Wyvernmire is about to make herself another enemy, and there's nothing you can do in here to stop it."

"Bulgarians?" Lumens says. "What are you talking about, child—"

"She's telling the truth, Professor," Atlas says. "The work we were supposed to do here has failed, and Wyvernmire has chosen other means to win the war."

Lumens pales and his hands begin to shake.

"You should leave," I tell him. "Feign illness or ask for compassionate leave. Before they get here."

Lumens turns to Atlas. "And you? What will you do?"

"Oh, we have a few ideas."

"The dragonlings . . . we cannot abandon them. Whatever you may think of me, Recruit Featherswallow, I never wanted to harm them."

"We'll deal with them," I say.

"But how—"

"Professor Lumens," Atlas says, "if you're going to leave, you'll need to do it soon."

"Oh . . . yes." Lumens begins rushing about the room, fetching paperwork and belongings.

"She won't let you take any of it," I say. "Everything inside Bletchley Park is classified."

He stares at me for a moment, as if trying to figure out who I really am. Then he drops everything in his arms back onto a desk. He nods at Atlas, once, and then turns on his heel and leaves.

Atlas walks toward me and takes my hand, but I shake him off.

"Why did you leave me that note? What have I done wrong?"

I ignore him. "I came to tell you that we might have convinced Muirgen and Rhydderch to join us," I say.

"Us?"

"The Coalition," I say softly.

A grin spreads across his face, but falters when he sees I'm not smiling back.

"What's wrong?" he says again.

"Chumana," I reply.

I watch his face for a reaction and catch just a hint of hesitation in his eyes. I take a furious step forward.

"When were you planning on telling me you knew her? Don't answer that," I snap as he opens his mouth. "You were never going to tell me because you don't trust me. Everything you said last night was just an attempt to get me on your side."

"Viv, no—"

"I told you I'd released a criminal dragon from the University of London and you *knew* it was her, but you didn't tell me you were sneaking off to visit her—"

"I wasn't visiting her," he retorts. "She came to me when she saw they had me in isolation. It's a freezing-cold bunker in the forest, and when she saw me there she lit me a fire through the bars. What does it matter anyway?"

"It matters because you *kept things* from me while I *bared my soul* to you!" I shout.

"I didn't want you to think we were conspiring against you!" Atlas shouts back. "Trying to get you to join the Coalition—"

"But that's exactly what you were doing."

Atlas shakes his head. "I know that's something you have to choose for yourself." He puts his hands on my shoulders. "Everything

I said last night and—and all that other stuff . . ." He blushes. "I meant every bit of it. I promise."

"And what if I'd stayed on Wyvernmire's side?" I say carefully.

He holds my gaze. "That would have been . . . difficult. But I still would have loved—"

He stops abruptly and lets his arms drop by his sides as his face turns red. I swallow, willing him to finish the sentence.

"Dr. Seymour just received a message from the Coalition," he says instead. "Wyvernmire's on her way back here and they're readying themselves to attack. They don't know about the alliance yet because Dr. Seymour's dracovol won't reach them until tonight. But it means they'll get to Bletchley before the Bulgarians do."

I nod.

"There's something else."

I look at him expectantly.

"The Coalition has located your sister."

My heart stops.

"I sent out a search request a couple of weeks ago, using Dr. Seymour's dracovol. The news came back with today's message. She's in a government-run home in Blenheim with other children evacuated from London."

Atlas takes my hand. "When we're out of Bletchley," he says, "we'll go and get her."

My heart thumps loudly in my chest.

I sent out a search request a couple of weeks ago.

Atlas was searching for my sister before he even knew I was going to change sides. He was searching for my sister while I was trying to break the code that would make sure the rebels lost the war.

"Why?" I whisper.

Atlas shrugs. "Families deserve to be together."

I melt into him, my arms round his neck, and he lifts me off my feet as I kiss him.

"When the Coalition gets here, how are we going to escape?" I murmur, my lips still on his.

Atlas smooths my hair back. "Your cousin had an idea."

I don't ask him how long he and Marquis have been secretly discussing escape plans. Instead, I let him lift me onto one of the desks and kiss me deeper, and as his lips find my neck, I stare over his shoulder at the open log burner, at the eggs as hot as coals inside—

"Atlas!" I say.

He jumps, his hands retreating as if my skin had scalded them.

"I'm sorry," he says, swallowing hard. "I got carried away—"

I roll my eyes. "No, not that," I say, half wishing he'd put his hands back where they were. "The eggs. And the dragonlings. We'll have to get them out tonight, with Karim."

He nods several times, like a drunk person trying to understand simple instructions. "We haven't got time to be . . ." He gestures to the desk beneath me and I smirk.

"There will be other opportunities," I say innocently.

He blushes again. "So tomorrow we go to our shifts as usual, and wait for the rebels."

"What if Wyvernmire finds out your dragonlings are gone?" I say.

Atlas glances round his basement workshop and I see a hint of sadness. First Dodie gone, then Lumens, and now the dragonlings.

"We'll blame it on Lumens," I say, answering my own question.

"What? No—"

"He'll be gone by then," I say. "We say that Lumens stole the dragonlings and the eggs, so no one suspects you. By the time she organizes her Guardians to go after him, the rebels will be here."

"All right," Atlas says slowly. "We'll need to remove the sonar blockers around the glasshouse. Otherwise, they might stop the rebel dragons from communicating when they fly over."

I nod.

"We meet at midnight," Atlas says. "Outside your dorm."

"Midnight," I repeat, pulling him toward me with a smile.

TWENTY-SIX

I get out of bed at a quarter to midnight. In the hallway, a floor-board creaks beneath the Guardian's feet as he readies himself for the end of his shift. Sophie sits up in the bed next to mine, lights the lamp, and glares at me.

You'll pay for what you did to me.

"We're going to get caught," she whispers.

"No, we're not," I say. "We'll go as soon as that Guardian leaves." I pull on my jacket and boots.

"How nice for you to be Wyvernmire's pet one day and a rebel the next," Sophie says. "Will you go back to being a Second Class snob when it's all over?"

"You were a Second Class snob, too, once," I say.

"But I didn't betray my best friend to get into university."

There's the pang of guilt again, the one that will never go away. How did I even entertain the thought that Sophie might forgive me?

"No," I say. "You're a better friend than I ever was. Now will you please get dressed?"

We hear the shuffle of footsteps going down the stairs. The Guardians usually have a cigarette break together in the courtyard before changing shifts. We have about two minutes to get out. I open the door a crack and jump as a face appears on the other side.

"All right?" Marquis says.

Karim and Atlas are standing behind him. When I slip out onto the landing, I let my hand brush against Atlas's. He has a large pack on his back.

"This is going to get us killed," Sophie says to Marquis as we hurry down the stairs.

Marquis shrugs. "Better than waiting for Gideon to come and murder you, wouldn't you say?"

We walk through the dark hallways and the kitchen, then out the back door and into the walled garden where Ralph broke my arm.

"You're meeting the dragon at the top of the forest," I whisper to Karim.

I wonder if Serena really is hiding in town. She must be terrified. For all I dislike her, I wish that she was here with us now, about to escape. We walk through the trees in silence and when we reach the glasshouse Atlas stops. He pulls the pack off his back and hands it to Karim.

"Give it to the dragon," he says. "She'll know what to do with it."

Karim gives Atlas a wary look, then opens the pack and almost drops it.

The three dragonlings are curled up inside, their tails entangled, and poking out from beneath them are two dragon eggs.

"Where did you—"

"This is what my and Dodie's work involved," Atlas says darkly. "Kidnapping babies."

"Keep walking straight up," I tell Karim, "until you reach a field. She's waiting for you."

He nods nervously as I turn to Sophie. "You should go with

him. Now's your chance to—"

"To live as a fugitive for the rest of my life?" Sophie glares at me, then glances at Atlas. "If his rebel friends burn Wyvernmire tonight, I want to be here to watch."

Next to me, Karim is locked in Marquis's embrace.

"Be careful," Karim tells him fiercely.

Marquis nods, his hands cupping Karim's face. "You too."

They kiss—one chaste kiss—and I stiffen. Marquis glances at me, as the secret we've guarded all these years finally emerges into the open. Then Karim walks up into the forest and I lean against my cousin.

"You'll see him again soon," I say.

He forces a smile. "I know."

It strikes me then that we could *all* go, Atlas, Marquis, Sophie, and I. Climb onto Chumana's back and fly away from Bletchley tonight. But I *want* to be here, I realize. I want to see the rebels with my own eyes, want to watch as Wyvernmire witnesses her stupid plan backfire.

And I want to be the one who makes sure she never sees a single translation of the Koinamens.

"Atlas!" a voice hisses.

I jump, then relax. A pale face, lit up by a lantern, is peering out of the back window of the glasshouse. Dr. Seymour.

We pile through the window, stepping through the mess of wires from the reperisonus machines, and Dr. Seymour hands Marquis a second lantern. He lifts it toward the two loquisonus machines on the sofa, their brass speakers glinting in the light. Next to them is a hammer.

Sophie's eyes widen. "We're going to destroy them?"

"It's the only way to keep them out of the wrong hands," Dr. Seymour says. She passes the hammer to Atlas. "That can be your job. Sophie and Marquis, I need you to move the sonar blockers. Get them as far away from here as you can. We have to make sure they don't interfere with any echolocation calls sent by rebel dragons flying over the glasshouse."

Marquis nods and he and Sophie creep back outside.

"And me?" I say to Dr. Seymour.

"The indexing system," Dr. Seymour replies. "And the logbooks. Every translation we've made has to go."

I feel my stomach drop. I glance at the box of index cards on the table, months of hard work. All about to be destroyed. Atlas looks at me, the hammer held between his hands. I nod. Then he lifts the hammer over his head and brings it down onto the loquisonus machine. It smashes into a hundred pieces, sending splintering glass across the sofa and floor. He lifts an arm to protect his face as glass continues to skitter, then brings the hammer down again. I wince at the noise.

"Where is Soresten?" I say to Dr. Seymour, realizing I didn't see a guard outside.

"I saw him talking to Muirgen this evening. He seems to have abandoned his post."

I feel a fizz of hope, then unease. Has Soresten deserted Wyvernmire to help the rebels? Or has he gone to warn Queen Ignacia?

"How do you want to destroy this?" I ask Dr. Seymour. "We can't light a fire."

But Dr. Seymour is already dragging a bucket of water toward me.

"Soak it all," she says.

I take a handful of index cards, each one covered in my hand-writing, or Sophie's, or Gideon's, or Katherine's. I read the lists of trills and skrills and sweeps and feel a strange rush of grief. I plunge the cards into the water. They float for a moment, then sink. In a few minutes, I'll be able to mash them to a pulp. I help Dr. Seymour push more papers into the bucket, ripping page after page out of the logbooks. I jump as Atlas hits the loquisonus machine one more time, then pulls the second toward him.

We don't have a choice, I tell myself as I stare at the most beautiful invention I've ever seen lying twisted and bent on the ground. Dr. Seymour, I notice, hasn't looked at it once.

Footsteps sound outside. I crane my neck to look for Sophie and Marquis, but no one emerges through the window. Instead, the steps go round the other side of the glasshouse. Dr. Seymour's eyes meet mine and we freeze. The door to the glasshouse bangs open.

"Dolores Seymour, you are under arrest for collaborating with the enemy."

Ralph is standing in the doorway, pointing a gun. When he sees me and Atlas, his mouth spreads into a smile.

"Three for the price of one."

I grab the last of the index cards and plunge them into the water as a group of Guardians storm in and seize us, snatching the hammer from Atlas's hands and handcuffing Dr. Seymour. Ralph grabs me by the hair and I scream as he pulls me to my feet.

"Get off her!" Atlas shouts.

"I should have known you'd be involved in this, too," Ralph says in my ear. "What will the Prime Minister say when I tell her that her best recruit is a spy?"

"The Prime Minister is working with Bulgaria," I say as a

Guardian wrestles my hands behind my back. "She's going to get us all killed."

Dr. Seymour is glaring at Ralph with pure hatred. "How did you find out?"

Ralph smiles and reaches into his pocket. He pulls out the dracovol, blood pouring from its nostrils, its eyes staring.

Oh no.

Dr. Seymour closes her eyes and lets out a shaky breath.

"We caught the blighter returning to its nest, no doubt after having completed a delivery?" Ralph sneers. "Passing messages to the rebels right under our noses. Perhaps I didn't give you enough credit, after all, Dolores."

He stares at me and Atlas. "Where are the rest of the recruits?" he barks.

Neither of us speaks.

"Are you going to tell me you have no idea where your cousin is?" Ralph snarls.

"I suppose he must be in bed," I say. "He's not involved in this."

"Liar."

"Do you really think we'd go looking for the other recruits?" Atlas says. "They've been trying to murder us!"

"Take them to Ravensloe," Ralph tells the Guardians. "Guardian 257, stay here and guard that machine. The rest of you, find out where the hell the fucking patrol dragon's gone."

They take us to the seminar room, where Ravensloe is standing by the desk like on the first day we met him. But any trace of his fake friendliness is gone.

"You dare betray your benefactors?" he snarls as we're lined up in front of him.

"Benefactors?" Atlas says. "Is that what you tell yourself you are?"

"You'd be dead without Bletchley, boy," Ravensloe says.

"We'll all be dead soon, Deputy Prime Minister," says Dr. Seymour. "How *could* you? How could you do this to Britannia? The Bulgarian dragons—"

"Silence!" Ravensloe roars. "I'll not be lectured to by you deserter scum." He jerks his head toward Ralph. "Where are the rest of them?"

"My team is still searching," Ralph says. "They're—"

"It stuns me how incapable you are of keeping track of a group of teenagers," Ravensloe says.

Anger flickers in Ralph's eyes. "They've been given too much freedom," he says. "The Prime Minister put her trust in the wrong—"

"The Prime Minister expects everyone to perform their duty, recruit and Guardian alike," Ravensloe says, staring at Ralph. "When she hears of this, she'll—"

His voice is drowned out by a loud whirring sound. Through the blackout curtains, lights flash. It's the sound of propellers. A helicopter.

"Oh, and here she is now." Ravensloe feigns a cheerful voice. Then he points at Atlas. "You. Have you *anything* to show for your work in Zoology? Any information to give your Prime Minister in the morning?"

Atlas snorts.

"I'm afraid not," he says. "I did pass on a lot of information to the Coalition, though."

The Guardian behind him lands a punch to his head, smashing his face against the floor. Dr. Seymour and I both scream.

"And you?" Ravensloe says, looking at us. "Have you cracked the dragon code? Or will I be sentencing you both to death this evening?"

I look at my friends, at Atlas's bleeding face pressed to the floor by the Guardian's boot, at Dr. Seymour's defiant glare saying one thing, but the hand pressed to her stomach another. We've lost before we've even begun. Ravensloe has us now, and Marquis and Sophie are out there in the dark. What if the Guardians find Karim and the dragonlings before they reach Chumana? Maybe we should have just waited for the rebels to get here, continued to play along . . .

I look from Ralph's goading face to Ravensloe's expectant one.

"Yes," I tell him calmly. "I've cracked the code."

Ralph's sneer disappears.

"Viv!" Atlas shouts. "Don't be stupid. You can't—"

"They'll kill us if I don't," I snap. I glare at Ravensloe. "Won't you?"

"If you fail to complete the work required of you, you will be judged for your crimes and punished accordingly, as made very clear to you when you accepted this job," Ravensloe says. "Unfortunately, those crimes now include treason, which is punishable by death."

"If we're guilty of treason, then so is the Prime Minister," Dr. Seymour says. "She's on the verge of putting Britannia under foreign rule."

I close my eyes. Marquis and Sophie might still live, but Sophie will spend the rest of her life in Granger's Prison as a class defector. Serena will be demoted or forced into marriage. And Gideon? I don't even know what he did to get here.

"She's lying, Deputy Prime Minister," Ralph says sharply. "She doesn't have the code."

"I'm not lying," I say. "I've been learning it for months, but I needed to be sure I was giving the Prime Minister the correct information. I'll give you the code and all of its translations, but only if you let the rest of the recruits go. Only if you pardon them."

"They failed to keep their side of the deal, Miss Featherswallow—"

"Giving Wyvernmire the code is the only chance you have at canceling this alliance," I say.

Hesitation flickers in Ravensloe's eyes.

"If it's confirmed, the Bulgarians will turn against the Prime Minister eventually. We all know that's inevitable."

I glance at Atlas staring up at me from the floor.

"So let Atlas and Dr. Seymour go, call off your search for the others, and I'll give it to you."

Ravensloe moves slowly out from behind his desk, his eyes on Ralph.

"Guardian 707, if I am not mistaken, your time in the German Freikorps taught you a wide range of persuasion techniques?"

Ralph stands up straighter. "Yes, sir."

"What were they?"

"The techniques were for use on dragons, sir," he says. "We couldn't use brute force, which was easily equaled by our prisoners, so we resorted to subtler, sharper techniques." Ralph removes a long, thin knife from his belt. "The fine art of cutting was one."

"Would you care to demonstrate?"

Ralph gives Ravensloe a stunned look, as if trying to gauge whether he is serious. Then he smiles. A Guardian grabs me from behind and thrusts me toward Ralph.

"No!" Atlas and Dr. Seymour scream together.

"Get off me," I spit, but the Guardian kicks my legs out from beneath me and lays me at Ralph's feet, pinning me by my shoulders.

He kneels down to my level and reaches toward me. I try to kick out, but another Guardian grabs my legs. Ralph lifts the sleeve of my jacket and shirt. He looks to the Guardian. "Hold her still."

"I'll kill you!" Atlas roars.

The knife cuts into my arm and I scream. Tears and pain blur my vision as I arch my back, but moving my arm is impossible. Ralph drags the blade along my skin and I scream again, nausea rising up inside me as I clench my eyes shut.

"I have information about the dragon eggs!" comes Atlas's muffled voice. "Please, just stop hurting her!"

Ralph lifts the knife and I feel the cool tip at my wrist.

"All she has to do is give us the code," Ravensloe says. "Will you do that, recruit?"

I keep my eyes shut, the dim light shining pink through my eyelids. I hear the door creak open and a gasp of surprise.

"Prime Minister Wyvernmire," Ravensloe says. "I wasn't expecting a visit tonight."

The knife tip disappears. My eyes fly open. Wyvernmire is standing in the doorway, dressed in a long green coat, her dragon's talon brooch gleaming at her throat.

"Whyever would that be?" Wyvernmire says sharply. Lines furrow deep across her brow, as if the past few days have aged her. "Did you expect me to sit in my rooms while you obtained crucial information?"

Ralph is still kneeling over me, staring up at his aunt like a little boy caught doing something bad.

"They were found sabotaging the contents of the glasshouse," he says. "You said to use any means necessary, Prime Minister."

"Indeed I did," Wyvernmire replies, her gaze finally falling on me.

I stare back at her, and for a brief moment I hope to see a trace of the woman who told me we were alike. But her face betrays not a trace of emotion.

"Except that is not the girl you will be torturing."

Ralph stands up. "No?"

"No," Wyvernmire says.

She moves aside with a swish of her coat to reveal a small, trembling figure behind her.

"This is."

I sit up, my whole body screaming in horror. The child stares at me, recognition flashing in her golden eyes. Then she stretches out her arms toward me and lets out a deep, desperate moan.

Ursa.

TWENTY-SEVEN

Someone is screaming, and I don't realize the voice is my own until Ursa barrels into my arms. No one moves to restrain us and for a blissful moment, as I press my lips to Ursa's cold cheek and breathe in the smell of her hair, everything around us falls away. My sister's tiny body shakes with silent sobs.

"Shh, little bear," I whisper into her ear. "I've got you. You're safe."

I'm surprised at how easily the lie comes. Perhaps it's because I know that I'll do everything in my power to make it true. Ursa burrows into me, her hands clutching at my hair, her dirty shoes pressing onto my thighs as if the ground is on fire. I scoop her up like a baby and hold her close as I stand up. Over the top of her head, Wyvernmire's face comes into focus. My chest fills with fire as I recall her words. Torture my sister?

Over my dead body.

The Guardians have pulled Atlas and Dr. Seymour to their feet and Wyvernmire surveys them with barely a hint of interest.

"What a disappointment you have all been," she says. She turns back to me. "You will provide me with the code, and all of its possible variations, immediately. Refuse, and Guardian 707 will continue his barbarous techniques on the child."

Terror prickles my skin. Wyvernmire nods at a Guardian, who

steps forward and pulls Ursa from my arms.

"No!" I scream as Ursa clings to my neck. "Please don't take her again. Just—"

But the Guardian lifts Ursa away by the back of her coat, depositing her between Dr. Seymour and Atlas as she sobs.

"I'll give you the code," I say breathlessly. "Just please don't hurt her."

"See, gentlemen?" Wyvernmire says with a cold smile. "There was no need to make things so messy. Love is the finest form of torture."

I glance at Ursa, hot tears streaming down my face, the air quiet except for the sound of her hysterical hiccups. Slowly, Atlas reaches out and takes her hand.

"Lock those three in the basement," Wyvernmire says. "And find the other recruits. I'll nip this miniature rebellion in the bud right now."

Any energy I have left in me disappears. My chest aches as the realization sinks in. We've been caught, and now, with Ursa here, Wyvernmire can make me do whatever she wants. I *have* to give her the code. I think of Ralph's face as he pressed the knife to my arm and swallow another wave of nausea. The thought of him anywhere near Ursa is unthinkable. The rebels haven't attacked yet, and in a few hours, I'll have signed the fate of the dragons and the Third Class over to Wyvernmire.

"There are reports of unidentified dragons in the skies," Wyvernmire tells me. "You must find out their exact location."

"I'll need to go to the glasshouse, then," I say. "To use the remaining loquisonus machine."

Wyvernmire nods. "Guardian 707 will take you. Once you

366

have identified the dragons, you will write out everything you know about the code on paper for him." She looks at her nephew. "See that it is delivered to me before daybreak."

Ralph grabs me by the arm.

"Let me take my sister with me," I say quickly. "I'll work faster if I know she's safe."

Wyvernmire purses her lips. "You'll work faster if you know she's not."

I swallow a sob. "I'll come back for you," I tell Ursa, feeling my jaw tremble. "I won't leave you again. Do you understand?"

She wipes her tears away with her free hand and nods bravely. Suddenly Atlas breaks free, lunging toward me and grabbing me by the shoulders. He kisses me, his lips like fire on mine.

"Don't give it to her," he whispers as he's pulled away.

"On second thought," Wyvernmire says, surveying the scene with amused interest, "take the boy up to the roof. He can have a last look at the dragons he failed to re-create before you push him off."

"No!" I scream.

Ralph pushes me from the room, his hand on the back of my neck, and Ursa's cries fill the air again.

"Don't do it, Viv!" I hear Atlas shout.

But he doesn't understand. There's nothing else I can possibly do. Blood drips down my arm as we stumble through the dark into the forest. I twist my body round to search for any sign of Atlas on the roof, but I see nothing up there except the shape of a patrol dragon flying above. Is it Muirgen or Rhydderch? Or have they abandoned us?

"I should have known you were a rebel," Ralph says as we reach the glasshouse. "I should have broken your other arm when I had the chance."

I want to make a quick cutthroat reply, or turn round and spit in his face, but I don't dare. Not after the threat Wyvernmire made to Ursa. Not now that I know the feeling of a knife on my skin, ten times worse than the sting of the switch. We push the door open and Ralph dismisses the Guardian guarding the loquisonus machine. I tread carefully through the broken remnants of its sister and place it on the table as Ralph shines a light. He pulls out a chair for me.

"Get to work, then, dragon whisperer," he says with a sneer.

I put the headphones on and twist the dial, willing my hands to stop shaking. The crackling sound fills my ears as I search for the right frequency and strain to hear the familiar clicks and trills of the Koinamens. Ralph sits across the table from me, his stare fixed on my face. I ignore him and close my eyes to listen.

There they are. A string of social calls. Whatever dragons are in the area have something to say. I listen closer. Are they talking about . . . landing?

"Explain this to me," Ralph says loudly. He's looking at what's left of the logbook, the pages we didn't manage to soak. "How do you know what the different sequences mean?"

I hold up my palm to tell him to shut up and feel a tiny stab of satisfaction at the look of shock on his face. My mind is spinning faster and faster, panicking as I realize I barely recognize a single call. A chill runs through me. What if these are Bulgarian dragons? What if Wyvernmire has already confirmed the alliance? We need the rebels *now*.

"I was able to understand echolocation by interacting with passing dragons, but without them knowing it was me," I lie. "I played snippets of echolocation recordings within the Bletchley perimeter, alerting them, for example, to an unidentified human, and listened to how they responded."

Thank God Marquis and Sophie moved the blockers before we got caught. Without it, the crazy idea forming in my head wouldn't work. Where is Atlas now? Have they taken him to the roof yet? My stomach fills with dread.

"I'm going to need to use those," I tell Ralph, pointing to the reperisonus machines.

I unplug the headphones and pull a wire from one of the machines, then plug it into the loquisonus.

"Why?" Ralph demands. "What for?"

"I'm transferring a previous echolocation recording of social calls back onto the loquisonus," I say.

That part is true. I press the tiny black buttons on the big machines, scanning the screen for the recording I labeled *Snake Maiden*. Then I send it to the loquisonus machine, followed by another I recorded a few weeks ago. Heart thumping, I sit back down in front of the loquisonus and glance at Ralph. He's staring at me intently. A bead of sweat trickles down my back.

"Now I'm going to play a part of one of the recordings," I say.

I flick the switch from *input* to *output* like I did the day I called to Chumana in the forest.

"I'm going to pretend to be a dragon, to see if any of the ones spotted nearby will interact with me. I like to call it the art of interception." I give him a level gaze. "I bet you'd be good at that."

A self-absorbed smile plays on his lips. I may just have bought myself some time.

I hit *play*. I can't hear them, but I know Chumana's calls are being converted back to their original frequency and hitting the air, which is no longer obstructed by sonar blockers.

Snake.
Maiden.

I count the seconds, enough for the first calls, then hit *rewind* and play them again.

Snake.
Maiden.

And again.

Snake.
Maiden.

"I don't hear anything," Ralph says, tapping on the speaker.

"The speaker, or headphones, plays incoming calls converted at an audible frequency for humans," I say. "But the output calls are emitted through vibrations in the air, imperceptible to the human ear."

Ralph leans forward eagerly as I press another button. I wonder how Dr. Seymour would have further developed the loquisonus machines had she got the chance. I imagine a smaller device, with a button for each individual echolocation call, or several devices designed to speak different dialects.

I press the button again, flicking back to the other recording. It's a call from weeks ago, when some of the patrol dragons were discussing protocol for an attack. Is the word recognized universally, or am I about to use a call that belongs to a dialect? I'm willing to bet it's universal.

I hit *play.*

Attack.

Ralph stares, his face a picture of confusion. I flick back and forth between the two recordings, hitting *play, pause,* and *rewind* as fast as my fingers can move.

Snake.

Maiden.
Attack.
Attack.
Attack.

"All right, that's enough," Ralph says, pulling the loquisonus machine toward him. "What did you say?"

"I sent out some ranging calls," I lie. I might as well make use of the fact that Ralph knows nothing about echolocation. "If you let me put the headphones on, when the calls bounce back, I'll be able to measure how far away the dragons are."

I want to laugh at the insanity of what I'm saying and the fact that Ralph clearly believes it.

"Forget about the dragons." He pushes the logbook toward me. "Give me the code."

"You don't get it," I say, shaking my head. "This language is complicated. It's not something that can be learned in a night—"

"For your sister's sake, it better be," Ralph snarls. He slams a fist down onto the logbook. "Look at this—why is nothing clear?" He points at my entry for Croon-246 and the hurried notes beneath it. "It says here that this call has six variants! And they all mean *to burn*! Are you deliberately trying to confuse us?"

It's simple really, I want to say to him. *The sound of the Croon-246 varies depending on the dragon emitting it. In Muirgen's dialect, the call has a slight inflection that doesn't appear in Soresten's version. And when Yndrir emits the call to Muirgen the tone is different, much deeper than it is when he uses it to talk to—*

"Answer me!" Ralph shouts.

I meet his eyes as he towers over me, his lips shining with spittle.

"What are you hiding?"

Atlas's voice rings in my head.

Don't do it, Viv!

Ralph's hand slips round my neck. "Answer me, or I'll cut that sister of yours into tiny pieces."

Did Chumana hear my calls? Did *anyone* hear?

"I already told you," I say calmly. "If you give me the headphones, I can—"

Ralph pushes me and I fall backward over the chair, hitting my head on the corner of the table. I stumble to my feet, wincing, as he comes toward me again.

"You've been lying to me." There's a dangerous edge to his voice, one I haven't yet heard—not even when he broke my arm. "I told the Prime Minister you weren't doing your job, but she wouldn't listen. What did you send out through that machine? Who are you communicating with?"

Blood trickles down my forehead and I wipe it out of my eye.

"No one," I say. "I just did what you asked—"

"Liar!" Ralph screams.

He pulls the knife from his belt. I back away until I'm behind the sofa, looking desperately among Dr. Seymour's empty coffee cups for something to defend myself with. All I can see is the dented speaker from the smashed loquisonus machine. I stumble toward it, but Ralph catches me by the back of my hair and I scream as he pulls a handful away. I dig my nails into his arm as he wrestles me onto the sofa.

"Let go of me, you bastard," I spit, bringing my knee up between his legs.

He lets out a pained cry, but thrusts me backward and straddles me, grabbing both my wrists in one hand and releasing the knife from its sheath with the other.

"In Germany, we used to slice the scales off dragons one by one," Ralph says with a smirk, the badges on his uniform glinting in the light. "They don't grow back, you see, so it was something we could take from them. And they're worth a fortune on the black market."

I struggle beneath him, but his grip is too strong. His eyes linger on my face, then slowly down the rest of my body.

"Now, I wonder what I could take from you?"

I gather up all the saliva in my mouth and spit in his face.

He laughs. "Bitch," he says, wiping his eyes with his sleeve. He places the tip of the knife at the corner of my mouth. "This will teach you to smile when I tell you to."

I scream as Ralph draws the knife across my skin.

"Where are the dragons you're communicating with?" he grunts.

"There aren't any—"

He cuts again and my mouth fills with blood.

"You brought this on yourself," Ralph says. "My aunt told me all about how you betrayed your friend. And now you're betraying your government, your country. You should be thanking me for not giving you worse, for not—"

"You're just bitter," I gasp, staring into his eyes. "Bitter that Wyvernmire brought you back from Germany just to be a useless Guardian, bitter that she didn't trust you to be a codebreaker or an aviator or a zoologist. Bitter that she chose *me*."

Ralph's nostrils flare as his face turns red, his mouth twisting into a terrifying, furious smile.

"You'll pay for what you did to me."

The words are like an electric shock. The exact same words Sophie used. Ralph leans forward, the sharp smell of his aftershave filling my nose.

"You think you can play the hero now, after everything you've ruined?" he whispers in my ear. "You deserve to suffer, Vivien Featherswallow. But you already know that, don't you?"

Terror rises up inside me. What if he's right? What if this is how things end for me, a retribution for all the awful things I've done?

I think of what Chumana did in Bulgaria and how she's dedicating her life to making up for it now. I think of how Mama told me that everyone must live with the consequences of their actions, and how I know, because I know my mama, that this isn't what she meant. I think of how much I used to hate myself because I couldn't see a way out of my own guilt.

"It's never too late to change, Ralph Wyvernmire," I whisper back. "Even *I* get a second chance."

I open my mouth as if to kiss him, then sink my teeth into his neck. He roars in agony and springs off me, holding his hand to his neck as I spit blood from my mouth. I roll off the sofa and onto the floor, then grab a shard of jagged metal from the ground.

"Don't come near me again," I snarl. "Otherwise, when the rebels win this war, I'll make sure the dragons know how you tortured their kin."

Ralph laughs, blood seeping out from between his fingers. "I'm not going anywhere except inside to make sure little Ursa knows the feeling of a knife on her soft skin—"

"Like hell you are," says a voice.

Someone moves in the shadows behind Ralph and then there's a *CRACK*.

Ralph jerks forward, his knife dropping to the floor with a clatter. His eyes roll back as he lands beside it. Marquis sets the butt of his gun down.

"Viv?" he croaks. "Are you all right?"

I stifle a sob and nod, and he holds out his arms to me.

"Where's Sophie?" I say as we break apart.

"In the forest," Marquis says. "After they took you, we tried to follow, but some Guardians found us and it was too dark to see anything. I hit one and got his gun, and then I heard you screaming." His voice breaks. "And then on my way here a dragon flew so low it knocked me over—"

"A dragon?" I say. "What did it look like?"

"Well, I hardly stopped to admire it, Viv—what are you doing?"

I step over Ralph and rush to the window. Through the trees, Bletchley Manor is on fire. And there's a dragon flying toward the glasshouse. I grab the loquisonus machine from the table and head for the door.

"Come on!" I say.

Out in the forest, I hide the machine beneath a pile of leaves.

"We might need it later to communicate with the Coalition," I tell Marquis.

We turn our faces toward the smoking sky and the tops of the trees tremble as Chumana lands beside us with a crash, black smoke billowing from her nostrils. She looks down at Marquis and me, her amber eyes burning.

"Never use that artificial tongue to talk to me again, human girl," she says.

Then she swings her huge head down to the ground and a figure jumps off her neck, landing with a thump on the frozen ground.

"Evening, misfits," Atlas says with a grin. "Ready for redemption?"

TWENTY-EIGHT

Atlas's triumph turns to shock as he sees the blood on my face.

"What did he do to you?" he stutters, tracing the cut that runs from the corner of my mouth to my cheek.

I ignore the question. "She didn't push you off the roof?"

"Oh, she did," Chumana says calmly. "I had to catch him like a dog catches a stick."

Marquis smothers a laugh and Chumana looks pleased.

"Where's Karim?" he asks.

"I was flying him to safety when I heard Vivien's calls," Chumana growls. "I left him on a nearby farm."

"We need to get Ursa and Dr. Seymour," I say. "Are they in the—"

"Basement," Atlas says with a nod, his eyes on the glasshouse. "Where's Ralph?"

"I knocked him out," says Marquis unapologetically. Then he turns to me. "Did you say . . . Ursa?"

But before I can explain, Chumana breathes flames from her mouth and nostrils. I feel the heat scorch my hair and pull Marquis back as we watch the glasshouse burn. Orange flames lick up the edges of the building and windowpanes shatter. Through the empty frames, I see the fire spreading, finding its way across the worn rugs and up the wooden tables, eating through the cushions and the plants and the magazine collection. Soon it will devour the last of my notes and the remnants of the first loquisonus machine.

"Ralph," I say. "He's still alive in there."

Atlas and Marquis look at each other.

"See, after what he did to you, Viv—" Marquis begins.

"Atlas," I say sharply. "Surely you're not going to—"

"No," Atlas says with a frustrated sigh. "No, I suppose I'm not."

He runs round to the secret window in the glasshouse and steps inside.

"Oh, for fuck's sake," Marquis says, going after him.

Chumana turns to me. "There is something you must know, something I failed to explain to you last time."

I wait.

"The Koinamens calls you hear through your machine, the ones that make us dragons sound like birds. They do not sound that way to dragons. The conversion to a frequency humans can hear distorts them and strips them of the crucial thing they carry."

There's a screech as the structure of the glasshouse begins to weaken.

I take a step closer to Chumana. "What thing?"

"Emotion," Chumana says. "Each call carries a complex emotion. A warning call will give the receiver a sudden sensation of fear, like an electric shock. And if the communicating dragons are closely bonded, are from the same family, one may even be able to see, momentarily, through the other's eyes."

I shake my head, struggling to grasp what she means. Marquis and Atlas reappear, coughing and pulling Ralph between them. But my focus is on Chumana's voice alone.

"The stronger the bond between dragons, the better they can understand each other. That is why dragons who don't know each other can only communicate using basic calls, calls that, without that emotional link running through their bones, they sometimes fail to understand."

I think of the way Muirgen and Rhydderch communicated so instinctively, yet could barely echolocate with Borislav.

"So that's what a familial dialect is?" I say. "A strong emotional bond?"

Glass shatters behind us again and Marquis puts a hand on my arm.

"Viv, we have to go."

"Yes," Chumana hisses. "And while it is possible to translate the Koinamens into human language, its emotion, and therefore most of its meaning, is inevitably lost."

"Every act of translation requires sacrifice," I murmur to myself.

"*This* is why humans must never be permitted to imitate it," Chumana says urgently. Her eyes are like golden suns, boring into me as if trying to read my mind. "To record and emit one of Muirgen's calls to Rhydderch on its original frequency would cause him to *feel* her in his being. It would be like playing your sister's voice to you inside your mind, as clear as if she were standing right beside you. You would follow it to the ends of the earth, would you not?"

Chumana lets out a loud, hot breath. "So would Rhydderch. And the Bulgarian humans *knew* this. It is why they wanted to exploit it, and it is why they are dead."

A loud roar rings through the night.

"Wyvernmire's dragons know you're here," Atlas tells Chumana, laying Ralph at the foot of a tree.

Chumana nods, watching me as I try to wrap my mind round what she has just revealed. Any human translation of the Koinamens would be a pale imitation of its original meaning. I glance back at the glasshouse. What we were doing in there was an impossible task. And yet even our feeble attempts could have had disastrous consequences. Now I understand Muirgen's fury and why Chumana flew all the way to Bletchley to make me see.

"I'm going for Ursa," I tell the boys.

Atlas nods. "And then we need to get to the Aviation workshop."

"The Aviation workshop?"

"That's how we escape," Atlas says.

"Can't we go on Chumana's—"

Chumana swoops upward, her wings beating just above our heads before she glides across the trees toward the manor. There's a sound like screeching metal.

"She's fighting," Atlas says.

"Am I hearing this right?" Marquis says. "Are you suggesting we escape by plane?"

"Yes," Atlas says impatiently. "You built it. Didn't you tell me you know it inside out?"

"Doesn't mean I can fly it, you bloody idiot!" Marquis replies.

"We're wasting time!" I shout. "Marquis, can you find Sophie?"

"She'll be at the manor," he says. "We agreed to meet there if we got separated."

We run through the forest, the sound of exploding glass echoing behind us, until we reach the garden. In the sky above the manor, Chumana collides with another dragon, sending it smashing into the roof.

"Fire!" a maid screams as she comes running out the kitchen door. "Dragons!"

We duck as a ball of flames hits the bush next to us and then two Guardians come running round the corner.

They both shout when they see us. "All recruits are to report to—"

Marquis raises his gun and shoots. The bullet skitters off the drainpipe, but it's enough to make them disappear behind the wall.

"Reckon you could do any better?" Marquis says to Atlas when he smirks.

"Absolutely not," Atlas replies.

He follows me through the door, but I stop as a group of people hurtle down the dark hallway toward us.

"Go back, go back!" I shout to Atlas, turning round.

"Viv!" squeaks a small voice. "Did you see the dragon catch that boy in the sky?"

I feel Marquis tense and Atlas fumbles with a light.

Dr. Seymour is standing in front of us, Ursa in her arms, and beside her, laden with guns, are Gideon and Serena.

"You've got to be joking," Marquis says.

"Thank God," I whisper as Dr. Seymour pushes Ursa into my arms.

"Did you see, Viv? Did you?"

I push Ursa's hair out of her face and laugh. "I did see. And here's the boy."

Atlas smiles and holds out his hand to shake Ursa's. "Nice to meet you, Ursa. I'm Atlas."

Ursa is already staring over my shoulder with wide eyes. Marquis falls into a low bow, his eyes suddenly wet.

"Long time no see, little bear."

Ursa reaches for him and I reluctantly let her go. I stare at Gideon and Serena.

"Where the hell have you two been?"

"Saving your sister," Serena says, her eyes flashing.

"It's true," Dr. Seymour says, adjusting her broken glasses. "Moments after we were locked in the basement, these two burst down the stairs armed to the nines."

Serena pulls another gun from her back and hands it to me, even though we both know I have no idea how to use it.

"Come to your senses, have you?" Atlas glowers at Gideon. "Not going to try and kill someone again—"

I put my hand on his arm and he falls silent.

"Thank you," I say to Gideon and Serena. "Both of you."

Gideon sniffs and hands Atlas a gun. "Anyone got a plan to get out of here?"

"It seems I've been promoted to pilot," Marquis says cheerfully, straightening Ursa's hair ribbon. "Shall we get on with it?"

Loud voices sound from outside.

"Wyvernmire's called for reinforcements," Serena says.

Dr. Seymour nods. "There's another exit through the ballroom. It'll take us out to the other side of the grounds, where the workshops are."

There's a loud screech, then a flash of blue out of the window. Muirgen?

"Go!" Marquis says as he moves to bolt the back door.

The whole house shudders and the wall behind the stove falls in.

"Can we go home now?" Ursa whines.

The house trembles again and a piece of plaster falls from the ceiling, narrowly missing Marquis's head. Adrenaline shoots through me as we run down the corridor and burst into the entrance hall as a group of Guardians come through the front door. I raise my gun, my finger feeling cluelessly for the trigger, but they stampede past us and up the stairs.

"The Prime Minister is being targeted!" one of them shouts.

We follow Dr. Seymour into the ballroom, then out a small door and into the grounds. I turn to look at the manor. Tiles and rubble are cascading off the roof and behind it the forest is on fire, flames surging up to the very tops of the trees as if to outshine the first tendrils of orange sunrise.

"Faster, Viv!" Marquis shouts as he streaks past me, Ursa bouncing on his hip.

Across the lawn in the courtyard, Rhydderch is towering over the Guardian cars. He swings his spiked tail, slamming into his opponent, a silver patrol dragon named Fenestra, who lets out an agonized roar. Guardians scramble for cover as the dragons fall against the cars, flattening them.

"He—he's with us!" I stutter in shock. "Rhydderch and Muirgen are fighting on our side."

A Guardian looks up from the rubble and our eyes meet. He shouts something at several others, who run toward me.

"Viv!" Marquis screams.

He and the others have already reached the workshops and Gideon and Serena are dragging open the tall wooden doors to one of them.

Atlas pulls me by the hand and I tear my gaze away from Rhydderch.

"Not much farther now," Atlas breathes.

I wipe sweat from my brow as we run and cough through a cloud of black smoke. Atlas's hand is hot in mine as we skid to a halt in front of the workshop. There's a huge crashing sound, followed by a rumbling like thunder. Across the grass, a dragon I don't recognize has smashed the entrance gates down. They land on the gravel of the courtyard and hundreds of people burst through. Soldiers and civilians holding guns, batons, and knives.

"Down with the government!" they scream.

"Down with Wyvernmire!"

"The Coalition," I whisper. "They're actually here."

Atlas's eyes glitter as he watches. The Guardians pursuing us fall back, redirecting their attention to the incoming invasion. And then come the dragons. They fly through the smoke from across the lake, a kaleidoscope of colors, their wings shielding the rebel humans from bullets as they swoop like birds of prey. We step inside the workshop, which is filled with rows of motorcars and Guardian trucks on each side. And in the middle, surrounded by tarpaulin sheets and tools, is a fighter plane.

"You built this?" I ask Marquis.

"Serena did most of the building," Marquis says. "Karim and I did the wiring and the engine. And," he says, pulling down the steps and clicking them into place, "Karim made this."

The metallic steps are covered in a blue fabric across which dance hundreds of tiny silver dragons.

"It's beautiful," I say.

"Yes, absolutely gorgeous," Atlas mutters impatiently. "Now get in."

Serena climbs into the cockpit and Gideon and Dr. Seymour follow her up the metal steps.

"Wait," I say. I look at Marquis and Ursa, their faces black with smoke.

"I can't leave Sophie here," I say.

"What are you talking about?" Atlas growls.

I spin round. "Did you think I was just going to climb onto this plane without her?"

Why did I think that she'd be here, waiting for us? Where is she?

"Viv," Marquis says slowly, "I told Sophie to get out if she couldn't find me. She'll have escaped by now, up through the forest."

"And we're just meant to assume that, are we?" I say.

"Yes!" says Atlas fiercely. "Viv, you've done everything you can. You destroyed your translations, and the glasshouse is gone. It's time to go now, to get away with both your cousin *and* your sister. This is what you came to Bletchley for."

I shake my head. "I can't abandon Sophie," I say. "Not again. After everything I told you, can't you understand—"

"*I'll* find her," he says.

"You?" I say incredulously. "But you're coming—"

A shadow falls across the workshop, and the first shaft of daylight peeking through the slats in the wooden roof is extinguished. Outside, the sky has gone dark, as if the moon has eclipsed the rising sun. The shooting and roaring stop as I run to the door. Then suddenly the dim light returns.

And the formation of Bulgarian dragons above us breaks apart.

There must be a hundred of them, all shades of black and red. They fly like a regiment marches, with sharp angular movements and swift turns in direction. As they head for the courtyard, I feel the hair on the back of my neck stand on end.

"I don't understand," Atlas says. "They weren't meant to be here until tomorrow. Isn't that what Wyvernmire said?"

No one answers him. We all just stare as the dragons advance across the sky. In the courtyard, the rebel humans and Guardians have ceased all fighting and are staring upward. Even the Bletchley and rebel dragons seem to hover midair, waiting. A burst of flames shoots from the Bulgarian formation and I feel a jolt of electricity in my chest.

"Serena!" I shout. "Start the plane."

I grab my cousin's arm. "You and Serena can fly this thing together, I know it."

"Get on the plane, Viv," Marquis says through gritted teeth.

I shake my head and Ursa begins to cry.

"I'll find you," I tell her. "I just have to go back for Sophie."

She kicks and screams as Marquis lifts her up the steps and Gideon catches hold of her, pulling her inside.

"Viv, please," Marquis says, tears in his eyes.

I reach up and kiss his cheek. "I promise I'll be fine," I say. "Take care of Ursa, okay?"

He holds me tightly for a moment, then climbs up the steps.

"Atlas?" I say.

He gives me a sheepish look. "You didn't think I was going to let the Coalition fight without me, did you?"

"Have you *seen* the sky?" I shout. "How are *you* going to fight Bulgarian dragons?"

"Look," Atlas says.

Chumana is flying toward the Bulgarians, flanked by Rhydderch and Muirgen, Soresten and Addax, Yndrir and a group of rebel dragons. There's only a small stretch of sky between the two opposing groups. What is she doing?

For a moment, none of them move, the Bulgarian army with scales like glass on one side, and a small group of dragons, already bleeding from battle, on the other. Are they echolocating? Is

Chumana trying to reason with them? Three of the Bulgarian dragons at the front of the formation jerk forward and Rhydderch reacts, leaping to shield his group with a warning snarl. The Bulgarians lunge for him and a scream rings through the sky as they pull his head from his body and blood sprays down like rain.

"No!" I shriek.

Monstrous screeches come from the Bletchley dragons as they attack in retaliation and the sky suddenly heaves with movement. Below, the gunshots and fighting resume. There's a ringing in my ears as Atlas's eyes meet mine and I see my own horror reflected back. A sea of fire streams down onto the courtyard, engulfing a group of rebel humans and Guardians. The plane splutters into life. The Coalition is ridiculously outnumbered. There's no way they'll survive this. How did we ever think we were going to fight an army of Bulgarian dragons? As the plane moves forward, Atlas grabs hold of me.

"Get on," he says.

"You get on," I retort.

"I can't—" He glances back at the burning courtyard. "I have to help them."

"What good are you going to do out there?" I say. "You're a seminarian, not a soldier—"

"We can't let Wyvernmire become more powerful, Viv. We can't—"

I grab his face in my hands. "Listen to me!" I shout over the deafening noise of the propellers. "It's too late. The Bulgarians are here and there's too many of them. There's going to be a real war, a—"

I stop as a memory appears amid the chaos of my mind. The sound of violins, a flash of feathers and fur, bubbles rising in a glass of champagne.

Language is as crucial to war as any weapon.

And it hits me.

"I've got to go back," I say slowly. "I've got to go back to Wyvernmire and give her what she wants."

Atlas pushes me out of the way as the plane jerks forward with a roar and Marquis stares at me through the cockpit window. I shake my head at him and he says something to Serena. Then the plane jolts forward again and hurtles out of the workshop and across the grounds before lifting into the air.

"What did you just say?" Atlas says.

"I've got to be Wyvernmire's translator," I say. "It's the only hope we have of controlling the Bulgarians—"

"That's ridiculous," he spits. "That's the opposite of what the Coalition stands for—"

"Look around you, Atlas!" I shout. "Soon there will be no Coalition left. The Bulgarians are here, and you can be sure more are coming. If Wyvernmire has no way of listening in on them, no possibility of control, then Britannia will become dragon country. You know as well as I do that this new alliance is just temporary. And this war we've been fighting, rebels versus government, is nothing compared to what will happen when Queen Ignacia learns she's been betrayed and the Bulgarians decide that Wyvernmire is just a thorn in their side. All we can do now is help our people, our country—"

Atlas seethes. "So we just give up? Bow down to the Bulgarians, to Wyvernmire?"

I'll never give the Koinamens to Wyvernmire, never let her know how mastering it could give her power she's only dreamed of. But I can use what I've learned to spy on the Bulgarian dragons, to make sure they can't betray her, to protect Britannia and the rebels at the same time.

"For now," I say gently. "Until we find a way to fight them. I'll give Wyvernmire a fake code, let her think that I'm with her, and when she realizes what she's done by letting the Bulgarians into the country, maybe she'll . . ."

The rest of my sentence is drowned out by the sound of Marquis's plane overhead. It circles once above the forest beyond, and as it rises, flames burst out from beneath the nose.

I can almost hear Marquis's whoop of triumph.

A fire-breathing plane.

"I thought *this* was what I was supposed to be doing," Atlas says. "That if it isn't to be a priest then maybe it's to fight for change with you. To defend people, *my* people, the Third Class and the dragons."

His voice breaks and I take his hands and kiss them.

"I know," I say. "And maybe it is. The Coalition—the rebel cause—isn't just here inside Bletchley. It's out there." I gesture beyond the fighting and the broken gates. "You're the man who risked his life to save just one person, when you hid him back in your church. Just because we've lost this battle doesn't mean it's all over."

He takes a step back. "But I've still failed. All this time, I was readying myself to lead the battle. We planned the attack for months—"

"That's just your pride talking," I say. "Believe me, I know."

He stares at me with red-rimmed eyes.

"There's another loquisonus machine, in the woods," I say.

"I thought they both burned in the glasshouse—"

"I hid the one you didn't get to break. But not for me," I say quickly. "It was to communicate with the rebel dragons, in case

Chumana didn't hear my message. But we can use it to spy on the Bulgarians, to learn their calls and make sure we stay one step ahead. Language—that's how we rebel."

"The Coalition's dragons will never agree," Atlas says. "How can you even suggest it, after everything Chumana told you—"

"They might if it's the only thing that can save us," I say fiercely. "And afterwards we'll make sure no human can ever use a loquisonus machine again. We can still beat the Bulgarians and win this new war."

Atlas's gaze fixes onto mine, wary of this last beacon of hope.

"I trusted you when you said that I should tell Sophie the truth, that I could be forgiven," I say. "Helping people, that's kind of your speciality, right? That's how *you're* called to love. Well, language is mine. You said so yourself, remember?"

I stroke his cheek as we remember that moment by the dragon-egg statue.

"Now I need you to trust *me*, Atlas."

He leans forward, his face like a bewildered child's, and kisses me.

"I trust you, Viv."

"Then we need to go back to the glasshouse."

Burning bodies and the corpse of a dragon litter the grounds as we tear back past the manor and into the forest. The trees around us are on fire, too, and in the middle of them the glasshouse is melted and black. There's no sign of Ralph. I cough and retch as smoke fills my eyes, kicking around in the undergrowth until I see it. The golden speaker of the loquisonus machine sticking out through the leaves. I check it's intact, the glass and metal almost too hot to touch, then turn to Atlas.

"We've got to find Wyvernmire," I say. "Her helicopter is still here, so she hasn't been evacuated, but she can't be inside."

Half the manor has already burned down.

"The basement," Atlas says suddenly. "It's fireproof because of the—"

"Dragonlings," I finish. "Let's go."

"Wait," Atlas says. "We don't even know if she'll agree to this yet. And if she doesn't, she could trap you down there. You're the one with the code in your head, not me. I'll go."

I hesitate but he's right. Wyvernmire has an army of Bulgarian dragons on her side, so Atlas and his zoology knowledge are now irrelevant to her. But if he can lead her to me . . . I take a breath.

"All right," I say, rising up on my toes to kiss him. "I'll wait for you here, where the smoke keeps me hidden."

Atlas nods, then turns and disappears through the trees.

Everything that mattered yesterday—keeping the code from Wyvernmire, joining the rebels, getting out of Bletchley—is suddenly irrelevant. A war is coming, a three-way war between Wyvernmire and the Bulgarians, Queen Ignacia and the Coalition. And our only chance of winning is to give our enemy something to fight an even bigger enemy with. Because if I've learned anything from my mama and her family's fate it's that Bulgarian dragons don't ally with humans. But I can help make sure this war isn't the end of us all. I can use my dragon tongues, my knowledge of echolocation, to save us. I can still give Sophie her life back. I stare at the loquisonus machine, at the remnants of the glasshouse, at the ashes of my life at Bletchley Park.

This is my second chance.

TWENTY-NINE

I crouch amid the smoke and listen to the fighting for what feels like an eternity. And then finally I see movement, illuminated by the light of the flaming trees. Atlas strides toward me, his hands balled by his sides, and behind him is Wyvernmire, looking triumphant. Where are her Guardians? The ground begins to shake and what I thought was a mass of black trees moves forward and out of the smoke. The only protection Wyvernmire needs. A Bulgarian Bolgorith.

Atlas comes to stand beside me as I stare at them, positioning myself in front of the hidden loquisonus machine.

"She didn't take much convincing," Atlas says quietly. "Half her Guardians have abandoned her and . . . just look at the size of that thing. Do you think she knows she's bitten off more than she can chew?"

Wyvernmire and the dragon come to a stop a few feet in front of us. It's the biggest dragon I've ever seen, with black scales encrusted with jewels. Mama has told me about this self-inflicted injury, traditionally found on Bulgarian dragons of high rank, those with the biggest hoards.

"Vivien," Wyvernmire says, "permit me to introduce you to General Goranov. He is our new ally in this war that Bletchley Park has failed to win."

The dragon surveys me through a black, glassy eye.

"Good evening, General Goranov," I say in Slavidraneishá.

The eye blinks once.

"I am yet to meet a human who speaks my mother tongue," the General growls. "Since my kind's rise to power, it has become somewhat unpopular. Did a dragon teach you?"

"English, please!" Wyvernmire snaps.

She gives the General a strained smile as his head swings round in her direction.

"You'll find that most of my troops do not know English," he snarls.

"Where did *you* learn?" I ask the General. "Did a human teach you?"

Atlas gives my waist a warning squeeze. I turn to Wyvernmire.

"What will happen now?" I ask. "You've made enemies of both the Coalition and Queen Ignacia. Britannia is in a three-way war." I glance at Goranov. "And soon it could be four."

"My government and the Bulgarian dragons will bring this nation back to order," Wyvernmire says. "There are more Bulgarian troops on their way."

Atlas snorts. "But in your attempt to crush one rebellion, you've created two."

"The Coalition and Queen Ignacia will be offered terms," Wyvernmire says. "A new Peace Agreement. I am not a cruel Prime Minister—"

"No one will want you as Prime Minister when they find out what you've done," I say.

"Oh, please," Wyvernmire says. "I am simply doing what's necessary to ensure that our great Britannia does not fall into ruin."

"You've brought ruin to its front door." I look at the General again. "You think *they* care for order, or peace, or prosperity?"

Goranov lets out a low growl.

"You are still too young to understand," Wyvernmire says. "I gave you an opportunity, Vivien, but you failed to take it. What you have in ambition, you lack in courage."

"Viv doesn't lack courage," Atlas says.

"The thing I've been working on," I say. "In the glasshouse? I can still give it to you. It's the only thing that will keep you—and the rest of Britannia—safe. It's the only advantage you'll have."

Wyvernmire's eyes narrow and I feel my heartbeat quicken. Does she see through my lie?

"You made it very clear you have no intention of sharing it, and only cooperated because I had your sister, who has now conveniently disappeared."

"As you can see," I say slowly, gesturing toward the Bulgarian dragon, "circumstances have changed."

Wyvernmire looks at the General. "Thank you for escorting me, General Goranov. I'll handle these recruits from here."

The General grins in my direction. "I will hear what your polyglot has to say."

I try my best to ignore the stench of his breath, the way his mere breathing feels like a strong blast of wind.

"I will remain at your side, as your personal translator," I tell Wyvernmire. "Think of it as insurance, in case things don't go the way you planned."

Her lips tremble the slightest bit, and I know she gets my meaning.

"But the glasshouse is burned—"

"I managed to salvage what is required," I say, stepping slightly to the side so that her eyes land on the half-hidden loquisonus. "But, in exchange, you must agree to the following conditions."

Atlas's arm tightens round me, making me feel bolder. A resounding crash and a dragon's roar come from the manor. The rebels are still fighting.

"You will order your Guardians and dragons—including the Bulgarian ones—to retreat."

The General's tail slices through the air like a whip and crushes a fallen tree trunk.

"No one orders my troops except me."

"You will let everyone on the opposing side, human and dragon, leave Bletchley Park," I continue. "The remaining recruits will be pardoned and their families liberated if you are currently holding them."

Wyvernmire's eyes shine with amusement. "Go on."

"Dragons will be reintegrated into society, given more rights, more land, and more prospects."

The General lets out a low laugh. "I had forgotten how tedious negotiating dragon and human equality is."

"The terms you offer to the Coalition will be fair," I say. "In this new society you intend to create, Third Class citizens will have the same rights as the Second Class. And you will abolish the Examination. It will no longer determine a person's position—"

"No," Wyvernmire says.

"No?" I reply, hearing my voice falter. "So you *don't* need me as your translator?"

"Translator for what?" the General snarls.

"You will do well to remember that you have already lost this battle," Wyvernmire tells me quietly.

"And *you'll* do well to remember that, without me, your government will be nothing more than a puppet state."

"I will agree to your first two conditions," she replies. "But not to the others. You could be great, Vivien, but only if you stop trying to play the hero, the role of savior to the Third Class. If only you remember that ambition requires sacrifice."

"Except it's always the same people doing the sacrificing," Atlas spits.

I feel as if I'm slowly shrinking, the courage that has fueled me all night dwindling. If I don't listen to the Koinamens for Wyvernmire, the Bulgarian dragons could wipe our entire country out. If she has nothing to use against them, then she, Queen Ignacia, the rebels . . . all of us will suffer.

"I will employ you as my translator," Wyvernmire says. "You'll work at the Academy, under the supervision of Dr. Hollingsworth herself, with a competitive salary and an honorary degree in Dragon Tongues."

As Wyvernmire speaks, two things happen. I feel Atlas move his foot backward, then forward, pushing a large stone toward me with the side of his shoe. And in the treetops, high above the General's head, I see a flash of pink.

I let Wyvernmire's words tug on the edges of my imagination. My family, safe and free in Fitzrovia. Sophie and all the other recruits pardoned. Me working at the Academy for Draconic Linguistics to keep the Bulgarian dragons in check. And Atlas . . . If we were to marry, he would become Second Class.

"Together we'll make Britannia greater *and* ensure its security. But only if you let go of your rebellious notions."

The vision vanishes, evaporating suddenly as I remember the way the Bulgarian dragons pulled Rhydderch's head from his body. The dead Third Class girl's bloody face. My father's eyes as he was led out of our house and pushed into a Guardian car. The images Wyvernmire's words have created are just an illusion, one that hides the ugly truth that my parents saw from the beginning.

"People shouldn't fear their prime ministers, Wyvernmire," I say slowly. "Prime ministers should fear their people."

Atlas snaps round to look at me, bewildered at the utterance of this rebel slogan. They are words I didn't understand until now. Wyvernmire's smile fades. I drop to the ground, seizing the stone at my feet, as the sky fills with fire. Chumana lands on the General's back with a terrible screech and Wyvernmire dives out of the way, slipping on the mess of dead leaves as flaming tree branches fall around her. I lift the stone and smash it through the top of the loquisonus machine.

Wyvernmire lets out a strangled gasp as the glass of the machine splinters, its insides split open. A dial flies off, landing in the undergrowth.

"Viv!" Atlas shouts.

He drags me out of the way just as Chumana and the General hurtle into the remnants of the glasshouse. Chumana's jaw is locked round the General's leg and he roars in agony as her teeth tear through his scales. From somewhere above comes the whir of a plane. The dragons suddenly lurch off the ground, hovering in mid-air, and as the General's talons rip into Chumana's side, Wyvernmire's hair is splattered with blood. She gets to her feet, shielding her face, and calls to me.

"Give me the code and I'll call my troops off."

She still doesn't see. That was the last loquisonus known to exist. She's just a pawn in a game played by Bulgarian dragons now. Atlas pulls me behind a tree.

"Look," he says, gesturing upward. "It's Marquis."

My heart jolts. Of course it is. Marquis's plane circles above us, gradually getting lower. Atlas kisses me.

"You were glorious, Viv."

I shake my head. "What are we going to do now? Without the loquisonus, the Bulgarians are just more powerful. They could take over Wyvernmire's government if they want to—"

"But *you* won't be part of it," Atlas says fiercely. "Whatever happens, you'll know that you refused to sacrifice people. We'll find another way to protect Britannia, one that doesn't involve becoming Bulgarian dragon f—"

Marquis's plane shoots a stream of fire down onto a tree, just missing the General's head.

"Your cousin's aim isn't the best," Atlas mutters as he peers through the smoky forest.

I slip my hands beneath his jacket and round his back, holding him close as the plane searches for a place to land. For a moment, I pretend we're not in the middle of a battlefield. I even close my eyes. I see the next few years together, conjured not by Wyvernmire's lies, but the smell of Atlas's shirt pressed against my face. Planning Britannia's resistance from the safety of rebel Scotland. Holding hands as we watch Ursa play in a dragon-filled countryside. Spending spring mornings asking the questions not yet scribbled in secret notes, discovering the parts of each other we don't yet know. Atlas twirls a lock of my hair round his finger as another dragon crash-lands a few feet away.

"Viv," he says carefully, "I have to stay here, to help the injured rebels."

I nod, my eyes still closed, because it's pointless to argue. Helping people is part of who Atlas is. I know he needs to prove to himself he can still do so, even without the priesthood.

"I have to look for Sophie, then go to Ursa," I say. "I won't leave either of them again."

He presses his lips to my forehead. "I'll find you when the battle is over."

We stumble backward as the fire spreads closer. It's all around us now, roaring so loudly it almost drowns out the sound of the plane.

"It's going to land on the tennis court," Atlas says, pointing to the clearing through the trees.

I flinch as gunshots sound and he pushes me toward the clearing. "You've got to go *now*."

"Wait, I—"

Guardians surge into the space between us and the tennis court, charging past Chumana and General Goranov and toward me. We turn to run, but there are more coming from the other direction, their white uniforms blackened from the heat of the naked flames. My stomach lurches and Atlas's eyes grow wide with panic. We waited too long and now they've found us—

I hear a long, low whistle.

The signal.

My head snaps up. Marquis? He's supposed to be flying the plane. How can he be signaling to me from—

There's movement in the tree above. A face appears among the leaves.

Sophie.

Duck! she mouths.

I don't think twice. I pull Atlas to the ground as a blue dragon swoops low over us and onto the Guardians, its huge wings stretched out like a giant net. Their screams are silenced by a roar as they are knocked backward and Muirgen's talons scrape across the General's back, forcing him to release Chumana from his jaws. Sophie drops from the tree. I feel Atlas's lips on my cheek as his grip on me releases, and before I can turn around, he disappears into the smoke. Sophie's hand finds mine. We run, her cold fingers interlaced with my burning ones, until we burst on to the tennis court.

Yndrir snaps at a Bulgarian's head and they both barrel through the tennis nets, flattening the poles that hold them up. There's the plane, flying as low and slow as it can above the court, a rope ladder dangling down. The screeches are deafening as Sophie grabs hold of the ladder and pulls herself up.

"Get on!" she shouts.

I scramble up after her and the plane begins to rise, pulling us higher. The freezing wind whips my hair round my face as I climb, burning branches falling past me. Gideon's face appears above, and then Sophie is pulled upward and inward. As I reach for the last few rungs, I cast one more look down at the smoke rising from the manor house. I see them then, in the garden. Ralph and Atlas. They're caught in an argument I can't hear. Dragons fly above them, as swift and sharp as the words I imagine being exchanged. Ralph lifts his gun.

Atlas jerks forward, then backward, as if his body has been pulled by an invisible string.

My foot falters on the rung. The shot is rendered silent by the sound of battle and yet it resonates through my body, the loudest moment I have ever lived.

Time slows.

Atlas collapses to the ground.

Voices above scream my name but my eyes are fixed on Ralph, advancing toward Atlas as my whole world goes up in flames.

"Viv!" Sophie screams. "Climb!"

I let go of the ladder.

THIRTY

Pain fills my chest and I gasp, desperate for a breath that doesn't come. When I open my eyes, I'm on my back, the plane circling above me. My chest spasms over and over and I choke, then wheeze as air finally fills my lungs. A dragon's talon almost crushes my arm and I roll over, pulling myself across the court on my stomach until I'm free of the flailing tails. I jump to my feet and run, crashing back through the forest to the garden. In the light of the dawn, Ralph is kneeling over Atlas.

"Get away!" I scream.

My knees give way as I reach him.

"Atlas?" I gasp.

His eyes blink rapidly as he tries to focus on my face. Ralph backs off, a silver revolver in his hand. I press my fingers to the gush of red spilling from Atlas's side.

"Your shirt is stained," I say shakily. I press down on the wound. "We'll wash it, don't worry."

He frowns, his face strained with pain. "You're supposed to be on the plane."

His blood, which coats my hands, is terrifyingly thick. I bring my face close to his as the trees around us spin.

"Help will come," I whisper. "A doctor will come. Someone will—"

My eyes land on Ralph, who is staring at us with a stunned look on his face. "I was aiming for his leg, not his—"

"Chumana!" I fling my head back and scream for her. "Chumana!"

The sky is eerily empty. Atlas reaches for my hand.

"Go back to the plane," he urges. "Ursa is waiting for you."

I shake my head, feeling the tears fall. In the forest and the courtyard, the battle rages on, but here in the garden we're alone.

Help isn't coming.

I squeeze Atlas's fingers as my mind clouds with panic. Footsteps sound from the forest and Wyvernmire emerges, flanked by several Guardians.

"Atlas," I say. "You have to get up."

He makes as if to sit up but winces. "Can't."

I wrap my arms round his chest and try to pull him upward, but so much blood pours from his wound that I stop. I lay him back down as I feel my breath coming in short, sharp surges.

"She'll have to give you the code now," I hear Ralph say behind me.

A shadow falls over us and Wyvernmire stares down at Atlas, then back at her nephew.

"Otherwise, he'll—"

"If he does," Wyvernmire hisses, "she won't give me anything at all."

Atlas cracks a smile, dead leaves crowning his head.

Wyvernmire kneels down beside me. "You shouldn't have

402

destroyed that machine," she says quietly.

I take a shaky breath and turn to look at her, my hand still in Atlas's. She's so close I can see the droplets of dragon blood on her face.

"Get him a medic, *please*," I tell her. "And I'll give you anything. I'll build you another machine. I'll—"

I can hear the despair in my own voice as it turns to uncontrolled sobs.

"My Guardians will help him, if you do the right thing—"

"Keeping echolocation a secret *is* the right thing, Viv," Atlas says.

I shush him and stroke his hair, terrified that speaking will cost him more energy than he can afford.

He looks up at me, his brown eyes shining. "She's wrong about you. You're brave and selfless and good. But *you?*" He laughs at Wyvernmire and brings his other hand down on top of my bloody one. "You're dead without Viv. She could have protected you, and the nation you claim to love, if you'd have just agreed to extend that protection to everyone. Even Ralph knows it—that's why he shot me. Because he thinks Viv will stay here with me, with you, instead of joining the rebels."

"I won't join them," I say fiercely, hot tears streaming down my face. "I won't leave you."

"You will." Atlas sighs, patting my thigh. "You're one of them, aren't you, my love?"

The rising sun shines onto his face, a spatter of gold on his dark skin.

"Atlas," I whisper, hiding my face in his neck. He smells of peppermint and dragonsmoke. "Please get up."

Wyvernmire is waiting patiently, like a mother might wait for a capricious child. Above the tennis court, the plane is flying away. Sophie can't save us now. I look around helplessly, then down at Atlas. His eyes are closed. I lean over him again, shielding him from Wyvernmire's view.

"I love you," I sob into his ear.

He doesn't move.

I kiss his mouth, his eyes, the stubble of his jaw. My tears drip onto his face and down his white collar. His chest rises, then falls. It doesn't rise again. I shrug my jacket off and fold it gently beneath his head. His hand is still on my leg. I kiss that, too, then let it drop to his side. I stand up and as I do, I notice a piece of paper poking out of his breast pocket. I unfold it and smooth it out. It's the note I left for him last night after we kissed in the basement.

> *I am leaving you one more note because, well, I feel like I should make up for the last one. Tell me, Atlas . . . if God turned the dragons into swallows to make them light and carefree, do you think He'll do something similar for us? This code, this language of dragons, has weighed so heavily on us all. I can barely bring myself to think of it, of the destruction it could cause. But there is one silver lining. The brightest silver lining I've ever known. The Koinamens—and all my dragon tongues—are what brought me to Bletchley Park. They are what brought me to you.*

And beneath it he has scribbled his reply.

> *Thank God for dragon tongues, Featherswallow. Thank God for you.*

I inhale a deep, shaky breath and put the note in my pocket. Then I turn round. Wyvernmire is staring at me, her jaw set in a hard line.

"Come with me now," she says. "This is the last death you'll have to—"

"Not the last," I say calmly. I look at Ralph and the hatred consumes me. "I'll make sure you don't leave Bletchley Park alive, you son of a bitch. I'll make sure you—"

Flames stream from the clouds, setting the vegetable garden and Ralph's coat alight. He drops to the ground, a tortured scream bursting from his throat. Chumana swoops onto the grass, positioning herself between me and Wyvernmire. Guardians shoot aimlessly, swarming round their Prime Minister and herding her toward the courtyard, where a helicopter is landing. Ralph, who has managed to douse the fire, limps after her. I crouch behind Chumana to avoid the bullets.

Kill him, I urge her silently as I watch Ralph escape.

But as the Guardians fall back, Chumana's head turns toward the fields. A car is hurtling past the lake. It drives through a bush, black smoke streaming from its exhaust pipe, and straight into the garden. I fall back on my elbows next to Atlas, wondering how Wyvernmire could have called for more reinforcements so quickly—

The back door of the car opens and a face stares out.

Rita Hollingsworth.

"Get in," she tells me sharply. "Before I'm seen."

I shake my head, casting a glance at the Bulgarian dragon that has appeared in the sky above. Chumana has seen it, too.

"Go with her, human girl!" she snarls.

I don't dare refuse, scrambling across the back seat of the car as the engine roars. I cast a look out the window as it reverses toward the lake. Chumana is battling the Bulgarian dragon from the ground, her scales glowing pink in the sunrise. And behind her lies Atlas's body. I sink backward, unable to breathe, and finally lose control. And suddenly Hollingsworth is holding me, engulfing me in perfume, her fur coat sticking to my tearstained cheeks.

"He's all alone," I sob. "I left him all alone."

As the car veers through Bletchley, past trucks full of injured rebels and dazed townspeople, the sun hits the windscreen. It shines onto my face, warm and taunting. Atlas won't see the sun again. He died before it rose. I lean my head into the shoulder of the stranger beside me and think of all the ways I have known him.

Atlas King.

Rebel, priest-in-training, defender of dragons.

The only boy I have ever loved.

And as I close my eyes I see his soul, seeking God as it slips among the burning Bletchley trees.

THIRTY-ONE

The car rolls to a stop outside a small farm, its yard dotted with chickens and guarded by a barking dog. The driver steps out and lights a cigarette without a word, and I suddenly realize who I'm with. The Chancellor of the Academy for Draconic Linguistics.

The woman responsible for my parents' arrest.

I lean back against the door, wiping my eyes, and stare at her. She's wearing dark-rimmed glasses and a string of pearls. Her hair is like silver gossamer, a perfect cloud round her head.

"What are we doing here?"

"Waiting for that plane." She glances out the window. "Chumana said it would be here."

"Chumana is a rebel," I spit. "Why would she tell you anything?"

I wonder if she's still alive, if Muirgen and the other Bletchley dragons survived.

"The Academy for Draconic Linguistics is full of rebels," Hollingsworth says calmly.

"How do you know?"

Hollingsworth spins one of the rings on her fingers.

"Because I am one of them."

I laugh furiously, stunned that I'm about to be forced to sit through more lies.

"You don't expect me to believe you're part of it?"

"As Chancellor, I am uniquely placed," Hollingsworth says. "My position keeps me close to Wyvernmire—"

"You got my parents arrested," I say. "You gave me my mother's research because you *wanted* me to crack the code, wanted me to *help* Wyvernmire win the war!"

Hollingsworth is shaking her head. "Your parents would have been arrested with or without me. The government had been watching them for months. But Wyvernmire was growing suspicious of me, and her request that I investigate your parents—and recruit you—was a test of loyalty. Turning your parents in renewed her trust in me, therefore keeping me in her inner circle."

Hot anger seeps across my skin, threatening more tears. Is she telling the truth? Or is this just a ploy to keep me distracted until Wyvernmire gets here?

"So you're saying the Coalition knew my parents were going to be arrested?"

"Yes." Hollingsworth raises an eyebrow. "Though they didn't count on you releasing a criminal dragon who broke the Peace Agreement in the aftermath."

"But then . . . the rebels betrayed their own."

"When your parents joined the Coalition, they agreed that, in the event that their position was compromised, the rebels would do what was best for the cause, even at the cost of their lives. On the condition that their children be protected. Helina and John didn't know who I really am, Vivien. Most people don't."

I think of the Hollingsworth I saw at the ball, how she made people's heads turn just by walking past. She rubs shoulders with the government's highest-ranking members, and yet she's telling me she's an undercover rebel, too?

"After your parents were arrested, I sent a dracovol to tell Wyvernmire that you weren't interested in a job at the DDAD. I did intend to recruit you, but *not* for her *or* for the Academy. A rebel group was dispatched to your house to pick you up, but you were already gone. When you released that dragon, Wyvernmire knew she could strike a deal with you."

"So if I'd have just stayed at home . . ."

Hollingsworth nods and pats her hair. "I was going to negotiate Marquis's release, but then we found out you'd convinced Wyvernmire to let him go to Bletchley, too. I'm afraid you made things easy for the Prime Minister."

"And my mother's research?" I ask. "Why would you give it to me if the rebels didn't want me to decipher echolocation?"

"I knew you had the potential to crack the dragon code," she says. "Forgive me for being so cryptic, Vivien, but giving you what you asked me for was my way of letting you know I was on your side."

"But—but how did you know?" I stutter. "How did you know I wouldn't give Wyvernmire the code? That I'd join the Coalition?"

"Atlas," Hollingsworth says simply. "He told me it was quite impossible that you would choose Wyvernmire over the rebels, and that you simply needed time to understand that for yourself."

I blink.

Atlas.

A low drone sounds outside and I peer out the window. Marquis's plane soars over us, looking for a place to land. I glance back at Hollingsworth. She wasn't lying.

"You're really part of the rebellion?" I say softly.

"Part of it?" Hollingsworth smiles. "Vivien, I *am* the rebellion."

The plane begins its descent above a field behind the farm.

"Where are we going, after this?" I ask.

"Me—back to London," Hollingsworth says. "If I am to continue my undercover work, then there must be no trace of my presence here at all. You—to Eigg."

"Eigg?"

She nods. "The Coalition Headquarters."

So that's where Dr. Seymour was sending the dracovol.

"There's something else," I say. "You took a piece of paper from my father's desk back in Fitzrovia. What was it?"

"A letter to the Coalition," she replies. "Warning us of the potential for a Bulgarian invasion. Thanks to him, we've had the opportunity to study Bolgorith battle tactics, which will serve us well in the coming months."

The plane lands and I see someone dart out of a barn in the yard.

Karim.

I reach for the door handle.

"Vivien," Hollingsworth says, "I *am* sorry, about Atlas."

I swallow. "He taught me that it's our choices—who we choose to become once we can see our mistakes clearly—that make us who we are. So I'm sorry it took me so long to listen when he told me not to give Wyvernmire the code. I was figuring out who I am . . . but I know now."

I step out of the car. Karim runs and flings his arms round me, but he doesn't ask why I'm here or who is behind the tinted car window. There will be time for that later. We wade through the wheat-filled field and climb the embroidered plane steps, and suddenly Marquis is holding us both and Ursa is clinging to my leg. As the plane propellers whir again and we reach the sky, I tell them all how Atlas died. The words coming out of my mouth barely make sense and I struggle to keep myself upright as silence fills the plane.

Dr. Seymour guides me to a seat with the same gentle touch that built the loquisonus machine, and Sophie, her eyes bright with tears, reaches for my hand. I feel myself go red, shocked at this simple gesture, when she has every right to hate me. I will myself to tell her one last thing before I succumb to the overwhelming pull of sleep.

"Thank you," I say. "For trying to get me out of there."

"You thought I'd forgotten the signal we used to use in those bunkers, didn't you?" she says.

I nod, watching Dr. Seymour fasten Ursa's seat belt.

"You've been the most loyal friend to me," I say. "And in return I've given you nothing but hell."

Sophie opens her mouth to reply, but I keep speaking, tripping over my words before I lose the courage to say them.

"I'll never ask you to forgive me, Soph. I would never expect that of you. But . . . I'm going to start trying to forgive myself. I don't know if I'll ever be able to, but I'm going to try. And I promise you I'll return the friendship you've given me. I'll spend the rest of my life making yours happier, and the lives of all the other people who have suffered because of the Class System and the Peace Agreement—"

Sophie holds up her hand to silence me, our childhood friendship bracelet still dangling from her wrist.

"I know you will, Viv," she says. "I know."

In the seconds before I wake, I'm floating in a soft nothingness permeated by a deep, steady voice so familiar to me that it could be my own. And then I remember. I open my eyes to the harsh light of day streaming through the plane windows. Atlas's voice disappears and I'm swallowed by a darkness worse than any I've ever felt. Sophie is asleep beside me and Karim and Gideon are dozing upright in their seats, the three dragonlings curled up between them. I hear the low voices of Marquis and Serena from the cockpit. Dr. Seymour smiles at me, Ursa stretched out across her lap, and points out of the window.

"Welcome to the Small Isles," she says.

I peer outside. Below, snaking through the stretch of gray-blue sea, is an archipelago of green mountainous islands dotted with rocks and sheep. And flying beside us, bloody and battle-worn, are—

"Dragons," Ursa whispers.

She appears beside me, suddenly wide awake, and I lift her so she can press her nose against the glass. The sky is full of them, Western Drakes and Sand Dragons and Ddraig Gochs, flying alongside Marquis's plane on both sides. I scan the clouds for any sign of a pink Bolgorith, but I don't see one.

Dr. Seymour puts a hand on Gideon's shoulder as he stares out across the islands.

"Dr. Seymour," I say, "Lord Rushby said Eigg was government-owned up until a few weeks ago. Where was headquarters before then?"

"The Coalition was decentralized until now. We have factions all over the United Kingdom. That's why there are offshoot groups—rebels who agree with parts of our cause, but not others."

"Like what?" Gideon asks.

"Some think the Peace Agreement should be abolished and not replaced. There's a faction in Birmingham campaigning for the right to hunt dragons again, and another that thinks we should strip each human and dragon of their property and divide it up among everyone. I'm afraid they've succeeded in delegitimizing us in the eyes of the public."

I've been living in a bubble, both at Bletchley and in Fitzrovia.

The dragons begin their descent and the plane follows.

"Fasten your seat belts, ladies and gentlemen!" Marquis shouts. "My copilot, Serena Serpentine, is about to land this plane!"

I strap Ursa in and fasten my own seat belt with trembling hands, glad that Serena's plane-landing experience is more extensive than my cousin's. I sit back as the plane picks up speed, hurtling through the air, then nose-dives, hitting the sandy beach with an almighty bang that makes Ursa scream. The propellers stop whirring as we slow and the plane falls silent.

"Let go of me!" Ursa whines.

I realize I'm grasping her so tightly that my knuckles are turning white. Marquis stands at the end of the plane, grinning from ear to ear.

"Reckon I did a good job of that," he jokes as Serena appears behind him, rolling her eyes.

I unbuckle myself and Ursa and she runs to Marquis.

"Ready?" he says.

He opens the door and kicks the steps down. Wind whips through the inside of the plane. I stare out into the bright sunlight. Waves crash against the shore, and across the water is another island, with dragons hovering above it. The air is cold and full of salt, and I breathe in deeply as my shoes sink into the sand. Dragons are landing beside us, hundreds of them alighting on the beach and making the ground shake, and people are sliding off their backs. Many of them are injured, and the dragons are all sporting deep wounds in their flanks or spots of missing scales. I turn to look inland and see more people rushing down to us from the clifftop.

So this is Eigg, the new Coalition Headquarters. Home to the cause my parents were willing to give their lives for, that Atlas *did* give his life for. Will I ever be as devoted to it as they were? Marquis appears beside me, hoisting Ursa onto his shoulders, and one glance at him tells me he's thinking the same thing. Our argument on the train to Bletchley feels like it happened centuries ago.

People are greeting each other, families being reunited with loved ones returned from Bletchley, and several nurses are already leading the injured away. They're all dressed differently, but I couldn't guess the class of any of them if I tried. Beyond the beach, up on the clifftop, are small stone houses.

"Dr. Seymour, how many people live here?"

"Barely a hundred," she replies. "Only the rebels most wanted by Wyvernmire's government came to Eigg."

"And Wyvernmire didn't try to take it back?" I ask.

Dr. Seymour shakes her head, scanning the crowds. "There's a clause in the Peace Agreement that forbids planes from flying anywhere near Rùm, so as not to disturb the eggs. It's a sacred space, a—"

She lets out a sigh as a man runs toward her, catching her in his arms and spinning her round. I watch as the wind stirs sand round them and the man kneels to kiss Dr. Seymour's stomach. How long have they been apart? What else have these people sacrificed for their rebellion? Behind them, two Sand Dragons are standing close together. I recognize their faces.

"Soresten!" I call. "Addax!"

414

The patrol dragon who guarded the glasshouse gives me an acknowledging blink as I walk toward him.

"Are you an undercover rebel, too?" I say.

"I am not," Soresten replies. "But when Rhydderch told me what Wyvernmire was planning, I decided to fight with you."

My heart sinks at the reminder of Rhydderch's brutal death.

"Do you know what happened to the others? To Muirgen and . . . the pink dragon. The one who was fighting the General?"

"Muirgen has gone to join Queen Ignacia," Addax growls. "She is still loyal to Her Majesty, despite her corruption."

Soresten lifts his head to stare out over the sea. "We have heard rumors that the Queen's court is feasting on the Isle of Canna. I have come to see if there is truth in it—"

"And the Bolgorith?" I say desperately. "Chumana?"

"We saw her make a kill," Soresten says, "before we retreated. I believe she survived."

I let out a shaky breath. Chumana is alive.

Soresten falls silent and I watch as the wound on Addax's chest knits together. The other dragons around us are doing the same. They can heal others, but not themselves because the Koinamens is a language, and language is an exchange. I don't know when I worked this out, but I hope Chumana isn't flying alone. I realize with a pang of sadness that the air must be full of echolocation calls that, now the loquisonus is gone, I'll never hear again. Addax's eyes narrow curiously as she watches me.

"The dragons are speaking of how you destroyed those machines. Some would probably like to kill you for using them in the first place." She pauses. "But know that your decision has not gone unappreciated."

I bow my head as they both turn and walk across the sand, people jumping out of the way of their tails as they head to the rocky caves at the end of the beach.

"You're welcome," I say quietly. "It was the right thing to do."

Dr. Seymour takes us to an inn called the Dragon's Den. We all have our own rooms, courtesy of the owner, a loud man called Jacob. I give Ursa a bath and tuck her into our big double bed in the middle of the afternoon. She's asleep moments after her head hits the pillow.

I go to the little washbasin and stare at my face in the mirror. It's black with soot, stained with gray tear tracks and blood from Ralph's knife. There's a burn on my chin and my hands are raw from the rope ladder. Sweat and smoke and the last trace of Atlas's touch cling to my skin. I place his note, the only physical reminder of our last moments together, in a pot on the shelf and try not to think of his promise.

I'll find you when the battle is over.

I wash the thought away in the hot, soapy water of the bathtub. My mind drifts to the last conversation I had with Chumana. All this time, my theory was wrong. The many versions of echolocation we heard through the loquisonus machine weren't different branches of one universal language, weren't dialects. They were simply the conversion of varying levels of emotion into sound. Dragons' understanding of each other, the calls they use to communicate, depend entirely on their bond. Soresten communicating with Addax sounded different to him communicating with Muirgen, because their bonds are different. One is the bond of brother and sister, the other of two dragons who happened to work together at Bletchley Park.

I stare at the water droplets on my skin. Dragon tongues may well contain familial dialects, like Mama's research suggests, but the Koinamens does not. That's because it isn't based on grammar or words. It's a language of emotion, a telepathy our human brains cannot even begin to imagine. All this time, I was looking at it from a linguistic point of view, basing my theories on the languages I know, assuming that they were the benchmark from which to begin.

I've always done that, I realize now. Assumed that everyone thinks like me, that everyone experiences the world the same way I do, that I could never be wrong. Yet, despite my good grades and recommendation letters and university place, there are so many things I *don't* know.

When I'm dressed in someone else's clothes and pulling a brush through my wet hair, there's a quiet knock on the door.

"Come down for food," Marquis whispers, his eyes darting to Ursa's sleeping form.

I set down the brush and follow him downstairs. People are crowded round the bar, most of them still in bloodied, burnt clothes. Someone I've never met hands me a beer with a smile. I sip the froth off the top, savoring the bitter freshness, and follow Marquis outside. There are several small fires burning across the grassy clifftop, and sitting round them are groups of dragons and people, talking in low voices. The sun is already setting and the sea and the sky beyond are a pale purple color.

Someone hands us some food as we walk by one of the firepits—a sausage between two slices of bread—and we eat like we'll never eat again. Karim and Sophie are standing on the cliff edge that overlooks the beach, and when they move apart I see Serena, Gideon, and Dr. Seymour sitting behind them, staring out at the sea. I feel a sharp pain in my chest. Three of us are missing.

"How is Ursa?" Karim says gently when we reach them, resting his head on Marquis's shoulder.

"Asleep," I say.

"Dreaming of dragons," Marquis adds.

I drain the last of my beer and sit on the grass beside Sophie. Her blond hair is clean and damp, her cheeks flushed, a dark bruise beneath her eye.

"What are you looking at?" I ask as the sun flings pink rays across the water.

"Gideon was showing us where Canna is," Sophie says.

I glance at Gideon. He's staring past the island directly in front of us to the one behind it.

"How do you know where Canna is?" I ask.

As far as I know, Gideon didn't grow up in Scotland.

"Cos that's where I was recruited from," he mumbles, his eyes still on the island.

I look between Sophie and Dr. Seymour to check I heard right. Canna is where criminal youths are sent, the place Queen Ignacia uses as her personal hunting grounds. It's where most of the recruits would have ended up if they weren't sent to Bletchley first.

"I was nothing but a pretty plaything to my father and his friends," Gideon says, eyes unblinking.

My heart sinks.

"But I had my revenge. That's what got me sent there."

"Is it true? What they say happens on that island?" I ask. "Do the dragons come to feed?"

Gideon gives one short nod, then gazes back out to sea. I set my glass down as we all fall silent. No wonder Gideon was so desperate to crack the code. He didn't want to go back to Canna.

I've been around a lot of dragons.

"The Coalition will put a stop to that," I say. I turn to Dr. Seymour. "Won't they? Can they get those kids off Canna?"

Dr. Seymour hesitates. "It's certainly one of our aims. But with the Bulgarian dragons' invasion, the country is about to crumble. The war is now on a much bigger scale than before. Wyvernmire has allied with the most hated dragons in Europe, making Britannia a threat to neighboring countries. The Bulgarians will occupy Britannia, with or without Wyvernmire's consent, and we may have to make some alliances of our own. That is where the Coalition's priorities will lie."

"So we could be looking at a full-blown world war?" Marquis says.

"It's possible," Dr. Seymour replies.

I lay a tentative hand on the shoulder of the boy who tried to kill me.

"Don't worry," I say. "We'll do something about it."

Gideon doesn't reply, but he doesn't pull away.

I look back at Marquis and he gives me a conspiratorial look. *We* know where *our* priorities lie. With the fire-breathing plane and my knowledge of the Koinamens no longer needed, we can't be of much value to the rebels on Eigg. But if we can get to London and find Dr. Hollingsworth, maybe she'll be able to help us get Mama and Dad and Uncle Thomas out of Highfall. And then I'll offer her my services, using my languages to help the Coalition in any way I can. My mind is still reeling from what I've learned about dragons' ability to communicate through language *and* emotion. And from the fact that I almost told Wyvernmire how to exploit it.

I lean into the warmth of Sophie's shoulder and remember

what the Chancellor of the Academy for Draconic Linguistics told me that terrible day I met her in Fitzrovia, before I knew who she really was.

I see a bright future for you, Vivien. But to reach it you may have to look in unexpected places.

I'm sitting on the edge of an island at war, in the company of the old friend I betrayed and new friends I have made, an ultrasonic dragon tongue permanently residing inside my head. I have made mistakes, terrible mistakes. But I'm forgiving myself for them, or at least trying to, and in the softness of the sunset I realize.

There is nothing more unexpected than that.

THE BLETCHLEY GAZETTE

BLETCHLEY PARK DESTROYED BY DRAGONFIRE
IN A REBEL ATTACK

Bletchley. Wednesday, December 26, 1923

TOWNSFOLK GATHERED at the scene of destruction at Bletchley Park this Boxing Day morning as emergency care was administered to government Guardians and Bletchley Manor staff. Firefighters fought valiantly against the blaze that swept through the park, destroying most of the nineteenth-century manor house and its surrounding buildings.

Prime Minister Wyvernmire, allegedly present at the scene for official purposes, and Deputy Prime Minister Ravensloe were airlifted to hospital, but are both said to be in a stable condition. It is likely they were the direct targets of this most recent rebel assault. MPs are already demanding an explanation for the sightings of over seventy Bulgarian dragons seen crossing the Channel in the direction of London during the night.

Bletchley Park, requisitioned by the government from the Leon family in 1918, is rumored to be the safehouse of several wartime secrets. A total of twenty-six victims have been recovered so far, including the bodies of four Bulgarian dragons, one Western Drake, and twenty-one members of the Human-Dragon Coalition.

By the time reporters arrived at the scene, the only remaining dragon presence was that of Bletchley Park's employed dragon force and a pink Bolgorith, spotted in the sky above the lake, carrying in its talons what seemed to be, according to eyewitnesses, the body of a young man.

ACKNOWLEDGMENTS

So much inspired this book: my bilingualism and work as a literary translator, the sound of my Nan's Welsh accent and my Grandma's rolling Scottish Rs, the cliffs of the English South Coast with its potential for dragons, my own personal experiences of love, faith, and forgiveness . . . But the most inspiring of all are the people who have accompanied me throughout my long writing journey—I'm honored to be able to thank them here.

First and foremost, thank you to my husband, Val, who supported me in every way possible during the writing of this book. *Je t'aime.*

To my parents, for a childhood full of magic and stories and for treating the prospect of me becoming a published author as a *when* and not an *if.* And to my stepparents for their excitement and support since the moment the much-awaited book deal news came through.

To my seven siblings, scattered across two countries, especially Grace, who has a newfound love of dragons but loyally insists mine are the best, and Harry, my first reader, my fellow fantasy fanatic, my very own Marquis.

To my Grandma, who nurtured my writing from the beginning and who showed me that motherhood and the intellectual life can fit together, with a bit of effort, like two pieces of an imperfect puzzle. And to my Grandad, who told me to *keep scribbling.* I miss you both every minute of every day.

To my friends and soulmates, who read my many manuscripts, lost their minds over every exciting update, and have always cheered me on and lifted me higher: Em, Hattie, Emma, Justine, and Meg.

To my writing group, the Cinnamon Squad, who make the land of first, second, and third drafts a less lonely place: Eve, Kate, Zulekhá, Anika, Lis, and Fox.

To my beloved agent, Lydia Silver, for taking me to lunch in Paris before making my representation dreams come true, for believing in every single book I have written, and for sticking with me through thick and thin . . . we did it! To Head of Rights Kristina Egan, for sending my dragons soaring across the globe, to my North American agent, Becca Langton, and to the rest of the incredible team at Darley Anderson Children's.

To my UK editor, Tom Bonnick, for your contagious enthusiasm for and dedication to this book, for giving me the whirlwind submission process of my wildest dreams, and for each thoughtful reread of every version of this story—I am so very grateful to be working with you.

To my US editors, Erica Sussman and Sara Schonfeld, for making me feel so utterly appreciated and valued. Erica, I've lost count of the ways this book has been improved thanks to your sharp editorial eyes.

To the whole team at HarperCollins Children's Books UK, including Cally Poplak, Nick Lake, Geraldine Stroud, and Elisa Offord, for giving me such a wonderful welcome and making me feel like a celebrity when I visited the London offices for the first time. Thank you to Laura Hutchison and Isabel Coonjah for their creative genius in sharing Viv's story with the online book world and also to Jasmeet Fyfe, Leah Wood, Dan Downham, Jane Baldock,

Charlotte Crawford, and Sandy Officer.

To my US team, Heather Tamarkin, Mary Magrisso, Meghan Pettit, Allison Brown, Lisa Calcasola, Abby Dommert, and Audrey Diestelkamp.

To Ivan Belikov and Nekro for the beautiful UK and US cover illustrations, to Matthew Kelly and Jenna Stempel-Lobell for the cover designs, to my copyeditor, Dan Janeck, and to my proof-readers, Jane Tait and Mary Ann Seagren.

To Steve Voake, an invaluable writing mentor and friend, and to his MAWYP alumni workshop groups for their invaluable feedback on the first draft of this book . . . you know who you are. To Jo Nadin, for being the first person to tell me to write YA with drag-ons many years ago. To Natasha Farrant, who took a chance on a young university graduate and introduced her to the world of book publishing and foreign rights. To everyone on the MA Writing for Young People course who treated me like a *real writer* long before I was ever published.

To all the people who pick up this book—thank you a thousand times and I hope my words bring you exactly what you need.

And finally, to God, who gave me all the things I thought I might never have, all at once.